Fr(

Western Lands and Western Waters

SALZWASSER
VERLAG

Frederick Gerstäcker

Western Lands and Western Waters

Reprint of the original, first published in 1864.

1st Edition 2022 | ISBN: 978-3-75259-176-7

Verlag (Publisher): Salzwasser Verlag GmbH, Zeilweg 44, 60439 Frankfurt, Deutschland
Vertretungsberechtigt (Authorized to represent): E. Roepke, Zeilweg 44, 60439 Frankfurt, Deutschland
Druck (Print): Books on Demand GmbH, In de Tarpen 42, 22848 Norderstedt, Deutschland

WESTERN LANDS AND WESTERN WATERS.

WESTERN LANDS

AND

WESTERN WATERS.

BY

FREDERICK GERSTÄCKER,

With Illustrations from Designs by eminent Artists.

LONDON

1864.

CONTENTS.

FREDERICK GERSTÄCKER.

THE prose writers of Germany are comparatively unknown in England; that is, if we take the popular acquaintance with French literature as the standard. This is not the place to enter on any inquiry as to the cause of this preference, but we may suggest that it probably arises from the greater solidity of the German school. It requires more thought to appreciate a German author, for even in his lightest moods the Teuton is weighty. Fictitious literature is continually receiving additions from the French—acknowledged or unacknowledged—in proportion to the morality of the translator, his reverence for mine and thine; the stage is the well-known reproducer of Parisian novelties; but it is only occasionally that a German book is "done into English," or a German drama mounted on an English stage. The result, however, of such an experiment is almost invariably encouraging.

Among German authors, the subject of this brief sketch holds a distinguished place. A few only of his versatile and numerous compositions are known either in France or England; the works selected for translation have, in some instances, been unhappily chosen, but the talent of the writer has been frankly acknowledged, and a popularity achieved somewhat akin to the high reputation he has attained in his own country.

Frederick Gerstäcker is the son of an actor, and was born at Hamburg, on the 6th of May, 1816. He received a moderate education, and does not appear to have exhibited any extraordinary ability during his schoolboy life. He was intended for commercial pursuits, and began his battle for bread in a counting-house at Cassel. But the dull routine of mercantile life was ill suited to his active temperament. He longed for novelty, panted for fresh air, thirsted for a free life, could not fasten himself down to the small details of the office. Plainly, he was not meant to be a pen-wielder in the sense of book-keeper or store-clerk. He was the sort of man who takes wallet and staff, and goes forth to seek his fortune. Very likely comes back again without having found it, and with nothing better to show than a worn-out stick and empty knapsack. Nothing better to show, unless you count knowledge of the world, experience of human society, enlarged views of the great family worthy of his toil and strife. Frederick Gerstäcker was determined to see] the world. America presented an inviting aspect; her broad prairies, her mighty rivers, her extensive forests displayed an attractive field to a young, vigorous, enthusiastic man. He was resolved on settling in the United States. First of all he would learn farming, then emigrate, then build him a log-house, then plant and gather, and sow and reap, beyond the reach of self-vaunting civilization.

About the year 1837, Gerstäcker embarked from Bremen for New York, and arrived safely in that city. He was lucky, or unlucky, enough to have some money, and gifted with a desire to see what there was to be seen. He lingered therefore in New York for several months. Where see you more of life than in a lounge up and down that wide, bustling street, stretching from the Battery Gardens to the avenues of the Upper Ten Thousand, and thence pushing its head into the open country, and known from east to west as Broadway? Irishmen, and negroes, and Wall-street merchants, and Yankee rowdies and Young America, with its collar turned down; ladies in all the colours of the rainbow, strong-minded women all of them in point of fashionable attire. No wonder that a man like Gerstäcker should observe the scene with singular interest. There was the New York upper ten to be seen driving in all its glory up the aristocratic avenues, and the New York lower ten shuffling ill-shod to the five points, squabbling and going to the bad, or locked up in the Tombs, the dismal city prison; and when all the squabbling and wrong-doing was over—laid to sleep in the Aceldama or Potter's Field—much was there to be seen then as there is now in New York city: bowling-saloons and ten-pin alleys, and bars innumerable; besides, there was the Bowery, and the Olympic, and Garden's, Niblo's, to say nothing of the oyster-cellars, always tempting, and the cobblers, and the juleps, and the—

Well. Gerstäcker spent every dime, and then began to wonder what he should do for a dinner. Not in the least particular, with no preconceived notions of being fitted for anything, and finding it quite enough to support himself without the extra trouble and expense of supporting his dignity, he was ready to accept the first chance of employment that offered. Under these circumstances he became stoker on board a steamboat; after this a sailor in the American river boats; then a farm-labourer; then a small farmer on his own account; then a gold and silversmith; then a wood-cutter; then a general dealer; then an innkeeper; "everything by turns and nothing long." Neither did he "locate" himself in one place; during these changes of profession he travelled all over the United States, seeing all that was worth seeing, and a great deal that was not, and mixing with all sorts and conditions of men, entering with equal spirit into the frigid entertainment of the republican *noblesse* or the boisterous humour of a negro breakdown.

Six years were spent in this way by Frederick Gerstäcker in the United States; at the end of that time he returned to Germany, and began the real business of his life: he wrote and he published. His first book was on the United States of North America ("Sweif und Jagazunge durch die Vereiningten Staten Nordamerikas). It was published at Dresden, in 1844, in two volumes, and the result was so far satisfactory that the author was encouraged to bring out another work in the following year. This he called a "Picture of the Mississippi." A second edition was issued in 1856. He also published a romance of Arkansas in the regulation three volumes, and the "Pirates of the Mississippi" also in three volumes. In 1849 he completed and published his "Pictures of Transatlantic Life." This was issued at Leipzig in two volumes, and met with considerable success.

Endowed by nature with remarkable powers of observation, a mind susceptible of the finest impression, and a memory singularly retentive, Frederick Gerstäcker's writings abound with the most life-like pictures. A style at once perspicuous and engaging, conveys, in the clearest manner, everything he has to express, while the experience he sets forth is strengthened by a solid judgment and enlivened by ready wit. That he should have risen rapidly in public estimation is no matter of surprise, when we remember his versatile experience. The very want of steady application which had marked his American career had provided him with the means of becoming one of the most fascinating writers of the day.

But it was not only in pleasing and graphic description, in sly humour, and in felicity of expression, that Gerstäcker excelled. There was much that was valuable to the naturalist—much that cast new light on various departments of physical geography. His acquaintance also with the social condition of the American settlers, life in the backwoods, the state of the Indian tribes—their habits and customs—all contributed to render his books of essential importance to the student, as well as to the practical man. He was therefore encouraged to undertake a journey of observation—to make special investigation into all matters relating to the welfare of new settlers, and with this object in view he quitted Germany in 1849, and proceeded to Rio Janeiro.

From Rio Janeiro, Gerstäcker went to Buenos Ayres, Valparaiso, and California. He also visited the Sandwich and the Society Islands, and the continent of Australia, returning to Germany in the year 1852.

The result of his travels was originally made public through two German periodicals, in a series of graphic articles—replete with instructive and amusing matter. These articles were subsequently collected and published as travels in five volumes.

Some of the most interesting and absorbing passages in the writings of Gerstäcker, are his descriptions of savage life, and the wild scenery of America. He tells us of the Savannahs and prairies, immense meadows watered by mighty rivers; of Llanos, the grazing ground of herds of wild oxen, and where the lakes and pools abound with gymnoti and electrical eels; of the wooded plains of the Amazon—the region of primeval forest; and of the southern Pampas and the mounted Indians who inhabit them, and whose only business is war. Amid the strangest and wildest scenery and people Gerstäcker revels, until the reader is apt to imagine him as one of the Barbaros, living on mares' flesh and milk, and loving nothing so well as a shrieking charge upon the Gauchos.

But the versatility of Gerstäcker's genius is one of his most remarkable features. He writes well on every subject, and he wields the pen of a ready writer. A list of his various published works would be no mean monument to his industry. We do not profess to supply the material for this memorial, but, as a contribution towards it, we may mention that sterling book of travel and of personal adventure—Narrative of a Voyage round the World; then the Wild Scenes in the Prairies; Travels in Rio Janeiro, Buenos Ayres, through the Pampas in Winter, Visit to the Cordillera; the book on the Two Americas; on the Adventures of German Emigrants; Echoes from the Virgin Forest; Wild Sports of the Far West; the City of the Quakers, etc. Add to these books the various fictions he has composed—many of them familiar in an English dress—the Feathered Arrow, or the Forest Rangers; Frank Wildman's Adventures on Land and Water; Each for Himself, or the Two Adventurers; the Little Whaler, or the Charles Hollberg; A Sailor's Adventures; the Haunted House; a Wife to Order; the Young Gold-digger; the Two Convicts; and Tales of the Desert and the Bush.

In concluding this brief notice we may remark that the works of Gerstäcker owe their popularity to nothing accidental or extrinsic. They claim attention on account of their truthful delineation, honest sentiment, genial humour, and perspicuity of style. The tales here printed have already appeared in the pages of "The Englishwoman's Domestic Magazine," and "The Boy's Own Magazine" during past years, and with those most excellent critics, English boys, Gerstäcker is a very considerable favourite; the honour in which he is held by them being little inferior, in fact, to the esteem he enjoys with all classes and ages in his own fatherland.

UP THE MISSISSIPPI.

UP THE MISSISSIPPI.

The Levee, New Orleans.

CHAPTER I.

"ON the 31st of July, at 10 A.M., the fast and splendid steamer, the *Oceanic*, G. Wilkins, master, will leave the Levee for St. Louis. For freight or passage apply on board, or to Smith and Richfield, agents, No. 52, Custom House-street."

This announcement might be seen in the New Orleans *Commercial Times* on the 29th of July, 184—, along with twenty similar ones of as many various boats, bound for the Mississippi, Red River, Missouri, Ohio, Illinois, or for the Gulf of Mexico.

The Levee was all alive, and boxes and portmanteaus, hat-boxes, beds, and all sorts of furniture were being carried in a great hurry to the steamer, from whose two immense chimneys thick clouds of smoke had been pouring out during the last half hour; for the first bell had been rung, and the *Oceanic* would start before the hour, as the captain assured several passengers while walking up and down before the cabin.

Fresh drays, however, still poured in—laden with sugar, coffee, molasses, cotton, and coarse salt—whose burden disappeared, almost as soon as it arrived, in the immense hold of the vessel, by the aid of some thirty firemen and sailors. A number of little wherries tossed and glided among the steamers, stopping chiefly near those that were just ready to start, in order to sell the fruit that was piled up in them to the passengers, partly to eat, and partly to carry with them into a more northern climate. These little gaily-painted boats presented a pleasing sight. One was pulled by a sun-burnt Spaniard, with a broad-leaved straw-hat and black beard, at whose feet lay, in picturesque confusion, pine-apples, oranges, figs, pomegranates, bananas, cocoa-nuts, &c., on which a parrot was constantly moving about, and appearing to invite the travellers to purchase by his noisy chattering; while, in the stern of the little boat, fastened by a thin chain, a monkey was playing all sorts of antics, and showing his teeth at the passengers of the various vessels past which his master pulled, and who tormented him by throwing peel and shells at him.

The bell had been rung for the second time, and passengers hurried up from all sides in order to reach it before its immediate departure, as they fancied. Many of them bore heavy burdens, and groaned along beneath them with the exertion of their utmost strength, while one even waved his handkerchief as a signal that he was coming. The captain turned away with a smile. Loaded drays still arrived with more freight for the vessel, and two-thirds of the hold were not yet filled, but the smoke rose thicker and blacker from the chimney, and that must be the surest sign of immediate departure.

Three boats had already left the Levee, also bound for St. Louis; but the *Oceanic* was notoriously a quick vessel, and many of the passengers preferred waiting half an hour to going on board another which they expected to be passed by her in a short time. The third bell was now rung long and loudly—almost always the sure signal for departure—and again fresh passengers flocked in, but at the same time fresh freight, and the chains were still fastened to the Levee.

"Captain, when do you start?" a Mississippi planter asked, who had just sent a nigger up into town for something.

"Well, sir," he replied, "hardly before evening—your freight is not arrived yet."

"Good, good!" he said. "It's all the same to me. I only wanted to know. Then I can go up to the St. Charles, and dine there?"

"Of course," the captain said, politely. "If the boat starts before night, I will send one of my people up to you."

The planter lounged on shore, and went quietly up to the hotel.

He had scarcely left the captain, when a poor emigrant, a German—who, with his family, were 'tween deck passengers—walked up to him, and asked timidly, in very broken English, whether he could go on shore, if he made haste, to buy some things absolutely necessary for his family, as he had heard the bell ring in the morning, and, for fear of being too late, had come on board without them.

"Good, good!" the captain replied, tired with the long address; "but make haste; the boat starts in half an hour, and I can't wait for you."

The man flew into the town—ran from one shop to the other—gave the price demanded, for there was no time for bargaining—and returned, fatigued to death, at the expiration of half an hour, to find the vessel in the same state of rest as when he had left it.

Thus the afternoon arrived, and the last boat bound for St. Louis, except the *Oceanic*, had just left the quay, in which many of the passengers would, undoubtedly, have sailed, had they not had their luggage on board the latter. So they were forced to stay; and the chief mate now informed all who asked him when the boat would really start, that the captain was on shore, but that their departure would hardly take place before morning.

Many of the passengers swore and abused, but to the majority it was a matter of indifference, as they now knew, for certain, that they would pass another night in New Orleans.

The heat was oppressive, and every one, whom business did not force to go out, remained in the cool of the houses; but those who had to attend to the shipping or unshipping of merchandize, lounged along the Levee, with their umbrellas up, to ward off the burning sunbeams.

Among the numerous bales piled up on the Levee, were hundreds of coffee-bags, waiting for vessels to carry them to Cincinnati, St. Louis, and Pittsburg. Around them a throng of women and girls were collected, busily engaged, as it appeared, in picking up the berries that had fallen out, and placing them in their little baskets; but, in reality, the majority of them had sharp little knives in their hands, with which they cut holes in the bags when they fancied themselves unnoticed, and so filled their baskets! These were mostly Germans and Irish.

The people on the vessels, however, for which the coffee had been brought down, were well acquainted with the tricks of these vagabonds, and attacked them now and then with whips, to drive them away; but, if scattered ten times in succession, they always returned, like vultures to their prey, and surrounded the wounded coffee-bags.

"Drat the Dutch!" the mate of the *Oceanic* at last growled, as he returned on board, bathed in perspiration, and quite worn out, after his sixth unsuccessful attempt to rout the feminine band. "I should like to know why Dutch, Irish, and musquitos were created? They're only sent to plague us!"

"And isn't it us who do all your work, honey?" an Irishman asked in his brogue, from another vessel. "Tell me, isn't it the Irish and Dutch who make your roads and canals, till your land, and build your houses? Now, sir-r, what have you to say to dat?"

"Go on with your work, Pat!" said the mate of his vessel, interrupting the scarcely-commenced discussion. "Don't stand there arguing. Work, boys, work! and get the bales aboard."

The sun was now setting, and the streets, which till then had been deserted, became suddenly full of life. People flocked in, in picturesque groups, to enjoy the coolness of the evening on the Levee. The ice and sherbet booths were filled with guests; crowds of coloured and remarkably handsome flower-girls traversed the throng, or seated themselves at the doorways of the hotels; and the whole city seemed suddenly aroused from a deep and unconscious sleep.

On the vessel itself, it seemed that the quiet, which had deserted the city, had taken up its abode. After the decks had been washed, the sailors and firemen went ashore, and the watch walked slowly up and down the forecastle, busily engaged in repulsing the attacks of the furious musquitos.

Gradually, deep silence again lay over the town; the lights were extinguished, the coffee-houses and hotels were closed, and only on the lower market, close to the Levee, the lamps of the coffee and chocolate-stands still glistened, which were attended by pretty young girls—nearly all of them Germans—who sold, through the whole night, hot coffee, tea and chocolate, and some, iced soda-water; and their bright coffee-cans, which glistened in the darkness—their clean stands, covered with white cloths—their plates of cakes, as well as their pleasant cheerful faces—formed a delightful contrast to the surrounding quiet and gloom.

In the still streets echoed the signals of the watchmen, who struck their heavy hickory sticks on the pavement; and groups of idlers or single wanderers, stopped at the stalls, drank their cup of tea, paid their picayune, and walked, laughing and talking, to another street, or to another market, to pass the night in the open air, and throw themselves, at daybreak, on their beds, to sleep a few hours.

At twelve o'clock, a number of sailors, who were somewhat intoxicated, came into the lower market, drank their coffee, and laughed and sang.

"Listen, Tom," one of them at length said to the noisiest of the group. "Don't make such a thundering row, or you'll spend the night in the calebouse."

"Hang the calebouse!" he replied. "I'm a white man, not a cursed nigger; and I'd like to see the man who'd put me in the calebouse! Here, girl, is your money! "He turned to the little one, who was timidly packing up her cups, through fear of having some of them broken. "Here—one, two, three, four, five, six, seven—here's half a dollar! Are you satisfied?"

"You've a picayune change to receive," the girl replied, modestly.

"Hang your picayune! I'll have a kiss! Now, come, don't be a fool!"

"Let me go, or I'll call the watch."

"Call and be hanged! I'll have my kiss!"

He tried to seize her, in spite of the advice of his more sober comrades, but the girl had scarce uttered a loud cry for help, when one of the watchmen, buttoned up in a coarse brown coat, with a helmet-shaped hat on his head, behind which, in sailor's fashion, a broad ribbon fluttered, while in front was a yellow number, came up, pushed back the disturbers, and ordered them to go away.

The sailors tried in vain to drag away their comrade; he used most vehement language to the watchman, and tried to take a stick from one of the bystanders to attack him. "K-r-r-r!" the rattle sounded; and the watchman sprang on the drunkard, seized him with the left hand, and said—

"You're my prisoner!"

The others drew back, and were surrounded in a second by some twenty well-armed and powerful watchmen. The drunken man gave in, and was led away, while the others quietly dispersed.

Now the first beams of day broke in the East, and the *Oceanic* became again all alive. The watch awoke the firemen and sailors; and, while the first kindled the fire under the boilers, the latter washed the several decks, so that they glistened and shone in the first beams of the morning sun. Breakfast was eaten, and again drays arrived with freight, or boxes and trunks belonging to passengers; the fruit-boats glided once again among the vessels, and once more the sound of the great bell was heard above all the noise of the port.

Little boys with newspapers, others with fruit, or baskets full of books, novels and stories; young negro and mulatto girls, with coloured handkerchiefs tied gracefully and coquettishly round their woolly heads, with large pewter cans filled with sweet or buttermilk, crowded over the narrow planks which connected the steamer with the shore, and tried to sell their various articles.

Two of the milk-girls, a mulatto and a negress, neither more than eighteen years of age, and both tall and graceful in their figures, had commenced quarrelling on board, and went on with it on shore. One word brought on another, and the mulatto girl at length put her milk-can on the ground, tucked up her sleeves, and challenged the other to fight it out. In a second, sailors and firemen rushed up from the vessels, and formed a large circle round the two girls, who now were eager for the fray. The negress had also tucked up her sleeves, and had boldly and successfully withstood the attack of the "yaller" girl.

"That's right, Mary," some one cried, guessing at her name; "that's right. Give it her!"

While, on the other side, might be heard such encouraging shouts as these—

"Between the eyes, Jenny! That was a famous blow! Now another! That's your sort!"

A man forced his way through the crowd, and, seizing the mulatto by the arm, tried to drag her away.

"Let loose—let loose!" five shouted simultaneously. "It's a fair battle! Let 'em fight it out!"

"She's my slave," the new comer said, angrily, while still striving to separate the two girls.

"Confound you and your slave!" cried a gigantic sailor, as he hurled him back. "Let 'em have it out!"

"Yes; let 'em fight it out!" the mob shouted; and the owner of the slave was obliged to leave her to her fate, unless he wished to be attacked himself.

The two fighters had given up their fisticuffs, and had seized one another by their woolly hair and clothes, so that the latter hung in rags; at length the negress saw an opening, seized the mulatto by both hands round the neck, and struck her own forehead with such violence against her temples that she fell down unconscious.

"Look at the nigger!" the mob shouted. "Well done, little one! you're a famous fighter! Your husband will have a benefit!" and so on, sounded from all sides, and they willingly made way for the girl, whose clothes hung in strips about her, that she might go home and receive a beating from her mistress for destroying her raiment, which, as much as herself, was her mistress's property; while the man lifted up his mulatto girl, threw her on one of the empty drays, and ordered the driver to carry her to his house. In two minutes the whole mob had dispersed, and no one thought any more of the occurrence.

Serious preparations appeared, however, now to be making on board the *Oceanic* for starting, and not merely the thick smoke poured from the chimneys, but the white steam rose in a cloud from the 'scape-pipe. The bell had been rung for the second time this morning, the chains were pulled in, and the vessel was only held by two thin warps; the paddle-wheels were working slowly against the current, and the mate sent two of his sailors out to stand by the iron rings on the quay, and throw off the ropes on a given signal.

The bell now sounded for the last time, with quick, re-echoing strokes. All who were still on board to take leave of their friends sprang hastily over the single plank, for fear of being carried off. Others, who were still on shore, jumped on board. The ropes were unfastened, the pilot stood in his little round-house, the two sailors ran over the plank on board, and some twenty men exerted themselves in pushing the vessel away from shore with long poles. The pilot rang his bell, the engineer answered by another bell that he understood the signal, and the immense vessel clove its way noisily through the fruit-boats, which quickly got out of its path, and in a few moments the steamer floated freely on the powerful river, dividing the waters with its paddles, so that they bounded high and foaming against the bow; and the wherries rocked backwards and forwards in the waves raised by the gigantic paddles.

But who comes running up the Levee, waving handkerchief and cap, and yelling and shouting, to the no small amusement of the bystanders, calls till he can no longer utter a sound, waves his cap till he has no strength left to lift an arm, and then seats himself—when he sees that the vessel is going further and further from him, and all his haste, trouble, and fear were in vain, desperately wringing his hands—upon the ballast that is piled upon the Levee?

It is a poor German, who arrived only three days before from his fatherland, who intends to go up to Missouri, and his whole family—a wife, three young children, and an aged mother, who would not be left alone in the old home—are on the vessel that is gradually disappearing in the misty distance. Many ask him what is the matter, many laugh at him, some pity him—he himself sits unsympathizing, and with his eyes fixed on the river. He understands no English, and, consequently, does not comprehend their questions, their ridicule, or their pity; but all he understands is, that he is alone, destitute, in a foreign city, and will never, never again see those who belong to him, and to whom his heart cleaves.

The poor fellow's wife scarce perceives that the boat has started, and knows her husband is on shore, than she rushes with flying hair, forgetting all else, to beg them to wait for him who may be nought to all the world, but is all the world to her. Poor woman! 'Tis the first time she has travelled in an American steamer; and the belief that anything would be done out of *charity* may be forgiven her—she knows no better!

"Don't understand!" is the reply she receives to her entreaties, accompanied, probably, by an oath, as she is in the way of those drawing in the cable. A German sailor, at length, hears her complaints, and runs to the mate, to represent the poor woman's situation to him.

"Go to the captain. I've something else to do. Why wasn't the German fool on board?" is the reply he receives. He runs to the captain, and tells him the story in a few words.

"Too late—too late!" says the latter, shrugging his shoulders. "The man had time enough to come on board."

"But, captain, his wife and children are alone on board, and don't speak any English. They have no one, therefore, to protect them."

"It's very bad; but I cannot help them. I cannot turn back five or six miles to pick up a 'tween-deck passenger, who neglected to come on board betimes."

Planter's House on the Mississippi

CHAPTER II.

THE *Oceanic* rushes with terrible velocity through the water, and the sailor is well aware that all argument is now useless. He goes down to the woman, and tries to console her with a sorrowful face ; but she runs back, shrieking and complaining to her children, and lamenting over the loss of her husband.

It would be, probably, not out of place to give here a short description of American steamers, as they differ materially, in every respect, from ours, and their internal arrangements may not be familiar to all our readers.

The American seeks, in all his undertakings and labours, to earn the largest possible sum in the shortest possible time ; and, starting on this principle, arranges everything accordingly. The building of his steamers is a proof of this.

To be able to employ the hull of the vessel solely for freightage, and not to lose the space where he can accommodate a great number of passengers, he brings his engine on deck, and builds over it a storey which is kept for the convenience of the cabin passengers and officers of the vessel.

The centre of the deck is occupied by the engine, of which the smaller vessels have one or two, the larger from three to eight, which stand in a row close together, the boiler being forward. The *Oceanic* had five boilers. Very frequently, vessels may be seen with two engines, which either each work a paddle-wheel, or turn one together, which is placed at the stern of the vessel, and is called the "stern" wheel; the latter, however, is never very large. Behind the engine, and occupying about one-third of the deck, is the room arranged for the transport of between-deck passengers; and, as we shall be obliged to descend thither several times, we will take a closer look at it beforehand.

Towards the front, or, rather, at the centre of the boat, this room is open, and on both sides run rows of berths, roughly made of planks, three together, one above the other, and broad enough to accommodate two persons, if necessary, while the single bunks are divided from each other by short cross-boards. In the centre of this deck is an immense stove, employed for cooking, as the 'tween-deck passengers are not boarded. When many passengers are on board, this is always surrounded by cooks, whose labours raise the temperature of the deck, especially during the summer months, to an insupportable heat. Here, too, the 'tween-deck passengers have their boxes and trunks, and can do just exactly as they please.

On the larboard side of the vessel is usually the galley, with a larder attached, in which is an immense stove, to cook for the 100 and more deck passengers, as well as the officers.

Above all is the cabin, to which small ladders lead up on either side. A large dining-room forms the centre of it, and on both sides are little sleeping-cabins with glass doors, and each provided with two beds close together. Towards the centre of the vessel are several little apartments for the captain, mates, pilots, engineers, and the book-keeper, near which there is usually a little "bar-room," which, on board the *Oceanic*, was elegantly decorated; and between the cut glasses and bottles, filled with different coloured liqueurs and adorned with gay vignettes, were piled up lemons, oranges, and pine-apples. In the middle of this little spirituous sanctuary—the whole was not more than eight feet broad and six feet high—was a piece of paper, framed and glazed, on which the words "No credit," in colossal letters, saved the passengers any useless inquiries on this subject.

The bar, as well as the dining-room, was decorated with a very elegant paper-hanging, and some engravings representing events in Napoleon's campaigns, and portraits of first-rate steamers, among which, of course, was one of the *Oceanic.*

Immediately in the rear, and only separated by a very large glass door, hung with red curtains, was the ladies' cabin, arranged in a similar way to the dining-cabin, with sleeping-cots on both sides; but the latter were decorated with tasteful drapery, while several rocking-chairs, for the convenience of the ladies, rendered it very comfortable. A little placard, however, over the door, with the expressive words "No admittance," prevented the entry of any gentleman unless they received the special permission of the ladies.

The deck, which runs over these cabins, is covered all down the centre by a species of case, which is made of glass and lets in the light of day, and, at the same time, forms the flooring of the third, or hurricane-deck, which is covered with a sort of coarse sand, that it may not catch fire through the continual sparks that fall on it from the chimney. In fine weather this forms the promenade for the 'tween-deck passengers, as they must not stop on or before the first cabin.

Upon this, and quite in front, almost between the two immense iron chimneys, is the pilot's little wheel-house, which is encased in glass, to guard the steersman from rough weather, and, at the same time, allow him a free prospect in every direction, to immediately perceive and avoid every threatening drift or every dangerous "snag." Ropes run down from this wheel-house into the lower deck, and along its roof to the rudder. These ropes have lately been exchanged for wire on most of the boats, as the vessel, in case of fire, could not be steered by aid of the common ropes, which so rapidly caught the conflagration.

Having carefully examined the vessel, let us now go up into the cabin, to take a glance at our fellow-passengers. The number of male travellers might be about twenty, and the greater part of them were collected in the front of the cabin-deck—which furnished free passage for the cool river breeze—and were admiring the landscape and the splendid plantations that they flew past.

The Mississippi planter, however, who had been to New Orleans to sell his cotton, sat, without noticing the beautiful scenery—which he had seen Heaven knows how often—with his legs stretched out over the balcony that surrounded the deck, and was reading the *Brother Jonathan*. Near him, with his feet also on the balustrade, but with his hands comfortably folded on his round paunch, and regarding the cotton and sugar plantations with a satisfied smile, sat a little, portly man, who also possessed a plantation on the Atchafalaya, in Louisiana, but was now going up to St. Louis on business. He was talking with a tall young man, in a plain brown surtout, who was leaning against one of the pillars, and frequently smiled at the little man's dry jokes; but still there was something melancholy in his glances, which his neighbour's conversation might, perhaps, momentarily dissipate, but not banish.

He was a Virginian, and his open, honest glance, his lofty forehead, shadowed with dark hair, and the sharply-delineated brows, which arched boldly over his dark eyes, formed a marked contrast to the pale face and downcast eyes of his neighbour to the right—a tall, thin man, whose features revealed deep, earnest reflection, and who sat biting his nails, and only raised his eyes at intervals to look timidly at those around him.

"No! deuce take it, sir!—what's your name though?" The little man again turned to the Virginian after one of his usual jokes. "My name is Simmons—and yours?"

"Gray," the young man in the brown coat replied, with a polite bow.

"Well then, Mr. Gray," Simmons continued, "you may say what you like, but you can't be angry with those confounded Irish, in spite of all their mistakes and nonsense."

"But, Mr. Simmons," Gray answered, "in that respect I do not at all contradict you. I never found more humour, more sound sense, more sharp, pointed wit, than among these Irish."

"Just listen to what happened to me the night before last, in New Orleans," said Simmons. "I was in company with some friends, and we had drunk a good deal, and the sweet pine-apple punch did not at all agree with me—in short, I took my hat and went down into the street to cool myself. Well, the fresh air did me good, and I felt quite well again after I had walked up and down a couple of streets. I was then going to return to my friends, but, deuce take it! the streets are all so much alike that I could not find the house where they were. The infernal French name I had also forgotten; and I therefore determined, as it must be past midnight, to return to my hotel, the St. Charles. But, as I did not know the way there perfectly—for I was out almost in the third municipality—I went up to the first watchman I saw, and offered him a dollar if he would take me to the St. Charles.

"'Jist come along, honey!" he said, with such a brogue that I could not mistake the Irishman. I therefore lounged along quietly by his side, until he suddenly stopped before a small house with green jalousies, and nodded to me to go in.

"'But, good friend,' I said to him, 'that's not the house where I live. I want to go to St. Charles's Hotel.'

"'And is it you that has to say where he'll go?' my hitherto leader asked in a loud voice. 'Isn't this the watch-house? and has not my mother's son brought you here?'

"'But, hang it! what crime have I committed, that I must pass the night in the calebouse?' I asked, half angry, half laughing.

"'Arrah, ochone!' the fellow now exclaimed, in the highest degree of astonishment at my audacity. 'Committed no crime? Didn't ye want to bribe me, sur?'

"That was too much, and I began laughing tremendously; he, however, was very angry at it, and pushed me, before I could recover myself, into the open door, where I was immediately received by a couple of others, and handed on.

"I was beginning to protest in all seriousness, and to explain the matter to the inspector; but, unluckily, at the same moment, a whole swarm of noisy drunkards was brought in.

"'I've no time to listen to every prisoner,' he said, sharply. 'Take him away.' And in a few minutes I sat on a hard bench behind an iron door, in the amiable society of rogues, drunkards, and thieves."

"And you spent the whole night in the calebouse?" the Virginian asked with a laugh.

"Do you believe, the fellows would not let me out again before nine the next morning. The Recorder, though, near killed himself with laughing when I was brought up and told my story in reply to the rogue of a watchman. I was obliged to laugh myself, and couldn't be angry; it was too comical."

"Can you, perhaps, tell me, sir," a very elegantly-dressed man said to Simmons, who looked him kindly in the face, "if there is much game in these parts? You seem to know the country, and I have come from New York merely for the sake of sport. I want to find out a place where there is plenty of shooting."

"Well, sir," said Simmons, with a shrug of his shoulders, "there's a poor prospect hereabouts; it's seldom we meet a stag, and the bears are quite extirpated."

"But there are plenty of turkeys?" the stranger asked.

"Not down here, where the river overflows the banks; but in the hills there may be a flock or two; but they are rare, too."

"But, good gracious!" the New Yorker said, in surprise, "I heard quite different reports in the New England States about the chase here. The swamps were said to swarm with wild beasts, and stags, and turkeys; and the buffaloes to stand and drink from the Mississippi while the steamers go past."

"Well, look sharp, then," Simmons cried, with a laugh. "You might shoot at your ease; but you want keen eyes, though, to see the buffaloes on the banks of the Mississippi."

"Is it better in Missouri, then?" the New Yorker asked, very despondingly. "I should not be disinclined to join a party to the Rocky Mountains."

"Then you've come, at any rate, too late for this year," the Virginian answered; "for, if I'm not mistaken, both the companies for the Rocky Mountains (one from Port Smith, in Arkansas, the other from Independence, in Missouri) start on the 1st of May."

"Stand by!" the captain cried from the hurricane-deck.

The *Oceanic* approached the right bank to take up some passengers from a plantation. The steamer's little boat, pulled by two powerful sailors, danced rapidly over the agitated waters, and stopped in a few minutes at a spot where several ladies and gentlemen had hailed the vessel by waving their handkerchiefs, and now waited for the boat.

Several negroes brought down boxes and portmanteaus from the neighbouring house. A gentleman and two ladies got into the boat; the luggage was soon handed in, and in a few minutes it reached the steamer, whose engine was stopped, and which was just commencing to go back with the stream.

"Go ahead!" the captain cried; and a young mulatto now went round, ringing a huge bell, to inform the passengers that dinner would be served in a few moments. The long table in the centre of the cabin was laid, the second bell sounded, and the captain, a tall, handsome man, simply but tastefully dressed, opened the door of the ladies' cabin, and led them to the upper end of the table, while he occupied the seat of honour before an immense roast turkey, so as to be able to see over the whole of the table, and satisfy the wants of each guest. The book-keeper, round whom the gentlemen were collected, occupied a similar post at the other end of the table; and mulatto and negro lads, with extraordinary white linen and woolly locks, waited at table, and handed round the various little dishes with which the board was covered.

In the American fashion, the meal was finished quickly and without much talking; and, soon after, black and tremendously strong coffee was handed round in very little cups, to suit creole taste.

After dinner, Simmons and Gray sat again together on the boiler-deck, and the former, stretching and yawning, declared he had eaten so much that he was unfit for anything that afternoon.

"The gumbo, which the French down here are so passionately fond of," the Virginian remarked, "doesn't at all suit my Northern stomach, and the cayenne-pepper, especially, with which they overload it, is enough to suffocate a healthy man with mere coughing."

"Yes—yes!" Simmons laughingly said; "when I came to this neighbourhood first, it was just the same with me; and my wife could not, for a long while, gain permission to put it on my table; but now I have grown accustomed to it, and eat the pepper like sugar."

"Here it may pass," said a young man, who appeared pale and wretched, and had come on board intoxicated the previous evening; "but a little further up, at Waterlow, where I lived a year, they put any meat in it] they could procure. I myself saw them use owls, hawks, and crows."

"Certainly a pleasant mixture," Mr. Gray thought.

"Well, owls or crows!" Simmons laughingly replied, "I've eaten so much that, if any accident were to happen to the boat to-day—and I shouldn't be at all astonished, for we are going like the wind, and there's the third steamer we've caught up already—it would be useless to think of swimming: I should sink like a stone!"

"Do you think there's any danger, sir?" the elderly gentleman, who had come on board with the ladies, asked, in a somewhat apprehensive tone, and in broken English, but very politely.

"It's of no consequence," Simmons said. "If the boiler were to burst, we should not perceive anything of it here; for we are sitting right over it, and should leave this world so quickly, that we should not have any story to tell about it in the other."

"Then the danger is really so great, as I was told in France?" the old gentleman asked, growing paler.

"By no means," Mr. Gray kindly interrupted him. "Accidents often happen through the carelessness of the captains and engineers, but I don't fear it with ours; for Captain Wilkins appears a very sober and sensible man, who would not hazard the lives of the passengers entrusted to his care, more especially as his own would run the same risk."

"I am much obliged, sir, for your kind explanation," the Frenchman politely replied. "I will now go and calm the ladies, who came on board, I can assure you, with great reluctance." With these words, he bowed and walked to the ladies' cabin.

"I should like to know," Simmons said, when he had retired, "whether he's got a life-buoy. I should be very much surprised if he and the terribly stout lady who came on board with him haven't got them."

The "Oceanic" at the Wood Yard.

"Are they always used on the Western boats?" the New Yorker asked.

"Certainly," Simmons answered; "there are few captains who would dare to start without life-buoys; but I don't think that madame there would require such a thing, for her two hundred-weight of fat ought, in any case, to keep her above water. If I were the captain, I'd make her pay excess-weight. But the boat's stopping to take in wood; I think it would do none of us any harm to take a little stroll on shore.

With these words he rose and left the boat with Mr. Gray, the New Yorker, and several others.

"Wood-pile—wood-pile!" the mate's voice now sounded through the 'tween-decks and the workmen's bunks, which were in a little room in the stern of the vessel, close to the rudder. "Wood-pile, boys, wood-pile!" And from every corner crawled out workmen and passengers, to carry on board the wood that lay piled up on the bank.

At the same time the mate carefully examined all the bunks, to see whether all the passengers, who had not paid to be dispensed from wood-carrying, were at work.

The passage-money is usually arranged after this fashion: the ordinary price from New Orleans to St. Louis is five dollars, without food or bed, and then the passenger has nothing to do with wood-carrying; but if he only pays four or three and a half, from New Orleans to St. Louis, about 1200 miles, he engages, at the same time, to help in carrying up and stowing away the wood, when the boat stops for it. The cabin-passengers have nothing to do with it, of course, and pay twenty to twenty-five dollars for the passage, including board and lodging.

"Heh! old fellow!" the mate cried to a rough fellow, who had retired into a corner and appeared to be asleep, as he seized him by the collar and shook him, "Do you carry wood?"

"What?" he asked sharply.

"Do you carry wood?"

"No!"

"Show your ticket, then."

He slowly produced a piece of crumpled paper from one of his deep pockets, and handed it to the mate.

"Confound you!" the latter cried. "Why did you say 'No!' when I asked you if you carried wood? You're only a third-class passenger!"

"And confound *you!* Why did you ask me if I carry wood, when I'm asleep in the corner."

"Be off with you," the mate replied, angrily.

"Well—well," the other laughed, as he got up and stretched himself, "I shall be in time." And he walked slowly to the forecastle to go to work.

"Do you carry wood, here?" the mate asked again, as he turned to a group of German peasants, who had just come from the old country, and did not understand what he wanted, as they made him understand by shaking their heads.

"*Nix romni heraus!*" the mate said, angrily, as he tried to imitate the German of the poor fellows. "Do—you—carry—wood?" And between each word, which he uttered slowly and distinctly, to be better understood, he gesticulated, as if to make them understand the species of work.

"What does the donkey want?" one of the emigrants asked the other.

"I really don't know," was the answer. "Only see what grimaces he's making!"

"*Nicht verstehen!*" a woman now said to the mate, halloing it into his ears as loudly as she could, probably because she believed that he would understand her better in consequence.

A German passenger, who spoke English, now explained to the people what was wanted of them, and, as they had bargained to help, they immediately obeyed the summons, laid their provisions, which they happened to have in their hands, back in the great chest that served as wardrobe and larder; and one of them said, while he pulled on his old shabby green jacket, "We're a-going," to which the mate grinned a reply of "Yah, yah!"

On the bank, where several hundred cords of wood lay piled up, the book-keeper had, in the meanwhile, measured off sixteen cords—the steamer expended, in the twenty-four hours, between thirty and thirty-five—and passengers, sailors, and stokers were busily engaged in carrying on board four or five of the light cotton-wood logs at a time—those accustomed to it could carry eight or ten—when they were received by others, who piled them in a regular heap. As the steamer had a great number of 'tween-deck passengers on board, nearly all Germans, who had arrived from Bremen in the *Gladiator*, and were now bound for Missouri, to settle there, the work was rapidly accomplished, and in half an hour every log was on board, the ropes and planks were drawn in, the vessel pushed off, and, groaning and puffing, the *Oceanic* again cleaved the yellow waters of the Mississippi.

Mr. Dalton's Escape.

CHAPTER III.

THE darkness of night now descended on the "Great Waters," and the pilot kept a little further off shore, to escape the numerous projecting "snags," while fires were visible on both banks, ahead of the vessel, to show the captain that at those points there was a wood-yard, in case he required wood.

Kindling these fires is a business peculiar to the negroes. As soon as they hear a boat coming—which they can, on a calm night and with a favourable wind, for ten miles—they light a fire, and, if the boat stops and takes in wood, they receive from their masters, by way of encouragement, a quarter of a dollar. But how frequently does the poor negro spring in vain from his hard bed, which he has sought, quite exhausted by his hard toil, to await for hours, by the side of his solitary fire, the arrival of the boat, only to see it—steam unheedingly past! Thus deceived in his expectations, he extinguishes his fire, crawls back beneath his blanket, and, notwithstanding the oppressive atmosphere, covers himself up, head and all, to obtain a little respite from the painful bite of the mosquitoes.

On the right bank, about a mile and a half ahead of the boat, a fire had been kindled, and a burning log swung to and fro, as a signal that passengers at that spot wished to come on board. The *Oceanic* is steered closer in shore, to inquire the number of passengers—stops, sends her boat ashore, and quickly returns, laden with passengers, and away steams the *Oceanic* over the waste of dark waters.

In the cabin the passengers were amusing themselves in various fashions—Mr. Gray was playing chess with a young man; Simmons had also found three acquaintances, and appeared highly delighted by a four-handed game of "eucre." The pale man, whom we have seen sitting on the boiler-deck, near Simmons, and who gave his name as Smith, had seated himself with the New-Yorker to a game of "poker;" and it was at least eleven o'clock before all sought their beds.

On the second day, at about six in the evening, the *Oceanic* drew near the town of Natchez, and the captain had the bell rung as a signal that he intended to stop.

As he had to take several bales of cotton on board, the vessel was brought to her moorings, and a multitude of visitors, scarcely waiting till the planks were run out, rushed aboard like locusts, and dispersed in every direction. They were followed by a number of white and coloured lads, with baskets, in which they carried newspapers, apples, hard-boiled eggs, oranges, and gingerbread, while five or six natty mulatto and negro girls, dressed in gaudy stuffs, brought on board most appetizing confectionery.

The freight had been shipped, several passengers had landed, others came on board, and the bell for starting was rung; the boat steamed away once more, raising an immense swell as it left the town.

"Hullo! I must get off!" a voice now ejaculated; and, accompanied by the laughter of all the 'tween deck passengers, a little fat man, in a white jacket, white beaver hat, and remarkably red face, forced his way from the depths below. "Stop!—stop the boat!"

The mate looked up from the forecastle to the captain, who was standing on the hurricane-deck, and had seen it all, but had only replied to the little man's speech with a quiet smile. When the subordinate found that his chief took no notice, and consequently did not intend to put the adipose individual ashore in the boat, he turned to his work, as if the matter no longer concerned him, had the planks arranged, the new freight put down the hold, and the deck swept, while the "Passenger *malgré lui*" ran from one to the other, and, in turn, prayed and expostulated with wonderful energy and perseverance.

"Pray be kind enough," he said, turning to one of the sailors, who looked in his face with a sly smile—"pray be kind enough to stop the boat; I must be in Natchez to-night, and you're taking me up the river at a furious rate. Stop her—stop her!" he continued, shouting to the captain; "I don't belong to the vessel—I *will* get out."

His cries were all in vain, however; not a soul took any notice of him; and at last, desperate and furious, he paced the deck, and anathematized the captain, the boat, Natchez, and, finally, his own stupidity, for setting foot on a miserable, ill-managed vessel like the *Oceanic.*

"But how far do you really mean to take me?" he, after half an hour's pause, asked the mate, who was calmly watching him as he wiped the heavy drops from his heated brow, and fanned himself with his white hat.

"To the first wood-yard," the mate answered, with the most complete coolness.

"And where is that?" the little man asked, as he stopped his fanning.

"Uncertain," the other replied, laconically.

"And I must pass the whole night in a block-house on the Mississippi, and haven't a mosquito-net!—the brutes will devour me!" the little man muttered in a most desponding tone.

"Very likely," the mate remarked.

Finding there was no way of escaping from his sad plight, the diminutive man forced a passage through the passengers, and huddled himself in a corner, where he waited, with a wobegone expression, the moment when the boat would stop. This took place at about eleven in the evening, and he sprang, with one bound, ashore, to escape as quickly as possible the ridicule of the other passengers.

Simmons was playing "eucre" again with his friends of the preceding evening, and told all sorts of anecdotes, so that he kept the whole company in continued laughter, after which they would go to the bar and "liquor" at the losing party's expense. Mr. Smith and the New-Yorker had renewed their game, while Mr. Gray stood dreamily on the boiler-deck, with his burning brow pressed against one of the pillars, looking out into the dark forest past which the vessel was racing, and whose pitchy darkness was illumined by myriads of fire-flies, which glittered like so many sparks.

They must have been melancholy thoughts that passed through his head, for his eye was moist, and heavy sighs found their way through his tightly-pressed lips.

At Natchez, among other passengers, a tall, powerful man had come on board, dressed in a light summer coat. He had hitherto taken no part in the conversation, and had remained in a corner, watching the game—more especially that between Smith and Bloomfield. He now rose, and, walking to Gray's side on the boiler-deck, he laid his hand on his shoulder, saying politely—

"Mr. Gray."

"Sir!" the latter answered, starting from his reverie.

"You'll excuse me," he continued, with a bow, "if I disturb you at all. I have only been a few hours on board, and should not like to commence a disturbance directly on my arrival; still I cannot but draw your attention to something I have been watching some time, and of which I am certain. The pale man, whom you, if I am not mistaken, called Smith, is a cheat, and must have swindled the other, who has no idea of it, out of a considerable sum."

"I thought so myself," Gray replied in a whisper.

"Let us go down again quietly, and watch the course of the game till we can catch him in the fact."

For half an hour they had been trying in vain to convict him, although he played all the time very suspiciously, when Bloomfield said—

"I wont play any more. I lost fifty dollars last night, and sixty again to-night. I must be decidedly unlucky; for when I hold three kings or three aces, you're sure to have four tens or four knaves in your hand."

"Just half an hour longer," replied Smith, insinuatingly; "perhaps fortune will turn; for it's true I've held extraordinary cards."

He shuffled again; and Gray clearly saw that he dealt himself seven cards instead of five, and very cleverly concealed in his lap the two that did not suit him.

Bloomfield held four queens and an ace in his hand. He staked a dollar. Smith two dollars more. Bloomfield threw a ten-dollar note on the table. Smith doubled it. They showed their cards. Smith had four kings and a knave.

"That's enough for to-night," Bloomfield said; and was just rising from the table, while Smith quietly stretched forth his hand to take up the money; when Gray, who had watched the whole proceeding with a beating heart, jumped up, laid his hand on the money, and cried—

"Sir, you've played false!"

An ashy pallor crept over the detected cheat's face, but his lips quivered with fury; and, almost speechless from passion, he shouted—

"Liar! How dare you——"

He did not finish the sentence, for Gray leaped the table at a bound, hurled the wretched man to the ground, and the two cards fell from his hand. In a second he was again on his feet; and, drawing a pistol from a breast-pocket, cocked it, and fired at Gray, before the latter had warning of the danger that menaced him. There was, however, too little time for aiming, and the bullet passed through the young man's coat-collar. Gray was again about to rush on him, when the man in the summer pâletôt held him back, and said—

"Stop—stop! Mr. Gray, don't soil your hands with the villain. Let him go. He wont escape the gallows."

"But he must give up his plunder," said Gray, calming himself with an effort, as if ashamed of his momentary excitement.

"Let him keep it and be hanged," Bloomfield said. "He has robbed me of a few paltry dollars, but I've had a lesson, and the experience has not been bought too dear. Let him go. His disgrace is punishment enough for him. I wouldn't, at this moment, change places with him for all the money in the world."

"Let's liquor, boys," now interposed Simmons, who had also sprung up with his friends to await the result. "Let's liquor. Hang the rogue! Our anger might be injurious to us, unless we wash it down. I've lost, this time. Brandy and sugar."

He turned to the barkeeper, and all followed his example—paying no attention to the cheat, who retired from the cabin with a heavy scowl on his features.

During the night, nothing remarkable occurred, except that the boat was sent off several times to take in or land passengers.

The next morning, at three, they stopped at Vicksburg, where a whole family came on board, with their furniture, bound for St. Louis. Two cabin-passengers here landed; and one of them looked in vain for nearly half an hour for his chest, which contained all he possessed in the world. The rogue Smith had stolen it, having landed ten or fifteen miles below.

As there were some trifling repairs to be done to the engines, it was bright day before the *Oceanic* could start afresh, and she soon stopped again at the Walnut Hills to take in wood; after which, however, she sped on up the river.

"There's a boat coming aboard!" the mate shouted to the pilot, as he ran up on the hurricane-deck—"just coming from that plantation, and they're making signs to us, as if they wanted to put their arms out of joint."

"There's another behind, Bill," the pilot cried, "and, by George! in the first one there's a young girl and a man. Call the captain! Quick!"

The mate sprang to the captain's cabin, and reported the occurrence.

"Stop the boat!" the latter cried, after looking for a moment at the two approaching wherries. "Lay by!"

The pilot rang, and the engine was stopped; still the vessel ploughed through the water with great velocity, until, at length yielding to the strong current, she appeared stationary for a moment, and then slowly drifted back, while the pilot kept her bow well up the stream. The first boat had, in the meanwhile, drawn much nearer, and was pulled by a young man, who appeared exerting his utmost strength to reach the steamer before the boat that pursued him. In the latter sat an old gentleman with two negroes, whom he seemed to urge on by words and threatening movements of his right hand, in which he held a huge whip, only stopping his exertions at intervals to wave a white handkerchief, to show the captain that he also wanted to come on board.

"Just look, Mr. Gray," said the captain, turning to the young man who stood near him, as he handed him his telescope. "Just look at the furious face the old fellow in the second boat is putting on. I'll wager my head those are lovers in the first boat, and the old man is after them with the hunting-whip. Heaven have mercy on the boy if he catches him!"

"You don't intend to give up the young folk?" Gray asked, somewhat anxiously, of the captain.

"I!" answered the latter, as if astonished at the question. "No, by George! if they were only on board; but I'm afraid they'll catch him—indeed, they're not fifteen yards apart!"

"Let us go and meet them in the jolly-boat," Gray cried, quite excited by the chase, and looking uncommonly interested in the successful flight of the young man.

"That would be of no use. I'll hold the boat a little more over," the captain cried, and shouted to the pilot to give the requisite orders. It all seemed useless, however; for both boats were still several hundred yards from the *Oceanic*, but scarcely two oars' lengths from each other; and although the young man had indubitably the lighter and swifter of the two, his strength was beginning to yield, while the negroes, urged by their unmerciful master to still greater exertion, were doing their utmost to catch the other boat.

"Stop rowing, you confounded rascal!" the old man could be distinctly heard to shout, from the *Oceanic*. "Stop, or I'll shoot you like a dog!" And he drew a pistol from his breast, and cocked it. The young man, however, though he saw his pursuer's act as well as having heard his words, made no reply, but only cast a melancholy glance at the girl, who sat despairing and wringing her hands in the stern of the boat, and rowed on, exerting all his expiring strength to reach the steamer, which was now hardly fifty paces away, while the second boat threatened each moment to come up with him.

The steamer was again in motion, and drew near the first boat, while her starboard side was crowded with passengers, looking with beating hearts upon the race. At this moment the second boat had overtaken the first, and the old man moved forward, with a pistol in one hand and the whip in the other, to spring from the bows of his own boat into the stern of the other, when his foot slipped, and he fell on the negro's arm, who fell back himself, and let his oar go. The first boat shot forward and reached the steamer, while fifty hands were extended at the same instant to help the young people on board.

"Go ahead!" sang out the captain; and the steam colossus slowly left the two boats astern.

"Stop that boat!" the old man shouted, after regaining his feet. "Stop, stop, confound you! Stop!" he continued, almost breathless with rage.

His shouts died away in the distance, for the *Oceanic* now had her full steam up, whereupon the old man was seen rushing like a tiger to vent his rage upon the two unhappy negroes.

The Collision between the "Oceanic' and the "Mazeppa.'

CHAPTER IV.

THE young fugitives, whom we have seen gain the friendly *Oceanic* in our last chapter, had, almost as soon as they were safely on board, been conducted into the cabin, where the ladies immediately took possession of the girl, pressed round her, and wished her joy, as if they had known her from her youth.

Mr. Gray took the young man into his own berth and gave him some clean linen, for he was so heated that large drops of perspiration continually poured down his brow and temples; Simmons, moreover, arrived with a tremendous glass of brandy-and-water, and did not rest till the other had emptied it, in spite of all his assertions that he never drank spirits.

"Hang it, man!" he exclaimed, "do you want to kill yourself? You're as wet as a rat, and wont drink any brandy! Gray, did you ever hear such a thing? He's been rowing himself almost to death's door, and behaving like a brave fellow, yet he wont drink any brandy! No, nothing of the sort," he continued, seizing the young man by the arm, when the latter, with a smile, had swallowed a portion of the fiery draught, and was going to put down the glass half full. "No, no; empty it; it will warm you. And now I'll go and give the young lady a similar dose to cure her fright." And, returning with the glass to the bar, he left the two men in order to carry out his charitable intention.

Off Vicksburg there came on board an old Missouri settler, who had been forced to remain in Mississippi State for several weeks on business, and was now returning to his Western farm. Although he appeared a substantial citizen, he was dressed quite in the fashion of the backwoodsmen, and wore Kentucky trousers and a simple leathern hunting-shirt. The latter, however, though duly fringed like the true Indian garments, was not, like them, decorated with beads or fantastic designs. From several remarks he had let fall, referring to game and hunting, he made Mr. Bloomfield his inseparable companion, who accordingly proceeded to overwhelm him with questions about the Western portion of the United States—about the nature of the game, the hunting there, and the dangers connected with it. The farmer, whose name was Stewart, displayed, nevertheless, a most exemplary store of patience in answering his pertinacious acquaintance politely and in detail, and appeared never tired of explaining to him matters which other men would not have thought of asking. Simmons listened quietly for a long while, but at last, fairly tired out, got up and walked away.

"No," he said to Gray, whom he found sitting despondingly in his berth, absorbed in thought, "may I be scalped if the man in the leathern shirt is not a martyr, and one of the most enduring of his class! He *has* got Christian patience! It is enough to drive one mad merely to listen to the questions put to him, to say nothing of the trouble of answering them."

"Yes, yes," Gray replied; "I observed him even before the lovers came on board. This Mr. Bloomfield is a confounded bore. But the stranger has a peculiar smile lurking about the corner of his mouth ; he'll humbug him splendidly before he's done with him, for he really cannot hold out much longer against such incessant questioning, even if he possessed Job's patience."

"Job !" Simmons ejaculated in astonishment—"Job was patient for one hundred and forty years, but must have lived four hundred and forty to display such patience as the leathern shirt has shown this morning. I never saw such a prodigy ! The New-Yorker asks question on question, and doesn't seem to have any mercy."

"Well, Simmons, what do you say to our chase this morning? That was interesting—eh?"

"I can tell you just this, that the breath in my body was clean gone when the old villain was going to jump out of his boat into the other ; and if I'd had a rifle in my hand at the moment, I really believe I should have fired at him."

"The young lady fainted when she was taken into the cabin," Gray said.

"No wonder," Simmons replied ; "at that particular moment she had little hope of coming on board with her sweetheart and escaping the old one's clutches. By Jove, what a whip he'd got !"

"Mr. Dalton (that is the young man's name) showed me a pistol he had in his belt," Gray remarked. "He told me he had made up his mind to blow his own brains out if the old man entered his boat."

"And what would the poor girl have done then?" Simmons asked, angrily. "Better have given the old man the lump of lead."

"The father of the girl !" Gray cried, in horror.

"Hang such a father !" Simmons said. "He himself would most certainly have ended the young fellow's days, had he not desired so greatly to take him alive. But deuce take me if I should have liked to be in the skin of the poor black devils who will have to pay the bill ! He flew at them nicely when his prey escaped him at the moment of capture. But, Gray," he went on, after a pause, during which the gentleman he addressed had been lost in thought ; "don't be angry with me, but there's something lying heavy on your heart —out with it. I am older than you ; and, although we have only known each other a little while, I have taken a fancy to you, and should like to know what troubles you ; for I might, perhaps, be able to help you."

"No, no, dear friend," Gray replied, with a melancholy smile, as he heartily shook the fat, good-natured little man's hand. "It's nothing—nothing at all. I—I am only a fool at times."

"Hullo! you want to get off the trail," Simmons cried. "No, no—nothing of the sort. I saw the salt water in your eyes last night, when I invited you to liquor. I should have spoken to you on the subject then, but the affair with that rogue of a cheat prevented me."

"I do not see," Gray said suddenly, as he rose and again seized Simmons's hand, "why I should not tell you what it is that gnaws at my heart and poisons my happiness. The story is simple and short, still long enough to render me miserable for my whole life. But this is not the place to tell it. There's the New-Yorker coming. Let us go on the hurricane-deck." And with these words he walked towards the wheel-house, and went up, followed by Simmons, and sat down in front of one of the colossal chimneys. For a few minutes he preserved silence, and looked thoughtfully at the green wilderness before him, and then began, rather speaking to himself than his friend—

"I am a native of Virginia. My father, a Scot, only settled in the 'old dominion' about six years before my birth, and then formed the acquaintance of a young German lady, whom he married.

"My mother bore him three boys in twelve years, but died in her last accouchement, and the child speedily followed her to the grave.

"We boys were now all that was left to my father, and he never ceased to toil indefatigably for us, so that his prosperity increased each year, and he, who had arrived from the old country with a few hundred dollars, soon possessed one of the finest plantations in Virginia, as well as nearly eighty slaves. Scarcely a mile distant from our house—the fields joined—was the plantation of a rich man named Taylor, who, himself childless, had adopted an orphan, and loved her as his own. We were playmates as children.

"Old Taylor died, and left everything to this girl, but placed her under the guardianship of his brother, to whom he entrusted Celeste —then nine years of age—on his dying bed.

"The brother had just returned from Mexico, where, it was said, he had kept a public gambling house, and had earned much money, if not in the most honourable manner. He had a son about my own age, and his plan was soon formed : to bring up Celeste for this son, and so obtain both plantations for his heir.

"This plan became, later, a necessity, because he lost nearly all his fortune through unlucky speculations, and the failure of several banks. We children grew up, in the meanwhile, and Celeste was sixteen, myself twenty-two, when the crafty man first perceived that the familiarity existing between two playmates might easily be converted into love.

"He took Celeste with him to Cincinnati, and placed her there in a school, under the pretext of perfecting her in feminine accomplishments, but, in reality, to separate us.

"It was too late. We exchanged letters; and that which we had not before dreamed of—or, at least, had not dared to utter to one another—we now confessed in our letters in the most glowing terms.

"One of these letters fell into old Taylor's hands; he opened it, and immediately went to Cincinnati in the greatest rage, to suppress, while there was yet time, those feelings which he had not imagined so deeply rooted in Celeste's mind.

"Where he expected timidity and obedience, he found an undaunted bearing and firm will; and soon saw that only severe measures could effect a change.

"He left the plantation in the hands of an overseer, and went to Georgia—I followed.

"Thence he went to Alabama; and there I found him out, and approached Celeste.

"His son, a repulsive looking fellow, with light hair and green eyes—who made Celeste almost mad by his importunate declarations of love—was everywhere their companion.

"I applied to old Taylor himself, and asked Celeste's hand, giving up any claim to her fortune, and handing him a written promise never to ask him for the estates which he seemed so fond of; for I possessed sufficient fortune of my own to live happily and independently. The old villain, however, sent me no answer, because he probably felt ashamed openly to retain Celeste's fortune—of which, as I then conjectured, he had converted a large portion to his own uses—and preferred retiring again secretly, and, on this occasion, to New Orleans.

"He had taken such excellent precautions to deceive me about his departure, that all my inquiries led me to believe him in Texas; but a letter which I fortunately received at the very moment I was going to leave Mobile for Huston, told me where they really were. I immediately changed my plans, and arrived a few days after them in New Orleans.

"There I was taken so ill, that the physicians who attended me despaired of my recovery. For weeks I lay in a terrible fever, which became frenzy when, in my sane moments, I thought that Celeste might be torn from me, and, perchance, compelled to give her hand to my hated rival.

"At length my powerful constitution gained the victory. I was scarce strong enough to leave my room, when I flew to Celeste's residence. She had gone months before, with her uncle, no one knew whither; some fancied to Texas; others to Mexico; many asserted he was in New York, while others insisted on his being at Cincinnati.

"I now returned home, and lived with my father; I slowly recovered from the effects of my illness, and intended to renew my inquiries as soon as I was in perfect health. The news suddenly reached our neighbourhood, in the spring of the year, that young Taylor had married Celeste—whose health had also suffered by a residence in New Orleans—and had taken his wife to England.

"This news immediately destroyed all the faint hopes I had, till then, secretly entertained; I devoted myself indefatigably to the business of my plantation, as my father was gradually breaking, and exerted myself to forget, in the labour and occupation of my vocation, all that had destroyed the happiness and peace of my life.

"In June I went on business to New Orleans, where I was compelled to remain some six or seven weeks; but conceive my sorrow, dear Simmons, when a mulatto woman handed me a letter, a few days ago, which Celeste had written to me when I lay in the dreams of fever, and in which she hurriedly told me that she was being taken to St. Louis, and entreated me to follow her and liberate her from the hands of her relatives, whose importunities and persecution had made life a burthen to her. The letter had not reached me then; and now—now, when it is too late—her trembling voice sounds on my ear, and tears open afresh all the old wounds of my heart."

"Then you're going to St. Louis?" Simmons asked gently, after listening to the young man's story with much sympathy, and seizing his hand as he turned to wipe away two bright tears that filled his eyes.

"Yes, I'm going to St. Louis. I will, at least, be certain about Celeste's fate. Perhaps I shall find her happy in her new circumstances—contented. If so, I may, perhaps, be able to endure what is inevitable."

He bowed his head on his hand, and looked fixedly down, while both were silent for awhile, each engaged with his own thoughts.

Thick mists had descended on the stream while they were conversing; and the steersman, who kept as close as he dared to shore, could only perceive the summits of the trees which emerged from the sea or fog.

"Stand by to stop her!" the pilot called down to the mate; "the mist's getting too thick, and I fancy I hear a boat coming down the stream."

"Ay—ay!" was the sharp reply, and the necessary orders were given on deck.

Young Dalton, who saw his darling entrusted to the care of all the ladies on board, and had taken advantage of Mr. Gray's kind offer to make use of his wardrobe, now walked up to the two gentlemen, and interrupted their previous conversation.

"I am afraid we shall have to lay by," he said, after a hasty salute; "the fog's growing thicker every moment, and just before us, there is a tremendous bend in the river, which has already been the destruction of many boats, through snags, sand-banks, and collisions."

"Our pilot is very careful," Gray replied; "and I fancy he's only getting out of the current to anchor, or——"

"Take care!—look out!—a boat!" a number of voices shouted together; and out of the thick mist, right in front of the *Oceanic*, the shape of a steamer became visible, which was coming down without using its paddles, and on which the bell was now being rung furiously.

Scarcely perceived, it came up with the *Oceanic* before the engine could be stopped; and a moment of terrible, breathless silence—during which the bows of the *Oceanic* ran into, or rather over, the side of the other vessel—was followed by a terrible crash, which was accompanied by shrieks of terror from a hundred throats.

The three men on the hurricane-deck had held on by the iron supports of the chimney, and observed, with bated breath, the result of the collision, but saw immediately, that if either boat were in real danger, it was only the one coming down the stream, for it was considerably the smaller, and was pressed down to the water's edge by the bows of the *Oceanic*. They sprang down—the one to calm his *fiancée*, the other to save or assist, if it were requisite.

The *Oceanic*, as we stated, had run its bowsprit on the forecastle of the *Mazeppa* (as the other boat was called), but had not done any considerable injury, for the captain of the *Mazeppa* had immediately torn the planks up, and found that the water was only coming in through a very trifling leak. He therefore sought to calm his passengers, who had, immediately after the collision, sprung on to the larger vessel.

Simmons, who was well acquainted with steamers, and saw at the first glance how matters were, took Gray by the arm, and, while leading him up the cabin stairs, said, "Come, come! in a quarter of an hour both vessels will be all right; and we'll liquor in the meanwhile, and calm the people up above. There is a terrible row in the cabin." With these words they entered the dining-cabin, in which the most terrific confusion prevailed.

"Hullo!" old Simmons cried, as he opened the door; "what on

earth's up here?" And he really had every cause to ask, for the *Oceanic's* cabin resembled a second Babel, in such wild confusion were Americans, French, Germans, and English running about laden with their traps, looking for their trunks and hat-boxes, to put them in a place of security. A picture of the most excruciating terror was presented by the stout French lady, who was rushing up and down the cabin with flying locks and ashy face, with an immense life-buoy fastened round her—which, however, hung still unfilled round her loins—shouting in a voice almost suffocated by terror, "Blow me out—blow me out!"

"But, Mrs. What's-your-name?" Simmons asked, opening his eyes to their fullest extent.

"Blow me out—blow me out!" the lady yelled.

"Gray!" said Simmons, who had been looking at her for a minute or two, and then fell back in a chair, while the tears ran down his cheeks from laughing—"Gray, I'm a dead man—I can't last any longer—the fat woman—the fat woman wants to be blown out to a still greater size."

"But she means the life-buoy," Gray replied with a smile.

The sight of that stout old lady, on whose forehead the perspiration of terror stood in huge drops, and the comicality of her position, were too much for both Gray and Simmons, and they, convulsed with laughter, left the cabin.

"If I die now, that woman will be my death!" cried Simmons, as he dried his forehead, and ran to the boiler-deck. "I feel as if I had broken something internally."

The captain had now entered the cabin, and, although he could scarce refrain from laughing at the confusion that everywhere met his glance, he at the same time soothed his terrified passengers, by assuring them on his honour that there was not the slightest danger.

In the meanwhile the little Frenchman had been looking for his own life-buoy. The moment had now arrived when he should employ it, and the cushion—which he had suspended over his bed, that it might not be out of the way—was missing at the critical moment. His eyes suddenly fell on Mr. Bloomfield, and he recognised his own life-buoy, but still unblown, round his loins, with which the New-Yorker, who now fancied himself quite secure, was walking up and down, scorning all danger.

"What are you do with my life-buoy, sar?" he cried to him. "Did I pay so moch money for it in New Orleans for you to save you life with it?"

"But, my dear sir," Bloomfield replied, who had seen the article in question hanging in the cabin he had in common with the Frenchman, and had regarded it as belonging to the vessel—"but, my dear sir, I did not know; I fancied that——"

"And you haven't even blown it out!" the Frenchman continued with a smile. "Do you think that the stuff will float you without air inside!"

"Ah! that was the reason the lady cried so for some one to blow her out," Bloomfield said, in surprise.

"Don't mention it, man!" Simmons shouted, who had returned in the meanwhile. "Don't mention the lady, if my life and the preservation of my bloodvessels are worth a cent in your eyes. But come, let's liquor," he continued, as he turned to the bar, where the bar-keeper was busily engaged in repairing the disorder which the first violent collision had caused among his bottles and glasses. "Come here, all of you," he cried in a louder tone. "We all want a drain to restore our equilibrium in some degree. I take brandy and sugar."

In the meanwhile the *Oceanic* had been again pushed off by the industry and exertions of the sailors and 'tween-deck passengers, and both vessels lay peaceably together near the bank, awaiting the rising of the mist.

"But, Captain Dundas," the captain of the *Oceanic* asked him of the *Mazeppa*, as they were seated in the cabin of the former vessel, while one of the waiters was going round the boat ringing a bell to inform the cabin passengers that, spite of accidents and dangers, dinner would be served immediately—"but, captain, what the deuce drove you down the stream, so that we heard neither engine nor paddles?"

"I heard your boat a short time before," the pilot remarked; "but soon after, everything being quiet, I fancied you had stopped.'

"The stupidity of some of my people is alone to blame, and I can't find out exactly who is the guilty party," Captain Dundas replied with a smile. "When the fog grew so thick that I was afraid of a collision, and heard you coming, I called to my mate to have the anchor ready; he gave the necessary orders, and my deck-hands set to work to carry them out. Some cleared the chains, others raised the anchor; but not one of the donkeys thought of fastening the anchor to the chain. When I fancied that everything was in order, and your boat came nearer, while the fog grew thicker, I halloed from the deck, 'Throw the anchor overboard!' 'All over!' was the answer I received, and at the same moment I saw the steam of the *Oceanic*. I immediately ran to the bell, and rang it with all my strength; but it was too late, and it is only fortunate that our collision was not worse than it was. But I see that the fog is settling down, and I'll be off again. I shall be obliged to stop at Vicksburg, and have my leak repaired—so good-bye, captain; good-bye, gentlemen." And with these words he went on board his own vessel, which was in readiness to start.

The *Oceanic* was also unmoored from the trees on the bank, and while the passengers were sitting down to dinner, it pursued its snorting and puffing course.

The company on this day were merrier over their dinner than is usually the case on American steamers, and there was much laughing at the various comical scenes and situations which had occurred during the apprehended danger, and which many of the passengers related themselves, for the sake of having a laugh even at their own expense.

Lynching a Murderer in Arkansas.

CHAPTER V.

THE vessel had now passed Louisiana city and the frontier of Arkansas, which lay extended on the left bank in all its green majesty, while the passengers, after dinner, walked awhile on the open deck, to get as much exercise as the narrow limits of the steamer permitted.

The wind had changed in the meanwhile, and black masses of cloud were collecting on the horizon: the aerial mountains rose higher and higher, in wall-like masses, and soon obscured with their shadow the friendly light of day, which struggled in vain against the dark masses, and was soon shut out by them.

A fine rain drizzled on the deck—at first a refreshing change to the oppressive heat—but, increasing into a tremendous shower, it soon drove everybody back into the cabin.

As nothing else could be done, Simmons had rapidly arranged a game of "encre," in which Mr. Gray, on this occasion, took part: Stewart, the Missouri settler, played also, as Simmons's partner, against Mr. Gray and Captain Wilkins. Mr. Bloomfield, however, had taken his seat close by Stewart's side, partly to observe the game, partly to address his incessant questions to the backwoodsman, and trouble him continually for stories, which, however, were patiently given.

Simmons had several times uttered some oaths, and entreated the New-Yorker not to interrupt their game every moment; but the latter, incurable in his passion, could only be turned from his purpose for an instant, and at length even produced his rifle and ammunition, which he showed the Missourian, asking him at the same time if he did not fancy that such large bullets would easily "floor a buffalo."

"A little bullet, sent home in the right spot, would floor him with equal ease," the Missourian quietly replied, as he regarded the New-Yorker with his bright, good-humoured eye; then taking up his cards, he threw a rapid glance upon them, and said to his partner, "I help."

"A little ball!" Bloomfield cried in astonishment. "A little ball for a buffalo, Mr. Stewart! You are really not serious?"

"Mr. Stewart, I wish you'd pay a little more attention," Simmons said rather angrily, while trick after trick was being made by their adversaries; "if you'd paid the slightest attention to the cards, we should have made the last trick and been out. You surely must have known that I should have played trumps if I'd had any in my hand."

"I presume the buffalo is fat," the indefatigable Bloomfield cried —"how can it be possible that a little ball can produce the requisite effect?"

"Deuce take large and small bullets!" Simmons said; "spades are trumps, and you, Stewart, are the elder hand."

"Now wait, Mr. Bloomfield," Stewart said quietly, as he played his cards; "as soon as this game is over, which wont take five minutes, I'll tell you a little anecdote of my small-bore gun."

"How many bullets to the pound?" Bloomfield asked.

"That's ours, and that's ours," Simmons cried; "the two highest trumps, the two black knaves. Encred, by Jove! Now, Stewart, let us have your story; but we'll liquor first, and the captain must pay—I take brandy and sugar—and then, Mr. Bloomfield, if you don't cease to bore Stewart, I give you my word of honour that I'll bewitch your beautiful rifle so that not a single bullet shall come out of it again as straight as you drove it in."

"It's just two years ago," Stewart began, after all had drunk, "when I shouldered my rifle one day, to make the rounds of my farm, as a quantity of squirrels were doing much harm to the Indian corn. I had one of our long rifles, which carry a small ball—one hundred and eighty balls to the pound."

"One hundred and eighty to the pound!" Bloomfield interrupted him. "Why! with that, the most you'd be able to shoot would be a squirrel—hardly a turkey."

"That was my own idea at the time," Stewart continued, without making a pause in his story. "At that time, too, there was nothing but squirrels in North Carolina: now and then we might catch sight of a deer; and, very rarely, a bear would come down from the mountains, in summer, to pay us a visit. Well, bear-tracks had been lately seen in our neighbourhood, and the old fellow had been followed, but, as nothing had been seen during the previous days, we all naturally thought he had gone westward. I myself, at least, would sooner have expected the sky to fall in, than to find a bear in the neighbourhood of my farm."

"But you don't mean to say you killed a bear with a rifle that carried one hundred and eighty to the pound?" Bloomfield again interrupted. "The balls are hardly larger than swan-shot."

"My field was close to the house," Stewart went on, without noticing the objection, "so that the buildings and a little garden formed its southern boundary, while it was surrounded on the other three sides by a high fence—ten bars high. I sauntered slowly along the western side, with my rifle on my shoulder, without having seen even a squirrel, then turned the corner, and went along the north side, looking cautiously round, without finding the least sign of anything worth shooting. I almost despaired of finding a head of game, when I reached the north-east side of my farm, near which was a little sassafras-thicket, through which a small cow-path led, and had scarcely arrived there when I fancied I heard a slight rustling in the leaves. Now, I had only loaded my rifle in order to kill a squirrel, if I saw one, but I never thought, on my honour, of anything larger; still I stopped in my walk, and listened attentively to the noise that drew nearer and nearer. I had cocked my gun, and was all ready, but still the thick sassafras-bushes hid the beast, whatever it might be: at length I saw the tops of the trees move.

"It came nearer, and suddenly appeared, hardly twenty paces before me, on a little path that led to my house, and in which I was standing."

"What did the bear do then?" cried Bloomfield, who had listened with breathless attention to the course of the narrative.

"A bear!" Stewart exclaimed in surprise; "what made you think of a bear! It was one of my cows, which was going home to be milked."

"And what did you really shoot?" Bloomfield asked, whereat Simmons began to laugh loudly.

"Well, you don't suppose I killed my own cow?" Stewart replied, with apparent surprise at the question.

"Let him finish his story quietly," Captain Wilkins cried, who seemed highly delighted at the disappointment of the New-Yorker. "He's got to go round the whole east side of the fence in order to reach his house again."

"Yes," Stewart continued, "it was one of my cows, which the less surprised me, as the six my wife keeps come home regularly about that time. So, uncocking my gun, as no game had been seen on that side for many weeks, I went on gently, naturally not expecting to have a shot here, close along the fence, and——reached my house in about ten minutes without seeing anything more."

"Ha, ha, ha, ha!" old Simmons burst out. "Let's liquor. Those smooth-bored rifles are really murderous weapons!"

"I am much obliged for the explanation," Mr. Bloomfield replied in a cold tone to Stewart, as he bowed politely, and went off without attending to Simmons's earnest entreaties not to expose himself to the cold night air without a drain of brandy in his inside; and left the players henceforth entirely alone.

"Give me your hand," Simmons said to Stewart, when Bloomfield had shut the door after him. "May I be scalped if you didn't 'sell' him beautifully. I took you for a sheepish Job, but, hang me, you humbugged that troublesome fellow gloriously. I take brandy and sugar."

Both Mr. Gray and the captain laughed heartily at Mr. Bloomfield's disappointed anticipations, and all seated themselves to the table again in the best possible spirits.

"Captain, will you be so good as to speak with the man on shore?" the mate asked, as he thrust his head in at the half-open door. "There's hardly half a cord of wood left, and that on the bank looks good and dry."

"Excuse me a moment, gentlemen," the captain said, as he laid his cards down. "I'll just see what the price of the wood is, and will return in a moment."

"That's what the mate calls looking good and dry," Simmons said, who had walked with the others on to the gallery. "The rain has been pouring on it for hours."

"What wood's that?" the captain cried from the hurricane-deck across to the bank, that was about a hundred yards off.

"Two and a-half dollars," was the answer.

"What wood is it?"

"About sixteen cords," the voice answered.

"But what sort of wood?"

"Yes, you can stop very well just under the cottonwood-tree."

"We must look ourselves what sort of wood it is," the captain said, laughingly. "The scamp doesn't or wont understand my question." And, seizing the bell-cord, he rang several times violently, as a signal that he meant to stop and take in wood.

"Wood-pile, wood-pile!" was now heard through the 'tween-decks, and the mate and his helpers went about with lanterns to drive out the by no means pleasantly-surprised passengers into the wind and rain to carry the wet, dripping logs of wood on their shoulders, down the steep, slippery bank, across a narrow, smooth plank, on deck.

The firemen carried burning logs ashore, and kindled two immense fires; and workmen and passengers thronged ashore to get the unpleasant task completed as quickly as possible.

A fireman had his load first on his shoulders, and walked with a firm step on the wet ground, whose sticky mud clung to his shoes. He reached the plank, and moved a few steps cautiously along it; but one of the logs slipped from his grasp, and, while trying to stop it, he fell with his whole burden into the rapid stream.

"Throw ashes on the plank," the mate cried. "Well, what are you all about?"

"A man overboard!" several shouted.

"The fool! It's his own fault. Lively, boys! carry the wood in!"

"Look after the man," the captain called from the hurricane-deck.

"He's swimming ashore," one of the sailors said. "He's on dry land by this time."

The man had again reached the shore, but would scarcely have made his way through the slime, had not the low branches of a tree assisted him. After having gained the high bank, he once more stepped over the plank, intending to dry his clothes on board, for the poor fellow had no other clothes save those he stood upright in; but the mate met him, and ordered him to help carry the wood in first; he'd have plenty of time to dry himself afterwards—concluding his remarks with, "Who told you to be such a fool as to fall overboard? There is the wood; get to work!"

The fireman, whom his accident had not put in the best temper, pulled out his knife, which he wore at his side like all the sailors, and swore solemnly he'd run it into the mate if he forced him to work in his wet clothing.

The captain now interfered, and would not allow him to work in his present condition.

For several hours the people worked with indefatigable zeal in carrying the wood aboard, while the mate had only to watch lest any one retired to the dark recesses of the 'tween-decks to escape the toil. Several Germans, indeed, attempted at first to retire into the forest at a little distance from the bank, and quietly wait there, reclining under a tree, till the others had finished ; but sharper overseers than even the mate of the *Oceanic*, drove them to work again—the musquitos, who attacked them in countless swarms, and forced them out of the oppressive atmosphere of the swamp.

At last the long-desired sounds of the bell were heard. "The mate's come on board!" sounded like music in the ears of the tired workmen. The planks were pulled in, the boat pushed off, and the *Oceanic* again clove the waters.

The rain ceased at ten o'clock, and the rising moon scarcely illumined the dark stream ; but the pilot was an experienced steersman, who, as he said, knew every inch of the river, and the immense vessel pursued its voyage with only a slight relaxation of speed.

At eleven they stopped at Napoleon, at the mouth of the Arkansas, to put passengers ashore, and to take in several who had come down the Arkansas. About mid-day on the fourth day, the captain and Mr. Gray, who were on the hurricane-deck near the pilot, saw, just when the white houses of Helena became visible, two boats coming down the river, and evidently racing. Both stopped almost in the same moment at Helena, the one to put passengers ashore, the other to discharge several hundredweight of lead.

With extraordinary speed, so as not to allow the other boat too great a start, the heavy masses of lead were thrown ashore, and the *Oceanic*, which did not intend stopping, came up just at the moment when the second boat, the *General Green*, again started.

Not fifty paces from shore, and scarce a hundred from the *Oceanic*, at the moment when Gray and the captain were looking for familiar faces on the vessel with their telescopes, white steam filled the engine-room, a terrible crash followed, and shattered corpses and fragments of the boat flew high in the air.

"Run aside of her," Captain Wilkins hurriedly shouted. "Let us save all we can, for the boat must sink immediately. Into the little boat, my boys—three of you—save all the human beings you can, but let the cargo swim."

With the speed of lightning, the *Oceanic* flew onwards, while the water round the unhappy vessel was crowded with living and dead beings, chests and timber. There was no time to lose, as those passengers who had escaped the explosion were still exposed to the danger of drowning; for the wreck was sinking fast. Several little boats also started from the town to furnish help.

The ladies' cabin was almost the only part of the whole vessel which had been spared, but the female passengers had already quitted it, and had taken refuge on the hurricane-deck, which was scarcely a few inches above the edge of the water when the *Oceanic* came np.

The bows of the vessel sank at this moment; and just as a plank was pushed over to rescue the ladies who were congregated in the narrow space, the wreck began to settle, and appeared about to go down with all on board.

Gray had been looking with a beating heart at the peril of the weak, helpless creatures, when he fancied he recognised a well-known form. "Celeste!" he shouted in horror, and still doubting. A pale face was raised to his. "William!" and the arms were stretched imploringly to him. The vessel sank at this moment, and the waters closed over the beloved face.

"Celeste!" Gray again shouted with a cry of horror, and, without a moment's delay, he sprang into the yawning gulf which had just swallowed his beloved.

The sailors did not like to be behind a passenger in courage. Five of them threw off their blue jackets and sprang after him, and for several minutes, when body after body rose to the surface, it could not be distinguished who was really saved and who lost in this chaos of dead and living things. The passengers of the *Oceanic* stood breathlessly on deck. Gray rose from the waters. On his arm he bore a lifeless body—it was Celeste—and he swam with powerful strokes towards the boat, into which he was pulled with loud shouts of joy from the *Oceanic*. With equal rapidity four other ladies were saved. The rest were never again seen.

Some wherries, too, which had started from shore, moved with practised speed among the fragments of the wreck, and saved from a watery grave many who were struggling desperately with the waves. After the others, a canoe had left the bank, and flew with the speed of wind towards a spot where a woman was struggling with the waves. "Save me," she implored; and one arm was raised in entreaty. The monster, however, would not have the useless burden in the canoe, but stretched out his hand towards a chest that floated near her, and lifted it into the boat. Once again a white arm gleamed through the muddy waves, and then sank, never to be raised again. The man, however, who, with cold blood, had suffered a helpless being to sink close to him without extending a hand to save her, moved about for a short time to fish up several other valuables and toss them into his canoe, and then pulled slowly, and, as it seemed, perfectly satisfied with himself, towards the bank, to place the fruits of his plunder in security.

But the villain was not destined to escape unpunished this time. The captain, as well as several of the passengers, had observed everything from the *Oceanic*, and, with a voice trembling with rage and indignation, Captain Wilkins gave orders to get the boat in readiness.

At the same moment when the man left his canoe, two sailors jumped on shore, and seized the fellow to deliver him to the authorities.

Helena had certainly the worst reputation of all the towns on the Mississippi, and robbery and murder frequently occurred there. Still, the better class of inhabitants were enraged at the villany, more especially as these had been witnesses to it; and the fellow, in spite of his violent resistance, was bound, with the intention of delivering him to the sheriff. This, however, the mob violently opposed.

"Hang him! hang him!" they shouted. "A rope is almost too good for him. Twist some withies, and hang him to the nearest tree."

"Stop!" a respected citizen of the town cried, as he pushed back those nearest him. "Stop! let us vote and see who is for and who against the immediate punishment of the scoundrel."

"Yes, yes, we'll vote!" shouted the mob.

"Well, then," proceeded the man who had just spoken, "those

who are for immediately hanging the murderer—for we can't regard him in any other light—must go to that side; those who wish to deliver him up to the authorities, who will box him up for a year, perhaps, and thrust him again on society, stay where they are."

"Hang him! hang him!" they yelled; and all moved away from the spot, with the exception of one man, who quietly remained where he was.

"I vote for delivering him to the sheriff, and punishing him according to the laws you have made yourselves," the latter said. "Don't take the law into your own hands, men of Arkansas, or you will be no better than this outcast of humanity whom you have just condemned."

"Don't listen to Davis," several said, with a laugh; "he's a lawyer, and must talk so. But we'll show these strangers that the inhabitants of Arkansas will not suffer such villains among them."

Captain Wilkins now interposed, and also tried to dissuade the mob; but in vain.

"Captain," the spokesman said, "these swamps are full of bad fellows, and you may easily imagine that the man who stands there so pale and downcast (for he knew his fate, from the instant you proposed to hand him over to the sheriff, although he laughed and put on a bold face) is not one of the best. If we set about imprisoning the several members of this band in our easily-broken-open gaols, we should do little else than give these villains cause to laugh at us afterwards; for on the very first night a band of his friends, who do not dare make their appearance here in broad daylight, would liberate him; but if he's once hanged we shall have peace, and the country will be spared the cost of keeping him, and lots of trouble. So, boys"—he turned to those around him—"get to work!"

"Away with him!" the mob shouted; and away they dragged the culprit, who now, perceiving his fate, turned in vain to Captain Wilkins, and implored him not to suffer him to be thus murdered against law and justice. It was, however, useless; the mob dragged him away; and when Wilkins returned on board, with Stewart and several other cabin-passengers, they saw the mob carrying the criminal by main force to an old tree. Several now clambered up the round, wrinkled stem, and bent down the boughs by their weight; others fastened the rope round the victim's neck, bound it to the top of the tree, and when they let it go, its elasticity again restored it to its proper position—but on it hung the lifeless body of the executed man.

Simmons was standing on the hurricane-deck when the captain returned, and from this elevation he regarded the whole scene; but he shook his head, and, turning to Dalton, gave his opinion—

"Very quick justice in this country, Mr. Dalton! deuced quick! spares the sheriff and the country a deal of trouble, and is, doubtless, very pleasant for the chief personage; for all the torture of examination and awaiting death are here done away with. I must, however, confess—though it's probably a prejudice on my part—that the judicial course would suit *me* better, if it were only to know how one really left the world. But what's the matter with you? Why are you looking so fixedly down the river? He now turned to the other, who appeared to be listening with the most eager attention to a distant sound, and was exerting his whole power of vision to look down the river. "What the deuce is the matter with you?" he again asked him.

"Mr. Simmons," the young man said in a half-suppressed tone, as he seized him passionately by the arm, "don't you hear anything?"

"Hear! why not? I hear the fellows down there making a horrid row, as if they were going to hang some one else out of fun. Well, they all deserve it!"

"Don't you hear a steamer coming up the river? Listen! Now again! Don't you hear it?" Dalton asked, timidly. "By Heavens! there's the white smoke rising behind the trees! I am pursued, and we are lying here quietly to await the arrival of the other boat!" In despair he pressed his hand against his brow, and ran up and down the deck.

"There's the captain coming on board," Simmons said; "we shall probably start directly, and then I'd bet ten to one that the white puffer behind us will never see us again. There! the bell's ringing. Courage, Dalton, courage! You behaved like a man when danger was near you, so don't despair now, because you see a little white smoke behind the trees."

The captain now came on the hurricane-deck, and when he saw the steam of the approaching vessel, and Dalton's despair, he seized the young man by the hand, and seriously begged him to be of good cheer, and not despond.

"Mr. Dalton," he continued, "you have reasons, as you told me, for not being married before you arrive at St. Louis; and I give you my honour that I'll land you both in good condition there, even if the old gentleman, as I strongly suspect, is on the boat behind us. It goes at a deuce of a pace, at any rate, and yet has only one engine," he went on, while protecting his eye from the sunbeams with his hands, and looking down the river towards the boat, which was seen just coming round a bend, though still several miles off. "Roberts!" he suddenly shouted down on deck to one of the firemen, a negro, "what boat's that? The fellow knows every boat on the river if he only sees the smoke." He then turned to Simmons and Dalton, who were looking through the telescope the captain had handed them, endeavouring to recognise the steamer, and to discover whether it was a fast or slow one.

"Can't see down here, massa!" the negro shouted from below.

"Come up, then, sirrah, and give us your opinion."

The negro reached the hurricane-deck in a few bounds, and, after attentively watching the coming boat, and listening to the puffs, which could now be heard more distinctly, he cried, with a grin which displayed two rows of pearl-like teeth—

"*Diana*, massa!"

"I thought so," said Wilkins, stamping.

"The fastest boat on the Mississippi!" cried Dalton, despairingly.

The German's Return to the "Oceanic"

CHAPTER VI.

"CONFOUND her! I'll try if she can catch the *Oceanic*, though!" the captain shouted, pulling violently at the bell, so that all who were still ashore ran on board, for fear of being left behind. "Let go the ropes!" he shouted down; "push off, men—push off!"

"But the lady whom Gray saved!" cried Simmons to the captain; "she is still on board, and did not appear to be bound for St. Louis."

The latter answered with a smile—"She must have changed her plans very lately, then; for, as far as I could understand Mr. Gray, she seemed very much inclined for a trip to St. Louis, and prefers the healthy air of the North to the yellow fever of the South."

The steamer left the bank, and glided along past the forests.

"Was the lady all alone, then, on the unhappy vessel?" Simmons asked.

"There were two gentlemen with her, I believe; but the one has disappeared without a sign, and the head of the other lies beneath that tree."

"Horrible, horrible!" Simmons replied, with a groan. "Yes; this shameful racing has cost many lives; and I consider it the greatest sin to patronize or even suffer it."

"On the other hand," the captain answered, "there is something remarkably attractive in it, that causes us to forget danger and death when every wish is felt to keep before another boat. I, myself, disapprove of this racing; but I openly confess there are times when I am only restrained by the terrible responsibility I have taken on myself—for hundreds of lives might be lost by my carelessness—from hazarding my life, and that of all the rest, to keep a couple of wretched boat's-lengths before another steamer. I was going once to New Orleans, and had a lady on board, who would only take passage with me on condition I promised never even to try to keep before another boat. I promised; but when we got below Bayou Tunica, we had nearly caught up a steamer during the night, and approached close to it the next morning; but the latter, being short of wood, threw fat under the boilers, as I could perceive from the black smoke, and then began going more quickly, and we could not gain an inch on it from that moment. At first the lady had appeared much terrified, and I was forced to promise her again not to try and catch the boat; but afterwards she said nothing more about it, and in the evening said, with a smile, she would give ten dollars if we could pass the other vessel. I had a couple of cords of pinewood on board for torches; this I had put under the boilers, for I was beginning to grow savage; and before dark we were up with her, and reached New Orleans ten minutes before her."

The *Oceanic* was now going at full speed; it shot through the sluggish water with the velocity of an arrow; and the tortoises that were lying on stumps in the warm sunshine dived down to escape the fancied danger; while the waves behind the vessel, rising against the steep banks, undermined, as if in sport, large masses of fertile soil, and swallowed them with mad merriment.

The firemen had soon recognised the *Diana*, which was trying to catch them, and did all in their power, without any further urging, to leave the swiftest boat on the river behind them. Spite of all their exertions, however, and the really terrible speed with which the *Oceanic* pursued its course against the powerful currents, it could not escape the pursuer ; the white smoke drew nearer ; and louder and more distinct sounded the measured puffs with which the steam was expelled.

The passengers had gone below into the saloon with the captain, and found Gray there, walking up and down in deep thought, but with a smiling face.

"I take brandy and sugar," he said to Simmons, as the latter entered the saloon.

"By Jove !" Simmons said merrily, "that is the selfsame idea I had at the moment, and a stiff glass into the bargain, for I feel quite queer after the hanging affair."

"Heaven be thanked !" Gray replied ; "I saw nothing of it—such a thing leaves a bad impression behind."

"And how's the young lady ?" the captain asked.

"She's asleep," Gray replied ; "but, captain," he continued, with a smile, "I am in your debt ; I paid my passage-money in New Orleans for myself, it is true, but I didn't know that I should end my voyage in such pleasant company, and——"

"Nothing of the sort," said Wilkins ; "the young lady is my guest. Mr. Gray of course thinks that I'll have people pulled out of the water, and then take passage-money of them ? Would to Heaven !" he continued, with a sigh, "we had the three other poor girls here, who now lie at the bottom of the Mississippi. I would gladly take them gratis to St. Louis, and back again to New Orleans ; but, alas ! they require no further help ; they are on a journey where the passage-money is paid—with life."

"But I shall not accompany you, now, all the way to St. Louis," Mr. Gray continued. "The business I had to attend to in St. Louis is now arranged, and I intend to leave you at Cairo, and take advantage of the first steamer up the Ohio, as far as Point Pleasant."

"If the boat behind us had any other name except *Diana*," Captain Wilkins replied, with a shake of his head, "I would say, you could wait for her in Cairo, but I'm almost afraid that we shall make acquaintance with her sooner than is exactly pleasant. Still, if Mr. Dalton——. But where the deuce is he? he was here just now," he broke off, as he looked round.

"He's looking after the other boat," Simmons said, as he stirred up the sugar in his glass, and by a rapid, clever motion sent the contents of the glass to the place where so many of the same sort had preceded it.

The mate now came into the cabin, and whispered something to the captain.

"Confound it!" the latter cried, starting up; "that wont do; I wont have my vessel blown up!"

"What's the matter?" all cried, simultaneously.

"Dalton," the captain said, laughingly, "is bribing my firemen, and has bought two casks of old fat from the cook, to be taken to the fire, and thrown under the engines."

"*Very good*," said Simmons; "if the young hothead has such a desire to blow himself and his Dulcinea into the air, I must most politely decline being one of the party. I have particular business to attend to in St. Louis, and should not like to be floated back piecemeal to New Orleans, instead of drinking my glass of brandy comfortably in the Mississippi Hotel."

"Don't be alarmed, gentlemen," said the captain, as he walked to the door; "I will speak myself with the engineer. I see, indeed, that it is useless. We cannot escape the *Diana*; and she must catch us, at any rate, at Memphis, for I must land passengers there."

Simmons, who had followed the captain, returned after awhile, and whispered something in Gray's ear, as he seized him by the arm and led him away—

"Hang it! it's very annoying; but, indeed, I'd give fifty dollars if we could escape. Still, I shouldn't like the captain to hear me say so, for I believe that he would be pleased that I, who spoke so zealously against racing, should now vote for it. But tell me, Gray, how was your charmer induced to quit New Orleans in August, leaving you to perish there, in all probability, by that accursed yellow Jack?"

"She told me all the circumstances briefly," Gray replied, shaking the old man's hand heartily. "She is not married; and they were shameful lies that Old Taylor spread about in our neighbourhood. But if she had been so, she would now be free; for Old Taylor is missing, and Hutchinson's head lies in Helena. The body had not been found, so Stewart told me, when we started. It was Taylor's intention to go to Matamoras, and thence to Mexico. What he intended to do there, I don't know; but his plans are confounded, and Celeste is mine. I intend to take passage with her in the first boat going up the Ohio. In a few days, we shall be at Point Pleasant, and my plantation is only 120 miles thence, in a south-western direction. And Simmons," he said, seizing his hand, "if you take half as much interest in my happiness as I believe you do, visit me when you have finished your business in St. Louis. I can give you some brandy that will astonish you. But, in any case, we shall find plenty of amusement to kill time."

"Done!" said Simmons, shaking Gray's hand. "I sha'n't go to Washington in autumn, and, as my son is now on my Atchafalaya plantation, I can get away for a couple of weeks. But, hallo!" he broke off, "what does that ringing mean? By Jove! there is Memphis, and there is the *Diana*, too," he cried, as he walked with Gray and Stewart (who had just joined them) to the boiler-deck. "I'm afraid we shall have a constable on board, if we don't make haste and get off again."

The *Oceanic*, when it arrived under the town of Memphis, that lies high on the precipitous banks, passed the first of the two wharves, to the upper one, to land her passengers, and take on board several others, who were dragging their chests and boxes down the hill in a great hurry; while the *Diana* stopped, at the same moment, at the lower one, some 300 yards from them.

The cabin passengers of the *Oceanic*, and especially the ladies, who took the greatest interest in the fate of the runaway young lady, were nearly all on the hurricane-deck—with the exception of Celeste, who had heard the poor girl's story, and now remained with her to console her.

Captain Wilkins had his telescope to his eye, and anxiously examined the passengers who sprang ashore from the *Diana*, to recognise the well-remembered figure of the old gentleman among them; while every eye was fixed, partly on his features, partly on the other vessel, although it was not easy to pick out an individual in the dense throng that covered her deck.

The bell on the *Diana* was rung, and all not belonging to the vessel sprang rapidly ashore, while the firemen closed the boiler down, and poked up the fire with their long prongs, so that dense masses of smoke poured from the funnels.

"Ring the bell, Mr. Blackheath," Captain Wilkins said to his mate; "I really believe the *Diana* intends to bring the old fellow aboard us; there's just such a figure standing on the boiler-deck. He may jump on board, but I'm hanged if he shall take the young folks from my vessel against their will; and it's not very likely that they'll go readily. If the old tyrant insists on remaining with us till we get to St. Louis, I'll put you and your lady, Mr. Dalton, ashore during the night, at Kaskaskia, or some other little town on the bank, and take the old man, while you are being married at your leisure, to St. Louis, where he may go look where I landed you. Go ahead!" he shouted to the pilot, and rang the bell again, while the *Diana* went past them; but from the other jetty, where she had lain-to, a man bounded, shouting and yelling, and frantically swinging his cap, which he held in his hand, halloing at the same time at the top of his voice, "Stop, stop! in God's name, stop!" and a shout of joy answered from the 'tween-decks of the *Oceanic*.

It was the German, who, separated from his family in New Orleans, scarcely hoped ever to find them again, but had taken advantage of the first vessel going up the river—fortunately the *Diana*, for no other could have caught the *Oceanic*—and who appeared now to have arrived only in time to see the boat that bore all that was dear to him in the world start again without him.

"Push off!" cried the mate from below; for the men delayed, and wished to wait for the German—"push off, hang it—push off!"

"Hold!" cried Captain Wilkins, who had heard the woman's cry of delight. "Stop! Take the man on board!"

"Ay, ay, sir!" the mate answered. The ropes were thrown ashore once again, and fastened to the wharf.

At this moment the *Diana* glided past.

"How are you, Captain Wilkins?" cried a tall young man who was standing on the hurricane-deck and waving his hat. It was the captain of the *Diana*.

Dalton pressed Gray's hand convulsively, and looked with a grateful glance to heaven, when the boat flew past with the much-feared father on board.

Attention was now attracted to the scene which was taking place in the forepart of the vessel, when the man left behind at New Orleans sprang on board, and his wife and children fell with joy on his neck, embraced and kissed him, wiped the perspiration from his brow, addressed innumerable questions to him, and would not allow him to speak; for they interrupted him again and again with fresh embraces and kisses.

The very firemen and deck-hands—rough fellows, hardened against all gentler feelings—did not laugh, although the whole was carried on in a language they did not understand. The pure, all-forgetting love of the poor people affected even their hearts, and some of them actually went up and shook the man's hand, who, scarce arrived in a foreign hemisphere, saw himself robbed, as if by some cruel destiny, of all to which his heart cleaved, and who now recovered all so suddenly.

The captain, Dalton, Gray, Simmons, and Stewart went down to him; and Stewart, who, as a native of Pennsylvania, spoke tolerable German, asked the man where the vessel had stopped, and if passengers had not wished to come on board, or made signals on shore, this side of the last city, Vicksburg.

"I don't know if any made signals," the German replied; "but an old gentleman came along in a boat pulled by two negroes, and waved a handkerchief and shouted, and an American told me that he wanted to come aboard. But we were a little too far off; and it was said our captain had laid a wager to reach Louisville in six days: he stopped nowhere to take in passengers, except where he had any to set ashore. From deck passengers," he continued, when he saw that all were listening attentively, though only Stewart understood him, "he took no money if they would only help to carry wood."

"Well, Mr. Dalton," the captain turned to the young man, with a smile, when Stewart had translated the German's statement to him, "now you are safe; for not a boat of all those that lay at New Orleans can catch the *Oceanic*, even if they were to burn pitch and sulphur. On the 7th, by the latest, we shall be at St. Louis; if your future father-in-law is a sensible man, he'll remain on his plantation; and if he wants to vent his spite on any one, he's got his blacks."

The *Oceanic* had, in the meanwhile, acquired her full speed, and behind her the buildings of Memphis were fading away, until they, at length, only gleamed in the twilight like a white streak, which soon became confounded with the surrounding scenery.

When it had grown quite dark, the boat stopped once more to take in wood, and then pursued its way through the numberless sharp curves which the Mississippi makes at this part (one of which is so large that the sailors call it the "Devil's Elbow," for it makes a circuit of twenty miles, and returns to within a mile and a half of the starting-point), towards the mouth of the Ohio.

Mr. Simmons, however, on this evening was obliged to look out for a fresh individual to make up his card-party; for Mr. Gray was too happy, too much removed from this world, to think of card-playing, and (which in Simmons's eyes was even worse) of brandy-drinking. He was sitting by Celeste's side, holding her hand in his, and telling her of all the suffering he had undergone, till the large dark eyes of the young lady grew dim; and smiling through her tears like a pleasant April morning, she returned his loving look, saying that nothing in this world should ever separate them again.

Dalton, in the feeling of newly-acquired security and peace, was spending equally blessed hours with his beloved; and rarely or never did the saloon of the *Oceanic* contain four happier beings than those who looked in each other's eyes, and replied to the inquiring glance of affection with joyful smiles, as the vessel raced up the river.

Not so romantic, but not the less cordial, was the happiness of the poor German family; and with not less attention than that with which Gray caught every word that fell from Celeste's lips, did the poor wife hearken to the description of his fear and trouble as he remained, alone and deserted, in the immense city.

"In despair," continued the poor German, "when I saw myself laughed at and ridiculed by all on the Levée, I ran back to the German inn where we had lived for the two days we remained in New Orleans; and after placing in a corner the coffee and sugar, and the milk I had bought for the baby, all of which reminded me more painfully of my loss, I sank into a chair and sobbed aloud. There were none but Germans in the room, but not a single one took compassion on me; and, instead of bidding me be of good cheer, and consoling me, they made their coarse jokes about my misfortune, and laughingly said that I should not have to bother about my family, for I should never see them again as long as I lived. But what consolation and friendly advice would, probably, not have effected, was done by the rage I felt at the shameful behaviour of my countrymen. I jumped up, and ran back to the wharf, fully determined to go on board the first steamer about to sail, and follow you, although I had not a penny piece, as all our money was on board, in the great red chest, and I had spent my last cent in making the purchases which I thought necessary on that unlucky morning. There was no boat at the wharf going up the river the same day—they had all left the Levée before the *Oceanic*—and mourning, and with gloomy thoughts, I returned to the inn, where I found the bar-keeper examining the things I had bought. I told him of my hopeless condition, and begged him to keep the things, and give me for them a bed and a bit of food. They were worth double; but he seemed to have no inclination; but at last was persuaded, and gave a lump of bread and cheese, and a bed for the night, but no mosquito-bar, so that the wretched vermin almost devoured me. Very hungry, I set out the next morning, and began again my inquiries about a steamer. Fortunately, the *Diana* was ready to start, and the captain took me, as well as all the other 'tween-deck passengers, gratis, on condition that we helped to carry wood. Oh, God! I would so gladly have been stoker, if they had let me, in order to catch you up the sooner, but there were workmen enough; and with frightful rapidity we steamed up the river, and caught every boat we saw. Oh! how my heart beat every time when I saw the white smoke rising before us, and hoped it was the right one! But now I have found you again, nothing shall ever separate us!"

He took his children on his lap, and kissed them, and the tears ran down his sunburnt cheeks.

Cotton Plant

A Thief on Board

CHAPTER VII.

THE 'tween-deck of the *Oceanic* presented, by the glimmering light of a single lantern that hung in the centre, a very picturesque scene.

Against both sides, on which the berths were erected in tiers, lay as many men as could find room; and strange and peculiar was the sight, as from the open bunks, here an arm, there a leg, there a head even, hung out, and snorting and heavy breathing sounded from every corner. The *Oceanic*, besides, did not possess sufficient berths for all the passengers; so on the chests and boxes, which were arranged in the centre, lay and hung all sorts of sleeping forms, frequently in the most neck-breaking positions, stealing from the god of sleep an hour of rest, in which they were continually interrupted by repeated noises and movements.

In one corner there sat, by the pale light of an almost expiring tallow candle, two men playing cards, with the silent, earnest manner of those whose fortune or ruin depends on the chances of the coloured pieces of paper.

The lantern had been put out, and gloom occupied the narrow space in which all, with the exception of the two gamblers, lay buried in sleep, when suddenly a head was raised cautiously behind the German's chest—in which he had foolishly stated his money was kept—a pair of restless grey eyes looked round for a moment, and were then fixed immovably on the two gamblers.

All was silence; only the uniform breathing of the sleepers, or the monotonous sounds of the engines, or, at times, a half-suppressed oath from one of the gamblers, broke the quiet.

The observer gently raised an arm, and carefully examined the padlock that fastened the chest, felt the keyhole, and then, almost noiselessly, produced a number of small keys from his pocket, several of which he tried. At length one fitted; the padlock yielded, and fell with a loud crash on the floor, as it slipped through the thief's trembling hand.

"Go to the devil!" a dreamer near him muttered, and stretched forth his long limbs on a chest, which was at the most three feet square, so that his head hung down at one end, his feet at the other.

The thief, alarmed by his own noise as well as the unconscious ejaculation of the sleeper, sank back, and remained motionless.

"There's something just fallen," the German's wife said, as she nudged him. "Get up and look!"

"It was something on the engine," the man muttered, half asleep, without paying any further attention to the remark.

The wife listened for a little while, but, as all remained quiet, she fell back again on her pillow.

The thief, after lying for a quarter of an hour nearly motionless behind the chest, opened the iron hasp very gently and cautiously, and, raising the lid a little way, thrust in his arm to feel for the money, which, according to the German's statement, was in it. After feeling several things in it, his hand suddenly fell on the desired object, which consisted of a small, heavy bag, containing the whole wealth of the poor emigrants. He slowly seized it, and pulled it, as carefully as he could, quite up, to take it out without a sound, when a long Kentuckian, who had been turning and twisting for a long while, woke up just above him, and stretching his limbs, rose on his elbow as high as the low roof of his bunk permitted.

"Confound the hard mattress!" he said, as he kicked his heel against the bed on which he lay, "and the carpenter too, who has not made the berth long enough for a man who is an inch or two above six feet to stretch himself comfortably. "Oh! oh!" he shouted, turning and rolling afresh, "I wish it was morning!"

With lightning speed the thief had withdrawn his hand, which held the booty he so confidently thought his own, and sank back again, grinding his teeth in the shade of the chest.

In a short while the former silence prevailed in the cabin, and carefully and quickly the hidden form of the thief again rose behind the chest; he gently raised the lid, pushed in his arm, seized the money —whose position he was now well acquainted with—and, holding the iron hasp firmly with his left hand, to prevent it rattling against the bolt, he pulled out his arm, clutching the treasure securely this time in his iron fingers.

He then let the lid fall, fastened the iron, and was just going to hang on and lock the padlock, when a fresh interruption again prevented him.

"I say, neighbour," a man stretched on the floor close to him cried, in whose face the feet of the man reclining on the chest repeatedly fell, "I wish you'd pay a little more attention to your long walking-sticks, or I'll bite 'em for you! Do you think I placed my brain-pan here for you to wipe your feet on?"

"Wood-pile! wood-pile!" the mate's voice now sounded through the 'tween-decks. "Wood-pile, boys! Get up here, get up!"

Then he walked round to the various bunks and shook the sleepers, taking little heed whether those he roused were bound to carry wood or not.

Stretching and yawning, the several passengers rose and rubbed their sleepy eyes, looking for their hats and caps—for, in other respects, they were quite dressed—while the mate stirred up the slowest to make haste or "get fixed," as he expressed it; but he still held the lantern close to the face of the other slumberers, to discover those who, in the darkness, would try to get off work.

The suddenly-aroused sleepers made extraordinary grimaces when they opened their eyes and saw the bright light not three inches from them.

An elderly man lay fast asleep, with his hands quietly folded over his chest, when the mate bent over him and cried, holding the lantern close to him—

"Do you carry wood?"

The man, hardly understanding the meaning of the words, but aroused by their sound, opened his eyes, and, seeing the bright light close to him, hulloed with all his lungs, "Fire!"

"What's up?" asked the mate, springing back in surprise and alarm at the sudden exclamation. "What the deuce are you hulloing so for?" he continued with a laugh, when he saw the other sitting before him, with staring eyes and widely-opened mouth. "Come, man, recover your senses—you wont be hurt!"

"What, in God's name, do you want?"

"Do you carry wood?" the mate asked.

"And all that horrid row on that account?" the other asked, opening his eyes still wider.

"Wood-pile—wood-pile!" said the mate, patting the German on the shoulder, who had also risen, but who, when he saw his chest open, rushed up to it, raised the lid, and with pallid cheek and fixed eyes, felt—alas! in vain—after the little treasure on which his future existence depended. In vain he looked through his poor clothing with trembling hands; the money was gone, and he stood, helpless and despairing, gazing with lustre-lacking eyes on the scattered articles of dress, while large tear-drops ran down his pale cheeks.

"Wood-pile—wood-pile, man! Lively! Throw your rags in—don't you hear me?" the mate shouted, when the former, paying no attention, kept his eyes fixed on the open chest.

"All stolen!" he at length muttered gently, and sank on his knees, exhausted by suffering, and covered his face with his hands.

"What the deuce is wrong now?" the mate said, looking round angrily.

"Some one has stolen his money," said one of the people, who understood German.

"Stolen!" the wife's yelling voice shouted, guessing the English word, as she rushed among the men with a shriek of terror. "Stolen—all our money? Heavenly Father!" she groaned, when she saw the open, ransacked chest, and her panting husband, a picture of dumb despair; and she sank on her knees by his side.

"Wood-pile! hang it," shouted the mate, "out with you! Why are you all standing here gaping? The boat has stopped; settle it all afterwards, but carry in the wood first."

The people who were bound to carry wood went out, but the German remained lying moodily by the chest, while, in frenzied haste, his wife again ransacked every portion of the huge chest, and threw everything out. It was useless. Equally unsuccessful was the result when several applied to the captain and requested a search, which was carried out when the boat started again; but the thief had quietly remained behind, preferring a short stay in a block-house among the swamps, to the strict examination to which he would probably have been exposed on board the boat. The search—which is always a most ungrateful task on board a steamer, where such numbers of dark corners render the recovery of small stolen goods highly difficult, if not impossible—was in vain; but day dawned before further attempts to discover the thief were given up as fruitless. All the passengers seemed to feel for the loss of the poor people, excepting the gamblers, who, without noticing in the slightest the noise around, or even inquiring into the cause of it, had remained seated over their game; and when morning, with her cold hand dissipated the shades of night, and the first timid sunbeams found their way through the doors and window, they blew out their dim, yellow-burning tallow candle, to continue their game by daylight. In the saloon, however, Simmons made a collection for the poor people, to protect them for awhile, at least, from the pangs of starvation.

The *Oceanic* pursued her course with extraordinary speed, and one bend after the other of the majestic stream appeared and disappeared again.

Interminable forests, miserably gloomy wildernesses, lay on both sides, only here and there broken by the little block-hut of a settler, who had retired to this comfortless solitude—almost cut off from all human society, and left to the mercy of the musquitos—to sell wood to the steamers traversing the stream: although neither the trees he felled nor the land on which they stood were his property, and his small, low house was almost invisible among the gigantic trunks of the virgin forest that encircled it. Nor without difficulty could the observer recognise, from one of the passing steamers, a clearing in the thick forest, had it not been that a little square of decayed trees, a shining grey shingle roof, that gleamed amongst them—and which, it appeared almost inevitable, must be destroyed by one of the colossal decayed trunks at the first puff of wind—as well as a strip of piled wood, close to the bank, revealed the abode of a family. This link in the chain of human society, made the spectator almost involuntarily exclaim, "What, in Heaven's name! could induce men—living, thinking, reasoning beings—even if they wished to retire from their fellows and live apart from all the world, to settle in such swamps, inhabited only by insects, reptiles, and beasts of the forest—where fever and pestilence rage—where the Mississippi overflows its banks, and they are forced, at certain seasons, to carry all their property to a boat, to save it from the greedy waters; while their laboriously-piled stock of wood, carried off and floated away by the wild waters, covers the surface of the river, which in rising left not a place where they could find even a dry spot to bury their dead?"

The blue smoke rose gently from these advance-posts of civilization, and disappeared, driven by the light breeze, amid the summits of the cottonwood-trees which enclosed the small clearing on all sides; while thick underwood and almost impenetrable creeping-plants filled the space between the immense trunks, and formed, as it were, a verdant wall around the spot.

The *Oceanic* was steaming past one of these clearings, which appeared, however, to have been only lately commenced, for the trees which had been blazed had not yet decayed, and no fire-wood was piled up; and only the glistening roof, formed of freshly-cut boards, as well as a few spotted cows, which were walking behind one another, along a narrow path near the bank—announced the neighbourhood of human beings.

"Hullo! Boat!" a voice shouted across, and a cloth was waved on a stick.

"Will you stop?" the pilot asked the captain, who was standing near him, and looking across to the spot whence the voice was heard.

"Let the boat fall off a little. There seems to be only one man: we'll ask him what he wants."

"Hullo! Boat!" the voice shouted again, more impatiently than before.

The captain rang the bell twice to let the person on shore know that he had heard him, and would stop; and the vessel went across to the spot where the man was standing.

"What do you want?" the captain shouted, when he got near enough. "Where are you going?—to St. Louis?"

"Ay, ay!" the man ashore shouted, as a sign that he understood.

"Do you want to come aboard?" the captain said, somewhat impatiently.

"Do you want to buy a rattling good canoe?" the other replied, as he held his hands funnel-wise to his mouth.

"You *don't* want to come aboard?" the captain shouted, half in surprise, half in anger.

"I say, do you want to buy an uncommon good canoe?" the hoped-for passenger again shouted.

"Get out with you!" the captain shouted furiously, and he nodded to the pilot to go ahead.

"Ay, ay!" the man on shore shouted, who did not appear to have understood the last reply, and turned quietly on the road back to his cabin.

"Bless my stars, captain!" Simmons grinned, when the former

came down into the saloon, "why didn't you take advantage of such a good offer? 'Pon my word, the canoe must be very good, if you went across the Mississippi to have it only offered you!"

"You may laugh; but what on earth could I do? If I had landed, the fellow would quietly have gone into the cane-brake, and Argus himself could not find him there. On such occasions it is advisable to put on a good face."

"Do you believe, then, that he only wanted to sell you?" Simmons asked in surprise.

"Well, what else?" Wilkins replied. "I cannot believe that a man would, in earnest, hail my vessel all across the Mississippi to offer me a miserable canoe, when he knows that all I could do with it would be to use it for firewood!"

"But then it was an uncommon good one!" Stewart said, smilingly.

"Don't believe it, captain," Simmons said—"don't believe it. The man was perfectly in earnest; and, if you had landed, he would have remained on the bank, in the firm idea that you intended to look at his canoe. What do you think a neighbour of mine, on the Atchafalaya, did lately? We had bet a gallon of whisky with a friend that a hog he had just killed weighed twenty score, and not eighteen, as the other stated; and they had agreed, as there were no scales in the whole neighbourhood, to leave it to the first comer to settle the weight, and take his verdict as final. The first thing we saw, then, was the *Black Hawk* steamer, which, like ourselves, was going up the other side of the stream; and my two friends regarded it as a sign from Heaven, not only to take the captain as judge, but also, at the same time, buy the whisky on his vessel, as it was the only way they could procure the liquor they so much admired—though, for my part, I prefer brandy. No sooner said than done. With wonderful energy they began waving their handkerchiefs; and, as the vessel had not many passengers on board, the captain, in the hope of earning fifteen or twenty dollars, stopped, and was not a little surprised to find he was only hailed to decide the weight of a hog. It is true he was violent in his remarks; but that was no use, and he was obliged to go on his way, furious at the impudence or ignorance of the fellows; while at the same time they, deceived in their expectation of getting the whisky, paid him all sorts of compliments."

"And were they stupid enough to do that seriously?" Captain Wilkins asked.

"Just as seriously as the man over there asked you if you wanted to buy a canoe, and who, I am quite convinced, will hail the next boat for the same purpose."

"Well, the Yankees are not altogether wrong when they cut jokes about the Westerns," said Wilkins; "and Mr. Bloomfield will have fine stories to tell about us when he returns to the Eastern settlements."

"Not so bad as you fancy, captain," Bloomfield replied, who had made it up again with Stewart. "The reputation the inhabitants of the West bear in the Yankee States is by no means that of blockheads. On the contrary, I always heard that the pedlars and clockmakers, who traverse all the States from the East, do less business in the West than in the central States."

"All respect for your clockmaker," said Simmons. "My father always said that a Yankee clock-pedlar would talk a man into buying a clock on his death-bed, and that the fellows would never leave a house they had once entered without disposing of some of their goods."

"Still the clock-pedlars are the best of the lot," Captain Wilkins remarked; "but just remember how the Yankees behave, with their wooden hams sewn up in canvas, which they sell by boatloads."

"Or the wooden nutmegs," Bloomfield laughed.

"That's nothing in comparison with a notice I found in a Charleston paper," said Gray, who had just come in, and drew the paper from his pocket. "It seems as if our Eastern countrymen are good in the manufacture of sausages. Only listen to the following:—

"'The sausages received from Hartford, Connecticut, consisting of finely cut red flannel and potatoes, may certainly be difficult of digestion, but they may pass; those, however, partly composed of brown paper are not even fit for dogs.'"

"Not bad!" Bloomfield replied with a loud laugh, in which all heartily joined—"not bad! My countrymen do not seem to retrograde in their industry; but, to make up for it, they are behind the Westerns in horse-dealing, especially in the Indian fashion of buying a horse, in which branch of trade Arkansas is specially distinguished."

"Well, I don't know if Missouri is far behind it," Stewart remarked. "There are regular confederations formed between the two States; and whatever is stolen in Missouri finds a ready market in Arkansas, more especially as lately the punishment for horse-stealing has been abolished, which used to make the fellows think twice before they set about it. How would it be, though," he broke off suddenly, and looked at Simmons, "if we were to have a hand of cards? The weather looks gloomy again, and we could not pass our time better."

"With all my heart," Simmons replied; "I was just going to propose it; but I must liquor first, for sitting down dry don't agree with my constitution. Bar-keeper, glasses here!"

Mr. Gray declined, however—by no means to Simmons's pleasure—and gave up his place to Bloomfield, whom he did not rightly trust since the hunting affair. Stewart's last story, however, had been a lesson to him, and he did not require a second reproof just then.

The vessel stopped at nightfall to take in wood, while the saloon passengers ate their supper. The meal was ended, the wood on board, and the *Oceanic* was again cutting through the rapidly-flowing waters, when a terrible noise was heard from the 'tween-decks, which seemed to grow fiercer every moment.

"Hullo!" Captain Wilkins cried, "what's the matter now? On this voyage, there are nothing but disturbances in the 'tween-decks. I must go and see, myself, what is the matter, or they'll be murdering each other."

With these words he got up from the card-table, at which he had just seated himself, and turned to the door, when the mate met him, with a young German, who, however, spoke English fluently.

"Captain," the mate began, "that cursed nigger, the cook, has been doing something wrong; but the man here can tell you all about it," he continued, pointing to the German, "for it was all talked over in Dutch, and I couldn't make it out."

"And what have you to say, sir?" the captain turned politely to the young man, who stood there pale, and almost, as it seemed, deprived of speech.

"The worst crime a negro ever yet committed," the young man began, his suppressed anger at length bursting out. "Gentlemen" (he turned to the cabin passengers, who were thronging round him), "listen to me, and then say, yourselves, what shall be done to the villain. Among my countrymen, who have all come, lately, from their old home, to find a new Fatherland in this hemisphere, there is a poor deaf and dumb girl, an orphan, who had been brought up by poor folk, and would not quit them when they emigrated. The child—for she is scarce fifteen—followed the black villain, innocently enough, to his cabin to-night, when the boat stopped to take in wood, and was there insulted by the fellow, who took advantage of the dumbness of the poor girl, who could not utter a cry for help."

"What!" cried Simmons and Stewart unanimously. "Kill the cursed nigger!—hang him!—throw him overboard!" sounded from the lips of all the horrified men.

"Where is the cook?" Captain Wilkins asked, biting his lips and stamping his feet; "by Heaven, he shall be hanged!"

"We have bound him, and he's lying on the deck," replied the young German, whose name was Ehrhold.

"Throw him overboard, then," cried Stewart; "that's the shortest way. The fellow should not be alive now if I were concerned."

"You *are* concerned, sir!" Ehrhold violently interrupted him. "You are concerned, as well as every white man on board; for I really don't believe," he went on, drawing himself up to his full height, and looking round sharply, "that there is a gentleman aboard this vessel who would not protect a poor deaf and dumb white girl against the insults of a negro, and avenge her shame."

"Captain Wilkins," Simmons said, seriously, "lately, when we saw the affair at Helena, I spoke in strong terms against Lynch-law, and didn't think it right that the people should take the law in their own hands; but the Almighty punish me if I would not vote *for* it now! Hang the villain, or drown him, or kill him in some way or other; for if he were to escape from the boat unpunished, which he will certainly attempt to do, you will have but poor thanks from the white population of St. Louis."

"Would it not be better to keep him in bonds, and deliver him to the authorities at St. Louis?" Mr. Gray interposed, for he saw that the captain was beginning to vacillate; "he could be well guarded, and his escape be made entirely impossible."

"There is no fear of his not being kept secure," the German said; "there are fifty men below who will not take their eyes off him—but——"

"You are never going to stand on ceremony with the black brute?" Stewart asked, angrily; "it's a sin every moment the villain still breathes."

"Yes, yes, captain," all the saloon passengers cried almost unanimously; "hang him!—make the boat fast, and hang him to the first tree!"

"Gentlemen!" the captain now said, as he drew himself up, "you are in the right; the fellow deserves death, and shall not escape fitting punishment; but there are two reasons which prevent me from punishing him directly, or on board—the first, and most important, is, that if we Lynch the nigger, I am the only man on board responsible for it, if it takes place with my consent; and if the authorities in St. Louis do not think badly of our conduct, still I shall be exposed to a number of disagreeable examinations, &c., and, perhaps, be punished in the bargain."

"Punished for hanging a nigger that has committed such a crime?" all said in astonishment.

"Besides this, gentlemen," the captain continued, quietly, "I have another reason; and that is, I have some twenty saloon passengers, besides my officers and hands, of whom the former have paid for their board, and the others work for it; and all these want to eat, and I am not an exception. This black scoundrel, however, is the only cook on the boat, and that must induce me to take him up to St. Louis, of course under strict surveillance, when the magistrates may punish him. And you know, gentlemen, that the inhabitants of St. Louis show little mercy in the punishment of blacks; it is scarcely half a year since they burnt a negro alive who killed his master."

"But, captain," Ehrhold interposed, "if you let the nigger go about at liberty and cook, he will certainly take the first opportunity and jump overboard, to swim ashore, as he knows what a fate awaits him."

"I'll be hanged if the villain should live two minutes longer," Stewart broke out, "if I were captain."

"Gentlemen, you have no responsibility," Captain Wilkins remarked, very quietly. "When the boat stops, you'll go on shore, continue your journey, probably to Illinois, and not be seen again; but I remain by my vessel, and all that belongs to me, for a time, and of course the magistrates will naturally make me answerable. Mr. Ehrhold," he turned to the latter, "you appear to be a suitable man, so keep the black villain under guard during the night, and to-morrow he can cook breakfast with twenty men at his heels, if you like; in the same way, dinner and supper, and the next morning early we shall be in St. Louis."

"Good, captain," the German replied; "we'll do all we can; but if he make the slightest attempt to escape, you may be assured he will be shot."

"Don't kill him, for Heaven's sake!" Stewart quickly observed; "that would be a kindness to him. No; fire at his legs, so that he can't run away, but leave his neck uninjured, that we may hang him afterwards; for I'm a rogue if the inhabitants of St. Louis will let the villain be ten minutes in prison, as soon as they have heard the nature of his crime."

"Very good, very good," said Wilkins; "if I only get rid of him, what they do with him afterwards is a matter of perfect indifference to me."

"Let us go below, and look at the brute," said Simmons; and all followed him as he went down the dark cabin stairs, through the engine-room, dimly lighted by two lamps, between bales of cotton and bags of coffee, to the 'tween deck.

There lay the negro, fastened to a pillar—his clothes hanging in rags about him—with swollen face and gleaming eyes, surrounded by all the passengers, who had bound him after violent resistance. Gnashing his teeth, he regarded the new comers.

"Captain," Stewart exclaimed, when they saw the horrible, blood-covered figure lying on the deck, "if you let that fellow cook another meal on board your boat, I'll be hanged if I touch a morsel of it."

"He certainly does not look very appetizing," said the captain, as he turned in disgust from the black, whose eyes rolled horribly.

"Bind him hand and foot, and throw him overboard: that's my advice," said Stewart.

"I really believe that would be best," Simmons agreed, while the 'tween-deck passengers demanded his death unanimously.

"I vote, however, for handing him over to the police," Mr. Gray's clear and powerful voice sounded through the noise; while the negro, with rolling eyes, and mingled fury and terror in his restless glance, regarded those around him. "He is now securely bound and carefully guarded, and it is better that he suffer his punishment at St. Louis, for that which is justice by the verdict of the jury would be murder here."

"I thank you, Mr. Gray," the captain said, as he shook the young man's hand; "that is entirely my view. And, as a proof that I am in earnest, some of my people shall watch him in turn, to prevent any chance of escape. The villain shall not escape punishment, but it shall be inflicted by justice."

The passengers now went up again to the cabin, while the captain made various arrangements to guard the prisoner, and calm the excited temper of the 'tween-deck passengers, amongst whom several Kentuckians, who had come on board at Memphis, insisted on throwing the nigger to the fish.

Several women also offered, as soon as they heard a cook was wanted, to undertake the office till they arrived at St. Louis, so that no chance might be given the negro to escape.

The Cook attempts to escape

CHAPTER VIII.

WHEN the night came, the passengers doubled the guard round the prisoner, who, with his hands bound on his back, lay on the ground silent and gloomy, and seemed to have yielded to his fate; for he looked with glassy eyes at the pale, flickering light of the lantern, till fatigue and exhaustion overpowered him, and he fell into a restless slumber.

The eastern sky had assumed a lighter shade of grey when the *Oceanic* reached the little town of Cairo, at the mouth of the Ohio, and passed from the yellow waters of the Mississippi into the clearer current of the former river, to fasten to the wharf.

The boat lay against the bank, the sounds of the bell had died away, the planks were pushed out, and Mr. Gray led his young *fiancée* down the cabin-stairs, accompanied by the captain, Simmons, Stewart, and Dalton. Upon the plank he turned once again, and took a cordial farewell of his newly-acquired friends, repeating his invitation to all, but more especially to Simmons, to visit him right soon, and convince himself how happily and contentedly he lived.

Simmons accepted the invitation, and the young man cautiously led his beloved Celeste over the narrow plank on shore, and up to the hotel, to await the arrival of a vessel bound up the Ohio; while the crew of the *Oceanic* took all imaginable trouble to get off the tough slime of the bank, in which it was securely imbedded.

The engine was reversed, and the whole crew summoned to the forecastle, to push her back with long poles into deep water; she remained perfectly walled in by the mud that formed the bank, and which was so soft and yielding, that the poles had no hold, and sank deeply into it, so that they could only be freed by the united struggles of several men.

"Call the deck passengers!" the mate now shouted, rendered quite furious by the useless toil—"call the deck passengers! and you fellows," he said to the workmen, "get closer together—hang it! don't lie on the poles as if you were going to sleep. Give her it, boys—give her it!"

The majority of the deck passengers obeyed the summons, and laboured at the poles with all their strength, in order, by their united exertions, to make one desperate attempt to push her off.

"There she goes!" the mate shouted, cheerily. "Be alive, my brave fellows—push away!" And, accompanying his words by a good example, he pushed with such force, while pressing his foot against the seat, that the perspiration ran down his brow, and his eyes seemed ready to burst from their sockets. At this moment a pole broke, which twelve powerful fellows had been pushing against; and, partly from their own impulse, and partly from the pressure of those behind, four men fell overboard, amid the cries of the others.

The prisoner had lain, in the meanwhile, almost deserted by all his guards, as the majority of the men had been required forward, to help push the boat off. Only two young German peasants had been left to watch him, and never took an eye off him. One of his lads now went past, to cut some slices of meat for breakfast from the joints hanging in the stern, and him the negro asked to give him a draught of water.

The young mulatto returned in a few seconds with a tin cup, and held it to the lips of the thirsty man, while the latter greedily swallowed the cooling draught.

At this moment the loud cry was heard which the sudden disappearance of the four men had involuntarily drawn from those around.

The two watchers sprang up in terror, and looked towards the spot whence the noise came; but the mulatto, employing the moment which might never offer again, passed the sharp knife he held in his hand over the cords that bound the prisoner, and before the two Germans—who were all amaze at the sudden freedom of the negro—could utter a single cry of alarm, the cook sprang up, seized the knife, which the mulatto willingly yielded to him, and leaped, with a wild bound, through the crowd of shrieking women, towards the stern of the vessel, to throw himself into the boat that hung there, or to save his life by swimming. At any rate, he was quite determined, as the brandished knife proved, to defend his newly-recovered liberty to the utmost. He, however, had scarcely reached the stern, and was just going to spring over the taffrail into the boat, when his wildly-rolling eye fell on a Kentuckian, who had retired thither into the cooler atmosphere, and troubled himself very little about the disturbance in the bows.

The shrieks of the women when they saw the negro rushing upon them with upraised knife first attracted his attention. Before, however, he could recover from his sudden surprise, the negro had bounded into the boat, cut one of the ropes that held it, and was just turning to the other, when the Kentuckian, who had rapidly regained his energies, soon perceived that decision alone would be of service. Despising the long knife of the desperate man, he rushed upon him, not only to upset him, but at the same time hold him fast. The pursued man soon perceived the enemy's intention, and, with a rapid motion, got out of the way of the other as he sprang on him; the Kentuckian consequently lost his balance, slipped on a thwart, and fell forward, exposed to the shining knife of his black and desperate assailant.

The latter was well aware how precious the few moments allowed him were, and sprang with a shout of joy on the fallen man; but at the moment of securely-fancied victory, a heavy bucket struck him on the chest, and before he could recover from the unexpected blow, the tall form of the young German followed, who seized his right arm, and tried to take the knife from him. The result of the contest would have been most inauspicious for the young man—for the negro, with great agility, exchanged hands—had not the Kentuckian by this time recovered from his fall, and, with the German, thrown down and firmly held the runaway, although he continually employed his disengaged armed hand, and wounded both men with his expiring strength. Several deck hands, however, sent down by the mate to fetch a pole to push the vessel off, also leaped into the boat, and by their united help the criminal was soon mastered, bound, and raised by a rope on to the deck.

Under the kicks and blows of the sailors, he was dragged again to his pillar, where they once more entrusted him to the charge of the passengers; while others—as the vessel was now pushed off, and the men who had fallen overboard saved—led the mulatto who had freed the prisoner and given him the knife, to the bows, and fastened him to a post. Under the directions of the mate, who appeared to take special delight in it, they flogged him with a heavy leathern whip until the blood burst from the wounds, and he fainted away under the punishment.

The women in the meanwhile bound the numerous, though not dangerous, wounds the Kentuckian and German had received from the black, and declared repeatedly that it would do their hearts good to see the villain hanged.

Captain Wilkins had also come below, and gave two of his people the special order not to leave the negro for a moment, and to fell every black man who dared to come within ten paces of him.

With this, though, the Kentuckian's countrymen and comrades

were not at all satisfied; and when the captain had gone up again to the cabin, and they were left to themselves, one of them walked forward and addressed the others as follows:—

"Boys! that black dog has not only insulted a poor deaf and dumb *white* girl, but has also spilled *white* blood; and although Cap'n Wilkins seems to have a great wish to take him in good condition to St. Louis, still I vote that we throw him overboard, bound as he is. The cat-fish can then see what they can do with his black hide."

"Wait a couple of minutes, till my arm is bound up," said the wounded American, "and I'll help. I should like to have a share in sending the villain to eternity."

"I believe myself it will be the best way," said Ehrhold. "The deuce take prisons! it may be possible for the fellow to escape."

"Overboard with him!—overboard!" several voices shouted at the same time, and the very deck hands who were left to guard the prisoner unfastened him from the pillar.

"Gentlemen!" the negro shouted in terror, who probably read his impending fate in the menacing glances of those around—"gentlemen, don't murder me in cold blood!"

"Dog!" shouted the wounded man, as he struck him in the face, "you shall drown!" And he seized him with his left, unwounded arm, and strove to drag him to the side.

"Murder!" shrieked the horrified prisoner. "Murder! Captain Wilkins, they're going to murder me!"

"Hullo, boys! What's up?" cried the mate, springing among them. "Don't be fools and run any unnecessary risk. The fellow shan't escape his punishment." And with these words he tried to remove the Kentuckian's hand from the negro's collar; but his comrades rushed forward, and one of them, as he thrust the mate back, said—

"Hang you! keep back and attend to your own business. This is ours, and if you don't like it, you can go!"

"Oh, Mr. Blackheath, don't let them kill me like a dog," the negro implored.

"Why delay?" the majority of the passengers now cried, as well as many of the deck hands and sailors, who had come up. "Overboard with him!—overboard!"

"Murder! murder!" he yelled, as he in vain tried to break his bonds, while the powerful arms of the Kentuckian and several Germans dragged him to the side.

"Stop!" the captain cried, who rushed up, having been called by one of the men—"stop!"

"One—two—three! Heave!" the Kentuckians sang, in boatmen's fashion, as they raised the prisoner in the air; and at the last "heave," which was uttered in a loud and powerful voice, the dark body flew several paces beyond the protecting side, and disappeared in the yellow foaming waves which were raised by the paddle-wheels.

At the same moment the engine was stopped, and the boat only went on by its own impetus; Captain Wilkins immediately sprang among the boatmen, when the dark figure of the nigger rose, writhing and hoisting, some twenty yards behind the vessel.

"Jump in the boat, my boys," he cried in horror, to his deck hands. "Ten dollars to the man who saves him!"

Not one moved, and all looked silently on the death-struggles of the black, who tried in vain to keep his head above water, and, prevented by his bonds from any motion, sank the second time with a curse of horror, which was half-choked by the water that poured into his mouth.

The vessel now appeared to be motionless, or rather, was carried slowly backwards by the current. Once again, though at a further distance, the black woolly head was visible, and then sank for ever under the turbid waves.

"He's gone!" Captain Wilkins said, with a groan, as he turned away and was about leaving the deck; but one of the Kentuckians stopped him, and laying his hand on his arm, said—

"Captain, you did all in your power to prevent the deed; you are free from any responsibility. Send for a constable as soon as we reach St. Louis, and have us four arrested—myself, my two comrades, and the young German. No one can reproach you for it, and you need be under no anxiety on our behalf."

"No; I'll be hanged if a hair shall be turned on you, my brave fellow," cried Stewart, who had come down, followed by Simmons. "Let yourselves be arrested, and call me false if you remain twelve hours in prison. I know St. Louis. The inhabitants are not the men to let anything be done to a white man who exercised justice on a black beast whose limbs ought in reality to have been torn one by one from his body. Don't be alarmed!"

Captain Wilkins had gone up again in the meanwhile, and went into the ladies' cabin to calm them; for they had been watching the negro's struggles from the window with horror.

All this time the vessel continued its rapid passage; but although all, passengers and sailors, regarded the negro's death as just and in order, the social tone that had pervaded the vessel appeared destroyed, and most of the men sat silent, busily engaged with their own thoughts. Even Simmons appeared not quite satisfied, and drank a greater quantity than usual of brandy-and-sugar.

About ten o'clock on the morning of the 7th, the passengers of the *Oceanic*, as the vessel passed one of the bends, saw the white houses of St. Louis in the distance, at whose wharves thirteen or fourteen various steamers were lying, partly for repairs, partly bound for New Orleans, Illinois, Missouri, or the Ohio; and the *Oceanic* soon made its way among them to the bank. The bell was rung, the ropes were thrown out, and all the busy movements connected with an arriving vessel now commenced.

Hundreds of visitors, draymen, and porters thronged on board, to greet acquaintances, get the papers, hear the news, or earn money by carrying goods and luggage; while the passengers had quite enough to do in looking after their own traps, lest a porter, as is frequently the case, might seize a box and quietly disappear with it in the crowd.

The confusion might have lasted an hour, and the majority of the passengers had quitted the vessel; the three Kentuckians, however, and the German remained on board, in accordance with their promise, and waited patiently for the constable, for whom the captain had sent immediately on arrival.

The constable at length arrived, and they followed him, after heartily shaking the captain's hand, who promised to do all in his power for them; and the former, on being informed of their crime, talked most kindly with them, and tried to give them heart by assuring them that they would not be eight days in prison.

"Eight days, man?" one of the Kentuckians asked, in astonishment, as he took a side glance at him—"eight days? St. Louis must be strangely altered if we are in arrest for eight *hours!*"

As the Kentuckian had prophesied, all the inhabitants of St. Louis, when informed by the passengers of the real facts, took the part of the prisoners, and went in a body to the magistrate to procure their liberty. The latter, however, reminding them of his office and duty, resolutely declined to give them up before their examination, and advised the St. Louisians to wait the course of justice patiently.

This unsatisfactory reply, however, did not suit the hot-blooded inhabitants of Missouri, and when it grew dusk, a mob of several hundred men went to the house of the gaoler, and as soon as he had opened the door to their knocking, requested him to give up the keys of the prison.

"Gentlemen," the man said, "I dare not give you the keys; you can *compel* me to do it, but my oath forbids me from yielding up the keys entrusted to me."

"Good; if you want compulsion," said a rough voice, belonging to a muscular, tall fellow, who had blackened his face not to be recognised—"if you must be forced, you shall have your will."

And with these words the giant drew a pistol from his pocket, placed it against the gaoler's chest, who was not in the least frightened, and then growled—

"Now, my dear sir, give the keys up, or I'll fire!" But, stooping at the same time, he whispered confidentially in his ear, "It's not loaded, Johnny!"

"Well, if I must, here they are!" said the latter, very calmly, as he delivered up the keys; "but you all, gentlemen, will bear me testimony that I only did so on compulsion, and in terror of my life!"

"Yes, yes—you are a brave fellow!" was heard on all sides; and the mob rushed with shouts to the prison, and carried out the four prisoners in triumph on their shoulders, not only into the open air, but through all the streets of the city, while they whistled "Yankee Doodle," and cursed and abused the negroes, so that the latter, who had heard the whole story, retired timidly to their houses, and did not dare to appear in the streets.

On the same evening the *Red Rover* steamer from New Orleans came in, and had the Mississippi planter on board, who was pursuing his son-in-law *malgré lui*. The young pair, however, had employed the short time of their stay in St. Louis famously, and had been joined by such a firm bond as all the planters on the tremendous river could not loosen.

* * * * *

"Gray," said Simmons, as he sat, in the autumn of the same year, in a comfortable parlour with him and his dear little wife, Celeste—"Gray, you ought to have been present when the St. Louis boys carried our four passengers from one grog-shop to another. The magistrates seemed quite satisfied, too, for no constable was to be seen; and the young German, who wanted to go up the Missouri to settle, walked two days later publicly about the city, without any one interfering with him."

"What can have become of Bloomfield?" Gray said, with a smile, as he thought of the anecdote about the "small-bored" rifle.

"I'd almost forgotten," said Simmons. "He went with Stewart to his farm to shoot deer and turkeys, and intends to make an excursion to the Rocky Mountains if he finds any companions."

"And Mrs. Dalton?" Celeste inquired, curiously.

"Is reconciled with her father, whose only child she is; and young Dalton, too, who comes of a most respectable family, appears to have made it up with the old Mississippian. At least, he assured me he intends, when winter comes, to carry his wife, who is not accustomed to this harsh climate, back to a more genial atmosphere—that is, to his father-in-law's plantation. But now, Gray, I've told you enough. Confound it! my mouth's quite dry from the everlasting talking. How would it be if we were to damp our throats a little? I take brandy-and-sugar."

THE WRECK OF THE PIRATE.

THE WRECK OF THE PIRATE.

Senora Fostero's mysterious visitor.

CHAPTER I.

THE PULPERIA.

IN the sitting-room of a small but by no means unimportant pulperia, or public-house, at the west end of Valparaiso, on the evening of the 5th of August, 1810, a considerable number of guests were assembled, discussing the most important events of the day. But Senora Fostero, the most famous living recommendation that ever sat behind a bar, and, at the same time, hostess of the inn, would certainly be vexed with us were we not to devote our first attention to her, if only to wish her good evening, before we join the assembled guests.

Senora Fostero, or shortly, "senora," as she was called by strangers, and "*tia mia*," or aunty, by the more intimate of her guests, weighed at least as much as two ordinary hostesses—not merely in caution and presence of mind in difficult circumstances, but also in real Chilian market weight; and thus could be regarded as a true, excellent hostess in moral respects as well, which is saying a good deal in Valparaiso.

Her youthful years had not passed so calmly and tranquilly as her old age, with a good income and famous health, promised to do. Twice married, she had lost both husbands. The first was a wild, unbridled fellow, who could not endure sitting quietly at home—as a married man ought—hence, through his restless habits, he bought a small schooner with his wife's money, and traded between the islands and the coast of Chili.

Affairs went on excellently for several years; but at last the usual period for his return arrived, and he did not come. His poor wife waited one, two, three years, still he did not come; and hence she was at length compelled to believe the skipper of another schooner, who, having left Otaheite with Lorenzo Fajardo, had, not far from the islands, been assailed by a fearful typhoon, which he only escaped with great difficulty and the loss of both masts. He said that he saw, two days later, the remains of another vessel, which, from the paint, he thought was Fajardo's schooner; and as the unhappy man did not turn up, there was no doubt that he had found a premature grave in the waves. His wife had by him only one child, a daughter.

Six years after the loss of her first husband, she married for the second time a Chilian by birth, Don Fostero. This marriage, however, was without issue, and Fostero died three years after marriage, by being thrown from his horse. The senora did not marry again, but carried on her business—more for the sake of employment than gaining a livelihood—and sent her daughter, Manuela, when she attained a proper age, to a sister of hers, living at St. Jago, to have her educated at the capital of the country; for in those days Valparaiso was not only a poor, paltry seaport, but a pulperia was not a suitable place to educate a young and handsome girl.

Only a few days previously to our story commencing, Manuela had come on a visit to her mother.

To wait on her guests, Senora Fostero had two girls from Quillota—Marequita and Juana—who darted about the small, gloomy room like wood-nymphs, to supply the required beverages or fruit—olives, oranges, and grapes.

The most cozy corner in the room was occupied by four persons, to whom I must first of all introduce my readers. One of them—by no means the eldest, but who, through his appearance, and perchance a slight peculiarity of attire, attracted the attention of those who entered after him (though they asked in vain the name and position of the stranger)—claims our first notice. He was speaking most, and, at the same time, treating Senora Fostero in the most intimate—I may almost say patronizing—manner, though he had crossed the threshold to-day for the first time. He jested, too, with the two waiting-maids, though his face was never crossed by a smile; and behaved altogether in such a free and easy, though perfectly respectful manner, as if he had been a visitor to the house for years; and yet no one remembered ever having seen him before.

He was acquainted with every country of the globe—he spoke of the most distant parts so that people imagined he was speaking of his native land; and his sunburnt complexion and harsh features, evidently marred by dangers and privations, as well as his powerful build, did not contradict such an opinion.

He was a well-built man, of the average height, certainly born in a southern land, with curly black hair, and still fuller, well-trimmed beard, which his left hand generally gracefully parted when the right hand bore the full glass to his lips.

A narrow black plaster ran across his forehead, from the roots of his hair to the bridge of his nose, which gave him a peculiar, and by no means amiable expression; and he had, therefore, been regarded by the two girls, since his entrance, with secret horror. His dark eyes, especially when he was speaking, revealed fire; but at times he would take no part in the conversation, and then, as if lost in thought, would cast long, inquiring glances round the room and the assembled guests, as well as the hostess—who did not feel at all comfortable, and feared to meet them. Then his eyes sparkled, we may say with a savage, uncomfortable lustre, beneath the bushy brows and black plaster, and even the charming face of Manuela, who had seated herself by her mother's side about half an hour before—though not for her sake—hardly lessened the fixed, cruel expression in the gloomy man's face, when his glance happened to fall upon her.

At the first glance he appeared dressed in the ordinary Chilian garb of the lower classes; for one of those common blue ponchos with a yellow and red fringe—such as only the peons and poorer farmers wear—hung over his shoulders, and entirely concealed the upper part of his body; but at the neck and opening of the poncho, through which the head was thrust, the collar of a fine cloth jacket and a snow-white shirt were visible; and under the poncho, almost to the ground, hung the tassels of a heavy Chinese-silk scarf, such as only the wealthier Chilians, or sailors who had visited the Chinese waters, are in the habit of wearing.

The second guest, who, though occupying a seat at the table, was more frequently by the senora's or Manuela's side, and only returned to the guests when Manuela, on household cares intent, left the room for a season, was a young man of five or six and twenty, with a light, almost blonde beard, chestnut hair, and light-blue, sharp eyes. His clothing, of the finest cloth, with the gold bands around his blue cloth cap, revealed the English naval officer. Edward Wilkinson was lieutenant on board her Majesty's frigate *Terpsichore*, but had been so dangerously wounded in a recent action with a French man-of-war, that the captain left him at Valparaiso when they reached that port, in the hope that he might recover with more careful nursing than he could obtain on board. His ship, which was stationed on the Peruvian coast, would call for him on its return.

He had recovered for some weeks past from the Frenchman's wound, but had been struck more dangerously and irrecoverably by another weapon—love for the hostess's fair daughter, whose acquaintance he had formed at St. Jago.

He was an orphan, but being in independent circumstances, he followed the sea more from fancy than as a profession. But the love for the fair creature, which was incompatible with a roving sea life, made the first breach in this fancy, and he was already forming all sorts of pleasant plans—to settle in lovely Chili with his young wife, and bid adieu to his native land for ever. But there was a most unpleasant, and seemingly insurmountable, obstacle to the fruition of these pleasant schemes. He was a Protestant and Manuela was a Catholic. The Spanish laws strictly forbade such mixed marriages; but had he gained the priest's consent, Manuela's mother—a strict and zealous Catholic—would ever have opposed it; and even the lovely, pious girl herself, fond as she was of the young heretic, sought, so soon as she recognised all these obstacles, with an aching heart, to overcome the affection, which had grown part of herself. She knew not how she loved him, and fancied the possibility of a separation, while her heart ever contradicted it, if secretly, all the more strongly. Senora Fostero, in other respects, liked the young man, and any one who learned to know him always liked him; but she wished that he had not formed her daughter's acquaintance, and it was only the hope zealously fostered by her confessor, nay, his orders, for the conversion of the heretic through the love he bore her daughter, that had hitherto prevented her from repulsing him.

The two other guests sitting at the table also belonged to the sea. They were not only masters of two small Chilian coasters, but also regular guests at Senora Fostero's whenever they could rest a short time from the fatigues of the sea.

Senora Fostero's house was one of the best wine-shops in Valparaiso, if not the best, and the sailors naturally patronized it for the sake of the liquor, though, perhaps, the pretty faces of the girls had something to do with it.

These three gentlemen we have described were sitting over a couple of bottles of Bordeaux, when the stranger, after hurriedly inspecting the guests and ordering a bottle of wine, sat down by the gentlemen with a polite bow, and from that moment seemed to direct the conversation; for the young Englishman's attention was engrossed by an object to him far more interesting.

The stranger seemed perfectly ignorant of the latest political changes in Chili, and, according to his statement, only arrived that afternoon from Manilla, *viâ* Tahiti, in a small schooner called the

Albatross; nor did he seem to take much interest in the topic, for he always turned the conversation to something else whenever politics were brought up.

One of the captains, who did not seem satisfied with the new state of matters, or feared they might disturb the commercial prosperity of the country, expressed his fears lest Spain might send a large fleet to blockade their port, and cover the country with soldiers.

"Bah! friend," the stranger said, as he filled his glass; "that is all nonsense. The Spaniards have not vessels enough to keep the coast free from pirates, much less——Oh, Marequita," he broke off suddenly; "come here, *carissima,* and give me another bottle of wine. *Tia mia,* the Bordeaux is sour, and I am sure you have better in the cellar."

Senora Fostero, as well as the guests, looked amazed at this familiar *tia mia.* The old lady was not accustomed to this address so soon from a stranger, but the latter proceeded as if not noticing it—

"Not far from here we were pursued by a rascally-looking schooner, and, had not a larger merchantman come in sight, which offered the pirate a better chance of booty, I doubt whether I should be spending the evening in your agreeable society. So much for your Spanish naval force. Thank ye, thank ye!" he then turned to the girl, who placed another bottle before him with a timid glance—"and come, were it the same bottle, Marequita, in your sweet hands it must have lost its acidity."

"You are the only gentleman who ever found fault with our wine," the senora said, much annoyed by the fault cast on her wine, and that, too, in the presence of her guests, in spite of the flattering *tia mia.* "We procure it from the best source, and at a high price."

"No doubt, aunt—no doubt," the imperturbable stranger said, as he tasted the new bottle with evident satisfaction. "But a bad cork will spoil the best wine, as bad wine spoils the best man."

"You were followed by a pirate?" The young Englishman now mixed in the conversation for the first time, as it had turned on a matter that interested him. "Whereabouts? and when?"

"I cannot describe the whereabouts exactly, senor," the stranger said, "for I am no sailor, and water seems all alike to landsmen; but it was about eight days' sail from here, and must have been to the south of Valparaiso, for I remember always to have seen the Southern Cross behind us during the last days."

"I presume your captain will lay the fact before the authorities?" the young man said. "At the present moment there are several men-of-war, both English and Spanish, in the harbour, and it would be worth while sending out a cruiser."

"What! have we another pirate in these parts?" one of the captains asked. "I thought the breed was destroyed with the destruction of Tenares and his band, or, at least, crushed for a dozen years."

"Ah, that Tenares is said to have been a wild fellow," the stranger remarked, emptying his glass at a draught. "Which were the ships that took him?"

"The *San Antonio* and the *Pendenciero*," the Englishman replied.

"The ships now lying in the harbour?" the stranger asked, carelessly.

"No," the old captain answered. "The *San Antonio* has sailed for Spain, and the *Pendenciero* is cruising on the Peru coasts."

"Hum!" the stranger muttered, as he nodded his head thoughtfully. "Well, what was I going to say? Oh, yes; what was the name of the merchant who bought the schooner when sold by government? Was is not Don Manuto?—I fancy so." He had again seized the bottle, and held it firmly resting on the glass as he looked at his neighbour.

"Yes; Don Manuto," the latter replied, as he also filled his glass; "that was the name of the former purchaser of the *Reconocido*."

"The former purchaser!" the stranger shouted, as the wine poured over the edge of the glass before he had time to collect himself, raise the bottle quickly, fill his glass and empty it.

"*Caramba amigo!*" the young officer said, regarding him with amazement, "you seem to take an interest in the vessel. Did you intend purchasing it?"

"Hum!" the stranger replied, now perfectly calm, as he dried his moustaches. "I had reason to take an interest in the vessel, for I have been in closer contact with it than ever I wish to be again with one of that sort. But my surprise was intended for the man, as I fancied the word 'former' alluded to his death, which I hope is not the case."

"You are right," the old captain said; "Don Manuto died, on the same evening that he purchased the schooner, of apoplexy. He was found to be insolvent, and the schooner, after knocking about the bay for some time, and being seriously injured, was put up for sale once more, and purchased by myself." Here he made a slight bow to the stranger. "But it is a long story, senor, and as it's rather late, I think it is time to break up. To-morrow I have to——"

"*Ah, caballeros!*" the stranger turned politely to his neighbours, "I am on land again to-day for the first time after a long voyage, and am too well pleased at having met such pleasant company to wish to part with it so soon. Juanita, *amiga mia!* two bottles of your best wine, my heart; and fresh glasses."

"I do not know, senor," the old sailor said, in some embarrassment, when he saw the girl coming toward them with two tin-foiled bottles, "really——"

"You must not be offended at my liberty, *caballeros*," the stranger interrupted him, imploringly. "You are all, it seems, water-rats, and unaccustomed to much ceremony; so pray allow a land-rat to remain at home among you for the few days he is permitted to remain on his native element. But to explain to you what interest I take in the *Reconocido*, and the reasons for it, I need only tell you that I lost my whole fortune through that pirate, and you may imagine it is a species of satisfaction to me to learn the close of his criminal career. Ah, Marequita *chiquita*, those are the right bottles—dear old friends from happier and better times. Ah! it is a glorious country, this Champagne—a real *Valparaiso!* And now, *caballeros*, A merry life, and no speedy death!"

The glasses were filled—the man had something so persuasive and lively in his whole manner, that the two old sailors felt unwilling to refuse his request—but the young Englishman excused himself by his still suffering state of health, and the three men emptied the tall glasses to the rather ominous toast.

"Well, if you take an interest in the pirate vessel, I can tell you the whole story in a very few words," the old captain at length recommenced. "The schooner lay here for months in the bay, and no one took any special interest in it—for it belonged to nobody, so to speak—and then it drifted on the reefs during a norther, and was so injured that any repairs were impracticable."

"That is a pity," the stranger remarked. "I have heard it was a splendid sea-boat; and on the Gulf of Mexico people could not say enough about its speed and the terror it occasioned."

"That was probably the reason why Don Manuto purchased it; but the norther spoiled this; and the repairs would have cost as much as a new vessel. When the schooner was put up for auction, then, no one would make an offer; so I purchased the wreck cheap enough, with the intention of getting back my outlay by using all in her that was serviceable. I have taken the masts out, which were in good condition, and intend to place them in my own vessel, as well as the decorations of the cabin, which are most tasteful; and I think, what with these and the tackle and chain-cables, which are chiefly on land, I shall repay my outlay and labour."

"I should much like," the stranger here said, "to visit the notorious vessel before it is broken up. I was so near being dragged as a prisoner on board it, that I should like to tread in greater safety the planks which so nearly served as my scaffold. Could it be managed?"

"Why not?" the captain replied. "If you are inclined, you can go aboard with me to-morrow morning; and I will meet you at ten o'clock, if you like. I have some preparations to make beforehand."

"*Bueno!*" the stranger said, nodding in acquiescence; "and double thanks that you have proposed so pleasant a place for meeting," he added, with a bow to the senora, while the two girls giggled at the curious stranger.

"There is a certain, though terrible interest," the young lieutenant here remarked, "in visiting a vessel on whose deck so much blood has flowed; and if you will allow me, captain, I will join you. Indeed, I had long designed to pull across to the wreck.

The old *Terpsichore* once followed the schooner half round the world without being able to catch it; and yet what would I have given to leap on its deck cutlass in hand!"

"It might have proved a dear amusement," the stranger remarked, "as I have heard this notorious pirate made many men leap down from his deck, but I know not one who leaped on it and lived to tell the story; except, at last, when an unfortunate shot—I mean unfortunate for him—from the *San Antonio,* laid low both his masts, and he could naturally no longer offer any resistance. It was always a riddle to me how they discovered him, for the position of the two ships could not have been the result of accident."

"You seem to be thoroughly acquainted with all the details," the lieutenant said.

"Only partially," the stranger replied, quietly; "I formed the acquaintance at Manilla of a young surgeon from the *Pendenciero,* who told me a good deal, but could not explain the reason of his being found."

"That is possible," the young Englishman said, "for the captains of the men-o'-war kept the affair secret when they left this port. They learned the hiding-place of the pirate through an accident; or, rather, through one of his atrocities—probably the last. He had plundered a vessel, tied up the crew, and bored holes in the hull, that she might sink. The cabin boy was not tied sufficiently securely, for he managed to loose his bands, but was unable to assist the others. He lay for several days in the water, on a spar, and was at last fished up by a Spanish cruiser. He overheard, accidentally, that the pirate was bound for Tahiti—for the crew did not trouble themselves with caution before people whom they expected would be at the bottom of the sea in half a dozen hours—and so the ships sent in pursuit fortunately found the pirate."

"Yes; there is great uncertainty in securing people," the stranger remarked, as he emptied his glass. "Strange," he then added, "how such things always come to light! The captain was hung, I believe; I think the doctor told me so?"

"Unfortunately not," the Englishman said; "no one knows exactly what became of him, for his corpse was never found. The crew defended themselves desperately, and Tenares received a cut on the head from the captain of the *San Antonio*; but then he disappeared, and must have found death in the waves, with the rest of his comrades, who jumped overboard to escape the rope. It is said that it was a terrible sight to see the sharks revelling among the victims."

"I do not know," the old captain said, "whether I would not sooner be hanged than spring among those accursed demons, the sharks."

"*Contra gusto no hay disputa!*" the stranger said, sententiously. "But, as I was going to say, the ships that brought in the *Reconocido* must have shared splendid prize money. *Caramba amigo!* he took in the Gulf of Mexico two ships worth a fortune. We ourselves, with a cargo worth 800,000 dollars, only slipped through his fingers; and the report was that he had enormous treasures on board."

"If that were the case," the Englishman replied, "he must have concealed them very cleverly, or thrown them overboard, for no money was fouud—which caused considerable surprise."

"And no diamonds?" the stranger asked. "There was a good deal of talk at the time, in the Gulf, about a ship he plundered which had a large quantity of Brazilian jewels on board, to be sent to Portugal."

"I do not remember hearing anything about it," was the reply. "No; the booty was very trifling. The *Reconocido* had lately been on the South American coast under false papers; and it is possible that the money so lightly got was squandered equally lightly there. The people who took her got more wounds than dollars."

The stranger's lips seemed to quiver with a smile, but it died away at once on his iron features, and he said carelessly—

"Yes, yes; that is usually the case in such affairs. Those who have a brave death before them, and a gallows behind them, always fight better than those who have their retreat free; and it would be the last thing I should wish, to board a desperate pirate, although I have had many a hard tussle in my time."

The two other captains now ordered in more wine, and the conversation turned once more from the pirate to things that interested them more closely; but at ten o'clock they declared they must go on board their vessels, and broke up.

"Then we meet again to-morrow morning, *caballeros*?" the elder of them said. "I shall be here precisely at ten." And the two men left the house with a respectful bow to the senora and her daughter, and a nod to the girls. The stranger also prepared to start, after sitting for awhile, gazing so fixedly on Manuela, that the poor girl began to feel alarmed, and was compelled at last to leave the room. Then he got up, emptied his glass, paid his account, and pressed his sombrero still more firmly on his brow.

"By the way, *tia mia*," he suddenly said, as he turned to the old lady, "you are now called Senora Fostero, but, if I am not greatly mistaken, you used to have another name, although I am not certain of it."

"My first husband was lost at sea," the old lady said, with a slight blush, but no longer so greatly offended by the "*tia mia*," for the stranger's generosity had reconciled her a little to him.

"And is Senor Fostero still in the land of the living?" he continued. "I have not had the pleasure——"

"He has been dead many years," the old lady said with a sigh; "but," she added more quickly, "how do you know me and my name, senor? I do not remember——"

"Oh, *carissima!* have you then entirely forgotten an old acquaintance?" the stranger said, shaking his head, and with a gentle tone of reproach.

"I do not know," the old lady replied, with some embarrassment, as she looked sharply in his face; "your features seem familiar to me, but I have been puzzling myself the whole evening as to where I saw you before; but I cannot remember. Have you ever been in Valparaiso before this time?"

"Oh yes, *tia mia!* and many a long evening in this same pleasant pulperia. But have not your books a better memory than you possess?"

"My books!" the senora said quickly, for that was attacking her on her weak side. "Oh, I hope that so worthy a gentleman has not remained so long in such bad company!"

A smile almost played round the stranger's lips, or, at any rate, his curly beard moved once or twice near them; but the upper part of the face remained as cold as before, and he said, with a sigh and a touch of comical seriousness—

"Goodness, *tia!* a man has sometimes to force his way in life amid strange company; but if I were no more in fault than that, I would gladly intrust the secret to my father confessor. A merry, jolly set used to meet here at that time; and yet I believe that every one of them is on the wrong side of your books."

"The Virgin protect us!" the old lady said, lifting her eyes to heaven, and laying her hand on that superficies of fat under which anatomy teaches us the heart must lie. "It is true; and a shame for men generally, and certain persons in particular. How little they care about swallowing the property of a poor widow! and do not trouble themselves to ask whether the woman who has supplied them so plentifully with meat and drink keeps a morsel for herself. They are not all so honest as you, *caballero*, who come, after so many years, to expiate your youthful sins. But what may your name be, senor?"

"My name!" the stranger said, thoughtfully, and stroked his beard—"my name is—— But we shall meet again, *tia mia*, and I will leave you a pleasant nut to crack this night—think over your list of debtors; and, to help you, I may say that the one against whom the largest sum is written is the man. But now, *buenas noches, senoritas!*" And with a friendly wave of his hand he left the house and walked slowly down the quiet street.

"*Ave Maria purissima!*" Manuela said, who returned at the same moment as he shut the door after him, and crossed herself fervently; "a stone has fallen from my heart now that man has left the room!"

"Yes; I felt uneasy," Marequita whispered, as if afraid he might be listening outside. "I watched him the whole time he sat there, to see whether he smiled once. But no; his face was as cold and frigid as the ice of the Cordilleras, and his eyes glistened under his dark brows and the odious black plaster which ran across his forehead."

"I only hope you did not look too deep into his eyes, Marequita!" the young man said, with a smile, who had now risen and was preparing to leave.

"Holy mother!" she said with a shudder, and cast a timid glance around. "How could you make such a remark, even in jest, Don Eduardo?"

"And what does Juana say to this extraordinary stranger?" the Englishman went on.

"That he is the most dreadful being I ever saw," the girl said, quickly, and almost violently; "he has a glance like a demon, and a face as if he had lain a week in the grave. The Virgin protect us! but I hardly believe it was a real man!"

The old lady had long retired to her room, and sat there brooding over her books, while striving to bring the stranger to the surface from the stores of her memory and the chaos of old names and figures. The girls were waiting on the few guests still left, and when Manuela went into the back room, Edward Wilkinson followed her.

"Good night, Manuela!" he said, as he offered her his hand, and looked with a more than friendly glance into her dear, bright eyes.

"*Buenas noches!* Don Eduardo," the maiden replied in embarrassment, and turned away from him.

"And am I to part from Manuela to-night with this cold word alone?" the young man said mournfully, and tried to seize her hand, which she left him for a moment, but then slowly withdrew from him. "Manuela, shall I have no consolation?"

"You know well, Eduardo, the only answer I can give you," the young girl said, seriously. "You are aware," she continued, with a blush, "that I love you; but both the law and my mother insist that a Protestant cannot marry a Catholic; and you cannot wish me to sacrifice my salvation, even through my love for you!"

"But Donna Fostero has always been friendly to me, and she knows what hopes I entertain. Could she be so were she quite opposed to them?"

"My mother deludes herself with a hope," the young girl said, sorrowfully, "which I have long resigned. No, Eduardo," she then added, in a softer, more tender strain, "our roads do not run together, however much it pains my heart. Your friends are probably strict Protestants, and would never consent to see you marry a Catholic, even if they reconciled themselves to the thought of recognising the daughter of a poor landlady. But not that alone—no; I will never so sin against our laws and our religion as to go to the altar with a man hostile to my faith, even if your priests allowed it."

"But who tells you, girl, that I am hostile to the Catholic religion?" Edward asked, quickly; "or do not esteem it as highly as our own?"

The girl fixed her large black eyes on him for a moment in surprise, but then said hurriedly, and almost imploringly, as she seized his hand—

"No, no, Eduardo! speak not so; you cut me to the heart! A man must have some belief, and you will never induce me to think so badly of you, even if you calumniate yourself."

"And you would love me if I resigned my religion and took yours, which you consider the only true one?" the young man said, seriously, as he looked firmly in her tear-laden eyes.

"Oh, if you did so through conviction," the girl said, quickly, and as if in a state of enthusiasm, "with what fervour—with what gratitude to the Supreme Being! But," she added, slowly and mournfully, "you must not do it solely for my sake, Eduardo; the priest says, indeed, that even in that case it would be an acceptable work to God; but it would ever appear to me a sin, and I hardly know whether I err or not."

The young man stood a long while silently, with his hand pressed to his forehead, and at length said in a low voice—

"Then you deprive me of every hope, Manuela?"

"I would not do so to my worst enemy, Eduardo," the fair maiden replied, gently, smiling through her tears—"how much less to you! No; I will pray, and that right fervently, that God may enlighten you; and be assured, Eduardo, that there would then be no happier being on the face of the earth than poor Manuela."

With these words she offered him her hand, which he took, and pressing passionately to his lips, quitted the room.

Visitors to the Wreck

CHAPTER II.

THE WRECK.

THE next morning Senora Fostero was sitting alone in the empty guest-room, and had her sewing materials on her lap; but the usually so busy needle rested idly in her hand, and she was gazing thoughtfully at nothing—a most unusual affair with her. To tell the truth, the stranger occupied her entire thoughts. She had, with Manuela's assistance, gone through, the previous night, the whole list of her debtors—and there was no small number of them—

Chilinos and Englishmen, French and Germans, Americans and Italians—a whole alphabet of defaulters—and had not found one of them who, in person or debt, tallied in the slightest with the extraordinary stranger. The old lady had an excellent memory; and there were few names in her books for which she could not summon up, with a few moments' reflection, the appearance of its owner; but the huge beard, and the hair falling so deep over the left side of the face, did not pass muster for one of them. The black plaster, too, running in a broad strip from the hair to the nose, concealed much of the little the beard left free. The worst of it was, that at the few names whose bearers she could not recal there were only small accounts of two or three dollars; and hence not one of them suited; for the *caballero* had himself said that his name figured for a round sum. Who in all the world could it be, then?

While puzzling over the mystery, the door opened, and her heart beat loudly as the stranger walked in, cast a searching glance round, and, as no one was present, walked straight up to her, offered her his hand, and asked, in the most friendly way, how she was.

"Well, have you found my name in your memory, or your certainly faithful books?" he at length said, as he took a seat at a table, nodded to Juana, who had just entered, and asked for a bottle of wine. "What is my name?"

"Senor," the old lady replied, in confusion, "you must come to my aid, for I can neither remember your name nor your account, and my books are in excellent order."

"Have you looked through them all, senora?" the stranger asked, as he filled his glass, and slowly swallowed his wine.

"All—at least the ledgers and accounts; but I really do not know——"

"Do you keep a book about what you owe other persons?" the stranger now asked, and held the glass to his lips so that his hand covered his beard, and his dark eyes flashed at this moment under his sombrero with such strange humour and peculiar fire, that the senora felt as if stabbed to the heart, and fancied, in her first alarm, that the eyes had done it. But the words the stranger uttered soon overcame the feeling; for they fell on her like a hundredweight.

He had been speaking, then, of what she owed others; that was the meaning of the round sum to which he had referred. Holy Mother! she certainly had not turned to those debts; and her blood stood still in her veins.

But before she could make any reply, the old captain and the young lieutenant entered the room; and as the former stated that his boat was waiting for them, and they must make haste, they left the house at once together.

The poor senora remained behind in a state of the most painful embarrassment; for she did not doubt for a moment that one of her "worthless husbands" had drawn a bill on her, and she, poor, betrayed old widow, would be called upon to honour it. But she soon made up her mind: not a dollar of her money would she sacrifice to hide the extravagant squandering of men who, as long as they were alive, had embittered her days, and now wanted to torment her after death with their unpaid bills.

"And there you come again with your *tia mia*," she suddenly exclaimed, after working herself into the proper temper; "but I will *tia mia* you, you scamp!"

Senora Fostero had grown very angry, and felt the more annoyed at having wasted the whole evening in studying old account books, which was in itself a most unpleasant, and, worse still, most ungrateful operation.

The three men, in the meanwhile, proceeded rapidly down one of the narrow streets leading to the water, got into the boat that was awaiting them, and four sturdy rowers soon brought them to the spot where the wreck of the former pirate, the once so feared *Reconocido*, lay bare and mournfully on the rocks, a melancholy image of departed greatness.

The captain was the first to climb on deck, and was followed by the stranger, who could scarcely control his impatience; and last came the young Englishman.

"Well!" the latter said, laughingly, as he swung himself over the gunwale after the stranger, "for a land-rat, as you called yourself last night, senor, you manage to climb a ship's side very smartly."

The stranger, however, made no reply; he probably overheard the remark. His eye was feverishly surveying the deck of the small, gracefully-built vessel, and he quitted the men, and proceeded to the quarter-deck, whence he gazed on the sea for a good minute. When he returned, his eye was as cold and calm as before, but his face had turned deadly pale, and he now said, as he carefully surveyed the build of the little schooner—

"It is almost a pity that the poor little thing should have met such a fate here. It is said to have been a famous sailer; and if employed for honest purposes, would have brought its owners large profits."

"Yes, it is a famous model," the old captain said, smilingly; "it was built in the United States, and was rigged quite in the Yankee fashion; and the Americans are unsurpassable in their schooners. But, as for it taking to sea again, it is, perhaps, better as it is; for I, for my part, honestly confess that I should not like to go to sea in a vessel which had been employed for such purposes as the *Reconocido*, and on which such horrors were committed as are told of its terrible captain, the bloody Tenares."

"Bah!" the stranger gave his opinion; "what's done is done; and the dead material can be used as easily for a crucifix as for a dagger. Of all those who might go to sea in the vessel, probably not one would think of what had previously taken place aboard her."

"Then, perchance, the ship itself might have reminded them," the old man said, laughing in a mysterious manner; "for all sorts of queer stories are whispered about it."

"Indeed!" the stranger hastily asked: "of what nature, if I may be permitted to inquire?"

"Oh, superstitious nonsense!" the old man replied, in some confusion; "I do not believe a word of it; but the people here are fond of repeating such tales. Thus, on the anniversary of the schooner's capture—by St. Jago, we shall have it here directly!—on the 8th of August, the terrible Tenares is said to visit his old vessel at midnight. Sailors who were rowing back from the cemetery (for you are aware, senor, that all dead bodies must be buried here at midnight,) swore that they saw him on board, with his ghastly, blood-stained face; and, whether here or not, I do not believe there is a single man in the town who could be induced by the wealth of Peru to spend the night of the 8th of August on board the *Reconocido.*"

"The strangest thing is," the young man said, with a laugh, "that he has been seen on every anniversary; and for the first two years it created considerable excitement; but as the story ran, that the ghost satisfied itself with standing on deck and looking over the side, no further notice was taken of it; and I do not believe it was seen by any one last year."

"I beg your pardon," the old man remarked; "last year, people belonging to my own vessel saw the ghost. My cook had died, and, as they rowed past, a few minutes after midnight, all was quiet and dark on board the old barque, and my mate purposely steered close by it. But when they returned an hour later—for the cook was a heavy man, and they had some difficulty in dragging his body up the steep hill—they saw a light."

"A light?" the stranger quickly repeated.

"Yes, a light," the old gentleman affirmed; "but no common light, as from a lamp or lantern, that emits a yellow or reddish glare, but more like the St. Andrew's fire. My mate, who is a bold fellow, and fears nothing, wanted to go on board, or at least see whether a boat were alongside the pirate; but I really believe, if he had promised each of the crew a hundred dollars, they would not have pulled to the schooner—for, close to the mast which was still standing, they could clearly distinguish a dim form; and one of the sailors declared, by all that was good and great, the shadow stretched out an arm towards them. My mate knew nothing of this; but he assured me that he saw the figure, or, at least, fancied he could trace its outline."

The stranger had followed this story with the closest attention, and looked searchingly in the faces of his companions, to try and see what their opinion of the affair might be. But though the captain asserted so confidently that the whole matter emanated from the foolish superstition of his crew, it was easy to see that he did not in the least doubt the probability of such an apparition, while the young and better-educated officer only concealed his ridicule through politeness to his older comrade.

"And what does the town say about the story?" he at length said to the latter.

"Not much," was the certainly evasive answer; "but, for all that, the wreck is generally known as the haunted schooner, and it is natural that people should try and bring supernatural and, as it were, avenging apparitions into unison with the great number of bloody deeds that were committed on board. But suppose we go into the cabin; I have never been below myself."

"Things look rather wild down here," the old gentleman said, as he preceded them after the manner of a host. "I have had several planks already removed, and there is not even a bottle of wine on board to offer my guests."

The two men did not even seem to hear the apology; for each was for the moment too much engaged with his own thoughts.

When they had descended the narrow cabin stairs, protected by an elegant bronze balustrade, a very pleasing odour of sandal-wood met them—and, in fact, all the pillars were composed of that expensive wood; the central compartments were formed of broad planks of mahogany, most artistically inlaid round the edge with ivory and mother-o'-pearl; and the old captain might be easily credited when he asserted that the decorations of the cabin in this small schooner had cost more than he gave for the whole wreck. Here everything had been left almost in the original state; but, on one side, workmen were already busy in removing the planks, to fit them into the old gentleman's own vessel. They were going to begin again that same afternoon, and completely remove the cabin without breaking off from their labour.

The stranger seemed peculiarly affected, his face had assumed an ashen tint, and he was compelled to sit down on a sofa, once covered with velvet, but now in a sad condition.

"Good heavens! senor, you are unwell!" the young man said, who was the first to notice his emotion. "You are more like a corpse than a living being—what is the matter with you?"

"Oh, nothing, nothing!" he said, as he motioned him back; "I have had it frequently lately—it is the strong smell of the sandal-wood, I believe; perhaps the excitement of visiting such a vessel as this. Oh, senor captain, is there by chance a drop of water on board?"

"Probably," the old man said, himself feeling startled at the stranger's pallor; "the carpenter has always a stone jar here, and—ah, here is a bottle of *aguardiente;* one drop of that will do you more good than a bucket of water."

He filled a glass with the liquid, and handed it to the stranger, who drank it at a draught, then sprang up, and walked hurriedly up and down the cabin. He held his hand firmly pressed to his eyes, and when he removed it again, he displayed the same cold, calm, almost indifferent features as before.

"Well, are you better, senor?" the old captain asked.

"Perfectly well again," he answered, politely. "I am only sorry that I caused you so much trouble—I really must consult a physician; for I have had these attacks more frequently than I like."

"Bah! what can a doctor help you?" the old man said, with a laugh; "such things happen at times to powerful constitutions, but pass off again directly—a rope starts somewhere in the brain, and a little thread breaks when drawn too tightly; but it always splices itself, and everything is in order again. Yes, that is a pity——" He broke off here, and walked to the stranger, who had stopped before a flaw in one of the panels, and was examining it attentively—"Some one must have struck it with an axe, or something of that sort; and the worst is, I cannot procure any of the wood at Valparaiso, so as to have it properly repaired, and I do not like to patch it, so I must leave the damage till a better occasion."

"Who knows what deed of horror may have been committed here?" the young man said, after examining the spot, and turning away with a shudder; "but the lips that could reveal it are eternally closed—the murderer and his victim sleep together beneath the waters. What is your opinion, senor? What can that have been?"

"Who—I?" the latter said, hastily. "Oh! it is an unlucky mark, but can be easily repaired. There must be a log of sandal-wood forward——Oh, excuse me!" he quickly interrupted himself, and the blood rushed to his head; "I really believed at the moment I was on board the same little vessel from which I landed yesterday. There the sailors had a lot of sandal-wood, if I am not mistaken, and you might purchase it from them, senor."

"Oh, yes! I should like that. What is the name of the vessel?"

"The *Albatross*, of Tahiti; but they have probably sold it already. So you are going to have everything removed here, and re-arranged in your own cabin?"

"Yes, it will do admirably. The size corresponds, and my cabin will be grand."

"There appears to be a trap-door here," the stranger said, carelessly, pointing to a small brass ring let into the flooring.

"Yes," the old captain said, as he opened it—for the table that formerly stood over it had been removed—"it must have been a sort of store-room."

"How spacious it is!" the stranger remarked, as he jumped down.

"Yes, and they chose wonderfully stout beams to bear the light cabin-deck," the old gentleman said, laughingly. "The gun-deck of a man-o'-war could not be stronger; and yet the rest of the vessel is built lightly enough. These beams attracted my attention some time back, for they do not run far forward, and hence cannot be intended to strengthen the vessel. Indeed, they seem to have been inserted afterwards, as you will see by the wood. The schooner herself is built of American timber, but this beam—look where the splint is off—appears to be a variety of that cedar-wood which grows so abundantly at Singapore. I have already told the carpenter to take out these beams first, and I will have them sawn into planks, for they will make first-rate doors."

The stranger had crept along in a stooping posture, and felt the edge of one of the beams, as if examining it. Then he climbed on deck again, and said carelessly—

"Yes, I believe the wood would be excellent for that purpose; but I think we have occupied enough of your time, senor, and would now go ashore."

"I should like to see the lower-deck," the young man now said—"that is, if I should not detain you gentlemen too long."

"It had no actual gun-deck," the captain replied, however, "and its armament consisted of two heavy swivels fastened on deck. They were said to have been magnificent guns, but the man-o'-war of course kept them, with all the ammunition belonging to them, and the name *Reconocido*, I believe, may still be seen on them."

The three men lounged about the deck for some time inspecting the vessel, so far as was possible in her present state, and then went back to land, where they separated, and left the crew on the beach.

"Antonio!" one of the sailors said, when they pushed the boat off again, and slowly pulled to the wharf, "I have seen that man once before."

"What man?" Antonio asked; "the lieutenant? I can believe it, for you can see him twice every day at the fat widow's, if you are inclined, and have any money to spend."

"No; I do not mean him," the other growled, as he shook his head, "but the black fellow with the great plaster on his forehead. *Caracho!* I have been bothering my head about him the whole morning, ever since he got into the boat, and nothing good was doing when I saw him—*diablo!* what a scowling face the fellow has. I should not like to meet him at night alone on the mountains."

"Has he been long in Valparaiso?" Antonio asked.

"Don't know," the other muttered, still in deep thought; "saw him here to-day for the first time; but I must rummage my memory-chest to see if I cannot find him in a corner somewhere His face is not so common as to be easily forgotten."

"Bah!" Antonio said; "you have knocked about men-o'-war for seven or eight years, and you see many faces there. You were present at that affair with Tenares. Pest! I wish our old man had pulled the wreck to pieces, for I am growing heartily tired of rowing backwards and forwards to her."

His comrade made him no reply, for he was too busy with his thoughts. The stranger's face bothered him; and when they at length landed and fastened up the boat, he went up the beach, and seated himself on a pile of wood, granting an audience to his thoughts, and awaiting his captain's return.

The Consultation at Senora Fosterc s Pulperia

CHAPTER III.

THE ALARM.

THE 6th and 7th of August passed, and our friends of the last chapter had not met again. Aboard the wreck the work was being pushed on as rapidly as possible ; and, as the labourers could rarely take the valuable material on board the other schooner the same evening, they usually slept on board the *Reconocido.* Four men did not fear a ghost so greatly ; but they did not go below ; they erected a species of tent on deck, beneath which they slept famously on these warm and dry nights.

On the evening of the 8th of August, however—a day they all knew too well—they arranged matters so that they finished up their work before nightfall, and went ashore with bag and baggage. The old captain was quite right: not one of them would have slept aboard the pirate *that* night—no, not for fifty days' wages. Everything they left behind, excepting their tools, was securely fastened; but, even had treasures been lying loose on deck, the boldest rogues in Valparaiso would not have satisfied their lust on that night.

On the evening of the 8th, then, nearly the same party of guests as before were sitting in the senora's public room, and being served by the ready hands of the two girls. At least, the old captain and our young friend had again seated themselves at the same table, not far from *tia mia's* usual seat; and as both had been kept away the previous evening by business, it was rather natural that their conversation soon turned on the stranger who had found them here on the last occasion.

"Has he been here since that evening, senora?" the young man turned inquiringly to the old lady, when all assured him that no one had set eyes upon him since.

"No, senores!" was the hasty reply; "and I should not be broken-hearted if I never saw those fine eyes again."

"Hoho, *tia mia!*" the old captain laughed; "what's in the wind? Did not the man say he was in your ledger? and have you not found him there?"

"I fear, I fear he is in many a ledger," the old lady muttered; in reality only angry because she could say nothing certain about the man; and quite determined not to speak well of any one who, as was evidently the case here, had to ask money of her.

"He was a curious scamp," the captain remarked; "and do you know what one of my men, who has served many years on board vessels of war, and was in the expedition against Tenares, declares? —that he saw his face aboard the *Reconocido,* and he was one of the leaders. But that is, so far, impossible; for not one of the crew ever set foot on land again; those who were not cut down, or sprang into the water, died at the yard-arm."

"Captain," the young man here observed—for a fresh idea seemed to shoot across his mind at this remark—"after all, your fellow is in the right. Did you not see how the man, generally so cold and gloomy, turned deadly pale when we went aboard the vessel? And may not his illness in the cabin be connected with it?"

"Well, one thing is strange," the captain said, laughingly: "do you remember, Don Eduardo, that he spoke of a piece of sandal-wood that must be lying in the forecastle?"

"Yes; the forecastle of the *Albatross*, in which he had come from Tahiti."

"But there was none in the *Albatross*," the old gentleman hurriedly continued. "I went aboard her that same afternoon, but no one knew about a lump of sandal-wood; and I was assured that they had none during the whole voyage."

"Did you make any inquiry about the man who was their passenger—what his name was, and whence he came?" the senora hastily asked.

"Of course I did," the old captain laughingly said; "you might suppose that, *tia mia;* but with no tangible result. He was a passenger from Papetu to Valparaiso, with a perfectly correct passport, in the name of Senor Alvarez, of Manilla; had paid his passage-money in gold, and behaved quietly and respectably during the voyage."

"And where did he get the wound on his forehead?" the young officer asked.

"That is the only thing that struck the people aboard the *Albatross*," was the reply; "for he wore the plaster when he came aboard, and they were four weeks out; the deuce knows what he has under it!"

"Alvarez, Alvarez?" the old lady muttered to herself, nodding her head; "I know three Alvarez, but he does not answer to one of them—if that is his right name: and he had a good passport?"

"Perfectly in order. But I am going away from what I wanted to tell you. Well, there was no sandal-wood in the *Albatross;* but where do you think I found some?—in the forecastle of the *Reconocido!*"

"*Caramba!*" the young man said, in a low voice, looking at the captain searchingly, as if surprised.

"Yes; but I cannot understand," another of the guests interposed, 'why you think it so curious to have found a lot of sandal-wood aboard the *Reconocido*."

"You don't understand it?" the old man shouted, smiting the table. "Looking at it in the most innocent manner, it is a very curious coincidence; for you do not know——"

They were interrupted by the opening of the door, through which a tall gentleman, with a large moustache, and buttoned up in a thick pilot coat, hastily came, cast a searching glance round the room, and when his eye fell on Don Eduardo, walked up to him.

He rose, blushing, from his chair; but the new arrival signed to him to sit down again; then saluting the old lady and the guests at the table, he drew a chair close to the young man's side, and whispered a few words in his ear. The latter replied in a similar low voice, though the captain sitting next to them could hear.

"No; and not for the last three nights, as I hear. Strange! We were just speaking of him; and there appears a remarkable coincidence in certain things."

"Then I may, perhaps, address myself to these gentlemen," the new guest said, in a rather loud key, but still so as not to be heard by the persons at the other table. Senora Fostero, however, took care not to be among the latter. "Gentlemen, you are aware that a strange man has been staying here for some days; or, rather, was seen here three days back; for his trace appears to be entirely lost since then, though he can be easily recognised by a large black plaster. Can any one of you give me any information about him?"

"*Senor capitano!*" (for the stranger was the captain of the Chilian frigate *Nuestra Senora*), the old master of the schooner here said, shaking his head, "we were just expressing our ideas about that man, though not one of us is able to give any information about him. There is certainly no good in him, I am convinced; and when you entered, we had just begun to bring him into some sort of connexion with the old *Reconocido*."

"Ho, then, our ideas agree!" the captain hastily said. "As I am told, Senor Wilkinson was seen rowing, a few days ago, with another gentleman and a stranger, to the wreck of the pirate; and I have come here to make some inquiries, as I expected to find my young friend here," he added, with a friendly side glance at the latter, which drove the blood into his cheeks, and induced the old lady to shake her head very discontentedly. "I will hence tell you openly—that is, for the present, in strict confidence—the reason that has induced me to do so. But we had better go into another room; for here," he added, in a low voice, "there are too many ears which might hear things which it is better to keep from becoming town talk."

"Senora Fostero will spare us the little back room for half-an-hour," the old captain said, with a friendly glance at her; and the lady, though so unwilling to let the guests out of her immediate hearing, was forced, *nolens volens*, to assent, and lights and wine were soon carried into the back parlour, which, adorned with a crucifix and sacred pictures, more resembled a chapel than a sitting-room, but was for all that the worthy old lady's boudoir.

Senora Fostero wished to remain in the room, to see, as she said, that they wanted for nothing; but the three gentlemen would not trouble her; and so she had no further excuse for granting her ears the certainly innocent satisfaction of hearing something prejudicial against the man whom she had well-founded reasons for suspecting to wish to extort money from her.

The old skipper told the captain of the *Nuestra Senora*, as concisely as he could, what they knew of the stranger, and on what they principally based their suspicions, and the young officer also told them what had struck him in the conduct of the strange, gloomy man. The captain listened to all silently, without replying a word, save now and then interposing a short question; but when he had heard all the men had to tell him, he said, after first casting a glance to the door, to see if any were listening,—and this precaution was not unnecessary, for *tia mia* was hurting her ear against the keyhole in striving to hear what was going on inside,—"Senores, from all you have told me, and from what I have heard elsewhere, which might appear unimportant under other circumstances, I have not the least doubt but that the stranger is no one but the terrible Tenares himself, who was believed to be dead long ago."

"Tenares!" the skipper exclaimed in alarm, and the young man gently nodded his head in assent.

"Not so loud, senor!" the captain whispered; "though the walls have no ears, the senora has them, and I am convinced she is making the best possible use of them at this moment. The reports spread at that time of his death are too vague—some declared he shot himself; others, that he leaped overboard. So much is certain: his body was never found, and we are all here well enough acquainted with the sea to know how easy it is for a man to float in the water for a long time, and be picked up by some passing vessel. Besides, the engagement took place in the neighbourhood of a small group of coral reefs, on which, I grant, not even cocoa-nut trees grow, but which on that account are entirely uninhabited; and on these, amid the seaweed—one or the other—the pirate may have concealed himself, in spite of our careful search. At any rate, it is not entirely impossible. But there are in this town persons who declare decidedly they recognised the man. Both were formerly sailors on board the *San Antonio*, which I had the honour of commanding at that time. One of them is now aboard of the schooner, senor; the other was invalided, and now lives in the town. The former rowed him aboard the *Reconocido*, and asserts that he perfectly well remembers the stranger fighting on the side of the pirates. But the other is an important witness, for he received the wound which robbed him of his right arm from Tenares himself, and is ready to take the sacrament that he met him in the town a few days back. He came straight to me, and assured me he was petrified with horror, for from the ghost story of the wreck, which you well know, he naturally believed, at the first blush, that he saw before him the spectre of the pirate. Tenares, however, as it seems, was far too much engaged with his own thoughts to notice him; he had just returned, I fancy, from the visit to his old schooner, and turned quickly into one of the streets running up the hill. The man, when he had recovered himself a little, and no longer felt the terror of the spectral presence, began to think over the matter, and was sensible enough to look me up directly, and tell me what he had seen. I myself know Tenares too well personally not to trust to my own opinion, if ever I see him face to face again; the old fellow, too, has been near enough to him, and has ample reason to remember him accurately. The possibility cannot be denied; and when I connect all this with the visit to the *Reconocido*, and the stranger's conduct, I begin myself to believe that we have the dangerous man once more alive within our walls."

"But what purpose could he have in returning here among his enemies?" the skipper remarked, with a shake of his head. "The affair still seems to me much too improbable. Or can he be connected with the schooner which brought him here?"

"No," the captain of the frigate said; "that was naturally my first idea, and the closest inquiries were made; but her papers are in perfect order, and no objection can be raised against her. No. Tenares seems to have come as a simple passenger from Tahiti, but the reason still remains an enigma."

"Which I, perhaps, can explain," the young officer said, who had been sitting for some time resting his head on his hands. "Do you remember that, on the evening he spent here, he particularly inquired whether much ready money and many Brazilian jewels were found aboard the *Reconocido*?"

"That is it!" the captain of the *Nuestra Senora* exclaimed; "there can be no doubt of it; he has some hiding-place aboard which we did not find, in spite of the most careful search, and has come here to secure his plunder. But where can he have been these four years, and why did he not come sooner?"

"*That* I cannot say," the old gentleman remarked; "but if it is so—and I believe it myself—what he intends to fetch is in the small lower hold, through which the two thick beams run; he sprang down there to examine it, and after that wanted to go ashore at once. Nothing else interested him. Yes; I remember perfectly well that he wished to remain astern when we proceeded to the bows. At that time, of course, I thought of no such thing, and it did not strike me. But what to do now? where is the fellow, and will he show himself again?"

"*Por vida mia*," the captain replied; "had I only heard sooner that the senor came here the first evening! for now he has probably all he desires, without any one entertaining the slightest suspicion, and is off again. But he cannot get away by land, and only one ship has recently started for San Janeiro."

"But he cannot have been on board the *Reconocido* since that time, for I have had carpenters there day and night; and though they might leave her for a few hours during the day, he would not have dared to go on board; and at night they have slept on deck, as I know for certain, for I lent them an old sail to make a kind of tent, because they did not care to sleep below."

"What is that noise in there?" the captain of the *Nuestra Senora* asked, listening to a confused sound of voices that reached him from the public room.

"Oh, nothing," the old man replied; "a couple to whose heads the wine is rising. But we are sitting here with dry throats." He seized the bell standing on the table, and rang it. "It is above all necessary that we should come to some decision," he added; "and I believe the best thing will be to put a permanent watch on board till we have captured the senor, or convinced ourselves there is nothing more on board to find. *Caramba!* captain, it will be a fortunate purchase for me if we really find treasure aboard."

"The prize money will have to be deducted first," the captain replied, with a laugh; "but, for Heaven's sake! we will not share the bear's skin till we have it. Oh, senorita! what was that disturbance just now in the room? I ordered some of my men here, and hope they have made no disturbance."

"No, senor capitaine," the girl said, with a smile; "it is only the old story of the goblin-ship—you know it."

"The *Reconocido?*" the old man said, leaping up from the table. "*Caramba!* what is the date to-day?"

"The eighth, and not one of us thought of it!" the young man replied, also springing up. "But what is the matter with the schooner, Marequita?"

"Oh, nothing, Don Eduardo," the girl said, with a smile. "A sailor just came in, and swore hard and fast that the ghosts were stirring again on board the pirate—he saw a light and figure on the deck. You know this is the anniversary of the old story."

"Senores, this time I believe it is more than a story," the captain of the *Nuestra Senora* said, also rising, and seizing his hat.

"Excuse us, senorita, we must be off. By Heavens!—the ghost!

This is indeed the day; but it is early for the goblin—it can be hardly eleven."

"Not quite, senor," the young officer said. "But what are your orders?"

"Simple enough," was the quick, decided answer. "Do you think, senor, that your men have remained aboard the schooner *this* night?"

"The carpenters?" the old skipper said, laughingly: "not if I had promised them a gold saw apiece for it. No; they are safe enough on shore, and I cannot imagine why that did not occur to me before."

"Good," the captain said; "then we can have no doubt but that Tenares, to whom you told all this, as I understand, will make the attempt this night, the only possible chance to carry out what he designs; but, fortunately, I am prepared. My two boats are lying off the pier, strongly manned, with which I shall reach the wreck within ten minutes. Before that, a signal, already arranged, will tell the officers on board my vessel what they have to do, and, as quickly as oars can bring them, four boats will hasten to our assistance. Not a rat, much less a boat, can escape from the bay; my only fear is, lest the pirate, on seeing himself pursued, may escape to land. If we have time enough to obtain the boats from the *Nuestra Senora*, every escape for him will be cut off; and hence I will post myself between this place and the wreck, in case we do not meet him under way, which I scarcely hope."

"What do you say, senor," the young officer asked, "to my taking to my own boat, which lies just off the houses here, and in the exact line he must follow, if he intends landing here?"

"Oh, of course, if you have a boat and like to volunteer," the captain hastily replied. "It is every brave sailor's duty to aid in annihilating this bloody pirate, and it will take five minutes ere I can get here. Is the boat quite ready?"

"I have had the oars brought up; we shall be ready in two minutes."

"*Bueno!* and you, captain?"

"My boat is also here," the old man said, "and I will help

Don Eduardo in cutting off his escape to land—that is, if it is agreeable to you."

"Perfectly; so good-bye for the present, gentlemen; and remember I am most anxious to catch the fellow alive. He made two of my brothers walk the plank, murdered their wives and children, in order to remove all witnesses, and, by Heaven! deserves no honest sailor's death. But now to work!"

Don Olinda, the captain of the *Nuestra Senora*, quickly quitted the room and the house, while the other captain ran down to the beach with his men, and Edward Wilkinson sent to his to wait for him here, and ran to his lodgings to fetch a brace of pistols. In a few moments he returned, sent his men down, and only hesitated a moment to bid adieu to Manuela.

The alarm had naturally spread among all the guests, and in a body they followed Don Olinda, who scarce reached the shore ere he shot up two blue lights, which were replied to in half-a-minute by one of the ships in the harbour. Senora Fostero's house was perfectly empty.

The young man had not to wait long for his beloved. She seemed herself to have sought the moment, and said, as she hurried up and laid her hand in his, without affectation—

"Eduardo, I have felt so terribly wretched this whole day. I had a foreboding of some misfortune, and could not give it a name. I know it now—you are going to meet a danger which is greater than you suspect."

"And if it cost me my life, Manuela, I would gladly give it, now that I see you take an interest in me," the young man exclaimed, as he kissed her hand, with flashing eyes.

"Oh, speak not so," the maiden implored; "that is tempting Heaven, and you are not yet prepared to appear before the Seat of Justice."

"Have no fear for me, my angel," the young man whispered, as he pressed her to his heart; "you frighten yourself more than the whole affair is worth. We have only to catch a criminal who has hitherto escaped from justice, and there are enough of us to board a vessel full of such fellows; so good-night, my darling Manuela; good-night, and may Heaven console you!"

He pressed his lips to the pale, cold, and unresisting lips of the lovely girl, and rushed off to his boat; but Manuela cast herself before the image of Him crucified, and her sorrow gradually subsided into soothing tears; but the terror remained in her heart, and with feverish excitement she listened for the slightest sound in the street.

The Signal.

CHAPTER IV.

THE PIRATE.

THE Bay of Valparaiso lay, on the evening of the 8th of August, as calm and silent as only a warm, balmy atmosphere, a pure, cloudless sky, and the mirror-like water, in which the stars were countlessly reflected, could render it. Not a breath was stirring; silence was only now and then disturbed by the oars of boats going to or coming from land; and the sound of merry music pealed across the waters from the brilliantly-lighted houses, in soft, harmonious strains.

The sharp, tinkling sound of "four bells" was heard from one of the vessels in the harbour at regular intervals and was answered by the other vessels in rapid succession. It was ten o'clock.

A quarter of an hour had thus passed, when a small, extremely narrow boat—hardly large enough to carry two persons, and which was paddled by one man, after the fashion of a canoe—glided from the west coast of the bay with the speed of light, and after passing several vessels, from which it kept as far as possible, cut across as if making for the usual landing-place. A little further on, however, the man altered his former course, and went southward, straight to the spot where the wreck of the pirate lay on the reefs. The man who paddled was perfectly well acquainted with his course, for he scarce reached the dark shadow the small vessel cast on the water than he fastened his boat alongside, and clambered, a few seconds after, on board, swung himself over the gangway, and disappeared below. It was our old acquaintance the stranger, whom we will now follow at his nocturnal labours.

The deck was only dimly lighted by the glimmering stars, but the between-decks was perfectly dark; and as the stranger descended the narrow stairs—for he only stayed long enough on deck to cast a hurried glance around—he produced a small dark-lantern from beneath his poncho, and entered the cabin.

He remained standing on the threshold, as if seized by an inward shuddering, and cast the light round the little room beforehand, as if he almost expected to find some one below. The destruction produced by the carpenters seemed to comfort him. On one side, all the valuable wood-work had been removed, and they had even begun their work on the other. The sofa had also been removed; and he quickly and cautiously clambered over the laths and boards piled up in the middle, towards the back of the cabin, where the trap-door led into the store-hold. At this moment the bright light fell on the left, hitherto untouched side of the cabin, and with an almost involuntary cry his hand moved to his belt and the handles of his pistols, while he let the rays fall full and brightly on a spot upon the denuded wall.

There was nothing to be seen that could disquiet him; but the lantern lit up the precise place which had so irresistibly attracted his glance on the previous day, and where the sharp mark of some weapon, hurled or struck, evidenced too clearly some deed of horror.

"Strange!" the man muttered gently to himself; "I could have sworn I saw a white shadow there—the light must have blinded me.

It is an absurd coincidence—the very anniversary of that mad hour! —and the fools in the town have seen ghosts, too! Haha! haha!" he grinned to himself; but it was a demoniac laugh—more a spasm of the muscles of the face than the flash of merry humour; the man with the death-pale face and glistening eyes did not look like jesting.

He quickly strode past the spot to the little trap-door. But here he found an obstacle which cost him some time. The carpenters had recently piled up all the woodwork at the back of the cabin. This had to be first removed; and the solitary labourer uttered many a bitter oath as he placed the lantern on the ground, and removed the wood as noiselessly but as rapidly as he could. At length he was able to raise the door, and leaped down with the lantern, without casting a glance behind him.

Scarcely was he below than he turned the full light on one of the thick beams. He had not to search long, for he soon detected a dark spot in the greyish-brown wood. With a small, peculiarly-shaped instrument, which he held in his hand, he pressed against it at two different points, and the snapping of a spring responded: a wooden plate was then easily pulled back, and from the interior he took out a small ebony casket, which must have been very heavy, for he needed both hands; and several larger and smaller bags. The smaller of these he concealed about his person, but all the rest he placed in a rather large leathern pouch, which he unfastened from his belt; and then thrust his hand once again into the recess, as if to convince himself that it was empty. He found something, which he pulled out and held to the light. It was a plain gold crucifix; but when the light of the lamp fell on it he started back, and made a movement as if about to throw it from him; but he held it tightly in his clasped hand, and then thrust it beneath his poncho, without daring a second glance at it.

"Pest!" he muttered gently to himself, as he pushed back the spring into its place; "ever and ever the remembrance of that deed!"

The moment, however, demanded action, not reflection; and so, seizing the leathern bag, to which he attached a small but strong silken cord, he took up his lantern and climbed up again into the cabin. Here he hesitated for a moment, and looked at the woodwork he had cast aside.

"Shall I arrange it again as I found it?" he asked himself, thoughtfully: "no one could then have the slightest suspicion. But of what consequence is it?" he broke off, and did not even close the trap; "before they can even suspect anything, I shall long have escaped them; and they can put it down to the ghost, the fools!"

He turned quickly to leave the cabin, when he clearly saw a tall, graceful form standing dimly in his path. He was not startled; for his nerves had been too strung by the excitement of the past hour to permit him such a feeling. His first move was to his weapons; but what would such things, made by mortal hands, avail against the pictures of his own fancy—the reminiscences of his conscience, which had assumed a visible form? Summoned up by time and the hour, he saw before him a phantom to which for years he had given form and colour in his dreams; and with painful interest, which seemed as if it would burst the nerves of his brain, he felt, rather than saw, the pale, suffering form extend an arm towards him. Its lips moved, and blood, pure red blood—every drop of which he could hear dripping on the ground with a clearness which drove the cold sweat to his forehead—poured down from the white dress."

"Josepha!"—the word unconsciously passed his lips; but then his old daring, his old strength of mind returned at once—"Devil!" he shouted; "you know that my brain is already full to bursting, and so you have determined to make me mad on this day! Back with you to your proper place!—you cannot terrify me!"

And letting the flash of light fall due on the spot, he walked unhesitatingly past. The walls were empty and bare, but his foot stopped in terror, for before him on the ground lay blood—blood as fresh as if just spilt—close to the blow on the panelling.

But it was only for a moment: the next he walked with a firm foot past it, and with a few bounds reached the deck. But he scarcely felt the fresh, cool night air blowing in his face than his entire energy and coolness returned.

"Succeeded!" he whispered, as he listened, triumphantly, and not a sound revealed that there was any life in the usually so busy bay; but on land, near the landing-place, he could hear voices, and see some lights moving through the streets. But what cared he for land? his road lay towards the entrance of the harbour, where a small but bright light shone from the peak of a small schooner anchored there. It was the *Albatross*, in which he had come from Otaheite.

Still, he had no time to lose; his boat yet lay motionless at the spot where he had left it, and heaving his valuable burthen overboard, he let it down cautiously by the silken cord; he opened and extinguished the lantern, which he had hitherto left on deck, and dropped it in the water; the sound was like the rising of one of the numerous fish in the bay. With another glance across the water where his course lay, he swung over the bulwark, when his eye was suddenly caught by two brilliant fireballs which rose on land and lit up the shore for a moment—he fancied he could see a crowd collected.

"Ha! what is the meaning of that?" he muttered to himself. "A signal—and answered over there, too!"

"But what care I?" he said gloomily to himself, as he sat quickly down, and thrust the canoe from the schooner's side. "Let them exchange as many signals as they please—I have torn the prey from their clutches." He gave a couple of strokes out into the bay, but then stopped for a moment in thought. The fireballs might be signals for boats to come ashore, and, in order to get out of their way, it would be better for him to keep over more to the west coast, in whose deep shadow he could easily escape any pursuit. The bow of the light boat flew round in a second, and glided like an arrow, guided by his practised hand, over the smooth water.

"*Caracho!*" the solitary paddler muttered between his clenched teeth, when he had gone about half-a-mile towards the landing-place, and allowed his boat to glide into the shadow of a vessel anchored there; for right in his way he saw a long, heavy boat.

It was not the boat itself which disquieted him, but he did not hear any sound of rowing: hence the crew had muffled their oars, and hence were engaged on some unusual expedition.

"But who on earth could know that I was out in the bay? That was not possible. Nonsense!" he muttered, "those fellows have their business and I have mine: we shall not interfere with each other."

He drove his boat about a couple of lengths forwards and held a little more to the north, to allow the other to shoot past and give him more sea-room, when he suddenly saw a second, rather further back, but both coming in the same direction; and now did not dare to go on, for he must not expose himself to the risk of being stopped by night, with what he had about him.

While pausing to make up his mind, he saw the first boat alter its course, and, as it seemed, come straight towards him. And it was so. In the stern-sheets was a young officer who cautiously surveyed the bay with a night-glass, and who hardly saw the dark spot, which he soon recognised as a boat, emerge from the shade of the vessel, than he immediately steered towards it.

"*Diablo!*" the man growled, as he turned his boat with one stroke of his paddle; "better the open bay;" and he was just proceeding towards the light hung up as a signal for him, when he saw two boats coming in that direction, and thus found himself completely cut off.

"*Carambo!*" he exclaimed, as he raised his head to survey the bay; "is the devil playing his tricks and intending to leave an old comrade in the lurch? Have the bloodhounds got scent—but through whom? No matter; but I know my way about better than you fellows may fancy, and though the capture would not be bad for you, you shall not have it cheaply."

With these words he quickly turned the head of his boat towards the reefs from which he had started, till he had the shadow of the wreck between himself and his pursuers—for such they now proved themselves—and then shot as quickly as paddle would take him towards the land, where houses jutted out into the sea, built on posts, in whose gloomy shadow he could laugh at any pursuit.

When scarce two hundred paces distant, and he had already chosen the dark arch he intended to run into, a large boat, pulled by four oarsmen, shot out. A broad, muscular form was standing at the tiller, and he must have been seen and watched by them, for they sought to cut him off; the steerer urged his men to lay on their oars bravely.

The pirate, however, knew far too well the speed of his own little boat to fear the least danger from the clumsy jolly-boat; all that troubled him was, that something lay in his way, and he must inveigle it to quit. As if afraid of being caught up by it, and preferring to put out into the bay, he turned his canoe round, and pretended to be growing exhausted. Not that it was so; he could have gone on paddling the whole night through, for his muscles seemed to be made of iron wire. In addition, a large empty bark lay here on a sprung cable; this he brought between himself and the boat, and as soon as his pursuers came close up to it, he turned his light canoe round, and, ere they could check the speed of their heavy boat, he shot back like an arrow; and neither the good old captain—who, on seeing his prey slip between his fingers, muttered curse on curse—nor the man-o'-war's boats would have been able to prevent his landing, had not at this moment Edward Wilkinson's boat—a light yawl, pulled by two powerful English sailors—shot out from before the houses, and cut him off.

"Are all the demons unchained to-night?" the pirate hissed, only able to escape the new danger, into which he had almost rushed headforemost, by rapidly turning his canoe's head round. "But take care, my fine fellows, take care; you are buzzing like moths round a candle; for you will never have Tenares alive, and, even dead, he will ask a heavy price of you!"

But though he had been so superior to the other boat in speed and activity, he found here an opponent who gave him all his work; while, himself surrounded by enemies, he hardly knew which way to turn, for the man-o'-war's boats had also come up so close, that he had no chance of escaping into the bay.

The clumsiest boat, and the one in which he least feared fire-arms, though he knew they would not readily be employed against him, was certainly the Spaniard's, who had succeeded in bringing her head round, and he pulled straight up to him. If he could reach land at any spot, he was so well acquainted with all the streets and buildings, that he did not the least fear escaping his pursuers, even if he had half the town after him. Hence, by turning the bow of his canoe further outwards, he again tried to make his foe believe that he intended to escape into the harbour. But the old captain would not be done twice in one night that way; and being aware that, within less than ten minutes, all the man-o'-war's boats must utterly prevent any escape in that direction, while he was unable to match the fugitive in speed, so soon as he saw him coming up he ordered his men to lie on their oars, ready to shoot to land at any moment.

It was an excellent place for him to watch the pirate's movements; for towards the land lay long spars of floating timber, and, holding on to the end of these, if the pirate tried to pass he must come within his reach, or run into the jaws of the boats, whose regular rowing could now be heard.

Tenares whose eye appeared to gain in sharpness the greater the danger grew, saw the wood in time to escape the trap, and put out really seawards, to throw his last and most dangerous enemy off the scent. Edward Wilkinson, however, was perfectly well aware that he could not escape in that direction.

"Back water!" he shouted to his men; and in a second the slight vessel lay as if anchored, while he turned her head, so as to be ready to start at once. But the fugitive had no time for manœuvring, and, trusting to the speed of his canoe, he turned back once more, to force his way ashore past the young Englishman's yawl.

"Surrender, senor!" Edward shouted; "your exertions are useless—you are surrounded! Surrender, or you will force me to extreme measures."

"*Caramba!*" was the only reply the pirate hissed through his teeth; "as if you had not already done your utmost to capture me; but *paciencia!*" and with rapid strokes he drove the bow of his boat straight towards the enemy.

"Back water!" the young man shouted, bounding from his seat. "Back water, men, for your lives!"

The two men pressed the whole weight of their bodies against the hurriedly-checked oars, and the elastic ash-wood bent as if about to break, as they suddenly stopped the way of the boat. But though it had hardly shot its own length forward, so effectually had the order been obeyed, still this slight distance was sufficient for the pirate to turn his light canoe and cross the bows of the yawl. Before the latter could have been turned, he would have been in safety; but Wilkinson, seeing at a glance the advantage the pirate had obtained, sprang on to the taffrail of his own boat, and leaped towards the canoe, which passed hardly a yard from him.

The pirate saw the movement, and turned the stern of his canoe as far as possible; but he could not prevent his foe clutching the gunwale, while the right hand clutched the pirate's waist-belt.

"*Diablo!*" Tenares shouted, and threw himself almost instinctively to the other side, while he let fall his now useless paddle, and drew his long knife. At the same moment, however, the little canoe capsized, and the two wrestlers sank into the water.

Wilkinson, in springing from his own boat, had naturally thrust it back a few feet, and as it was in the act of turning, this movement turned its head round completely, and hardly a minute had elapsed ere the sharp bow shot over the spot, and the oars backed where the men had sunk, and the agitated water still heaved. The little capsized boat drifted like a nutshell on the surface of the water towards the land.

A head, and only one, at length appeared on the surface; but, whichever it might be, the sailors at once clutched at the long hair floating on the water, and the next moment the body was lifted into the boat.

"Have you caught the pirate?" was the young officer's first exclamation when able to speak.

"He has not yet come to the surface," was the reply of both men, who kept their eyes fixed on the water, and paid no attention to their officer, whom they fancied all right.

"Look! look!" the young man groaned, and sank back unconscious in the boat.

Though the events described took so few moments in their performance, all the other boats had assembled round the spot.

A few words from the sailors to the captain of the *Nuestra Senora* explained all that had happened, and he gave his orders in a quick but distinct voice. All the boats would cruize in the bay and along the coast, and examine most carefully every empty boat, every float of timber, and be careful that the pirate did not escape by swimming. In the town the police had already turned out, and it seemed impossible the pirate could escape them. The captain then gave his orders to ship their oars, and he proceeded towards land.

"But where is Don Eduardo?" he suddenly asked, as he gave his crew a sign to stop. "What has become of him?—is he saved?"

"I fear he is dead," one of the young man's sailors replied, who had bent down over him, and felt the warm gushing blood on his hand. "At any rate, he is severely wounded, and has fainted."

The captain's boat shot up the next moment alongside the officer's yawl. He was carefully taken out, and then they proceeded to the nearest point of land with all possible speed.

He, however, did not follow the enemy's movements; he was fearful of some new feint, and wished first to be quite certain of the direction he intended to take. By this the pirate certainly gained a slight start, but if the English still held the inside, he must pass before or behind them to reach the land. He tried the latter first, but Wilkinson's attention foiled it, and the two boats ran alongside for some two hundred yards, hardly two boats' lengths apart.

Tenares makes himself known to Senora Fcstero.

CHAPTER V.

THE RECOGNITION.

THE police of Valparaiso, at the period of which we write, were not so excellently organized as is now the case; still, mounted, and with a sabre at their side, and a lasso on their saddle-bow, they traversed the streets at night, or stood at their appointed stations. The sabre was only an honorary weapon, however—just as our courtiers wear a sword—for they wore it more to make a noise than for actual service; but the lasso was all the more dangerous to nocturnal evil-doers, who, in their flight, did not find quickly enough a corner into which they could crawl. The servants of the law galloped after them, and it was all over with them if they came within reach of the never-erring lasso—the noose flew out five-and-twenty or thirty paces behind them, and once in its rough clutch, they hardly ever succeeded in liberating themselves from it.

The chief of the police—or, at least, of the quarter where Donna Fostero's house stood—received orders from Don Olinda to scatter his men along the beach, and arrest every suspicious person, no matter who. To the crowd that had collected around he also offered a reward of five hundred dollars for those who caught the fugitive; and it may be easily imagined that police and *peóns* did their best to gain this magnificent reward.

Four of the crew, by the captain's order, in the meanwhile, bore the wounded man to the Donna's house, where he was sure to be kindly treated, while another went to summon a physician. When all this was arranged, he sent his boat off again, in charge of a midshipman, to join the others, and, at any price, prevent the pirate's escape to sea; while he remained on land, to see the measures he had ordered strictly carried out.

Mourning and lamentation now brooded over the Donna's once so merry *pulperia*. Manuela had sat, ever since her lover's departure, in painful expectation; before her mental eye ever glistened the pistols he carried in his belt; he had gone to meet a mortal danger, and she feared—nay, awaited, with a heart-breaking that threatened to burst her breast—that the sound of distant firearms would reach her ear at every moment. She could not weep—the deadly apprehension mercilessly restrained the soothing flood of tears—and she sat, with clenched hands and death-pale face, at the window, looking out on the bay, while her cold lips moved in gentle, but, oh! how fervent prayer.

Suddenly a noise was heard in the streets—a number of voices shouted in wild confusion—they stopped at the door of the house, there was a knocking, and the next moment the four sailors bore the young officer's senseless body into the house.

Donna Fostero shrieked in horror, and smote her hands together over her head; even Marequita and Juana stood speechless with terror at the so sudden death of the young man, who had left the house in such spirits a few hours before; but Manuela was collected. So long as the danger still threatened, her heart almost broke through the terrible fear of meeting it; but at the moment that fate assailed her existence so coldly and seriously, and destroyed her fairest blossom of hope, all weakness and despondency disappeared, and she made the necessary arrangements with a calmness and thoughtfulness that filled even her mother with astonishment and admiration.

The wounded man—at first they had believed him dead, until the sailors assured them there was still life in him, and a physician would arrive directly to examine his wound—was carried into the small back-room (the quietest in the house), where a bed was hurriedly prepared for him; and Manuela with her own hands took off his coat in order to stop the bleeding, until the physician's help could do more for him.

A number of curious persons had entered the *pulperia* with the wounded man, and from them Donna Fostero soon learned all they knew about what had taken place; but while their story was reaching the culminating point, a *peón* rushed in and told them that *senor capitano*, of the *Nuestra Senora*, offered five hundred dollars—a perfect fortune in that country—for the capture of the pirate, and there was at once such a zeal among the population to get hold of a man of whom they did not yet know the slightest harm, and whom they had probably never seen in the whole course of their lives, that, five minutes later, not a soul was left in the house, but all rushed in wild haste to the beach, in order to help in gaining the offered blood-money. The warning example, however, which they had just seen, told them, at the same time, what they had to expect in case they rushed too carelessly into danger, and many of them came to the certainly most praiseworthy resolve of keeping a very careful eye on their own skins in this affair.

The physician had, in the meanwhile, arrived, and Manuela had sent for a priest to give the dying man extreme unction, in case he desired it. She forgot that he belonged to a religion strange to her; she only saw in him a beloved one departing this life; and her own bleeding heart yearned with feverish excitement, even at this moment, for the consolation of the Church—for was there any other consolation left her in this world?

The priest soon arrived: meanwhile the physician declared the wound very serious, and probably mortal, and the young man opened his eyes for the first time, with a faint smile, as he saw Manuela's beloved features bent over his bed. The Franciscan refused, point-blank, to give a heretic the Holy Sacrament, or the last consolation of the only saving Church, unless he returned to her bosom first, as a penitent sinner; for he regarded all Protestants merely as back-sliding children from the real Metropolitan Church.

Manuela was kneeling, in speechless grief, by the bed of her dying lover—her excited fancy summoned up all the fearful terrors of her religion before her mind, which the souls of the condemned were exposed to in a future life. With all the fervour of her Southern blood she loved the man who must now be hopelessly lost to her; and by her side stood, in his white sacred robes, a priest of the God of love—the only man who could yet save him, and pluck him back from the fearful abyss—and he refused to stretch out a hand to him.

The physician, who saw her growing desperation, and probably feared the consequences for herself, if she gave way to any violent emotion, now tried to console her, and begged her to grow calm. The young man's wound was certainly dangerous—it was still possible to save him—but he could promise nothing if she excited him too greatly. But the eye of love could not be deceived by such words—it saw death imprinted on those features—and the words of consolation, instead of calming her, only shook her more violently.

"No!" she suddenly exclaimed, as she threw herself on her lover, and covered his pale lips with her kisses; "no! you shall not go alone into the fearful night of eternal condemnation, my poor, unhappy friend. You have not a being in this wide world now to take interest in you—not one to let a tear fall on your grave, save me—and it shall not be said that I was yours only in joy and happiness, and wished to walk with you in the sunshine. I could have resigned you—resigned all the blessedness I felt in your heart—if I knew that you were happy, or saw the possibility before me that God might enlighten you and lead you in his paths. But now that is past—you are alone and deserted—the whole world has rejected you, the Church itself repulses you, and you shall not—no, by Heaven! you shall not—die in desperation. Manuela is yours—as she was in life, she is in death; and by that spectral moon, which now shines upon you—by that mysterious world whose secrets none of us can fathom—I swear to you that the religion in which you die shall be mine, the God you believe in shall also be mine; and you shall not alone endure the darkness and torture of condemnation, for Manuela, who belonged to you in life, will not leave you in death!"

The physician was deeply affected by this love, which was able even to dare those terrors of eternal condemnation at which the pure heart of the lovely child had hitherto trembled; but the priest, in pious horror, made one cross after the other in the air, which was desecrated by such sinful words, and at length even seized the maiden's hand—which she, however, immediately drew back—to withdraw her from this dangerous place, which seemed to imperil her own salvation.

At this moment the wounded man, who had listened, with a sweet smile on his face, to the passionate words his beloved uttered, gently lifted his hand, and tried to raise himself in the bed. The physician sought to prevent him, and begged him to speak as little as possible, as it would be dangerous in his present condition; but his patient shook his head with a melancholy smile, and whispered—

"I *must* speak, dear doctor. I have but little time to lose here, and wish to procure myself a happy moment, by pouring consolation and hope into the pious, faithful heart of this poor girl by my side. Reverend father!" he then turned to the priest, with a voice which had almost entirely regained its vigour and expression; "will you fulfil the prayer of a dying man, who, before his death, desires to be received into the bosom of your Church, and to die with the consolation your sacred religion can impart to him?"

"No, no, you shall not do it for my sake!" Manuela shrieked at this moment; for though her face was illumined by an almost supernatural joy on first seeing the meaning of her lover's words, the old, numbing pain returned. "You shall not part from this world in bitter remorse, and make such a sacrifice in vain. Do not try to deceive yourself. Your God would not and could not pardon you if you implored His mercy through such motives. No, no, it is too late; in your heart you are still a Protestant. They are merely sounding words, which cannot reconcile you to your Creator, and you wish to deceive yourself and me by a hypocritical consolation. But fear not for me, my beloved," she said, with an enthusiasm which imparted even greater lustre to her eyes; "I bring you no sacrifice, but I will no longer struggle against what is impossible. Without you even Heaven would be a torture to me, and God must tear asunder my poor heart, if He strove, even in eternal life, to separate it from thee."

And with this pious heresy on her lips, she sank on her knees, sobbing loudly, and her tears poured abundantly on Edward's hand. The dying man again slowly raised his head, till the moist glistening of her eye met his again, and then said, with a smile, but in a firm voice—

"Listen to me, Manuela, and then say if you can call my present action a sacrifice, and if God will not receive into His arms an erring child, who is longing to be clasped to His paternal heart. I feel that you would be miserable were I to die without the blessing of your religion; but could I depart satisfied with the consciousness that I left you, whom I loved more than my whole life, in such a state? But not that alone: the religion to which a heart so faithful and pure as yours, Manuela, can be devoted, must bring consolation, and salvation, and peace. Will you blame me because my soul thirsts after its blessing? God knows and sees my heart, my Manuelita. He knows what earnest motives induce me to take this step, which I intend to take with the aid of this reverend gentleman. Will you still reproach me, then, or believe that the All-Merciful will refuse me His mercy?"

It only required a few consolatory words from the priest—who seized, with pious zeal, the opportunity to save a soul he already thought lost—to reconcile the maiden to the idea that her lover had entered on the path of salvation through internal conviction; and, with a rejoicing, thankful heart, she sank on his bed again in fervent prayer.

While this scene had been taking place in the upper room, Senora Fostero had listened for some time at the door, but had been restrained by a peculiar feeling from disturbing her daughter, whose deep sorrow affected even her own sluggish heart; and hence, when the priest began questioning the dying man, she withdrew quietly from the door.

The streets had, however, become so animated, that she began to feel apprehensive about the safety of her own house, which was now quite unguarded. She therefore went into the lower rooms, looked if the house door was securely bolted and the shutter properly fastened, and was just going to look at the little back door, to see whether her girls, in their alarm, might not have forgotten to shut it—for she had sent them off to bed long before—when the door, which led to a small courtyard behind the house, suddenly flew open, and the old lady stood motionless and speechless through terror, when she saw before her the terrible form of the stranger, who everybody said was a fearful pirate, and one of whose victims lay bleeding in her own house.

Tenares, the terrible pirate of the South Seas, looked really very terrible in his present condition, hunted like a beast of prey, and would have alarmed even a bolder woman than Senora Fostero as to the injury he might inflict on her person or property. His face was deadly pale; his long black hair hung in thick, wet masses over his temples, and mingled with his dripping beard; his eyes looked like glistening coals of fire; and on his forehead, from which the black plaster had been washed away by long exposure to the water, was a broad, blood-red scar, reaching far down between his eyes.

His clothes were wringing wet; the water poured from him in many drops; his hat he had lost in his flight; and only his right hand held convulsively, and like the last means of defence, the long, sharp knife with which he had already disposed of his first foe.

But though his position was so desperate, he acted with rapid decision. A threatening motion of his armed hand towards the trembling woman revealed to her the danger to which the first cry for help would expose her; then he quickly closed the door behind him, but only turned the key, for he did not intend to barricade himself there—he only wished to secure himself from a surprise; then he bolted the other door which led to the stairs, listened for a moment to the noise in the street, and then removed the long wet hair from his face with a deep-drawn sigh.

"So!" he then said, with a contemptuous smile, which rendered his features perfectly fiendish. "For the moment I am saved, but not entirely—now, *tia mia,* I please you thus, do I not? Yes, darling, the times have changed since we last met. An hour ago I was a millionaire, and now, through the hasty leap of a maniac, I am a beggar. But you will give me a bottle of wine on trust, eh, aunt? Silence!" he added, seriously, as she was about to utter an exclamation—"silence, my dove; I am not disposed for jesting this evening; yet I should not like to do you any harm."

With these words he seized a full bottle standing on a shelf, knocked off the neck with the back of his knife, and poured the wine into one of the already used glasses standing on the table.

"Hem!" he said, after emptying it at a draught, and filling it again, "that does good, and gives the muscles fresh strength—but it was wanted; for I really believe that the whole town is after me. But now to work, *tia mia;* I have a request to make of you which you will not refuse: I must beg of you the brass key of the little yellow room—you know what I mean—be quick, *carissima!* for, by heavens! the pursuers will not let my trail grow cold. I have escaped them for the present. The rogues had me in the lasso; but a scoundrel, I verily believe, saw me turn into a little side court, and I fancy I can hear the bloodhounds in the next house. But I have no objection to their finding my trail here; for you know, *amiga mia,* that I can escape easily from the yellow room, if I have any luck, in a direction which they will not suspect; and while they fancy me still in the house, I shall be over the hills and far away."

Senora Fostero, at first startled and terrified by the pirate's appearance, forgot, at this moment, all her fears in the one feeling of amazement; for the secret of the key, she was certain, was known to no other living being than herself. Who was this mysterious being, who assumed, on the first day of his appearance here, a degree of coolness as if he alone had to give orders, and who now, possessed of her deepest, and, indeed, only secret, demanded her aid in his flight, as if she were bound to afford it to him, and not betray him to his pursuers as soon as his back was turned? or would he murder her so soon as he had the key in his possession? The thought drove the blood with icy coldness to her heart, and, in timid haste, she looked round for assistance.

The pirate may have read in her disturbed and pale features what was passing in her mind; but he no longer dared to run the risk of any delay, for loud voices were now heard in the adjoining house, and at any moment his pursuers might rap at the door, which would afford no long obstacle if force were used. He therefore said, in a quiet but suppressed voice—

"Have no fears for your life, *carissima!* I have other means to purchase your silence; but the time for masquerading is past. Hang it! Beatriz, I was always vain enough to believe that when I had lived on such intimate terms with a woman as man and wife are usually on, I should not be so easily forgotten by her."

"Holy Mary! Lorenzo Fajardo!" the woman groaned, in a suppressed voice, for the pirate raised his finger in warning—and sank on her knees, overcome by surprise, but also by internal horror.

"Yes, yes!" the man whispered, as he nodded his head, and looked fixedly at her; "that was the name I used in former, I really believe happier times. But that is past," he said, drawing himself to his full height. "Yes, Beatriz, I have led a wild and dangerous life since my star—I may call it my evil star—led me from this coast; first pursuing, then pursued; at last overpowered and robbed at one blow of all that I had earned by years of danger and—much blood. Then I escaped, was captured again, and kept a prisoner at Manilla, with wild thoughts in my brains, which often threatened to burst my veins. Again I escaped, and, when on the point of getting all my own again, was hurled to the ground. There you have, in a few pencil-marks, my whole course of life. I meant rightly by you, had my plan succeeded; but it was not destined to do so. The wheel of fate turns incessantly, and I am now once more at the bottom, but the next turn will lift me to the top; and they have not yet laid hands on poor Lorenzo Fajardo, whom they despised here, but who, as Tenares, drove the blood from their cheeks when his mere name was mentioned—no, by heavens! and they shall not have him so long as he can move an arm or brandish a knife. But now, *carissima!* there is no time left for gossiping," he suddenly broke off, while thrusting back into its sheath the knife he had still been holding; "give me the key, for I hear voices in the street. If they break in here, and find the wet marks here where I

Bay of Manilla.

have been standing—and you cannot well hide them—tell them I have been here, and probably escaped through the back door. Not another soul knows the way over the roofs; I can easily escape to the mountains, and, before daybreak, I shall have reached my protecting ship, in spite of their boats and signals. Pest on them! Tenares is too tough to be stopped by a party of policemen, or be lugged from his own element, the water, by a couple of boats of dirty sailors—the key, *carissima,* the key!"

The old lady had, in the meanwhile, regarded the speaker in silent horror, and through the tangled hair and beard, which he had never worn before, and which now covered his entire face, she saw—oh! it was a fearful truth!—the features of the husband she thought dead, in the hounded, bloodthirsty pirate. His danger, however, soon restored her to consciousness, and she quickly went to a little cupboard, and produced from a secret drawer a small brass key. But, on the point of handing it to the fugitive, she started back, under the influence of a new thought.

"Great heavens, Lorenzo!" she whispered, hurriedly, "you cannot go upstairs. In that room lies the officer mortally wounded by your hand; and Manuela, a priest, and a physician are with him."

"*Diablo!*" the pirate said, stamping on the ground with savage fury. "Well, he said, furiously, as he tore the key from her and held it tightly in his hand, "there are only two who can stand in my path—good night, Beatriz!"

"In the Saviour's name, shed no more blood in my house!" the woman shrieked, falling at his knees in mortal apprehension; "you have caused a greater misfortune than you imagine already—and one of them is a servant of the Lord."

"Be calm: there is nothing to fear; but your shrieks will bring in people from the street. Ah! I hear voices on the stairs." He opened the little door quickly and gently.

"Stay!" the woman implored; "you must meet them."

"Hist!" the pirate whispered, for he knew the ground here too well not to form his plan directly; "they are coming down, and I will hide myself here under the balustrade. Open the door again when you hear them coming down: the bright light in the room will dazzle them; I will keep out of the reflection. Good night, Beatriz, good night! If I escape you shall hear from me again." And like a serpent he glided through the door, which he closed again, while slow and heavy steps could be heard descending the stairs.

The poor woman, in her terror, did as her husband bade her—she opened the door, so that the light fell on the lowest stairs; but then she was overcome by the thoughts of all that had occurred during the last hour, and sank, sobbing loudly, on the nearest chair, and hid her face in her hands.

Immediately after this, the *pater* and the physician entered the room. The priest was in front, and, when he saw the bowed-down form of the woman, he stopped by her side, and, laying his hand on her head, said, in a consoling, almost gentle, voice—

"Weep, weep, poor oppressed heart, that will afford you consolation and alleviation; but trust to Him, who will lead you in the right path, through night to light, and through morning to salvation. His ways are marvellous, and He guides all for the best. When the dagger of the evil one mortally wounded a straying lamb, God laid His hand on the victim, and illumined him with his redeeming love and mercy. He is happy now; he has gone to his eternal rest, reconciled to his God, and blessing the hand of the murderer, which opened for him the path to salvation."

The woman, whose tears had flowed more copiously at these consoling words, although she did not yet understand their meaning, now looked up to him wildly and haggardly. Of whom was he speaking? But the physician, who also believed that she was weeping for the unhappy young man, who would once have been more closely connected with her, but would, probably, find some consolation in his reconciliation to her religion, said, gently—

"He died easily and softly, and joined your creed before his death. Your daughter seems to have found marvellous consolation in it, and is perfectly calm—so pray calm yourself too, senora. It is a melancholy event, but who knows whether it is not all for the best? The ways of Providence are inexplicable."

The poor old lady, to whom the past now came back, hid her face once more in her hands, and said—

"Poor, poor Manuela!"

A violent knocking at both the doors at once interrupted her here; confused cries were to be distinguished; and while the physician who heard from without the summons, "In the name of the law!" walked up to the door and pulled back the bolt, the lock of the back door was broken in by the pressure of the crowd, who were trying to force an entrance. Police stationed themselves, however, immediately at both entrances; and, while they summoned the crowd to surround the house, and allow no one to go out, either in male or female attire, they only allowed a few persons to enter the room. Among these were Don Olinda, two of the lieutenants of police, and several armed sergeants—one of them wounded in the arm, who had been brought here because a surgeon was known to be present.

"Senora!" Captain Olinda said, as he entered the room, and cast a hurried glance around, "it is most painful to me to disturb you in this way in the middle of the night; but the pressing nature of my business must serve as my excuse. The flying pirate whom we seek, and who escaped us in the bay, is said to have entered this house; he was seen by two persons, and we are therefore compelled to search the house from top to bottom; but you can go quietly to your room, and I will be responsible for your property with my whole fortune. Ah, doctor! and how is the patient? I trust not —poor Eduardo!" but he suddenly broke off on noticing the surgeon's gloomy shake of the head—"what, is he really dead? Ha, by Heaven! the measure of this criminal's iniquity is overflowing, and it is time for him to be brought to a reckoning."

The old lady had in the meanwhile risen and walked to the stair door; her heart beat terribly, for she heard voices above—the desperate man had not yet escaped; and, good heavens! suppose he were captured in her house! Obeying her feelings more than any settled purpose, she tottered up the stairs.

"Now, gentlemen," the captain said, turning to the police authorities, who stood with uncovered heads before him, "are you certain he cannot leave the house without being seen and captured by your followers?"

"All the streets are occupied, senor," one of them replied; "my men and a number of volunteers occupy all the neighbouring houses and courts, enticed by the handsome reward you offered for the capture of the criminal. If he cannot fly or leap from roof to roof like a cat, we must catch him—but what is that?"

He pointed to the ground, where the wet marks of the stranger's dripping clothes were still distinctly visible.

"*Caramba!*" the captain hurriedly exclaimed: "we are on the track; but no—the water runs towards the stairs; it comes from the clothes of the unhappy young man who was just now brought here, dripping with wet and severely wounded."

"But the bottle here?" the policeman asked, who had been looking searchingly round the room, and who was naturally struck by the empty bottle, and the neck still lying on the floor. "Some one drank wine in a great hurry, a good deal has been spilt, and there is a broken splinter in the glass—that looks suspicious."

"You are right," Don Olinda said, as he hurriedly walked up: "in that case he cannot escape us."

"Here are the wet footprints of a man," another policeman said, who had been looking about; "the wounded man could not walk, and it must be——"

A loud shriek above interrupted his remarks.

"There he is!" Olinda shouted. "Give the alarm round the house—and now to help!" And while one of the men sprang to the door, and shouted that the fugitive had been found, and they must look out, the others, led by Don Olinda, who was armed with a pistol, bounded up the stairs into the place whence they had heard Manuela's loud, piercing cry for help.

"I wish you luck with your capture," the wounded policeman said, who, being in the hands of the surgeon, bit his lips together from pain. "It is not a man, but a tiger. Till now, when a man was so snug in the lasso as I saw him, I always fancied that we had him; but he cut the tough leather through as I would a bit of twine, and, before I could jump out of his way, I had my allowance—a little more to the right, and it would have been all over with me."

The Pirate reaches the "Yellow Room."

CHAPTER VI.

MANUELA.

WHEN the priest and the doctor slowly walked down the stairs together, the fugitive was so near them, with his knife in his hand, that the father's white robes grazed him; the slightest side movement the latter had made would have brought him into contact with the body pressed against the dark wall. But the pirate did not tremble for his own safety, as he knew that no greater danger now threatened him than since the first moment of the pursuit, and an almost devilish smile played over his gloomy features, when the thought flashed across his mind, with what marvellous calmness and security the reverend father walked close past his yawning grave; for he was quite decided on stabbing both of them, so soon as they discovered his hiding-place, because, by following, they would greatly impede his flight. The pious man did not really suspect that his life at this moment hung on a movement of his elbow, or he would not have walked so comfortably, or with such a perfect feeling of safety, through the narrow passage. His hour, however, had not yet come; he walked unconsciously past the danger, and immediately entered the room, followed by the doctor.

It took some time, though, ere they walked sufficiently far from the still open door for the fugitive to dare to trust himself on the lower, brilliantly-lighted stairs, although the broad form of the priest hid the treacherous gleam.

He still hesitated; for, had one of them looked round, or the stairs creaked, nothing could have saved him from discovery. But at last he dared not lose any more time, for his practised ear, sharpened by danger, already heard the voices of the approaching enemies.

"Confound them! the danger of detecting me is on their side," he muttered, "and the consequences on their heads;" and he then lightly swung himself on the stairs and went cautiously up them, unnoticed. On reaching the landing, he gently opened the door of the room the two men had just quitted, and hastened through it, closing it after him. The scene here presented to him bound him for a moment, as if paralysed, to the spot.

On a mattress on the ground lay the corpse of Edward Wilkinson, covered by a snow-white sheet, the upper part of which revealed a broad dark-red stain. At his feet, and so arranged on a low chair that the dying man's eyes could fall fully upon it, stood the iron flower adorned crucifix, which usually had its place on the little altar in the corner of the room; and by the side of the bed—the cold, dead hand still in hers, as the dying man had left it—knelt Manuela in fervent prayer, with her head bowed over the corpse.

Even the pirate was affected by the holy, inexpressibly touching picture; he cast a wild, shy glance round the room, and with his left hand (for the other unconsciously held the knife) he parted the long wet hair off his brow, and pressed it to his temples, as if thus wishing to expel wicked, torturing thoughts.

Suddenly the voices grew loud below; the back door was broken in, and he must act. But at the first step he took, the kneeling girl, whom the sound disturbed from her devotions, raised her lovely pallid face, and looked on the murderer, whose eyes were fixed on the ground. But she was not alarmed—the horror was accomplished—even the fearful form, holding a glittering knife, which seemed to have sprung out of the earth, no longer terrified her; and for the moment she scarce believed the reality of the apparition.

Tenares stood for a moment as if undecided; the fixed, almost unconscious look of the unhappy girl cut through his soul with a long-forgotten feeling of reproach. But he must employ this first moment of surprise, for the way to the door which would lead to liberty passed close by her. But he had hardly taken the first step towards her when the maiden stretched out her hand to him, and said, in a gentle but firm voice—

"Back, murderer! back from the corpse. Are you not afraid to appear before your victim with hands still red with his blood? Or are you not satisfied? Here, stab me to the heart! I do not fear your knife! You have done your worst."

"Sooner should this hand wither, Manuela!" the pirate replied, in great agitation. "No; fear nothing, girl; you are the last in this wide world of whom I would injure a single hair. I fear, too, I have done thee an ill service this night, child; but the madman forced it on me. I had never done him any hurt—indeed I liked him. But time is slipping away; let me pass, Manuela—I will do you no hurt."

"Back, murderer!" the maiden now cried, listening in increasing amazement to the fearful man's words, but hardly appearing to understand them; but when he advanced to the corpse, she gained her entire presence of mind, while the voices below told her what had brought him here. "Back from the corpse of the man you murdered! Ha, listen! the avengers are approaching, and woe, woe to the guilty!"

"Be reasonable, Manuela," the pirate said soothingly, as he advanced to her. "You know not what you do. I am——"

"Help! murder!" the desperate girl now shouted, raising her

voice to the utmost. She foresaw a danger, but could not clothe it in words. But Tenares had no time for explanations.

"Fool!" he hissed, as he threw her with a giant's force out of his way; "do your worst, then, and endure hereafter the stings of conscience when you learn the truth."

And with one bound he reached the little door so well known to him, which he had, indeed, made for smuggling purposes. In a second it was opened; and while Manuela, who knew not the existence of this door, stood speechless with amazement, he disappeared.

But now she heard the noise of the men rushing up stairs, and her repeated cry for help urged them to increased speed. At this moment the room-door was torn open, and her mother rushed in with agitated, deathly-pale features.

"Help!" the terrified girl again shrieked on seeing her mother; "help, mother! the murderer is——"

"Thy father, wretched girl!" the woman groaned, and concealed her face in her hands.

Manuela stood as if petrified by the fearful word; her dull eyes were fixed on the form that told her such horrors, and she held her arms outstretched, as if keeping it at bay; but when Don Olinda sprang into the room, pistol in hand, she threw up her arms, gave an insane laugh, and sank senseless on the ground.

In a second the room was filled with armed men; but, though every corner was searched, every window examined, not a trace of the fugitive could be found. Had he really been in the room? The windows looked out on the shed, which was crowded with men. The second door was locked within, and there was no hiding-place visible. Olinda looked despairingly at Manuela; she was the only one who could give any explanation, and she lay motionless in the arms of her mother, who was bowed over her in agony.

"Pest!" the captain muttered, and stamped his foot; "women will always faint at a trifle, and at the most improper seasons. Poor Eduardo! and shalt thou lie unavenged in thy bloody grave? No! I do not yet give up all hope, for he cannot disappear into the earth. But there is nothing to be done here." And at a sign from him, the rest silently and noiselessly retired from the room of mourning to continue their investigations in the other apartments.

The whole house was surrounded, every street occupied, and, in fact, nearly the whole town seemed to be on the alert; for any man whom curiosity did not draw from his bed was dragged from it by fear. The report of the return of the pirate not only penetrated to the most distant parts of the town before an hour had elapsed, but it grew rapidly with every street, like the rolling snowball. It was no longer one pirate, who was hunted like a wolf, and trying to escape his judges—no, a piratical fleet had anchored in the bay during the night, and their hordes were plundering and firing the town, and dragging women and children into slavery.

It did not occur to them that five or six men-o'-war were lying in the bay, and that such a surprise was impossible—at such moments, and when supported by fear and suddenness, there is nothing so improbable but that it will obtain credence.

"They have him—they have him!" was now heard from every throat. "He fled into the house, and cannot get out again." One told the other, with sparkling eyes, as if they were playing an amusing game, and not a human life at stake, "He is up there in that room, where the shadows are moving about; he has murdered all the women in the house." Another said, "Heavens! how they shrieked for help!—that is a bloody sign, *caramba;* and I would ride a hundred miles to see him hanged."

Curses and jests were heard among the crowd, who were thirsting for their victim's blood; while, at this very moment, he was gliding along above their heads, in a deep gutter which ran from one house to the other. At length he turned the corner of the houses, clambered up the roof of the next, and so on to the next, and thus reached slowly, but with great caution, the steep clay-bank which, on this side, incloses the seaport, and terminates in long, barren hills, furrowed by deep ravines.

So soon as he reached them, the pirate felt himself free, the first time for several hours: he clambered a short distance up the first ravine he came to, and, on reaching the top of the hill, could survey the scene of his past adventures—the bay at his feet, and to the right, in the shadow, the town, through which lanterns still flashed. Even the sound of voices reached his ears; his pursuers were still astir, but the prey had long escaped from their clutches. For a moment he listened to the sounds; but while a gleam of wild delight traversed his face, he turned quickly towards the bay, for he was far from being in safety yet; and over there, in the east, he fancied he could already distinguish the first faint gleams of dawn.

He had now to go a short distance, perhaps half-a-mile, along the hills, in whose dark shadow he could defy any pursuit. Further above, a rocky promontory jutted out into the bay, and, if he took to water there, he would have hardly half-a-mile to swim. The light still glistened from the peak of the *Albatross*—to him a faithful star,—there was liberty, safety for him—there he could brood over his plans of vengeance; for he was agitated by the most furious feelings of passion; and, once on board, he knew he had no discovery to fear, even if the vessel were searched from stem to stern, which was most unlikely.

It was true that not only his flight, and the exertions of the night, but also the terrible excitement in which he had been kept, had fatigued him; but he could swim this short distance, as several vessels lay between the coast and the schooner, which he must pass, and he could rest on their anchor-chains, if he found it necessary. He had nothing to fear from these vessels; they were merely merchantmen, who, in the first place, probably did not know the occurrences on land, and always have their boats in such regular disorder, that it would be impossible to let them down quickly, even if they wished to take the trouble.

The moon, however, illumined the quiet, noiseless bay more than he liked, and the strong ebb-tide that set in towards morning warned him of another danger, of which he was perfectly cognizant, of being carried by the current past the vessel he wished to reach, before he could lay hold of the cable, or a rope be thrown to him; for he knew that on board the *Albatross*, where the confusion on shore was known, a watch was being kept for his boat. Hence he did not dare go too far down the beach; and, on reaching the point he thought most suitable, he lay down in the shade of a lofty rock to rest a few minutes, and convince himself that all was safe.

No boats could be seen, so far as his eye could discern in the half-light—not the slightest sound of oars could be heard on the water—all the boats seemed to have gone to the land during the night, to take part in the sport, or, at least, to satisfy their curiosity—and from this side he apprehended no danger. But it was time for him to start, for the gleam in the east grew momentarily more distinct; there was no mistake about it, day was breaking; and he knew that the crews of the merchantmen in port were usually aroused at that hour. He therefore rose to proceed down to the beach, when his sharp ear detected a slight sound on the water, as if oars were being cautiously lifted and dipped again; it came nearer, and, two minutes later, a small boat glided along close to land, and in the direction of the promontory where he was.

His heart beat impetuously and joyfully—that was help in need; the *Albatross* had certainly sent the gig to find him, if that were possible. But he must go to work cautiously, lest he might perchance betray himself to an enemy. There were three persons in the boat—two pulling and one steering—but their faces could not be distinguished. If they belonged to the *Albatross* they must know the appointed signal; and, as the boat passed in front of him, he gave a gentle whistle, or cry, like the mews resting on land often utter at night.

The steerer's hand, in a second, checked the oarsmen, and the whistle was cautiously replied to, but not exactly in the same note.

Tenares, in his deceived hopes, clenched his teeth, and his hand sought almost involuntarily the handle of his knife. That was not the appointed answer, though it resembled it, perhaps accidentally; but his ear could not be deceived by such a clumsy stratagem, and he remained motionless against the stone on which he was leaning.

For a time all was quiet. The boat lay about thirty yards from him, and if he had risen they would have discovered him, but now the shadow of the rock completely concealed him.

"Jack," a youthful voice suddenly said in English, though in a suppressed key, "was that a bird or a man?"

"It was most likely a mew, sir," a rough, deep voice growled in reply. "When you answer them they always keep quiet; and it sounded just like one."

"Yes; but it did not seem so loud as usual."

"Still it must have been one, sir," the other said; "it is but poor fun pulling up and down this coast the whole night through, and watching those boats load or put off—and not a drop o' grog aboard either."

Hunted to Death.

CHAPTER VII.

A SWIM FOR LIFE.

THE boat had, during this conversation, been drifted back some distance by the powerful ebb-tide; and, though the sailors dipped their muffled oars again, it was at least a minute ere they brought the boat back opposite the spot where the signal had been given. The young man in the stern sheets now rose, and carefully surveyed the mconlit shore, although his men did not leave off pulling.

"I wish I had brought a night-glass with me," he said, as he fell back on his seat; "it is impossible to see what is going on upon land."

The boat slowly left the spot, and pulled along the beach towards the town; but, from what he had heard, Tenares knew that, so soon as it had reached an appointed spot, it would return here with the current, and so he hardly found himself out of the sight of his enemies in this quarter than he crept down the beach and into the water, firmly decided to swim straight for the *Albatross*.

The boat was the same in which Edward Wilkinson had pursued the pirate on the previous evening, and it had been given in charge of a young midshipman belonging to an English man-o'-war, to guard this part of the coast, in case a boat might come in for the pirate, or, after he had escaped from the town, he was to put off in any boat left here for him.

As, however, it appeared highly improbable that he would make any such attempt at flight, Don Olinda had thought it quite sufficient to entrust this duty to a midshipman, a mere youth. But, to be prepared for all eventualities, he had several rockets on board as signals, and received the strictest orders to give an alarm at the slightest thing at all suspicious, so that the other boats might immediately hurry to his assistance.

Though close to the beach, the blocks of stone lying there concealed the pirate from every eye that looked that way from the water—hence he glided noiselessly into the sea, and with slow and regular strokes he soon left the land behind him, and reached that portion of the bay where the scattered vessels broke the light on the surface of the water, and rendered any discovery still more difficult. The tide was so strong, however, that the swimmer was obliged to put forth his utmost strength not to be carried too far out to sea; and when he reached the first vessel—an English merchantman lying at anchor—he was glad to be able to rest for a few minutes on its chain, and collect fresh strength. This vessel lay about three hundred yards from the shore, and twice that distance would carry him to the *Albatross*.

In order to rest his arms, he twisted his right leg round the taut chain, and thrust his left foot through one of the links—in this way he was able to draw a long, reviving inspiration. But, in trying to rise a little higher, his foot glided off the slippery chain, and, though he held on as firmly as he could with both hands, he could not prevent a slight splash in the water, and a rattling of the chain. He let himself down into the water as far as he could, and listened whether any one was awake on board before he recommenced his voyage.

A head was bent over the bow of the ship and peeping down—it was the mate, who had just left his cabin, and, with sleep still in his eyes, was looking at the time and weather, and was just about turning back, with a yawn sufficient to dislocate his jaws, to wake the crew—for it was daybreak.

In the midst of his yawn he heard the noise in the water, and went forward and peeped down through the hawsehole. But all was quiet again ; and, as the moon was in the north-east, and the starboard anchor was down, he could see nothing there.

"Well," he said to himself, as he turned away, "if that was a fish, it ran very roughly against the cable ; why, the whole ship shook—ah !"

This exclamation was produced by a fresh noise he heard. The swimmer below, having heard no one on deck, and feeling secure against discovery, moved slowly round the bows of the vessel towards the larboard side—for the vessel lay under the influence of the ebb-tide, with its bow turned towards the south and the town.

The man on board stood quietly leaning over the side, and, as he heard nothing, he was just going back the second time, when he recognised the dark form of the swimmer below, who was trying to leave the ship's side with slow but energetic strokes. The mate at first believed—for he had no idea of what had taken place on shore—that it was one of his own sailors trying to desert, and shouted to him—

"Hallo, Bill, where are you going, eh ? Ah, my man, where are you bound for ? Below there !"

But he received no reply, and the swimmer appeared in haste.

"It can't be one of our men," the mate thought ; "perhaps the fellow has been ashore secretly. Well, I don't care—what does it concern me?"

"Hallo! the ship!" a shout was now heard in a sailor's voice from shore.

"Hallo!" the mate said, looking in the direction, and troubling himself no longer about the swimmer; "what's up there? Ship ahoy!" he shouted in reply.

"What was that you hailed just now?" was heard again, and a small boat hurried up from the land.

"Don't know," the mate replied; "a man in the water, I fancy."

"A swimming man?" the voice asked quickly, as if to convince himself of the truth of what he heard.

"Ay, ay!" the mate responded, and then muttered to himself, "It may have been a dog. But, hallo!" he added, in surprise, as a pistol was fired from the boat, and three rockets blazed up; "they're in a hurry. Well, I'm blessed! what crime can he have committed?"

"Hallo! the ship!" the clear, shrill voice of the midshipman asked, as the boat shot past the Englishman's bows, "which way was the man swimming?"

"Down east!" was the careful reply of the mate, as he cast a hurried glance in the direction.

"Thank you!" the voice replied from the boat, and followed in that course, while another rocket was fired to show the spot where he was.

The flying pirate knew what impended over him; he had feared little from the crew of the merchantman; he knew their indifference about everything not immediately connected with their own vessel; but as soon as he heard the shout from land, which reached his ears only too distinctly, he felt that the decisive moment had arrived, and, on the shot being fired, he left off swimming.

Oh! how near was the vessel that would save him! and must he now, when he had almost gained his object, and had succeeded in escaping his most dangerous foes—oh! must he be driven back by the hand of a boy, nay, almost a child?

Perhaps, though, the signal was given to boats lying on the beach, and, till help arrived, he should be in security. He hoped to escape the observation of one enemy, for, in the past night, he had foiled the compact mass of his pursuers.

Hence he swam on again, but had not proceeded a boat's length when he noticed not only the inutility, but also the danger, of such a proceeding. The ships were beginning to display some excitement, and he could distinctly hear the splash of hurrying oars. His only chance of salvation was in returning to land, and the current would easily carry him out of reach of his enemies. But, as he turned back to carry this into effect, he saw his pursuers' little boat steering down upon him. They had not seen him yet, however, that was certain; and so he dived, and allowed the boat to pass right over his head. When he rose again, the boat was a good cable's length from him; and, as the steerer was anxiously looking forward, he hoped to escape unnoticed. Once again on land, he intended to remain in hiding till the next night, and then he would be enabled to reach the *Albatross* with the greatest ease from the extreme end of the bay.

But he was destined to see no morrow, for one of the sailors noticed in a moment the dark spot his head formed in the water, and his sharp cry checked the course of the boat. The next minute the powerful ebb-tide drove it back, and it lay motionless on the water.

"Did you see him?" the midshipman said, as he quickly turned the bow of the boat in the direction indicated by the sailor.

"Just then I saw a dark spot like a head," the man said, as he turned his head round; "but it may have been only a kedge."

"We must inspect it, at any rate," the boy replied, no little imbued with the importance of his present position, as he had given the signal for the other boats; "he must be somewhere close by, for there are the other boats coming to meet us. Lay on your oars, my boys, with a will all;" and the sailors, excited by the chase, and spurred on by the thought of avenging their young lieutenant, laid so heartily to their work, that the boat sped on like an arrow.

"It was here!" the sailor shouted, as he peered down in the water; "but there's no buoy here, so it must have been the pirate."

"There he is again!" the midshipman cried, springing on the thwarts to survey the surface of the water. "By George! boys, there he is swimming; push for your lives! we shall have him!"

"You had better give one of the other boats a fresh signal, sir," one of the sailors said, who wished to proceed with greater certainty; "he is a crafty and a savage fellow, and now driven to desperation."

The young man would have preferred the sole honour of the capture, but he could not venture to neglect this reasonable warning. Again a rocket blazed in the sky, showing the boats the fresh course they had to steer. But, when they looked round again for the swimmer, he had disappeared, and, after resting on their oars a short time, they saw him appear again in a different direction, and much nearer the land than they had expected.

"If he reaches the land," one of the sailors said, tugging away vigorously, "he will be off."

"And that he shall not, if we can prevent him," the midshipman cried; "there are the boats coming to our help; we must get betwixt him and the land."

Tenares was a splendid swimmer, and his muscles seemed to be of steel, so indefatigably had he passed through all the immense fatigue of the past night; but he now felt too clearly that his strength was beginning to fail him. He could not dive for so long a time as before; and, even were he on land, would he be able to escape from his pursuers, when the day was breaking more and more through the clouds, and filling the bay with its weak but rapidly-increasing light?

He was scarce fifty yards from land, but the current was rapidly sweeping him to the end of the bay, when he saw the little boat that still headed his pursuers hurrying up to him. If he could render this harmless, salvation, he thought, might still be possible, for hope only leaves poor human hearts with life.

Again he sank beneath the surface; but the boat was not stopped this time to await his re-appearance, but tried to reach the coast as quickly as possible—thus cutting the fugitive off from land, until one of the man-o'-war's boats, that was coming up at full speed, could come to help the midshipman. Suddenly the pirate's iron hand seized the starboard oar, as it was dipped in the water, and pulled it, with one tug, out of the hands of the astonished sailor.

Of course, the boat swung round directly—the stern turned towards land in an instant—and the pale face of the pirate, with the fearful blood-red scar and flashing eyes, rose at the same moment, and almost unconsciously, to the surface; for he was busy in thrusting away the oar he had captured, and so stopping the boat's course. The young midshipman, who had heard the almost involuntary cry of the sailor, and really believed, at the moment, that the pirate designed a desperate attack on their boat, took up one of the pistols lying by his side, and, almost without aiming, fired it at the wild face staring at him from the water.

"He's here—he's here!" he then shouted—swinging his cap, and seizing the other pistol—to a boat's crew hardly a hundred yards off; "quick—quick! or he will escape; we cannot go a yard further."

The pirate, at this moment, disappeared once more under water—he dived, and attempted to swim along, but his strength failed him—the bullet had traversed his right shoulder, and deprived him of the use of his arm. With a few strokes he could have reached the shore, but he felt that his time had arrived.

When he again rose to the surface he was no longer sensible of his danger—his senses were leaving him—and only the instinct of self-preservation drove him mechanically to the surface to draw breath.

"There he is again—there!" the young midshipman shouted, furious that he could not proceed with his boat, and springing into the bows, while the other sailor followed him with his oar, in the hope of getting back the one floating in the water.

"I see him!" was the reply of the lieutenant from the first man-o'-war's boat, who was also standing in the bows with a pistol, while a midshipman was steering.

The pirate's eye glazed as they looked upon him—he saw the enemy, but no longer recognised him—the scar on his forehead stood out like a fresh gaping wound, and his body rose out of the water almost up to the shoulders.

"Surrender, senor, or I fire!" the lieutenant shouted, as the boat flew up.

The body remained for a minute, at least, motionless above the water.

"Bring him to the larboard side!" the lieutenant shouted to the steerer; "stand by, my men, and lift him into the boat."

But the corpse slowly sank from between their hands, escaping its enemies even in death; and only a dark stream of blood revealed the spot where it had disappeared.

The boat glided past, and then returned to the old spot; but the water did not give back its victim.

The lieutenant uncocked his pistols, thrust them in his belt, and turned to the midshipman, whose boat had recovered the oar, and had now come up.

"Merriman, my boy," he said to him, "I congratulate you! you took a capital aim at the fellow!"

The boy turned deadly pale, and hid his face in his hands—it was the first human blood he had ever shed!

STEVENS AND HIS DOG POPPY.

STEVENS AND HIS DOG POPPY.

A Strange and Tragical Story.

INTRODUCTION.

"A HANDSOME Newfoundland dog, belonging to Mr. Floyd, an attorney in Holmfirth, drowned himself in the river that runs close behind his master's house, after evincing remarkable sadness for a few days previously. He was seen to throw himself into the water, and try to sink, by keeping perfectly tranquil. He was taken out and kept chained for a little while, but he had hardly been let loose before he renewed his attempt, and, after several trials, which exhausted his strength, he at last succeeded in carrying out his design, by holding his head resolutely for some moments under water. When he was again brought to land he was quite dead."

Some years ago, the previous anecdote about the strange suicide of a dog appeared in nearly every paper, and though doubted by many, the fact could not be contradicted. But how the poor animal was driven to a degree of desperation which usually only manifests itself among civilized beings, is an affecting history known only to a few, which I will here impart.

CHAPTER I.

THE CABIN.

FAR in the West of the United States, where the Missouri pours its muddy waters into the powerful Mississippi, and at the foot of the pine-crowned hills which enclose the fertile bottoms, stood an unpretending cabin, built of rough planks, and covered with shingles.

It was very rarely, however, that human eye perceived it, or human foot—with the exception of the owner's—entered it, for it was situated deep in the forest, and surrounded by the magnificent backwoods, while a small, scarcely perceptible footpath was the only thing that connected it with the world without.

It was a wildly romantic neighbourhood, and a man, as well as the wild beasts, found shelter there at no great distance from each other, for a solitary hunter had settled here, to pursue the chase more at his ease, and not be disturbed by the hideous forms of his fellow-men.

The hut itself, however, is worthy a short description, before we proceed to its inhabitants, as, through a peculiar whim, the interior was furnished in the most curious fashion. The space contained within the rough-hewn boards was about fourteen feet square, but little of the wood could be seen within, as immense buffalo-hides hung down over all the walls, and the floor was covered with large long-haired bear-skins. The half of one side was occupied by a deep chimney, covered with a coat of plaster, in which a cheerful fire crackled. Opposite to this was a raised bed of skins laid upon each other, and at its end another little bed, upon which a few gnawed bones revealed the resting-place of a dog. Above the low door lay a long rifle, suspended on two wooden pins, and behind the door hung the bullet-pouch and powder-horn, in whose broad leathern sling a small scalping knife was stuck in front, and an awl behind.

The only articles of furniture consisted of a roughly-framed table, that still bore the marks of the axe, a board fastened to the wall in a most artistic fashion, which held a wooden plate, a small iron kettle, and a tin pot, a chair covered with bear-skin, and a piece of a hollow stump, which stood in a corner, filled with peeled maize. Besides these, a harpoon glittered over the chimney, and several empty bags made of deer-skin hung from the cross-beams in the roof. But who were the inhabitants of this peculiar domicile? We will examine that subject in the next chapter.

Stevens at Home.

CHAPTER II.

THE INHABITANTS.

BEFORE the fire, upon the lately-described chair covered with bear-skin, sat the lord of the house, a powerful, ruddy-cheeked veteran, with snow-white hair and blue eyes, busily engaged in sharpening his long hunting-knife on a small whetstone. His costume was that of a hunter. Leathern leggings and mocassins confined his legs and feet; a wide hunting-shirt of the same lasting material, decorated with pointed fringe on all the seams, fell over his shoulders; and an old beaver hat, battered into all sorts of shapes by wind and weather, covered his brow. His neck was bare, notwithstanding the cold autumn wind that whistled without through the leafless trees; and a broad leathern belt bore the knife, a little tomahawk, and a second fur cap; while a rolled-up woollen blanket lay at his feet. The man was evidently equipped for hunting, and was just trying the edge of his trusty knife, to see whether it was sharp enough, and fit for use.

Before him, however, sat the second inhabitant of the cabin, not upon a chair covered with bear-skin, but upon his own hind-quarters, and looking up impatiently with his large, fine eyes in the hunter's face. It was a powerful, long-haired Newfoundland dog, with broad chest, and heavy, muscular frame. Broad scars, however, everywhere disfigured his beautiful, glistening coat, and proved how bravely he had, by his master's side, fought many a perilous battle. He knew, though, in what estimation he was held by the hunter; and never had man and dog been better, more inseparable friends. He looked up seriously to the old man, who had just completed his task, placed the hone upon two hooks in the wall, and returned the knife to its sheath.

"Poppy!" said the old man confidentially, as he looked down to his faithful comrade in the chase. "Poppy, shall we go hunting?"

The dog was certainly no longer a puppy, but he had retained the name of his youth, and seemed perfectly satisfied with the affectionate title; for he scarcely heard his master's loving voice before he laid his head a little on one side, showed his glistening ivory teeth, and began wagging his tail in a really dangerous fashion.

"Poppy," the hunter said once more, "are you inclined?"

"Wau," said Poppy, and laid his broad paw upon his master's knee.

"Where shall we go, then, to-day, Poppy?" the old man asked again, and laid his hand on the faithful animal's head. "Now, why are you whining? Shall we shoot a turkey, eh? You don't feel disposed?"

Poppy had taken his paw from his master's knee, and looked down on the ground; he did not seem to feel any inclination for turkey-shooting.

"Or shall we look up the great stag that we saw in the osier-bed? What does my dog say to it?"

This did not seem to affect Poppy either; he scratched the ground with his paw, as if impatiently, and then remained quite quiet.

"Well, Poppy, then I don't know anything better than for us to go on to the hills and look whether we can find an opossum—that's not bad eating—eh ?"

Poppy looked for a moment most seriously in his master's face; but, as he did not say anything more, the dog got up, growled angrily, and then walked to his bed, on which he lay down in high ill-humour.

The old man had observed his clever dog with a smile of delight; but when the latter closed his eyes, and did not appear desirous of hearing anything further on the subject, he addressed him once more—

"Poppy !"

Poppy did not hear.

"Poppy ! I don't care for opossum !"

The dog pricked his ears.

"Poppy, shall we go down the river ? Shall we look whether the bear has crossed the stream again ?"

In a moment the dog was by his side, and regarded him with his large bright eyes, as if dubiously.

"Go bear-hunting, Poppy ?" the old man said; and, with a loud bark, the dog bounded with mad joy up to him, and licked his hands. At last he seated himself, and howled in a heartrending fashion.

"Very well—that's enough !" the hunter said with a smile. "Come, behave yourself, Poppy—good dog !—right so !" and with these words, he put on his bullet pouch and blanket, took the rifle down from the hooks, and walked in front of the house, accompanied by his dog, and closed the door from without by pulling out a plug.

"Wait, Poppy !" he now said to his dog, as the latter started in the well-known direction and trotted towards the bottom. "Wait, Poppy. First we'll look at the smoke-house, to see if all is in order."

With these words he approached the store-room, which scarce deserved the name of house, for it was nothing better than a species of shed, of palisades driven into the ground side by side, which a thick bark roof protected from wind and rain, while some sixty sets of antlers, piled upon it, kept the single pieces of bark from slipping off. A low door, firmly closed with a wooden plug, formed the entrance, and the interior was the store-house of the industrious hunter. Several sides of bear-bacon, a row of smoked deer-hams, and two bags filled with honey, formed the chief supply; and on the ground were several stumpy, hollow trunks of trees, called gums, filled with maize and salt, and on some cross poles hung dried pumpkins, the best vegetables of the Western States.

Stevens—for this was the hunter's name—was just going to close the door, after a contented glance into the interior, when he suddenly regarded a row of deer-hams, and then bent down to one of the palisades, evidently busily engaged in counting the notches cut in the wood.

"One, two, three, four, five, six, seven, eight, nine—right—and inside," he continued, as he rose again—"one, two, three, four, five, six, seven, eight—h'm," he said, and looked seriously at the empty spot where the ninth smoked ham had hung; "but that is strange, Poppy! Doesn't Poppy know what has become of the ninth ham?"

Poppy, who had again joined his master, seemed not to have heard the question; for he was entirely engaged in regarding a sun-bleached bear-skull, to which he devoted all his attention.

"H'm! it's strange," Stevens growled between his teeth; "no mark of any living creature but Poppy and myself, and the ham is gone! Can I have made a mistake in counting? But that's the third time I've missed something. Poppy, Poppy, you must pay more attention," he continued, as he turned to his dog; "I can't stand that any longer. If I miss anything more, I'll make your bed in the smoke-house."

Poppy threw a timid glance up to his master, and then bounded, when the latter closed the door and raised his rifle to his shoulder, merrily before him, towards the bottom, to look for the promised bear-trail.

Patz has a Fall

CHAPTER III.

THE HUNT.

WHEN Poppy had once got the house in his rear, he began wagging his tail tremendously; he was a famous dog on a trail, and found himself in his element as soon as he trod the forest ground—which always took place, by the way, at the same moment as he crossed his master's threshold. The latter set a proper value on his dog's excellent qualities, and let him do as he pleased in every respect; and no one had ever heard an unkind remark exchanged between them; they understood and respected each other, and love and friendship can only emanate from mutual respect.

Poppy was on a warm bear track, and he stopped many times,

looking back to his master with a friendly eye, as if he wished to say, "Are we not a couple of jolly fellows, and wont we have a famous piece of fun?"

The old man would then merely nod his head, and say, with a smile—

"Right, my dog! excellent beast!"

It was Autumn; the white oaks bore ripe fruit, and the bears climbed the trees to break down the weaker branches and devour the acorns. This neighbourhood is still one of the best in Missouri for sport. There are a large number of bears; but the poor bruins will soon be driven thence, and be forced to leave the land of their fathers, in order to let themselves be hunted in the "happy hunting-grounds" by the spirits of the extirpated Indians.

"Poppy!" the old man suddenly said, gently and cautiously; "Poppy, stop here—I hear something."

Poppy, however, had an equally good ear, and a much better nose, so he raised the latter in the air, waited a moment, and then returned to his master and scratched his leggings with his fore-paw.

"Yes, my dog! I know it," the latter said, smilingly, and patted the animal's head—"I hear it too; but come, be cautious; to-night we shall have bear-meat to eat."

They then crawled—hunter and dog—towards the sound, which continually grew louder and more distinct, and could not be mistaken—it was the sound of heavy branches being broken off, which, when they fell from any height, echoed far through the silent forest. They soon reached the dry bed of a little stream, whose steep banks brought them close to the tree, without the bear who sat upon it discovering the least signs of them. About a hundred and fifty paces from the tree, the hunter, however, stopped, and, after making a sign to the dog, rose carefully up, to watch the careless feeder, who, on his lofty eminence, did not dream of such dangerous enemies.

The bear was standing about ninety feet from the ground, on a rather stout branch, and was busily engaged in drawing down a small twig that grew above him, and breaking it off by his weight;

but the elastic wood withstood all his attempts, and he was evidently afraid to advance any further, as he did not dare trust his heavy carcass on the frail support. Stevens had cocked his gun, but saw, by all the beast's movements, that he felt very comfortable up aloft, and would not so soon hasten down, and consequently did not fire immediately, but determined to wait to see in what way the black fellow would act in breaking down the branch. Poppy, though, who could see nothing of all this in the bed of the stream, became impatient, and began scratching at his master's legs.

"Poppy!" Stevens whispered, with a gentle menace.

Poppy had taken a seat, and was restlessly swinging from one fore-paw to the other, but obeyed for a while his master's intimation, till he began to grow tired, and again scratched the old man's legs, as he bent his head back. The old man raised his foot, as if he was going to kick. Poppy was not to be daunted in this way, though; he knew very well that his master would not kick, and he remained in his former position, without revealing the slightest fear. The bear had, in the meanwhile, perceived that the branch which he so much desired to acquire could not possibly be broken off, as his standing-point was too dangerous to allow him much motion; he therefore climbed somewhat higher, and stepped upon the longed-for twig, which bore a quantity of splendid acorns at its extreme end, and tried to bend it towards him; but, quicker than he expected, the wood bowed beneath his weight, and with great difficulty Patz saved himself on an adjacent branch, where he now seated himself with great self-contentment, and scratched his head.

Poppy had started up on hearing the branch crack, and looked with fixed attention to his master, but the latter did not yet make the slightest preparations for firing; for the bear had just pulled towards him the broken bough, and swallowed the hardly-gained acorns with evident satisfaction. But now the dog's patience was exhausted; he seized the leathern fringe on his master's hunting-shirt, and tore at it with such violence that he cried in alarm, "Poppy!"

The sound reached the comfortably-masticating bear; and, becoming attentive, he paused in his repast, looked cautiously down on all sides of the tree, and began to feel less at home on his lofty station.

Stevens knew now that the right moment was come, for the bear had not yet moved, as he wished first to discover from which side the suspicious sound had reached him. The hunter raised the death-bearing weapon quickly and surely, took aim, and the thundering echo of the rifle pealed through the surrounding hills. The oak branch slipped from the beast's paws and oscillated back and forwards, but the animal itself remained firmly for a few seconds in the same position, then nodded once or twice, and soon fell, head foremost, down from the giddy height, upon the moss, so that the ground shook.

Directly after the shot was fired Poppy had reached the open ground in a few bounds, and now howling with delight, rushed to the tree, at whose foot the mortally-wounded bear was writhing in his blood. After a few convulsive movements, all was over; he stretched himself out, and was a corpse.

However impatient Poppy might have been previously, he now behaved calmly and respectably. He licked the blood a little, and then lay down peacefully by the side of the bear, to wait till his master had cut him up, and was ready to drag him home.

Stevens had not taken a horse with him, for the only one he could call his own was wandering about the woods, and had not come home for two days; the sun, consequently, had nearly set before he reached home with his last load, when he hung up the meat and the sides of bacon in the smoke house, stretched the skin, and broiled for his own supper a few ribs and some other delicate morsels.

"Here, Poppy," he said, as he cut off a large piece for the dog, and held it out to him; "here! you wouldn't eat out there, perhaps you'll like it now." But he did not like it now, for Poppy smelt at the meat, shook his head, and laid himself upon his bed. Stevens looked at him seriously, and asked him, compassionately, "Are you ill, Poppy?" Poppy, however, did not think it worth while to answer him, and had soon fallen into a deep sleep.

CHAPTER IV.

THE STRANGE ROBBERY.

THE sun had risen high above the summits of the trees before Stevens got up the next morning. He would not hunt on this day—it was a Sunday—and he prepared his breakfast in great tranquillity, ate it, and then seated himself by the fire to mend his mocassins a little.

Poppy had again spurned all food, and the old man threw many an anxious glance towards his favourite, who, however, seemed to pay very little attention to it, but lay rolled up, with his eyes closed.

"Poppy, is there anything the matter with you?" the old man asked, after a pause, during which he had been attentively regarding the dog. "I'm hanged if he is not wounded!" he suddenly cried, and sprang from his chair to examine his injuries. It was not an actual wound, however, but the hair appeared rubbed off on one side, as if by a blow or scratch, and the skin itself was torn in two places.

"The confounded bear!" the old man said, sorrowfully, as he patted the faithful animal's head; "so he gave you one, after all! I fancied he was dead; but wait, Poppy, we will soon help you. Pure bear-fat on the wound, as you know, cures all such injuries."

Poppy cast a restless glance towards his master, wagged his tail a little, then got up and followed him out of doors. When Stevens opened his smoke-house, his first glance was directed to the smoked hams, one of which, he feared, had been stolen the previous day, and he counted the row.

"One, two, three, four, five, six, seven," he said, in a long-drawn tone; "seven, Poppy! They've really stolen another ham. No! I cannot stand it any longer. You must sleep, for the future, in the smoke-house, Poppy—do you hear?"

The dog wagged his tail, as a sign that he comprehended, but appeared not to take much interest in the smoke-house, for he was again lost in deep examination of the old bear-skull, while his master walked carefully round the smoke-house, and looked everywhere, to see if a palisade was loose, or a piece of bark removed from the roof; but all was secure, and no strange trail could be seen.

"This night you'll sleep in the smoke-house, Poppy," the old man repeated once again. "I can't stand this any longer; and, if you notice anything suspicious, you'll make a noise, and perhaps we shall catch them."

Said and done. Poppy, from this night forth, slept upon soft skins spread out for him in the smoke-house, and the thefts ceased; but the dog's health seemed wonderfully improved by this change of air, for his side grew well, and his appetite he recovered in a most extraordinary manner. He ate all that came in his way, bear-meat and venison, and even did not turn up his nose at turkey, which he usually despised from the bottom of his heart.

After about fourteen days, during which nothing remarkable had occurred, Poppy seemed to have no inclination to use his new bed-room any longer, for he came to his master's bed, and lay down at the foot of it.

"All secure, Poppy?" Stevens asked; "all secure? Wont you keep watch out there any longer?"

The dog appeared to understand his master's question, for he rose and passed his paw over his mocassin.

"Good dog!" Stevens said, and patted his head; "excellent dog!"

Both were now agreed to leave the smoke-house, for this night, to its fate. But how astonished the hunter was, the next morning, when he looked after his smoked hams, and only found six. That was too enigmatical. He had shot four more stags in the last few days, whose legs were also hung up, but the nocturnal thief preferred the dry, smoked one, and did not touch the other meat.

"Poppy," said Stevens, "the matter's growing serious. I must watch through the night. The moon shines; and I can cover the smoke-house from my bed if I pull back the skins; and you, Poppy—but come here, and leave that confounded old skull alone—and you, Poppy, shall sleep, not in, but by the smoke-house—if anything approaches you'll have better scent, and can follow it."

For three nights in succession Stevens kept watch—for three

nights long Poppy walked round the smoke-house in the moonlight—but nothing was to be seen; on the fourth, when both sought their beds, fatigued by their long watching, the thief came again, and on the next morning there were only five hams hanging up. The patience of a saint would not have held out on such provocations, and Stevens was only an ordinary Christian; he therefore stood with the door of the smoke-house in his hand, lost in amazement, upon the threshold, or, at least, on the spot where the threshold should have been, and declared that "he would be hanged if he knew how it was done." Poppy did not know either, for he stood close to his master's side, and looked up with equal surprise at the empty rack. Both shook their heads in great amazement.

CHAPTER V.

THE DREAM.

STEVENS began to feel uncomfortable about the matter. There was something inexplicably mysterious in the whole nature of the robbery, and he determined to watch one more night, and on the next morning go and ask the advice of his nearest neighbour, and get to the bottom of the matter, if possible. The nearest neighbour certainly lived at a distance of twenty miles; but then his horse had been grazing in that direction, and he intended to look him up at the same time, and so kill two birds with one stone.

When he again entered the house, he took down his rifle, cleaned the lock, poured some fresh deer-fat into a hole made for the purpose in the stock, cut a pair of new legging-straps, and melted some lead to make bullets. The dog, in the meanwhile, when he saw his master busied with his rifle, had seated himself in front of him, and was looking at him with his large, black eyes, as he probably expected that they were going directly into the forest. The poor beast was tired, although he had slept the whole night; his eyelids fell down after a few moments, and he nodded first on one side and then on the other.

"Go to sleep, Poppy," said the old man, "we shan't hunt to-day. You can lie down quietly." Poppy did not wait to have this told him twice, but got up, and stretched out first one hind-leg and then the other, scratched his head with extraordinary agility, mounted his bed, turned round on his axis the three usual times, and then lay down to "do a sweet sleep."

Stevens had, in the meanwhile, taken down his bullet-pouch from the wall, and examined its contents, to see that all was in order for the morrow's march. Five bullets and one in the rifle were six—that would be enough for three or four days—the pricker, three flints, a piece of tinder, some rag to clean out the rifle, and a piece of fine leather for wads, a turnscrew, a turkey-call, and a little bag of salt—all was in order, and he was just putting some powder into his regular horn from a larger one, when Poppy became restless on his bed, and began whining softly—he was dreaming.

"Hem!" said Stevens, looking laughingly at his comrade, "the old Indian with whom I lately shot the bear, told me that, if you put your handkerchief over the head of a dreaming dog, and then lay it under your own head and go to sleep, you'll have the same dreams as the dog has just had. Shall I try it with Poppy?"

Poppy now began kicking out all his legs, as if he was in some tight orifice, and would be glad to get out, and whined pitifully.

"I'll—I'll try it," the old man said, took off his handkerchief, laid it over the sleeping animal, and carefully observed all his movements. For a long while he lay perfectly motionless; his quicker breathing alone showed that his mind (not his instinct, for the instinct cannot dream) was at work. At length he began scratching with his fore-paws, then lay awhile again quiet, writhed with all his energy, and made no further movement. Stevens gently took the handkerchief off him, placed it under his head, and was also asleep in less than five minutes; for a real hunter must always take advantage of a time of rest, that he may have no lead in his eyes at the moment when it may be requisite to remain awake and attentive.

The autumn sun shone warmly and cheerily down upon the hunter's cabin in which the inmates were slumbering.

Evidences of Poppy's Guilt.

CHAPTER VI.

THE DISCOVERY.

IT was about two in the afternoon when Stevens at length awoke. Poppy, who had been busy before the hut for the last half-hour, had again come in, and lay quietly on the old spot. Stevens, however, seated himself upright on his bed, and looked down on the ground for a long, long while, as if lost in reflection: then he regarded the dog, sighed once deeply, as if in bitter sorrow, shook his head, and exclaimed—

"Poppy!"

Poppy was awake, so he immediately raised his eyes and wagged his tail proudly at his master; but the latter only shook his head the more, and turned a reproachful eye upon the dog, which he kept fixed on him. Poppy seemed to feel uncomfortable; for he rose up, lifted his head, and looked first in one corner and then in the other, but always with his master's eye fixed upon him; so that, at last, as if moved by some internal impulse, he went up to him, rubbed against him, and tried to lick his hand as it hung down. Stevens however, withdrew it, and uttered his warning—

"Poppy!"

"Wau-wau!" the dog barked, and scratched the old man's knee with his fore-paw, as if he meant to say, "Come, don't play any such tricks—I don't like them;" but the latter thrust him back, let his feet down so that he sat upright, and addressed the attentively-listening dog in the following strain:

"Poppy! for four years, since you were quite a little thing, we have lived in close friendship together. I never beat you but once when you ran after a rabbit when we were on the track of a bear, and afterwards once again, when you would not leave the tree up which the wild cat had climbed, and I had only *one* bullet by me. Have you not always had enough to eat? Have you ever wanted anything while with me? Did we not, on one occasion, when I did not find a head of game for three whole days, share the last morsel honestly, and then *starve* together? Can you contradict this?

Poppy had, in the meanwhile, looked at everything else in the room except his master's face, and did not appear to feel at all comfortable. He even cast a melancholy glance once or twice over to the door, as if to say, "If I could only get away!" Although the door was open, he did not move from the spot—he had an evil conscience.

"Poppy!" the old man continued, after a short pause, "you are an ungrateful, wicked dog! You have ill-used my confidence, gained my affection, and now you steal! Yes, Poppy, you steal! Do you see this loose board in the chimney corner? You creep out there at night. You deny it!" he continued, in anger, when Poppy got up, as if quite innocent, and smelt at the board. "You deny it? Hear, then, what I dreamed of you this day, while following the old Indian's advice. I had scarcely got the handkerchief that had received your dream beneath my head before I also slept, and found myself, the next moment, in the most extraordinary position, with my body half through that hole, and head first, from which I freed myself with terrible difficulty. My side pained me when I reached the ground, but still I ran, and, to my surprise, upon all-fours, to the door of the smoke-house, and pulled out the plug with my teeth, instead of doing so, as usual, with my hand. Poppy, I am almost ashamed to tell you what I did then. I climbed on the Saltgum, pulled down one of the smoked deer-hams from the rack, and carried it before the door; then put the plug in its former position, and carried the deer-ham into the thicket, close by the fallen red oak."

With a deep sigh, the old man here stopped for an instant in his narrative, and nodded his head reproachfully at Poppy; the latter, however, knew no rest; he moved from one foot to the other, looked into every corner, scratched the ground with his paw, and turned longing glances to the open door, though he had not the heart to leave the room.

"Then," the old hunter continued, in a melancholy tone, as he wiped two large tears from his eyes with the back of his hand—"then I lay down with both hands on the ham—it seemed to me as if they were paws—and gnawed the meat from the bone; then I hid the remainder under moss and leaves, and returned through the hole in the chimney into the room, when I, to hide my disgraceful deed, pushed back the board which closed the hole, went to my bed, turned round three times in a very peculiar fashion, and lay down. Stop here, Poppy!" he now cried in a loud voice to the latter, who had approached nearer and nearer the door, and now was on the point of withdrawing from the conversation, that was proving unpleasant to him—"stop here, Poppy! Are you not ashamed, you wicked, ungrateful dog? But stay! we will first have the proofs of your crime. Come with me to your hiding-place."

He then took a rifle and bullet-pouch (for a real hunter never goes ten paces from his house without his gun), and bade the dog to follow him; but Poppy, who had already probably acquired some suspicion by his master pointing to the chimney-corner, scarce perceived the direction in which his master walked, before his ears fell, he put his tail between his legs, and followed most despondingly. Twice he stopped on the road, and looked back longingly to the house; but Stevens paid close attention to all his movements, and he could not escape. At length they reached the spot at which Stevens had hidden the bones in his dream. There lay the tree, there were the old roots, covered with a thick growth of sassafras and sarsaparillà, and, close under the tree (Stevens pushed the moss and leaves aside with his rifle), lay the proofs of the robbery—the remains of the stolen hams.

Had Poppy been able to creep into the ground at this moment he would have done so with the greatest pleasure; he felt so wretched, so humiliated; he saw himself discovered, convicted, and knew that the eye of his generally so kind master was fixed upon him in anger and contempt. Poppy indubitably considered himself at that moment the most unhappy dog in Missouri.

With hanging head, quivering limbs, and half-closed eyes that were fixed despondingly on the bright leaves before him, he stood for a long while, and awaited his master's rebukes, or even punishment. To his surprise, nothing of the sort took place. Old Stevens looked at him for a long while sharply and sorrowfully, then shouldered his rifle, and walked silently into the forest. Poppy followed, downcast, at his heels.

Night came on, and both camped under the outspread branches of an oak; but the former friendship existing between them was annihilated. Poppy tried, it is true, to make it up; but Stevens pushed him away, and said, "Go along, you are a wolf!" and he could not have called him a more opprobrious name, for he detested nothing in the world so much as a wolf. Poppy went back sorrowfully, and laid himself beneath a tree, far from the fire and his master.

CHAPTER VII.

THE PUNISHMENT.

ON the next morning Stevens marched further at daybreak, and reached the Missouri at about ten o'clock. His plan had originally been of a horrible nature. As he had loved his dog so dearly before, the cunningness of his nature had the more outraged his feelings, and he had intended at first to shoot him; but he could not gain the heart to do it, so he preferred carrying him to the next settlement, and making him a present to some one there, though he knew how difficult it would be to prevent the dog from returning. As he sat there gloomily, and was undecided what to do, he heard one of the steamers coming down the stream, which go up it at intervals, partly to carry the hunters of the Rocky Mountains a further distance into the interior, and partly to take the skins and furs of the trappers, as well as the productions of the country-people, to St. Louis. A few hundred paces from the spot where he was sitting the steamer stopped to take on board several loads of wood, which had been prepared by a settler who lived close by.

Stevens went towards it.

"Hullo! old fellow, that's a splendid dog," said one of the passengers, a tall, light-haired man; "do you want to sell him?"

"Sell him!" Stevens replied; "no! not for my life—but if you like to have him, and promise me to take him far away, and treat him kindly," he said, with a side glance at Poppy, who stood very despondingly by his side, "then you may take him."

"Really!" the stranger said, surprised and delighted, whom the large, long-haired animal greatly pleased. "Well! I'm going with the next vessel from New Orleans to England. Is that far enough for you?"

"Take him," Stevens said, and turned away. At this moment the bell was rung on board, the Englishman quickly fastened his handkerchief round the neck of the unresisting animal, and soon after they left the land.

Poppy, borne down by an evil conscience, and frightened by his master's silence, had, till then, behaved only passively; but when he saw the distance between himself and his former owner grow gradually larger, a prescience of his fate rose before his mind, and he howled and yelled, as in the old time, when summoning his master to the chase. This the hunter's gentle heart, which parting from the dog had so much pained, could not resist; he turned and shouted—

"Poppy—my dog—come here!" and, with a loud howl of joy and

delight, Poppy was about to obey; but his new master might have foreseen something of the sort, and the poor beast, struggling with all his strength, was soon chained up.

"Poppy! Poppy!" the old hunter shouted in deep agony; but Poppy's form faded away in the distance, his cry was no longer heard, and the steamer puffed and snorted down the stream.

CHAPTER VIII.

THE PURSUIT.

FOUR days later a rider galloped through St. Louis in a leathern hunting shirt and a rifle on his shoulder, his horse jaded to death, to the landing-place, then threw himself from the saddle, and asked one of the carriers standing at the water's edge for the steamer *Yellow Stone.*

"Went to New Orleans yesterday," said the man, as he loaded his last cask of flour, and drove into town; the rider, however, stood for an hour on the banks of the broad Mississippi, and looked at the rushing stream. He then slowly mounted his horse again, and rode, without deigning to throw another glance upon St. Louis, back into the forest.

L'ENVOI.

THE conclusion is soon told. Poppy was carried to England and treated by his new master with untiring kindness and attention, for he had grown terribly thin on the voyage, through grief and sea-sickness. Poppy noticed it all, and thought a great deal of his new master, but took no interest in anything—ate what was offered him, and lived through the autumn and winter in England as calmly and contentedly as a poor dog could do after being violently torn from his fatherland. But when spring arrived with its new buds and blossoms, when Nature assumed a happy face after her long winter sleep, when the swallows returned to the houses, and he thought of the wood-birds at home—when all was verdant and blooming, when the birds twittered and the tame turkeys began to cackle—ah! then poor Poppy's heart broke; he thought of his forest, of the now green and glorious bushes, of the silvery stream that foamed and rustled past the cabin; he thought of the chase by the salt lake, where he had watched so many nights with his master; he thought of the free, splendid, forest life—how much bluer the sky looked when seen through the green trees, how much brighter the stars gleamed when looked up to through the thick foliage; he thought of the tracks of the wild beasts, of the contests with bears and panthers, and his heart broke—he became melancholy, put his tail between his legs, and went about as if bewitched.

His master was even once fearful lest Poppy had gone mad, and placed a dish of water before him; but Poppy lapped it up, for he was always fond of drinking. In vain, though, the children, who loved the great, good-tempered animal, brought him all sorts of sweetmeats; he certainly ate them, but remained melancholy and desponding. One day his master received a chest from St. Louis—for he still had connexions with America—and opened it in Poppy's presence. He took out of it, one after the other, one—two—three—four—five—six—seven—eight—nine smoked deer-hams.

That was too much—old, sorrowful reminiscences recurred to the dog's mind—he thought of his former master who had loved him so dearly—how shamefully he had robbed him, and how terribly he had been punished for it—and he threw himself into the river that ran behind the house, with the determination to put an end to a life that had become insupportable to him. The rest, too painful to repeat, has been made known by the newspaper reports; we must add that he was taken out of the water, though unhappily dead, and received an honourable burial.

Poor Poppy! thou liest now in a foreign land, in a strange soil and a single fault drove thee from thy home.

But the master? what became of thy poor old master? Silent and solitary, he returned to his cabin, and for many months the rifle lay untouched and unnoticed on the hooks above the door. Old Stevens was ill, and a violent fever had thrown him on his bed, which he only left at intervals, to crawl to the stream and fetch himself a draught of cold water.

Week after week he lay there, silent and alone, upon his solitary couch, and the illness gnawed at his heart; not illness alone, but the thought of the last friend whom he had lost in such a sorrowful, painful manner. And when the reminiscences of past times overcame him, and he felt that he could never again give his love and his confidence to another being in the world, he often fancied that he had closed his accounts with the world, and it would be far better for him to stretch himself out where he lay, and sleep the last, long sleep of earth.

But he regained his health again; his powerful, uncorrupted constitution was this time the victor, and only the silent sorrow still gnawed at his heart—hardly allowed him to rejoice that he was once more strong and healthy. But when spring returned, the old man felt too lonely, too sad in his formerly-so-cheerful cabin. He cleaned his rifle from dirt and rust, took his hunting accoutrements, saddled his horse, and rode far, far to the West, among the distant prairies. All, however, that he took with him from his old dwelling to his new home was a bear-skin, which he rolled up and fastened behind his saddle—the same bear-skin which he had obtained when he hunted with his dog Poppy for the last time.

THE SILVER MINE
IN THE OZARK MOUNTAINS.

THE SILVER MINE IN THE OZARK MOUNTAINS.

Lying in Wait.

CHAPTER I.

THE thunder rolled hoarsely and menacingly over the lofty summits of the Ozark Mountains,* fiercely challenging its echo from the gloomy ravines and precipitous mountain slopes. The lightning gleamed wildly, giving the whole wild landscape, in the pale light of parting day, a peculiar and melancholy illumination,

* This is a mountain chain of North America, extending south-west, in a direction parallel with the Appallachians, from the Missouri, near the Osage, to the Red River. They belong neither to the Appallachians nor to the Rocky Mountains, but from their coincidence with the former in geological structure and direction, they are related to them in physical origin.

and the rain fell in torrents on the thick leafage of the oaks and hickories, but was speedily sucked up by the thirsting earth before it could reach the deep-lying bed of the little Hurricane River, in which the water stood in isolated small pools.

At the moment when the storm seemed to have reached its highest pitch, and peal on peal, redoubled by the echo, growled through the ravines, two hunters, wrapped in large white woollen blankets, which covered the whole figure nearly down to the fringed mocassins, clambered down the precipitous slopes which frown over the Hurricane from its source to the spot where it falls into the Mulbury, and did not stop till they found themselves on the lowest, terrace-shaped promontory, whence they could survey the rocky bed of the river.

"Confound the storm !" the elder of them at length exclaimed as he stopped, and, after throwing back his blanket, examined the leather-covered lock of his rifle to see whether it was dry and in good condition; "it howls to-day among the old trees as if it wanted to tear up the whole forest by the roots. I am heartily glad that we have reached the river, for my legs are almost giving way from the hurried march, and the sharp stones have torn my mocassins and feet."

"Then you know for certain," the younger, whose name was Thompson, asked his comrade, who was at least ten years older, "that you are on the right trail, and the Spaniards have gone this way?"

"This morning, at daybreak, I saw their watch-fire below, at the little osier-bed, about a mile and a half from here, and heard the bells of their mules," Preston answered.

"And how many men, do you think, were there?" the other asked, thoughtfully.

"I have already told you," the elder replied, crossly, "that, as often as these strangers have been seen here, never more than two men went upwards from the mouth of the Hurricane, although eight or nine awaited the return of the two who preceded them at the mouth."

"I cannot understand the affair at all," Thompson replied, with a shake of his head, "and I should like you to tell me all you know about it, once again; for, as we are about to risk the adventure together, I should not like to be groping in the dark."

"Good," his comrade replied; "the rain has abated considerably; so we will go down to the waterside and camp there; the story will be much better told by a good fire and a properly broiled piece of venison; and, to tell the truth, we shall require all our strength between this and to-morrow morning. It is beginning to grow quite dark down here, and we shall want the twilight to set the wet wood alight—so, on."

With these words, and without awaiting a reply from his comrade, he walked down a narrow deer track that led to the stream, and soon stood by the stony bed of the Hurricane, at a spot where a basin of water, usually clear, but at this moment disturbed by the rain, is formed by a subterranean spring.

The storm now yielded in intensity, the thunder resounded in the distant north, and, in many places, the blue sky peeped out through the grey masses of cloud which, driven by a fresh south-east wind, moved athwart the valley in long strips.

The two men, however, seemed to have little pleasure in the beautiful evening, but were busily engaged in kindling a fire, not merely as a protection against the by no means mild evening breeze, but to prepare for supper a few pieces of raw venison, which Preston took out of a freshly-stripped skin. Thompson now struck fire, and lighted a patch of linen, well rubbed with powder, while Preston brought some little dry splinters which he had cut out of a fallen, decayed tree; in a few moments a weak flame rose, aroused by their united blowing and fanning, which, being carefully and quickly fed with additional sticks, soon gave out a bright, glowing flame.

The hunters now hung their blankets to dry, on poles which they fixed in the ground; collected several pieces of bark from the half-rotten trees that lay around them, which they laid on the ground to keep them from the wet; then placed their strips of venison on sharpened pieces of wood near the glowing ashes, and employed the time during which the meat was broiling, in drying and resting themselves a little.

Both were dressed in simple, dark-blue hunting-shirts, made of coarse homespun, but the younger had a species of ornament on his consisting of narrow yellow fringe, which was attached to the collar, the sleeves, and all the seams. They wore leathern leggings and mocassins, and in the belts which confined their shirts were broad long bear-knives. Preston's head was covered with an old, shabby beaver hat, while Thompson had a gaily-coloured handkerchief bound tightly round his temples.

Their long rifles, with bullet pouches hanging over them, they had leant against a young tree, and now threw themselves, fatigued by the exertion they had undergone, upon the strips of bark near the fire, so that the steam rose from their damp clothes in clouds.

"Now, Preston," Thompson began, after he had taken one of the pieces of meat from the fire, cut off the part that was broiled, and returned the rest, "tell me your strange story once again; calculate the risk and possible gain, and then I will let you know if I will share it with you or not."

"Let me know—share it or not?" Preston asked in astonishment, as he raised himself on his elbow, and looked inquiringly at his younger comrade. "Have we come hither through storm and tempest, that you may now be in doubt what you will do or leave undone, and only, perhaps, wait for a less favourable description to return home quietly, and leave to me alone the discovery on which, as you are well aware, I have set my life?"

"Well, well," Thompson said, with a laugh, "be not so angry—out with it; you know I am usually the last to give up a thing on which I have made up my mind; come, tell me clearly and frankly what we have to hope, so that we may take our measures quickly and surely."

"Spoken like a man," said the elder, as he fell back into his comfortable reclining position; "and now, then, learn all that I know of the mysterious conduct of the Spaniards, whom I have been following for years. But never has a fox made a greater fool of a hound, or more frequently led one from the scent, than these cursed Señors have done, even though I have followed them with equal fidelity and willingness.

"You know that, for many years, the Cherokees have spoken of a silver mine, which is situated somewhere on the waters of the Hurricane, and is said to be extraordinarily productive, but no imaginable promises could induce one of them to describe the place more closely, as, according to their laws, death is the punishment of treachery, although the secret can no longer be of service to any of them. A few Spaniards, however, must be in possession of it, for, during many years (and for the last three, I have watched them myself), several dark forms, wrapped in long Mexican serapès, come with three or four mules to the mouth of the Hurricane, when the greater portion camp in the almost impenetrable thicket whence the river derives its name, while two with the beasts mount the hill on the left bank of the river, cross the second terrace from the top and the 'flat mountain' opposite the little thicket which lies about a mile from here up the stream, return to the valley after leaving the mules hobbled in the thicket, and then look for the mine, which must be somewhere in this neighbourhood, for, in twenty-four hours, they usually return with heavily-laden beasts to their company, and then disappear for twelve months. For three years I have been watching them, and followed their trail when they retreated, with indefatigable care, searched the precipices on both sides of the river from top to bottom, and left scarce a stone unturned, as if all the bears in Arkansas were looking for worms, and all in vain. From the osier-bed they had gone several hundred yards up the mountain, but had afterwards kept so entirely among the rocks, that every trace disappeared, and my eye, which is far from being one of the worst, could not follow their trail any further. For two years in succession I have been making these fruitless attempts, and to my shame I must confess that a fear my neighbours had impregnated me with caused me to refrain from insuring to my researches the proper success. They tell all sorts of horrible stories of these black Spaniards; for instance, that they do not care about shedding human blood to preserve their secret, and once murdered a solitary hunter who accidentally surprised them at their task, and such like terrible tales.

"When I was alone, an almost womanly fear seized upon me involuntarily, and I would then look timidly, expecting to see behind each projecting rock or overthrown tree, the cocked rifle of one of the black-eyed villains. Now it is quite different—there are two of us and two of them; if we find the place where they are digging, and they discover us and prove hostile, well! our rifles will shoot as surely, or perhaps more so, than theirs; if they listen to reason, all the better; I don't wish to spill blood, and there will be silver enough for all four of us; but I must know the place, and I shall not have wasted years in following them without gaining my end."

Preston ceased, and brooding over his scheme, looked thoughtfully into the glimmering ashes, while Thompson also maintained silence for a few minutes, and dug all sorts of figures in the ground with his broad hunting-knife. At length he half turned his head to his comrade, and asked, as he wiped the point of his knife on his leathern leggings and picked his teeth—

"When shall we start?"

"As soon as the moon rises, and that will be at a quarter past twelve," was the reply; "then we must follow the course of the stream till we reach the osier bed, and wait there until the Spaniards return to their animals laden with the precious metal. They will have to make several journeys, and it will depend on our cleverness to settle the whole affair peaceably—that is, undiscovered—or, in a hostile manner, if we are detected. They have no dogs with them, so we need not fear them; and if we find the place, we are made men."

"Good!" Thompson said, placing another piece of meat before him, an example which his more serious companion now followed. "Good! I am with you. There's little trouble and danger, and a prospect of immense gain; I cannot resist it. We will now refresh ourselves heartily, and sleep for half an hour, for who knows how much we shall require it? When the moon rises we shall have fresh strength to endure all that crosses our path with fresh spirits."

Silently the two men ended their meal, then piled up the fire, which burned brightly through the dry wood they heaped on it; wrapped themselves in their blankets, and tried to recruit their bodies for the exertions that awaited them.

The younger soon slept, and his deep, regular breathing proved how little he knew the danger he was going to incur, or, if he knew it, how undauntedly he awaited it.

The elder also wrapped himself in his blanket and seemed to slumber, with his head laid on a piece of decayed wood, but his eyes were open, and he looked up thoughtfully at the myriads of stars which trembled peacefully and cheerily in the dark sky.

At length the sky grew bright above the eastern chain of mountains; Preston then rose from his hard couch, stretched his limbs, aroused his comrade, and then walked to the river, which was only a few paces distant, to bathe his hands and face in it, and commence his dangerous task with clear eyes and senses.

Thompson sprang up and followed his example; both then rolled up their blankets and hung them over their shoulders, took up their rifles, strewed fresh powder in the pans, and were thus prepared for anything that might oppose them.

"Had we not better go through the valley?" Thompson now asked, as he saw that Preston was climbing up some precipitous masses of rocks to reach one of the terraces. "We shall have, in any case, a better road, and can get along more quickly; for, deuce take it, it is a very unpleasant matter clambering in the night among sharp stones with torn mocassins! my feet already burn like fire."

"We must keep among the rocks for the same reason that the Spaniards select the roughest part—to avoid leaving any trail. If we remain unnoticed, we will retire gently and cautiously, and not excite the suspicion of the enemy, who, assuredly, even if they do not follow the road through the valley, will look and see whether they can discover any dangerous footsteps there."

With active steps, and without uttering another word, the elder walked in front, and Thompson, clearly perceiving that his more experienced comrade was in the right, followed him, only now and then, when he stepped on a very sharp stone, assuaging his pain by a half suppressed curse.

They had advanced in this way for nearly an hour, the moon poured its silvery rays on the forest, when Preston stopped, and, pointing before him, whispered to his companion that this was the osier-bed, and he fancied he heard the sound of a bell.

The fine, pure tones of a few small bells now distinctly reached the ear through the silence of night, and the men stopped to discuss their future movements.

"Are they on the right or left bank of the river?" Thompson gently asked his comrade, who was listening attentively to the sound of the bells, in order to discover how many animals they had with them on this occasion.

"On the right," Preston whispered; "at least, their footmarks have always been on that side. But," he suddenly turned the conversation, "only listen; how many bells can you hear? They seem to me five or six."

With great attention, they now both listened to the mixed sounds which reached them from the valley, till Thompson at last broke the silence, and gently muttered to himself that he certainly heard four different bells.

"I fancy there are five," Preston replied, equally gently.

"Well, hang it, let them be ten," Thompson said, angrily; "we are here now, and it will make no difference about a couple of Spaniards, more or less; we are standing on Uncle Sam's own ground, and if the strangers, in case they discover us, have hostile designs, they must blame themselves if we are liberal with our lead. But what have you got there?" he said to his companion, who was stooping down and carefully examining the ground.

"A footmark, as true as I am alive, and belonging to a booted foot!" Preston cried; "they must have gone up here."

"Pst!" Thompson whispered, seizing his arm and holding it firmly, "I hear steps."

They both listened with fixed attention, and the sound of a man slowly walking towards them became more and more distinct.

They laid themselves on the ground, behind some scattered masses of rock, and awaited the figure, which, wrapped in a long brown cloak, and the head covered with a broad-leaved black sombrero, slowly scaled the terrace at whose edge the hunters lay, then halted, looked all around cautiously for about five minutes, and uttered a gentle though distinct cry, in imitation of an owl.

It was answered once from the thicket, and after this all was silent as the grave for half-an-hour; then the same cry sounded again from the valley. The sentinel—for the tall, dark figure that leaned against a tree and listened for the slightest noise could be nothing else—answered as on the previous occasion, then walked down the path by which he had come, and in a few minutes, when his steps had died away in the distance, the whole neighbourhood was as quiet and deserted as if it had never been desecrated by a human foot.

The two men remained in their hiding-place for a quarter of an hour, but then, as all appeared safe, and they might believe that the strangers had again retired, Thompson raised his head, looked for a moment down into the valley that was brilliantly illumined by the moon, and then turned to his elder companion, who had also risen, and again inspected the lock of his rifle, to see whether the powder had not fallen from the pan through laying it down.

"Well, Preston, what do you think of that apparition? It did not please me at all; I had a great desire to spring forward and stick my knife into the long fellow—it would have been one less!"

"That would have been as foolish as it would have been dangerous," Preston replied in a half-suppressed tone, "and might not only have spoiled our whole scheme, but have exposed us to the vengeance of all the brown villains. No! I now understand it all. The fellows must come down into the valley with their booty in the rocky bed of the mountain stream, else I should have found their traces in former years; and this long fellow was merely stationed here to guard them against any surprise from below, while they, in the meanwhile, carried their booty to the camp, and load it there afterwards at their ease. But we have no time to lose now, for who knows if they make more than one journey? and, if we don't find them engaged in digging, so that I can mark the spot, all our trouble will be of no avail."

"But it is impossible that they can find all the best ore by night, and they must surely continue their labours after daybreak," Thompson replied.

"What they acquired yesterday they will now secure, and then destroy all the traces which they may have left," Preston replied.

"No, no! we must not wait for daybreak; and, besides, it seems to me that they scent danger, which the sentry sufficiently proves. So now come down into the valley; we will creep through the osier-bed, where they have hardly left a guard, and will quietly follow the course of the stream. If we find them busied at the mine, we will mark the place and retire as quickly and gently as possible; for I conjecture, not without reason, that they have come this time in larger numbers than usual. Let them take away what they have collected; when they return next year they will find it more difficult to fill their leathern saddle-bags than has yet been the case, without the silver is found in lumps upon the mountain."

The hunters now went cautiously down in the narrow valley, crawled like snakes into the little osier-bed, which was not very thick,—paying the closest attention, at the same time, to the slightest thing that might menace them with danger or discovery. But there was no watch left near the mules, which grazed quietly, and did not appear to pay any attention to the crawling visitors; and, drawing a deep breath, the hunters again reached the open forest above the osier-bed, where Preston was about to hurry forward, when Thompson took him by the arm and asked whether they had not better first look for the silver which the Spaniards had already carried to some place near them.

"Go to the deuce with your nonsense!" Preston replied, angrily. "What! waste our time here with child's play, to find out a thing which we dare not even touch without fearing immediate discovery? Come, come, we may at any moment meet the villains on their return, and it would be desirable for us to leave them before they have any idea of our vicinity."

With these words, he loosed himself from Thompson's grasp, and glided with noiseless step over the smooth round pebbles in the bed of the river, accompanied by his comrade with equal precaution, like two dark shadows that had lately quitted their graves.

They had continued their progress for nearly a mile, undisturbed and uninterrupted, without hearing the slightest sound that could betray the vicinity of living creatures, when they suddenly heard voices close before them, and they had scarcely time to throw themselves in the shadow of a fallen plane tree, before five dark forms, with small sacks on their backs, which must have been of considerable weight, judging from the stooping position of the men, who came straight towards them, and walked noiselessly towards the osiers, stepping from one large stone to another.

When they were only a few paces distant from the hunters' hiding-place, the leader stopped, and addressed a few words in Spanish to his followers; but soon after he went on, and disappeared with his comrades behind a rock that formed a curve in the course of the Hurricane.

"Did you understand what that long scoundrel muttered in his beard?" Thompson asked of his companion.

"Not a word," the latter replied. "It is the first time I ever heard Spanish spoken; but come on quickly, we dare not lose a moment; perhaps we can discover the mine before they return, for, hang it! there are more of them than I expected, and the fellows wear long, sharp knives."

Quickly and gently the two followed the course of the little stream for some thousand paces, when Preston, who was in front, suddenly stopped, and pointed to several picks and spades that lay scattered about in a dried-up part of the bed of the river.

"There, by Heaven!" he cried, seizing Thompson's shoulder convulsively, "we're in the nest."

"And what's that dark object lying under the bush?" Thompson asked, as, with outstretched hand, he walked up to the place in question, and stooped down to look at the object that had excited his attention. But, with a cry of terror and surprise, he sprang back, for at only the distance of a few inches the dark eyes of a man gleamed, who sprang to his feet at the same moment with a brandished knife, and uttered a loud cry for help.

"Devil!" Preston shouted, who had also drawn his knife from his belt on the enemy's first movement, "Devil!" and rushed on the Spaniard.

The leap would have been his destruction, however, had not accidentally the rifle which he held in his left hand warded off the foeman's sure blow, and at the same moment the hunter's broad knife was driven home in his breast, and he fell to the ground wi a loud yell; but in his fall he tore a pistol from his belt, and fir it at his enemy.

The bullet missed the man for whom it was intended, but shattered the left hand of his comrade, who was standing close l him, and had just raised his arms to finish the enemy with a bl from the butt-end of his rifle. Thompson's arm sank powerless l his side, and his rifle rolled down among the stones. Still he fl like a tiger on the mortally wounded man, and drove his kni thrice into his breast, till Preston seized his arm and drew him ba

"Away, away!" he cried; "he has had enough, but we shall so have the other devils on our track. Away! I would not, for the silver mines in the world, form the acquaintance of their knive

After the Fight

CHAPTER II.

DEATH STRUGGLES.

"I AM wounded," Thompson whispered, with suppressed pain; "my hand is smashed."

"Better your hand than your head," Preston growled, raising the rifle from the ground and handing it to his crippled comrade. "Come; in five minutes it will be too late." And, with hurried steps, he hastened, followed by Thompson, who perceived their imminent peril, for a short distance along the bed of the stream, and then bounded up the rocky wall to the right, probably to reach the summit of the hill before the pursuers, and then carry on their flight successfully on the other side of the ridge, under the protection of night.

With his shattered arm hidden in his bosom, Thompson remained close to Preston's side, and in a few moments they both disappeared in the shade of the forest. At the same instant, however, the bushes rustled, and five dark forms broke through the branches on to the battle-ground just deserted by the fugitives.

They uttered one cry of terror when they saw the body of their murdered comrade, and cast inquiring glances around to discover the performers of the deed and sacrifice them to their vengeance; but then a quick, authoritative movement from their leader warned them to silence, and, like so many figures carved out of black marble, the men stood breathlessly and listened.

For a few moments the silence of death prevailed, till the sound of a cracking branch reached their ear, when, unanimously, and with a loud shout of joy—like dogs that scent the proximity of their flying enemy, the panther—the five powerful men sprang up the almost perpendicular rocky wall that inclosed the narrow defile, and, with revenge and blooodthirstiness in their glances, followed the direction in which they had heard the noise.

The two fugitives, who had brought the pursuers on their track by a fall on the part of the wounded man, had already reached the sixth terrace, and were hurrying with rapid steps towards a thicket of chestnut trees, which lay darkly before them, when they heard the steps of the swiftest of their foemen close behind them. At the right moment, Preston pulled his comrade into a small ravine, formed by a spring that burst there from the rock, and close to which, at not two paces distant, a dark abyss yawned, as a tall, dark figure sprang past them and hurried towards the thicket. He was followed rapidly by a second and a third, and the two last had already climbed the edge of the terrace, and were about following the same direction, when one of them, guided either by chance or by an instinct that betrayed the presence of a foe, sprang towards the dark spot that contained the two fugitives, and which probably appeared to him suspicious, and looked attentively in.

The moon, at this moment, shone out from behind a fleecy cloud, and the glistening rifle-barrel must have betrayed the hidden men, for a "Ha!" of surprise escaped the Spaniard's lips. But it was his last sound, for Preston, when he saw that they were discovered, had calmly raised his rifle, and, on the crack of the piece, the Spaniard fell, with a heavy sound, among the rocks.

"Kill the other villain quick, or he'll escape!" he now cried to his comrade, who leaned against the rock, pale and breathless.

"Take my gun; I cannot raise it now," he whispered, and handed him the rifle, which Preston seized with feverish excitement, in order to render the other foeman harmless. But the latter stepped behind a large oak, which covered him, and his shout soon brought the others back to the spot, who had been stopped in their career by the crack of the rifle, and now obeyed the summons with wild shouts of joy.

But Preston had not been idle in the meanwhile, and, as he saw that the Spaniard was out of his reach, he laid down Thompson's rifle, reloaded his own, and was shaking powder into the pan, when the dark shadows of the pursuers became visible as they rapidly glided among the masses of rock and trees.

In a few words, the Spaniard that had remained behind described the hiding-place of their enemies, and showed them the new victim who had fallen by Preston's unerring hand; but only a loud, wild shout of revenge—on hearing which the two pursued men involuntarily recoiled—was the reply, and, like tigers, the Spaniards rushed on their prey.

Preston held his rifle in readiness, and the first, who rushed upon him from behind a rock, with a pistol in one hand and a knife in the other, fell, shot through the heart; then, throwing down his rifle, he seized his comrade's, and aimed with lightning speed at the nearest man; but his finger pulled the trigger in vain! the sparks certainly flew down into the open pan, but the powder had been scattered on its fall, and the iron struck the flint to no purpose. The next moment, a flash burst from behind a closely adjacent rock, and Preston fell back upon his comrade with a shattered skull.

Thompson sprang forward with a drawn knife, and defended himself with wild desperation against the three assailants who rushed upon him, as if he despised wounds and danger; but a blow from the butt of a pistol caused him to stagger, and, while he tried to clutch the rock with his wounded hand, he fell, with a heavy crash and a loud cry of agony, into the deep, yawning abyss at his side.

Three days had elapsed when a hunter from the settlements on the Hurricane followed the track of a deer, and saw swarms of carrion crows hovering over one of the terraces.

In his curiosity to see what species of game had fallen a prey to the ravenous birds, he drew near the spot, and found on the mountain one, and in the abyss a second, skeleton, but, at no great distance from the first, a newly-made grave, and upon it, as a tomb-stone, a broad-leaved sombrero, fastened with a long knife upon the hurriedly thrown-up mound.

Although he hurried as quickly as he could back to the settlements, and on the next morning brought all the neighbours he could collect to the scene of the contest, and thence followed the easily-guessed criminals in order to punish them, they remained in vain for days, with the keen scent of Indians, on the track of the mules. The crafty Spaniards had shipped themselves and all that belonged to them in safety in canoes, and only sent one of their number, with the beasts of burden, by land, in order to lead those astray who, they were sure, would pursue them. The latter had then sold the mules, and had disappeared without leaving a trace.

From that day, none of the Spaniards have dared again to scale the mountains, where the vengeance of the wild frontier men awaited them; but the Silver Mine on the Hurricane has not yet been discovered by the dwellers upon that river, and in vain have the hunters tried to penetrate a mystery in the preservation of which so much blood was shed.

A BEAR HUNT IN THE WESTERN MOUNTAINS.

A BEAR HUNT IN THE WESTERN MOUNTAINS.

The Entrances to Three Caves.

CHAPTER I.

THE BEAR CAVE IN THE MOUNTAIN.

ON a clear, bitterly cold afternoon in the month of February, when the sun, surrounded by a fleecy veil of clouds, had not sufficient strength to warm the piercing breeze that blew across from the north-western prairies, and even a thick coat of ice, a very unusual thing in Arkansas, covered the rivers, three men were climbing the precipitous slopes which surround the sources of the "spirit creek," and selected the roughest and most inaccessible tracks that could be found in the whole neighbourhood. Although narrow strips of level ground often lay before them, they constantly skirted them, and sought again the bleakest, wildest walls of rock, where rugged masses of stone, hurled in strange forms upon each other, rendered their progress almost an impossibility.

The three hunters, for other people could not have anything to look for in such a chaos of rock, kept a few hundred paces apart, carefully examining the soil and plants upon and over which they walked, and they moved forward very slowly. Suddenly a cry from one, an Indian (the other two were white men), attracted the attention of his comrades, and on his signs and movements, which showed that he had found something, they climbed down to examine his discovery.

The Indian was a young and active man, about thirty years of age, tall and graceful, but powerfully built: at least, the naked arm which he stretched out from beneath his woollen blanket, to give the others a signal, revealed extraordinarily strong muscles and sinews.

His legs were clothed in leathern leggings, his feet in mocassins of the same stuff, but his hunting-shirt, composed of thin parti-coloured calico, was in reality only held together by his belt, for it hung down from his shoulders in strips. His head was uncovered, and his long black hair hung down over his brow and temples, and his face displayed none of the usual disfiguring paint, but only his own dark, copper-coloured hue, from which a pair of sparkling eyes looked boldly out. On his left shoulder his long rifle rested, and his belt held, under the blanket, a knife, tomahawk, and a tin cup.

His two companions were dressed in the same fashion as himself, except that they wore leathern hunting-shirts, their blankets were rolled up on their backs, and one of them, a tall, thin man, whose light hair revealed the Northern, had a rough, hairy cap, coarsely made from the skin of a Polar bear, pressed deeply over his forehead, while his comrade, on whose shoulder a short German rifle hung by a strap, wore a woollen nightcap as head covering.

Accustomed to the rough road, they sprang actively down the

precipice, from rock to rock, and soon reached the side of the Indian, who, when he saw that his signal was obeyed, awaited them, wrapped up closely in his blanket. When they reached the place where he was standing, he stretched out his hand once again, and said, as he pointed to the ground and to several little lately-torn bushes, "The bear loves sassafras, for it makes a soft bed; if the weather was warm, there would be a track from here to the water's edge."

"Unless we spoil it in the meanwhile, Tessakeh!" said the tall hunter, as he carefully examined the signs which betrayed the abode of a bear in their immediate neighbourhood. "But where is the black fellow? He must have his hall-door somewhere close, and yet I see no cave."

"Wah!" said the Indian, as he pointed to a hole, which went perpendicularly downward, just where he was standing, and was scarcely large enough for a strong man to enter.

"And how shall we get down?" the German asked, as he held his head down to the orifice and tried to look down. "Confound it, it appears to be very deep, and is perfectly dark." With these words he threw a pebble, and its hollow murmur and splash showed that it had fallen into water.

"Water down there?" the American asked, as he bent forward and listened. "Indeed, and some twenty feet deep. The deuce take me if I would go in if the fattest bear-meat lay there that had fed on the acorns in the forests of Arkansas. But there is no bear there, for the old fellows are not so stupid as to choose a wet bed when there are so many dry ones all around."

"The bear is cunning," Tessakeh replied, as he threw down another stone and listened to the sound, "very cunning; he manages to find a place where he can lie secure and dry, but the white man hangs with his eyes on the clouds when he should look at his feet. Did he break off the twig on which he is standing?"

"In truth," said Redham, as he took up and examined a little withered sassafras-twig that lay close to the mouth of the pit, "the bear must have dropped it here, and that is a tolerably sure sign that he is in there. But we shall hardly be able to trouble him down there; even if we killed him, we should have to bring him out piecemeal, and I fancy we should have to go down to him in the same fashion."

Without making any further reply, Tessakeh looked sharply round for a moment, and then climbed up to a young, thin hickory, which rose, tall and gracefully, to a height of about forty feet, and only a few inches thick, felled it with a few blows of his tomahawk, so that it fell close to the two other hunters; freed it from the branches, which he, however, cut off at a distance of about six inches from the trunk, and, with the assistance of the German, who soon understood for what purpose it was to be employed, lowered the quickly-formed ladder into the cave. As the trunk was longer than they required, they took it out again, cut off about eight feet from the lower, branchless end, and were all prepared to enter the cave.

"Well, Redham, wont you come down with us?" the German asked, as he threw off his blanket and shot-belt, and fastened his powder-horn close to his body with a strap. "We shall have plenty of fun, and it would really be a pity to leave you all alone here."

"I don't begrudge you your fun, Werner, in the least," Redham interrupted him, striking fire at the same time. "Go down now, and bring me up before evening a piece of the bear, for I am really hungry, and we ate the last of our meat this morning. I will keep up a good fire in the meanwhile, and guard the entrance."

Tessakeh had also thrown off his blanket, and taken out of his belt a short, thick wax candle, roughly moulded from the yellow comb of a wild-bee hive, while Werner unwrapped from his blanket a similar piece, though considerably larger. The Indian then bound his long hunting-knife tighter, and laid his rifle down by the fire, which already burned up brightly under Redham's practised hands.

"Then I must only take my rifle?" Werner said, on seeing Tessakeh preparing to open the campaign without his.

"Tessakeh has a long barrel, and if the loading-stick is pulled out, it is four feet longer," the Indian replied.

"Well, if this lair is as narrow as the last one we crept in together," said Werner, with a laugh, "mine will also be too long to reload; but forward, Tessakeh, forward! we will show this good man up here that we're not afraid of a deep hole and water at the bottom. If there is a bear in, then we shall have meat this evening, and that's a thing we stand in great need of."

With these words, he prepared to go down first, with his rifle suspended on his back. Tessakeh, however, pulled him back and said, as he pointed to the mouth of the gun, with a shake of his head—

"White man has the safe end. Tessakeh will go down first, and if my brother feels an inclination when down there, he can show his wax-light first to the bear."

Without awaiting any reply, he disappeared in the hole, while soon after Werner followed his example. Redham had only time to call to him—

"Take care, Werner, take care; don't shoot unless you are certain of your mark, and remember that in such a cave, the bullet leaves the barrel with remarkable ease and quickness, but is preciously difficult to put in again with a proper charge, especially if you have to fight with a wounded bear."

Werner nodded to him once again, cried, "Much pleasure to you," and also disappeared in the narrow chasm, paying great attention to his rifle, lest it might be discharged by holding it carelessly.

With great agility, the two men clambered down the tree, and Tessakeh soon stood at the foot of it, in water, which he examined beforehand, and found to be only six or seven inches in depth. Werner soon stood at his side, and, holding up their candles, which threw a dim light around, they examined the space in which they found themselves. It was a species of vault, about nine feet high, and sixteen to eighteen broad, and two passages led into the mountain, one at a height of about five feet from the ground, the other under water.

Tessakeh climbed, with Werner's assistance, to the upper opening, and finding there traces of bears and other wild beasts, he crept further in, to see whether the inhabitant of the cave had taken up his quarters in the dry or wet passage. Werner was obliged to remain behind, as, without other help, he could not have reached the narrow entrance at such a distance from the ground, encumbered as he was with his rifle, and stood up to his ankles in cold water, in a by no means pleasant position. At length, after long waiting, and when he began to shiver with the cold, Tessakeh again appeared at the opening of the upper passage, and assured him that it grew so narrow further up that a large bear could not possibly live in it; the old fellow must, consequently, have selected the lower, wet passage to reach a dry spot higher up.

The entrance to the second cave, however, looked terribly uncomfortable; for, although the passage was some twenty inches in height, and a man could crawl along it comfortably, still, it was filled with water to a depth of nearly six inches, and the dark opening yawned with a terrible aspect before the two hunters.

"There's a bear in there," Tessakeh at length broke silence, after both had regarded the opening for some minutes seriously—"there's a bear in there; but will my brother risk his life by attacking the beast in his well-defended stronghold? It is cold; the stag is looking for acorns, and Redham is a great hunter. He will have meat before the sun again stands in the east."

"It is true, Tessakeh," Werner said, casting a repugnant glance at the dangerous awkward entrance; "but we are here, and, in all probability, we can find and kill the beast by a little perseverance. Will you follow me, then, if I go first and open a path, or wait here? for I must and will try it."

"My brother is brave, and can make the attempt, but when he turns his head, wherever he may be, he will look into Tessakeh's eyes," the Indian replied; and, without wasting another word, Werner knelt down in the water, close to the opening of the cave, and held his candle in. No special obstacle seemed to be in his way, and, holding his rifle, with the barrel pointing in front, on the left shoulder, with the left hand, in which he also held the light, he rested his weight on his right elbow, and crawled slowly into the narrow entrance, followed by Tessakeh, who could move with greater ease, as he had left his gun behind.

Although Werner's head and left arm alone projected out of the water, and he was compelled to hold the sling of his powder-horn between his teeth to keep it dry, he boldly and undauntedly followed the dangerous, gloomy road, and reached, after he had crept some thirty or forty yards in this uncomfortable fashion—wet through and trembling with cold, though otherwise in good condition—the dry portion of the cave, which sloped upwards and divided into three distinct branches. Tessakeh was by his side at the moment when he rose and entered the open space, and shook himself like a dog that has just left the water; then, cautiously raising his candle, he examined, with great care, the soft ground in which a mass of different tracks was visible, and then turned with a smile to his white friend, who had unfastened his belt, taken off and wrung his hunting-shirt, and was now examining his rifle to see that it had not been wetted by some incautious movement on his part.

"The hunters have often found the cave, but my brother and Tessakeh were never among them; they have lighted their fire at the entrance, but not one has carried a spark thus far; they are like the wolf, that crawls round the camp of the sleeping hunter—they smell the game that has been hung up, but they fear the eye of a man."

"In which of the three caves can the beast be?" Werner asked, as he again pulled on his hunting-shirt, and refastened his belt with the knife in it. "They all appear alike, and, confound them, all three equally uncomfortable."

An Unexpected Danger

CHAPTER II.

THE HUNT.

TESSAKEH had, in the meanwhile, continued his observations, and now, pointing to a broad track which led into the left-hand opening, and where the entering traces were embedded in those the animal had made on going out, he cried, as he carefully inspected the marks with his light, and held the knuckles of his right hand upon them, in order to estimate the size of the enemy by it, "Here!" and, holding out the bent fingers of his right hand to his comrade, he continued, "He is large and heavy; his paws went in to some depth, and he is asleep!"

"Well, if he's asleep, Tessakeh," Werner replied, who had now finished his preparations, and was putting on a fresh percussion-cap, to be sure of his fire, "then we have an easy game, and it will cost us more trouble to bring the old fellow to daylight than to kill him. But," he continued, as he raised his light from the ground, "we must lose no time; Redham will be terribly tired of waiting, and I should like to see a good lump of meat boiling at the fire for supper."

"For supper!" Tessakeh said, with a smile. "Our brother will again see the sun rise over the mountains, and still be lying at the fire and waiting for us. The cave is narrow, and we shall have to work hard before we get our burden out of it."

"That is a poor prospect," Werner muttered, whose wet clothes, which Tessakeh did not appear at all to notice, hung far from comfortably on his person. "Here, though, there is no other road but forwards. To work, then; the longer we dawdle here the later we shall finish. And now, Tessakeh, go a-head!"

"Will my brother trust the short rifle to me, and follow my trail?" the Indian said, as he stood still.

"No, no; I did not mean that," the former replied. "I will crawl on, and I'll be hanged if you see any trace of fear in me. No; if the prospect of a long fast did not suit me for a moment, it was by no means through fear or other anxiety. Pay attention to the light, that we may see what we are about. And now, here goes."

At the last words he had approached the entrance of the cave, and crawled, as he pushed his rifle before him, and holding the light in his left hand, forwards, followed by Tessakeh, who, when he saw his companion determined on going first, did not utter another word, and seemed quite contented that the young man voluntarily undertook the greatest danger.

The cave was, at the outset, so spacious, that both men could crawl along on their hands and knees, but after some fifty yards, it became narrower every step they advanced, and the upper part was only about twelve inches from the lower; so that Werner, who had a broad chest and wide shoulders, could scarce crawl through. Still he pushed on, as he saw in the moist soil that the bear must have passed through this narrow place, and soon reached a part that was several inches higher.

But here a new difficulty opposed them, for, although the passage went straight on into the mountain, a well-like abyss yawned close before them, which, if not broader than the passage in which they were crawling, was at least three feet long; Heaven knows how many deep; for Werner, who held his candle down at arm's length, could see nothing.

"Does my brother hear the bear?" Tessakeh asked, when he perceived that his comrade did not progress.

"No; but there is a hole here," the German whispered, "and I should like to know how deep it is before I venture across it. I really don't know in what way, either; for I cannot see the bottom, and have no stone here to throw down."

"And no bullets in your pocket?" the Indian asked, laconically.

"Right, Tessakeh; I did not think of them. I shall surely not fire five down here," Werner replied, and, at the same time, took one from a flapped pocket in his hunting-shirt, which he dropped into the pit.

It must have been some thirty feet deep, for it was a long while before the hollow sound of its fall into water reached their ears. By no means calmed by the result, he growled—

"Hallo! that's a bad look out; for if I get across by holding on to both sides, how the deuce shall we bring the bear back? I really don't know what to do."

"Forward, if it is in any way possible," Tessakeh replied. "It is difficult to wing a bird when he's flying in the air. When Tessakeh sees the blood of the dead beast, he will know how to bring it to daylight."

"Good! If you think so," said Werner, "I am agreeable; but you shall take the responsibility if all our trouble and labour are lost."

With these words, after hanging his rifle round his neck, he pressed both his elbows and knees against the rough walls of the cave, and, almost hovering in the air, with the deep pit beneath him, into which the failure of a sinew would have precipitated him, he advanced cautiously, inch by inch, and reached the other side, or, rather, the continuation of the passage, which was so narrow that he could scarce turn round towards the road he had traversed. Without waiting for the Indian, whom he fancied behind him, he crept further and followed the track, which was clearly imbedded in the soft soil, some hundred yards further, till suddenly he heard a gentle, whining sound at no great distance, and in that part of the cave that lay before him. He listened, and distinctly heard the sound which the bear utters in his winter sleep when sucking his paws.

"Tessakeh!" he now whispered, turning his head—for the passage had grown somewhat wider—"Tessakeh! I hear the bear."

He received no reply from his companion. Unbroken darkness lay behind him.

"Tessakeh!" he now cried, louder, as he fancied that the Indian must be somewhat further back; and again he listened for his comrade's voice in answer. Only the distant whine of the bear broke the death-like stillness, and, desponding, he threw himself on his left side, to rest awhile, and consider if he should continue his road alone and dare the encounter, or turn back, to see whether an accident had happened to his comrade.

"H'm!" he at last muttered softly to himself. "If he had fallen down the pit he would have called for help, and if he remained on the other side, to let me finish with the bear alone, I will, at any rate, show him that I do not want him to fire a gun. The bear can do no more than eat me."

With this consolation, which had something undeniably reasonable about it, he began again to move forward, and drew nearer and nearer to the whining, which momentarily became more distinct.

The cave was no longer so very narrow, but such a quantity of stalactites hung down from the walls and projected from the bottom, that it was rendered a very difficult matter to advance, and Werner's knees and elbows pained him frightfully.

In this part of the cave there also were a quantity of bats hanging to the roof by their hind feet, and indulging in their winter sleep, from which they were disturbed and disquieted by the light that moved beneath them, and which they proclaimed by a shrill hissing sound. The bold hunter paid little attention to them, however, and was just on the point of turning round a bend in the cave, behind which the bear must inevitably lie, when he saw an immense rattlesnake coiled up on his right hand, and in such a position that he must touch it as he passed. Disturbed by his approach, it opened its little gleaming eyes, but, blinded by the light, it closed them again immediately, and, bending back its head, while its sharp double tongue played restlessly backwards and forwards, it raised its tail and sounded the warning rattle.

Werner drew back involuntarily, and was undecided what he should do, for, although he did not fear the snake, still its neighbourhood was far from pleasing to him, especially as he did not dare shoot it, as it would have been an impossibility to load again in the narrow passage.

As he lay there still undecided, he saw, to his uncommon satisfaction, Tessakeh's light slowly approaching, and the Indian soon came close to him and asked why he delayed.

Werner told him, in a few words, what the matter was.

"Does he show his fangs?" the Indian whispered.

"No, but he has warned."

"He is like a hound on the trail of a bear! He warns—but when the enemy approaches, he draws back. My brother may crawl boldly past him—he will close his eyes and sleep."

Werner obeyed, though very reluctantly, the advice given him, and, pushing his rifle cautiously before him, he was soon by the side of the snake, which tried to open its little eyes several times, and rattled more loudly and menacingly. At length he lay close to it, and, although he pressed closely to the opposite wall, the space was so narrow that his right arm almost touched the coiled-up form of the enemy.

He slowly drew his knee up and was about to advance, when the snake opened its eyes again, and seeing the bright flame close before it, with its head drawn back for a spring, opened its mouth wide, in which, white and glistening, the poison-filled fangs lay on both sides of the quivering tongue, while its eyes sparkled with green fire.

In horror Werner tore his knife from the sheath, but at the same moment he felt Tessakeh's arm on his loins, and his tomahawk, guided by a firm hand, whizzed down upon the snake, which writhed in its blood.

Although Werner knew that it was now harmless, still he shuddered when it rolled in the death spasms in the narrow passage, and its cold scales touched his burning cheek. He hurriedly removed it, but Tessakeh seized the quivering body and carefully cut off the rattles, which he fastened to his belt.

When this was accomplished, Werner was about to continue his progress, when he suddenly felt himself checked by Tessakeh, who whispered gently to him—

"Take care—I don't hear any whining—the bear is awake and his eyes are open. When he scents us we shall hear something of him; but the smoke of our candles flies backwards."

"In truth you are right, Tessakeh," Werner replied; "the old fellow must be awake, and will make no pleasant face when he sees the lights. The cursed snake claimed my attention so thoroughly, that I did not think of the bear; you were just——"

"Hist!" the savage said, raising his hand, "I hear the bear—he is becoming restless."

Both listened for a couple of minutes, but the deepest silence prevailed, and not a sound could be heard. Still Werner looked at his rifle, to see whether the cap was all right and the priming not spilled, cleaned the sight-piece from the clay that had adhered to it, and advanced again, gently, followed by his comrade.

A slight growl reached his ear, and, soon after, the dark form of the bear came out from the gloomy cave, and his eyes sparkled in the light, like red-hot coals. Growling, he inhaled the air, and raised his nose to discover the nature of his visitors; but, although the breeze carried the scent backwards, and he could not properly sniff out who his enemies were, still they were too near for him not to perceive that there was something wrong, and, puffing and snorting, he drew back again before Werner had time to take aim at the black fellow's continually moving head.

Both the hunters knew that the moment for action had now arrived, and moved without a sound over the rough ground in pursuit of the retiring beast, whom they soon caught up again, and, indeed, as Werner perceived to his horror, at the extreme end of the cave, which was here so spacious that he could rise on his knees; but there was no other exit except the one where they cut off every chance of flight for the desperate bear by the intervention of their own persons.

"Wah!" said Tessakeh, as he rose up by Werner's side, who was just engaged in bringing the sight-notch of his rifle in a direct line with the restless animal's sparkling eye. "Wah! a comfortable

A Sudden Charge.

wigwam, but a bad fighting-ground." And then, noticing the direction of Werner's rifle, he whispered to him—

"Don't shoot at his head; if you miss we are both lost, and the brute does not keep quiet a moment. Aim at the breast-bone, and, if the bullet does not hit the heart, he will be mortally wounded, and less dangerous to us. But wait; I will keep Blackie quiet for a moment, and then may my white brother aim surely and hit him home."

Tessakeh had scarce uttered these words when he imitated the bleating of the young deer. The bear listened attentively when he heard the shrill, unexpected sound, and, at the same moment, the massive vault re-echoed the thundering crack of the rifle. But, as if struck by an electric shock, and before the smoke dispersed around the barrel, the bear rushed upon the hunter, who had not even time to throw down his gun and draw his broad knife, but, hurled backwards by the terrible strength and force of the beast, his head struck against the rock near him, and he became unconscious.

Tessakeh, however, who was lying on his stomach, with the sharp blade in his hand, saw through the smoke the rush of the animal at the right moment, and, conjecturing that the bear had no hostile intentions, but desired to reach the open air, he kept close to the ground, and drove his knife to the hilt into the beast as it bounded over him and disappeared in the darkness.

Werner was stunned by the blow, but recovered almost immediately. Still, he could not remember for the moment where he was, for the darkness of night surrounded him. He suddenly heard a knife struck against a flint, and a consciousness of his situation returned to him.

"Tessakeh," he cried, "where are our lights?"

"If the bear has not taken them with him, they must lie near us, the Indian replied, laconically; "but my face is wet, and I taste blood. Tessakeh's blow is sure, and the bear will not return to see whether the enemy is resting in his bed.

He had, in the meanwhile, lighted some tinder, then tore a piece of his hunting-shirt off, and a cheerful light soon shone once more around them. They now examined the place where the bear had lain, and found thick, black drops of blood up to the spot where Tessakeh wounded him, and from thence the blood was scattered all round the cave. The Indian was quite covered with it. Werner was about to load his rifle again, but Tessakeh prevented him.

"The shot was a good one," he said; "and if the blood did not flow directly, my knife opened a road for it. We shall not have to search far."

"Why have you blown out your candle though, Tessakeh? The immoderate brilliancy surely did not blind your eyes?"

"Does my brother know how long we shall have to stay in the

cave? If the bear has fallen in the narrow passage which is between here and the pit, the tall man at the fire without will see the sun rise and set before we can return to him."

"Confound it!" said Werner, "I did not think of that. If he sticks there, we are shut up. Ha! I feel as if the air were already growing thicker. Come, Tessakeh, let us hurry. I shall not feel comfortable till I know what we have to fear."

Silently the two men crawled along the path by which they had come, and reached the abyss without finding the bear, though the thick, curdled blood they found showed that he was severely wounded, and could not have fled far.

"It would be shameful," Werner muttered, who now crawled behind the Indian, "if he is lying at the bottom of the pit, for we should have had all our fun for nothing, and, devil take me, if I follow him down."

"Wah!" Tessakeh cried, who, with Werner's candle in his hand, as he wished to save his own, which was the shortest, held it for a moment down into the pit, and then looked across to the opposite side, where they had crossed at the risk of their lives, "Wah!"

"Is he at the bottom?" the German asked hurriedly.

"I wish he was," the Indian muttered to himself. "Our lights will burn down, and we shall hunger and thirst, but not reach the other side of the pit."

"But, Tessakeh, what is there to prevent us? Why shall we not reach the other side?" Werner asked in terror, as he strove to crawl up to the Indian's side and find out what caused his remark.

The latter drew close to the rock, and, holding his light over the abyss so that the beams played on the other side, he said, "Here is the pit, but where is the passage out?"

The more tranquil German himself uttered a cry of horror when he saw the opposite passage so thoroughly blocked up by the body of the dead bear, that there was not the slightest prospect of getting across without falling down the chasm, as there was not an inch of firm ground on which to rest either hand or arm.

"Tessakeh!' Werner at length broke the silence that was growing painful, "we cannot stop here, and we cannot expect any help from

Redham, for he has no candle, and would never find his way in the dark through the water, nor, if he really found it, would he venture it if twenty lives were at stake; and I cannot blame him, for I shuddered, though I had a light. But here our situation is growing worse every minute, for our candles are burning away; so, with God's help, I will make the attempt. If I cannot reach the bear, but fall into the pit, it will look very bad, and we shall be buried alive; but if I succeed, I will then move the old fellow out of the way."

Round the Fire.

CHAPTER III.

BEAR MEAT AT LAST.

THE Indian made no reply, and Werner laid his rifle and po
horn aside, removed his wet, heavy leggings, to have no
about him that could impede his movements, and, as on the pre
occasion, pressing elbows and knees against the sides of the ca
hovered over the gloomy abyss, and in a few moments reache
other side. But in vain he tried to move the heavy, helpless ca
of the dead bear; the monster lay motionless, occupying the
space, and an object of terror to his murderers even in death.

With all the strength which Nature had given him, and whi
fear of death augmented, he now made with his right arm
attempt, as he could not remove the left from the rock, for f

losing his balance. At this moment his right foot slipped from one of the projecting stalactites: missing its support, his body followed, and he would have infallibly fallen down the pit had he not seized the rock at the right moment with both hands, and saved himself, though his whole body hung in the abyss.

This certainly afforded him but consolation, and only appeared to delay his inevitable fate for a few moments, for he would not have been able to endure this painful position long, exhausted as he was by hunger and fatigue: but Tessakeh, quickly perceiving his danger, called to him to hold on for a few moments—he would try to save him. Placing the light on the ground at the edge of the pit, lest it might go out and leave them in perfect darkness, he commenced his passage over the chasm, but, warned by Warner's accident, backwards. He succeeded in fixing his feet close by the side of the bear. By this he was at least saved from slipping down; and he then set to work, with the strength of despair, in crawling through past the bear, for his body was much more slightly built than the German's.

The cave was terribly narrow, and the beast very powerful and fat, still he succeeded, after several minutes of almost superhuman exertion, and soon found himself on the other side of the animal. But it was almost equally difficult to move it and drag it towards him, for he could not spare a moment to rest if he wished to save his comrade. The projecting stalactites were a great assistance to him, however, and against these he planted his feet, and drew the heavy animal towards him.

The perspiration poured from him in streams, and he was stopping for a moment to draw breath, when Werner's weak voice reached his ear, assuring him that he could not endure his position half a minute longer.

"Courage, courage!" Tessakeh cried; "the brute is moving, and my brother will be able to breathe freely in a short while. Courage!" and with renewed strength he tried to drag the colossus. It gave a little —a little more. He took a fresh hold, and then drew the lifeless carcass at least a foot towards him. With lightning speed he forced his way past the body, and seized Werner's wrist with his right hand.

"Swing yourself up, so that I can seize your belt!" he cried to him. Werner was unable to do it, and whispered faintly, "I cannot hold on longer, I must let go!"

His strength was gone, and Tessakeh saw it. Losing no more time in words, he left hold of the white man's wrist, rapidly cut a hole in the skin of the bear, in which he inserted his left hand to have a holdfast, and then bent down, and seized Werner's belt with the other. The latter scarce felt the weight taken off his stiffened arms before he exerted his strength for one last attempt. He raised himself, and soon lay with the upper part of his body in the cave, supported by the Indian.

He could do no more, for the carcass of the bear still closed the entrance to the passage; but in this position he was, at least, able to rest a little, and no longer feared that he must fall into the pit. Tessakeh, in the meanwhile, recommenced his attempts on the bear, in order to move it into a more spacious part of the cave.

At length he succeeded, and Werner swung himself entirely up. Both men were, however, exhausted to death, and the German, who was worn out not merely by corporeal labour, but by his fear of death, lay for half an hour almost unconsciously by the side of the Indian.

Tessakeh, who himself required rest, at least, for a short space, was the first to recover, and cheering his comrade, warned him against giving way too utterly to his feelings of exhaustion.

"Our way is long and fatiguing," he said, "and my brother will not be able to endure the gnawing pangs of hunger. Can he eat the flesh raw? Before the cave a fire burns, and a warm camp invites us to rest and refresh ourselves. Here the air is damp, and darkness will surround us in a short time. Our candles are nearly all burnt out!"

Werner, who himself saw how little they must delay, unless they desired to look for their road in perfect darkness, thought with horror of the cave filled with water, collected his strength, and through their mutual exertions, they moved the heavy mass of flesh —Werner pushing and Tessakeh pulling—further forward, where the cave widened so much for a little distance that they were able to sit upright.

Here the Indian quitted the white man, who required rest more than he did, and crawled back to the abyss to fetch Werner's clothing, rifle, and the candles from the other side. The light was almost burned out, but he had retained his own small piece to light them on their onward track, and he quickly returned to the German, in order to finish the tedious task of moving the heavy carcass forward in the narrow cave.

Werner proposed that they should skin him, and merely take the hams and ribs, wrapped in the skin, away with them; but Tessakeh would not listen to it, and asserted, not quite without reason, that they would be able to move the bear to the entrance of the cave in as short a time as they would require to skin and cut him up.

"But how shall we get him up?" Werner objected. "Nothing will be left us but to perform the business we now defer in the water. We three together could not possibly bring the heavy beast into daylight without cutting him up."

"My white brother will see how easily we shall secure our booty, and say Tessakeh is right," the Indian replied, and, without wasting their time in further discussion, they commenced their task, after Werner had again put on and fastened his leggings. Slowly, very slowly, they advanced, yet they reached the rather wider part of the cave, and soon came to the spot, without exchanging another word, where the water commenced, and where they must wade through it again before reaching daylight once more.

Till now, their waxlight had also served them faithfully; but it burned down, flickered, and expired! Darkness surrounded the hunters, and, for a few minutes, neither of them dared to speak!

At length, Tessakeh broke the silence by saying, "It is good! we should have been forced to leave the light behind us, for my brother has not three hands—two to drag the bear with, and one to hold the candle. We will go to work."

"But, hang it, Tessakeh! wade into that dark hole filled with water, and no light! it is, indeed, no trifle," the German replied, somewhat despondingly.

"Did my brother think before catching hold of the rock when he was falling into the pit?" the Indian asked.

"Think! that was a pretty time for thinking," Werner said, with a laugh. "What else could I have done?"

"And what else will my brother do here? My ear is open, and listens to the voice of the white man."

"You are right, Tessakeh," Werner said, somewhat ashamed; "now, as you always are; but that you may see that I will make up for it, let me go first. There is my rifle, do not throw it down when you pass; I will fetch it afterwards. Now, though, we must take care not to miss our road."

"The cave is straight, and there is no side passage," the Indian said; "there will be no room for my brother to leave the right path, and the warming fire of the 'tall man' will soon welcome us."

Werner had crept in front, and, feeling his way, with Tessakeh's assistance, he dragged the bear into the water.

Night covered the two men as with a mantle, and their situation in a narrow cave, not two feet in height, and half-filled with water, was by no means one of the most enviable. Still their hearts had been steeled in the open forest by continuous dangers and privations, and without a word they continued their road, slowly, but surely.

Although their tour in the water was, on the one hand, so unpleasant, their burden could be moved all the more easily in it, and it cost them scarcely any further difficulty. After hardly a quarter of an hour's exertion, the blessed daylight shone above them, as a reward for their heroic perseverance, through the chimney-like opening, when they reached the foot of the tree that served as a ladder.

"Hullo!" Werner cried with all his strength, and holding his hands funnel-wise to his mouth to increase the sound, "Hullo, up there!"

At the same moment the entrance was obscured, and Redham's cheerful voice sounded down, "The deuce take me if I'm not glad you've come at last. I fancied you had made up your minds to settle down there."

"Not a moment longer than was absolutely necessary," Werner cried, as he climbed up the rough tree with the agility of a cat. "But, hallo!" he said once more, and this time in surprise, for, round a tremendous fire, five backwoodsmen were lying. Horses neighed, dogs barked, and the men sprang up to greet him.

He quickly clambered out of the gloomy hole, and drew a deep breath in God's free and glorious Nature. Tessakeh was by his side almost at the same moment, and both found themselves speedily surrounded by the strangers, who shook their hands cordially, and wished to know how the hunt had come off, for both the Indian and Werner were almost smothered in blood. Werner, however, stood on tiptoe, and looking over their shoulders towards the fire, where several dainty pieces of venison and large lumps of juicy turkey-meat were roasting, he pushed all the inquirers on one side, pulled out his knife as he seated himself by the fire, and attacking the provisions, he assured them, with full cheeks, that he would be as dumb as a fish till he had appeased his raving hunger.

The others laughingly followed his example, and it was not till all the meat roasting at the fire was consumed, and fresh pieces, spitted on fresh splinters of wood, promised a second meal, that Werner's tongue was loosened, and, he began to tell the men, who listened attentively, about the difficulties and dangers they had undergone, and how Tessakeh had saved his life, twice. With these words, he offered the brown son of the forest, who was gnawing the leg-bone of a turkey very contentedly by his side, his right hand, and pressed the Indian's greasy paw very warmly and heartily, as he said—

"Tessakeh, you have done me a service I shall never forget, and it will not be my fault if I do not try to requite it by doing the same for you."

"My white brother speaks well," the Indian replied, as he withdrew his hand from the German's; "but it is not the first trail we have followed together, and it will not be the last. When Tessakeh camps at night, the buffalo hide will always guard two men from the rain. Tessakeh and his white brother are one!"

"And did your candles last to the end?" Redham asked. "Confound it, you were more than eighteen hours in the hole!"

"They went out, and we were forced to work in the darkness," Werner replied. "I tell you, Redham, the darkness was so thick down there that you might have cut it with a knife; and then the voyage by water—brr! I shudder, even now, when I think I must go through it once again to fetch my rifle."

"Have you got the bear close to the entrance?" one of the hunters asked.

"It lies by the tree that we put down."

"Why ever are we lying here then, and looking at the clouds?" another cried, "when, scarcely a hundred feet from us, such glorious bear-ribs can be found. Give us a lift, my lads!" he continued, as he sprang up and unfastened a long rope from the neck of his horse, "Werner can go down once more and fasten the rope round the bear's body—he is wet through already—and while he is fetching his rifle, we'll bring the old fellow to light."

"Good!" said Werner; "I'm agreeable; but have not any of you a candle? for I should like to have a light; and, besides, I do not know if I could find the opening again in the dark."

"Here's one," said a hunter, as he took a taper from the folds of his blanket, "and if you want company, I'll go with you."

"Thank'ye, thank'ye," said Werner, as he lighted the candle and approached the hole, "that is unnecessary, and you would get wet through for nothing; the distance is short, and I'll soon cover it. Throw me down the end of the line."

With these words he again disappeared in a narrow hole, and soon gave the signal to heave; but Tessakeh, who feared lest the single line might break from the tremendous weight, let down another, which Werner, by his directions, fastened round the fore-paws and body of the beast, and, with united exertions, and the merry shouts of the hunters, the prey acquired with so much difficulty lay near the fire, saluted with loud barks from the pack of dogs, who surrounded and licked the carcass. Soon after, when the improvised ladder had again been let down, which they had removed for greater convenience in hauling up the bear, Werner also made his appearance with his rifle, and found in the ribs of the bear a slight reward for the dangers to which he had been exposed. And both he and Tessakeh declared that they would not descend into the cave again if there were twenty bears in it, for it was, as the Indian not unjustly remarked, "too much trouble and too little meat."

THE WILD MAN OF THE WOODS.

THE WILD MAN OF THE WOODS.

Stewart brings news of the Menagerie

CHAPTER I.

NEARLY in the centre of Arkansas, and on the banks of the St. Francis river, there is a small squatters' town, called Francisville, founded more through speculation than through any actual necessity, for the three houses which formed the central, and, indeed, the entire town, had stood for years as when the first immigrants settled there. A couple of broad roads intersect the forest, and, bearing the haughty names of Main Front and Washington streets (as was indicated by a small board nailed to a tree), were, in addition to the City Hotel, really all that might induce a stranger to believe that he had exchanged forest life for that of a town, and was no longer in the utter wilderness—the best hunting-ground in the United States, where he need feel no astonishment if a real live bear met him in broad day in Front-street, or disappeared in the scrub of Washington-street or the market-place.

Wolves, bears, and panthers frequently at night imprinted their footmarks on these chief streets, and the next morning mine host of the City Hotel, leaving the business in the care of his wife and a small negro boy, would set off with a pack of dogs in chase of his uninvited guests, frequently the only ones, though, he had. The neighbourhood was composed of a wild, careless, and independent people of squatters and hunters, who rarely had a cent of ready money, but often brought in the produce of the forest, such as bear's fat, honey, smoked deer-hams, skins, and bear-hides, which they exchanged for powder and shot, whisky, and the other luxuries of forest life. But, for all that, the traffic of this little place was far from inconsiderable, especially in the summer months, for the main road from Memphis, the capital of Tennessee, to Little Rock, the chief town of Arkansas, ran through it; nor was there any other road than this to the Northern White River, Batesville, &c. In winter, however, and in truth for nine long months, the whole district, a flat bottom land, was under water—the postman was the only person to pass along the roads for weeks, and the host then had his "winter sleep," as his neighbours called it.

The people who principally used this road, even in summer, were nearly all pioneers, engaged in their usual western wanderings, with wagons and beasts of burden, with now and then a travelling pedlar from the Yankee States, with wooden clocks, or a chest of "all sorts," calicos and ear-rings, spoons, tape, combs, needles, buttons, thread, &c.; and even these formed a subject spoken of as something extraordinary. Once, indeed, when one of these pedlars carried a shot gun—a French double-barrel, with the proper shot for it—and offered it for sale, the report of it spread in every direction, and folks came in a long distance along the country road to see the man who had the "thin double-barrelled rifle," and shot from it a handful of bullets as small as rape-seed.

They behaved, in fact, in all extraordinary matters, like children with playthings, and treated them often just as recklessly—as the reader will soon see from this slight sketch.

It was in the summer of 1852 that a hunter, followed by four famous dogs, rode into the little town at a greater speed than people were accustomed to see any one arrive; and the landlord, forgetting his greeting, stood in the doorway, anxiously awaiting to hear what had brought him so quickly.

"Bless my soul, Wilson," the backwoodsman said, fully answering the expectations he had raised, "there is coming along the road behind us the most remarkable thing this child ever saw; and if you don't soon have the most wonderful visitor that can be imagined, may I go out hunting for the rest of my days with a smooth-bored gun, and not know how to distinguish a wolf's trail from a dog's!"

"What does it look like?" the host asked, who wanted to form an idea of the object, and really believed that it was some remarkable beast that had shown itself for the first time in the forest; "has it teeth and a long tail?"

"May I be hanged if you haven't hit the nail on the head!" the hunter said, leaping from his horse and removing saddle and bridle, which the nigger boy carried into the house. "It looks like a wild beast, has a large beard, and chatters like a blue jay; but what it has got with it is the most wonderful. Only think, Wilson, a little Frenchman is coming along the road with a whole parcel of wolf's traps on four-wheeled carriages."

"Wolf's traps!" Wilson said, and his face was drawn into a broad grin of delight—"wolf's traps, Stewart? And a Yankee is bringing traps into our settlement? That's capital—does he expect to catch anything?"

"Catch!" the backwoodsman said in amazement; "they're all

full, I tell you, of the most astonishing beasts that you can imagine in the world."

"Full!" the landlord repeated incredulously, as he shook his head —"full? nonsense! What do the Yankees know about setting a trap, though they are so clever in selling onions, or humbugging a poor backwoodsman to buy a clock?"

"I tell you again, it isn't a Yankee," the hunter replied; "it's a Frenchman. But what I was going to say, Wilson—have you ever seen a man feed a catamount?"

"Feed a catamount!" the old man repeated contemptuously; "Stewart, you must have a precious large whisky bottle at home to have lasted so long; for you haven't been at my house for at least a month."

"Well, I give you my word he has one with him, and feeds it as I do Dick, and Bob, and Jerry here," the hunter said, eagerly. "But you will witness it yourself this evening," he added, "for I can see the dust of his carts rising there among the trees. The fellow intends to stay a week in Francisville, and give exhibitions, to which he intends to invite the whole neighbourhood."

"Invite!" the landlord said in surprise. "What! is he going to kill the beasts and serve them up to American Christians? Deuce take the French pagan!"

"Well, he will have company enough," the other replied, with a laugh; "for the day after to-morrow is court day, and they will come in from all sides, so he'll have no want of guests."

"But he shan't sell any liquors," the landlord said, with a hearty curse; "my licence costs me heavily enough. But whoever likes can be his guest, though I do not think many of our fellows will accept the invitation."

Such were the ideas of the backwoodsmen about the astounding procession which had just become visible and was rapidly approaching; and when a couple of neighbours joined them they also puzzled their brains as to what the stranger was going to begin in the forest with such an amazing cargo. That he intended to show what he brought with him for money did not occur to one of them; and, indeed, could not, for only very few of the farmers and hunters had a quarter-dollar in cash in their cabins, probably lying on the mantelpiece to pay for any letter that might arrive by accident. The postman would not take bear-skins and deer-horns, except at scandalously low prices.

The stranger, in the meanwhile, drew near. The dogs began barking, and Watch, an old bear follower, which had now got scent of the animals, raised his nose high and inquisitively—he sniffed, sneezed, and then crawled off cautiously into the scrub, after looking round for his master.

"Ha-ha-ha!" Stewart laughed, who had been following the movements of the dog. "Look, Wilson! the old boy has got scent of the catamount! Watch, my boy, here! back, I say, or the Frenchman will laugh at you, stupid beast, for having the best of you. Here, Watch, to heel!"

A horseman at this moment galloped up the road on a black, active, long-haired pony, in front of the train; and, at the first, moment, the barking of the dogs quite drowned any question or salutation. The Frenchman, in the meanwhile, lifted his hat very politely, and, riding up to the men, who were shouting at their dogs, and rendering the confusion worse, he asked them, when he could get a word in, where would be the best place to pitch his camp for a week or ten days.

"The best place, sir? why, anywhere!" Stewart said, with a laugh; "there, at the corner of Sycamore and Washington streets, or here on the market-place, when Wilson has removed his wood: it's all the same where you find a place."

"Corner of Washington and Sycamore?" the Frenchman repeated, rather amazed, looking all around; "corner of what, gentlemen?"

"Well, the sign is large enough and clear enough," Wilson, the landlord, said, partly piqued that his town was insulted by the difficulty of finding the streets, and, besides, rather alarmed whether the stranger did not intend to open an opposition to him with his caravan of traps and other objects, which now slowly approached, drawn by oxen, along the road.

"Ah, then, very good, messieurs," the little old man said, turning his horse to the indicated spot, and rode round it, when he found it suited him, and then bowed gratefully to the men, who were wa ing his every movement. Then, giving the spur to his active l animal, he went to meet the approaching train.

Stewart had certainly some reason for feeling surprised; Monsieur Bertrand was, in fact, the first human being who had attempted to introduce such a cargo of living animals, partly obtai from their own forests, to the inhabitants of Francisville; and he the Frenchman was not wrong in his conjecture, that the inhabit of this forest district would find an interesting sight in the anir that peopled the woods around them, but whose movements t never watched so calmly and safely as they could now do behind iron bars. But M. Bertrand was soon to learn that feeling a pleas and paying for that pleasure are two different things.

The wagons were drawn, by his directions, so as to form a se circle, or, rather, to inclose three sides of a square. When this done, the men unyoked the oxen, took off their yokes, and allo them to graze at liberty, while M. Bertrand began arranging cages on the carriages, which were, however, carefully covered w hangings.

The dogs had, in the meanwhile, collected around, and execu such a barking and howling that it would have rendered any comn man deaf; but the little Frenchman did not drive them bac indeed, that would have been labour lost—but regarded them, some measure, as a cheap announcement of his curiosities, and t their owners' attention would be more attracted by it.

Nor was it long ere Wilson overcame the unjust prejudice he l at first formed against the stranger, and walked, with Stewart, look at the Frenchman, who was putting up a cage, and screwing the iron bars.

When they arrived at the cage, it really seemed as if the d would fall on the contents, and tear in pieces everything that ca in their way, so fearful was the noise they made; and it was imp sible, at the beginning, to enter on a conversation; but when noise had, in a degree, lulled, Wilson began—

"I say, sir!"

"Monsieur?"

"Eh, what?" the backwoodsman said, to whom the word was strange.

"What can I do for you, sare?" the Frenchman corrected himself, thus evading the foreign word, but speaking in dislocated English.

"Where are you going to, if I may ask?" the landlord inquired; for he could not believe that the Frenchman had come direct to Francisville with such a cargo, and then meant to go back again.

"To Little Rock, and from there down the Arkansas, to Napoleon and the Mississippi."

"Ahem!" the backwoodsman said, who did not exactly comprehend why a man was proceeding *from* the Mississippi with the intention of reaching that river; "but the other way about"—pointing with his thumb over his shoulder—"would have been nearer."

The Frenchman laughed, and replied with a shrug of his shoulders—

"Certainly, monsieur—sare, I would say; but to get through the world a man must not always choose the most direct route, but go round about and in and out."

"Yes, yes; it is the same in hunting," Stewart confirmed him; "but it must be very awkward with such a heap of chests—quiet, Dick! quiet, Watch!—you're bursting the drums of my ears with your whining."

"And what may there be in them?" Wilson now said, as he walked up to one of them, and tried to peep under the oilskin cover. "Bless me, if these are not famous wolf-traps—only in our country no wolf would trust itself behind the iron bars—but there's something tapping there."

"I must beg you, sare, leave it alone," the Frenchman said; but the curious backwoodsman had already lifted the cloth a little with a stick he held in his hand, and started back as if struck by lightning, for a brown hairy paw passed through the bars, and seized the stick.

Wilson stared as if he had seen a ghost.

"Bless my soul, what was that?" he shouted, and fell back involuntarily a couple of paces, as if not certain whether the paw might not emerge again and seize something else. "Does he bite, old fellow!"

The Frenchman, whose object it was to have the marvels of his show spread about the forest as quickly as possible, decided on delighting the two backwoodsmen with a sight of the ape, just as he had shown Stewart the catamount on the road, and he therefore suddenly drew back the curtain which had hitherto covered the barred prison of a large chimpanzee, the most valuable specimen in his menagerie.

"Darn my buttons!" both men exclaimed on noticing the marvel, "if that don't blow the lid off the pot."

"Jimmy! where did you catch it?" Stewart shouted, employing the first name that occurred to him, while he bent down before the cage, and put his elbows on his knees, to have a better look at the monkey. "Is it eatable?"

"By this and by that, if it isn't a wild man!" Wilson interposed. "He was caught down there in the Cash swamps. Prince was after him twice, but couldn't come up with him."

"And there's no fall in the trap," Stewart said, now examining the cage carefully on all sides. "I should like to know how he got in."

"It is a monkéh—an ape," the little Frenchman remarked, revelling in the amazement of his spectators—"comes from India, lives in a very hot country, very warm, and has much *ressemblance* with men."

"Much what?" Stewart said, gazing at the stranger with open mouth.

"Much *ressemblance*," the latter continued; "much, much like you; *comprenez?*"

"Ahem!" Wilson said; "he can climb up trees?"

"Yes, climb up trees; and many other animals here—extraordinary beasts."

"Well, out with 'em, old fellow," Stewart encouragingly said—"out with 'em; I am much inclined to pass them in review."

"*Non, non!*" the little Frenchman said, stepping before him as he prepared to examine another cage; "not this evening; no more; to-morrow evening, *grande entrée*—grand exhibition in Francisville—see all when all in order; this evening see nothing, for nothing in order."

"A—wh—ch!" the catamount yelled at this moment from its cage.

"Seize him!" the old hunter shouted, almost instinctively, on hearing the sound; and the dogs, which had till then been hardly restrained, made a furious attack on the cage, tore down the curtain, but soon flew back howling from the sharp claws of the catamount, as the Frenchman interposed with all his people, and drove back the raging animal.

"By Jingo, a catamount!" Wilson shouted in triumph, as he saw the curtain torn down. "Out with him; give him a fair start—Jimmy! hu—pih!"

And once more the dogs, encouraged by the shout, were about to bound on the imprisoned animal, and the men could only keep them at bay with poles and sticks. At length, however, the little Frenchman succeeded in mastering them with a heavy hunting-whip, and driving them out of the square. Then, after covering the cages, he ordered his men to make a fence round the wagons to keep the dogs at bay, and prevent them rushing in at the moment of exhibition.

Wilson and Stewart now went back to the hotel, for they soon found that the little Frenchman was not inclined to make further concessions to them. But the whole conversation in the little town that evening, irrespective of the court-day and the coming election, turned solely on the stranger's collection of traps; and the most improbable suppositions and conclusions were arrived at as to why the strange man took the beasts about the country—whether he wished to eat them, or show them to the people, in the hope of receiving commissions to catch more. Stewart and Wilson had a bet of a deer-skin as to the place where the Frenchman caught the "wild boy;" Stewart asserting that he had been brought from Leckie's Elbow—a curve in the Mississippi, far down in Tennessee, where one was said to be living in the swamp—while Wilson insisted he was nailed, in some way or other, in the Cash Swamps; and he should himself have captured him on one occasion, had not his foot slipped and plumped him headforemost into one of the numerous bayous there.

Thus the next day arrived—a Tuesday—and the morning passed

calmly and peaceably. The Frenchman had completed his arrangements during the night, and spanned a species of tent over the wagons, which completely enclosed his little menagerie, and allowed nothing to be seen during the morning. In the afternoon, however, the little town grew very lively, and visitors rattled in from all sides, on little ponies, or on splendid horses, which the backwoodsmen were in the habit of breeding.

The next day was the first Wednesday in September, and a court-day for the county, so that the farmers and squatters came in from all the country round; some as plaintiffs or defendants, others as witnesses, but the majority to see the sport. Of course no other conversation was heard on this day save the marvels of the tent; for the Frenchman was still, at three in the afternoon, in the menagerie, and the door was "tied up," and thus closed to every stranger and uninvited visitor.

At length, when some thirty "neighbours" had collected from the whole country and every point of the compass, while new arrivals came in every quarter of an hour, the canvas door was drawn back, "Monsieur Bertrand," as Wilson called him, stepped out, fastened a large poster near the door of the tent, and nailed a smaller one to the side of the hotel.

A few seconds later a crowd was assembled round the bills; and some who managed to read the enormous letters now announced to the others, with a shout, that the whole affair was a menagerie, and that Monsieur Bertrand had solely come to Francisville to exhibit it to them.

"Hurrah for Bertrand!" the crowd shouted; "he is a fine fellow; hurrah for the Frenchman!" and the jolly fellows were about to rush to the tent, when Wilson's eye, which had been carefully studying the bill, to see if there was anything in it about eating and drinking, suddenly fell on the price of admission, and he stopped their advance by a loud shout of admiration.

"Bless me, boys!" he said, pointing with his left hand to that part of the bill where the ominous words were, "it costs something to see the traps!"

"Costs!" the crowd shouted, incredulously—"what can it cost, then? Of course we will treat him to a quart of whisky. That wont ruin us; so come along, boys."

"Stop a minute!" the landlord shouted; "here it stands in print: Every one who wishes to go in must pay a quarter-dollar in money or money's worth. Hallo! Monsieur Bertran'—you there!—is that correct?"

"*C'est vrai, Monsieur,*" the little Frenchman replied, as he came up with a smile and a bow. "It is all in order. A quarter-dollar *entrée*, for entrance to see and admire the menagerie. Very little."

"Indeed! and so we are to pay a quarter-dollar for very little?" an old backwoodsman here interrupted, who had been gazing on the stranger with the most unbounded amazement. "Well, I'm hanged if that isn't cool! Comes here, puts up a tent in the middle of our town, and instead of behaving like a friend and neighbour, as we might naturally expect, he asks a quarter-dollar before any man can cross his threshold. It's wonderful what impudence strangers have!"

"But much to see, monsieur," the little Frenchman replied; "a monkéh, a catamount, four little monkéhs, two other little monkéhs, an African leopard, and a lama, an animal from South America—very far, very far—and only a quarter-dollar. Beasts eat many, very many, quarter-dollars."

"Eat quarter-dollars!" the old man said, his eyes and mouth growing momentarily wider—"did ever a Christian hear the like of that? The Frenchman feeds his beasts on quarter-dollars!"

It took a long time before the little man could explain to the crowd that collected around him the nature and character of his collection. But not one would expend a quarter-dollar, payable in deer-hides, furs, or bear-skins, before he knew exactly what it looked like in there; and, as Monsieur Bertrand entertained a very strong suspicion that they would not pay afterwards, he proposed a compromise, and offered to show the marvels of his menagerie gratis to a deputation of two men, and leave it to them to pay him the admission, if they thought it worth it, and to make a report of what they had seen.

Unanimously the old squatter and the judge of the nearest township were chosen; and the old man declared his readiness, "for they couldn't frighten him;" but if they fancied they would induce him to pay "angtray," or whatever they called it, they were wofully mistaken. Of course he would give his quarter-dollar's worth of bear-skin if the affair inside seemed worth it, but not otherwise.

The Frenchman now led the deputation into the interior of the tent, and they remained about half-an-hour in it, while those standing without heard nothing but the strange growling, purring, and whining of the animals, or a loud cry of amazement from Smithly, the old squatter. At length the curtain was drawn back, and the old man, shaking his head, and smiting his fist on his hand, a perfect image of amazement, stepped out into the open air, followed by his equally astonished companion.

"Gentlemen!" he began, so soon as he had reached neutral ground, and the others pressed round him, "here is my hat; and, indeed, monsieur, you have earned it; for I'll be hanged if that doesn't beat cock-fighting! A quarter-dollar! I'd walk ten miles to see what I have just seen, and I wouldn't do that for a quarter-dollar."

"Then it was fine, Smithly?" "What did you see?" "How did it look?" "What is there in there?" "Are we to go in?" These, and a thousand other questions, were heaped on the old man. The Frenchman could not have selected a better man than the squatter for his purpose; for the mere amazement depicted on his face spoke volumes to the curiosity of the backwoodsmen, although they could not yet comprehend how anything was to be paid for going into another man's house and looking round it: that was quite contrary to nature.

"If I only knew where he caught that little specimen of a man!" the old squatter said, to whom this was the most remarkable thing in the whole business. "Confound his traps; they have no fall or cover, yet they shut quite tight."

"Well, didn't you ask him, Smithly?" one of the bystanders said.

"Asked? yes, but it was no use. Bless my soul, what stuff that fellow talks—you can make nothing of it. And the wild men he calls monkehs—what he means by it I don't know; for we call them simple forest men, or wild men—chattered and shrieked, and the spotted panther howled, and an old vagabond of a catamount he has there—devil take the beast, why don't he kill it?—whined and yelled enough to drive one mad."

"And has he really wild men?" one man, rushing forward, turned back to ask.

"Wild men?" the squatter repeated, gazing on him in surprise; "you ask if he has wild men—why, he has a whole nest of them! We only saw one and a heap of young ones, and they look—the Lord knows what strangers we have not got in our forests!"

The questioner did not stop to hear the end of the speech, but ran at full speed, followed by several others, back to the hotel. There he had left his various articles of barter, and did not wish to lose a moment in inspecting the marvels with his own eyes.

The Frenchman did a good stroke of business that afternoon; for when the first reluctance to pay was overcome, the squatters went not merely once, but twice or thrice, into the wild beast show, as they called it, and had so much to tell each other, and were so desirous to show new arrivals the wonderful sight, that there was a perfect crowd in the tent; and M. Bertrand had his hands full with his extraordinary treasury, into which he took the most wonderful objects—which, however, possessed a double value for him as trader—and allowed their former owners admission into the menagerie

The thing that puzzled them most was the monkeys' tails; for they insisted, in spite of the Frenchman's protestations, on their being wild men. The stranger was so stupid that he did not know what he had caught; and they, the backwoodsmen of Arkansas, must surely be allowed to know what a wild man of the woods looked like.

It is, certainly, a peculiar circumstance, that the rumour of "wild men"—that is, of men who have turned wild, who then rush into the forests, and cannot be removed from them—should exist in the Western Forests, in spite of the fact that seldom, or never, such a thing comes to light. Frequently, after being quiet for months, the rumour breaks out afresh, and one hunter or the other declares he has found the trail of a wild man, and traced him to his home in some cave or hollow tree on the mountains. The most terrible stories are then told of former captives—how they defended themselves, used their teeth; and how Bill's father, or Jem's grandfather, in the settlement, nearly lost his life in struggling with the apparently weak mannikin, whom they were always compelled, in the end, to shoot, and could never catth alive.

And this little thin fellow of a Frenchman had caught a whole nest full—who would have expected that of the little withered stranger?

Well, as I said, they could not agree about the tail, and Stewart at last asserted (and confirmed it not only with a curse, but by an offer to bet three bottles of whisky), that the wild men were descended from the Hasscolds (neighbouring squatters), for they had all such precious long backs, that they might easily grow into a tail. This explanation seemed far too probable for any of the other men to venture the wager.

A report may appear as incredible and absurd as you will, but there is always some foundation of truth for it; and there have, in reality, been wild men, not only in Arkansas, but in many other countries. It is a remarkable fact that men, if lost for any length of time in the forest, are entirely deprived of their reason by fear and excitement; and finally, when found by others, instead of rejoicing at their salvation, leap into the nearest thicket, and try to escape man as their most dangerous foe. As proof of this, I will here tell a story of an old backwoodsman, who spent all his life in the forest.

I have forgotten his name, which, however, is not necessary for the story, but he lived in the western part of Tennessee, not far from the spot where the town of Randolph is now built, and had a small farm at the foot of the hills which run down into the Mississippi Valley. He lost his way, one cloudy day, while hunting in the enormous swamps of that district, and, instead of lying down and going to sleep quietly, as is the hunter's rule, in order to choose the direction in cool blood and perfect collectedness, he allowed himself to give way to his first impulses of fear, and began to run backwards and forwards. Hence, growing more and more excited, he at length lost consciousness. He ran day and night over the morass, and at last he formed the mad, but fixed idea, that he somehow crossed the

Mississippi, which was at least a mile wide, and must return to the other bank in order to reach his home. He had been missed, however, and his friends set out to look for him. They found him at last, though almost driven to desperation by his zig-zag trail, on the bank of the Mississippi, busily engaged in making a raft, on which to cross to the pathless wilderness of the opposite Arkansas swamps, At first they did not know what he was about; but when he heard them coming, he leaped into the reeds, and they were obliged to drag him home by force. On reaching his log hut he did not recognise it, and looked wildly around, as if meditating a fresh flight; but by degrees his senses returned to him, and the recollection of all that occurred to him.

Such men, who now and then grow quite savage, are pursued by the hunters, and even killed in self-defence; and, though it may happen so rarely, it seemed as if the truth of the story were confirmed by the presence of such creatures, just as they were thought to be in these extraordinary beasts.

The hanging of the "Catamount."

CHAPTER II.

AT first, then, as I said, the Frenchman's business went on gloriously; and the spotted panther, as they would call the leopard, however much the Frenchman might object, excited considerable interest. But the people were not satisfied with merely seeing; they also drank heartily of the whisky; and some of them began to play tricks with the animals, to tease the panther and leopard, and shake the monkeys' cages, so that the poor creatures, in their terror, clambered up the bars, and then, by gnashing their teeth, and other comical expressions of fear, caused the rough crowd to break out into noisy bursts of applause and hearty laughter.

M. Bertrand considered it at length time to close his exhibition, especially as it was growing rather difficult to make the intoxicated men pay the entrance-money; and he wished, also, to keep expectation on the stretch for the morrow, before the people grew tired of looking at the animals. Hence he requested his visitors to retire; and, when they good-humouredly obeyed, he began to fasten up the canvas, and thus, as he believed, cut of all further communication with the external world for this evening. But in this he had made a mistake.

"Hu—pih!" a fresh band of young fellows shouted, who had just gallopped into the settlement, and at the first house heard the wondrous news of the exhibition. "Hu—pih! boys. Where is the beast collection? How with it? Here comes the company that wishes to see it!"

"The steamer has just started, gentlemen," one of the men just turned out said, with a laugh. "You are a day after the fair—fire-works can't be let off twice."

"Hullo, mates! who's dead, and what's to pay?" one of the new arrivals asked him.

"The shop's shut, gentlemen!" he said, delighting in the disappointed expectation of the late comers, and inexhaustible in similes —"shop's shut, and key fallen overboard."

"Don't bother yourself about the key, Bob!" the other replied, as he leaped from his horse and gave it to the little nigger. "Confound the key! if the door is still there, this child will get in. And you, boy, look after my horse; rub him down, and give him some hay in half-an-hour, or I'll hang you up by your ears."

"Joking aside, Ned," the other went on mocking, "the exhibition is over—the ladies and gentlemen have all gone home, and the lights are put out."

"Hurrah, boys! who'll go with me?" the first shouted. "I'll be hanged if I go to bed till I have seen the beasts! Let's climb over the fence and show them to ourselves."

It required no great persuasion to get the half-drunken and curious fellows to follow. They rushed upon the Frenchman's tent —who met them with his usual invincible politeness—and demanded admission.

"Pardon, messieurs," was the reply; "no more this evening. Monkéh very tired—seen too many people to-day."

"Monkey be hanged!" the leader of the band shouted; "we want to see your wild man, old boy; so pull open the canvas, unless you want us to cut it into strips."

"No *entrée*, gentleman!" the Frenchman objected, as he barred the way—"no *entrée*. I must fetch Justice of Peace if you employ force. I am here in my house."

"Oh, go to grass with your house!" the first speaker, a rough, wild fellow, said; and, hurling the Frenchman on one side, he pulled out his bowie-knife, and cut through the cords that prevented entrance. With one bound, then, he reached the interior, still holding his knife in his hand, and the whole band followed, in spite of the violent and passionate protestations of the stranger, whose rights were thus invaded.

Although the better-thinking portion of the townsmen saw very clearly that, in the present state of matters, they could not alter what had happened, or induce the savage men to make any concession, still they did not wish the stranger to be treated unfairly on their soil, and now demanded that the intruders should at least pay the admission-money. At first the Frenchman would not accept it, and insisted on their retiring; but when he found that he was not in a position to enforce that, he put up with the payment, on the condition that they should only remain half-an-hour, as it would be dark by that time. As some of the new arrivals had really silver-money about them to pay the lawyers, and were not in a condition to be chary of it, Monsieur Bertrand was soon perfectly satisfied, and began to explain his animals to his audience for, at least, the fiftieth time that day.

But, like the former spectators, the present audience only cared for the chimpanzee. They hardly deigned to bestow a glance on the "spotted panther;" and it was not till one declared it was painted that attention was drawn to it. Of course he wished to convince himself of the fact, so he wetted his finger, and, passing his arm through the bars, rubbed the leopard's skin. He fared badly in consequence ; for the brute turned with lightning speed, and not only tore up his sleeve, but also his arm—thus making, once for all, a serious protest against any investigation of its spots.

"And yet it is painted!" the wounded man shouted, as he held his arm and looked boldly, though at a respectful distance, at the animal ; "and if I only had the brute out here, I would prove it with my fists in its face."

"Gentlemen!" Ned now shouted over the laughing and confusion, which seemed to increase every minute—"gentlemen, that is a real wild man ; for I met one once at White River exactly like this. You have no idea what strength such a harmless-looking creature possesses."

"And I can whip the spotted panther and the dirty wild man in the bargain," the wounded man shouted, who had now bound a handkerchief round his arm. "Deuce take the scratching brute ; let it out, so that we can stand face to face."

"*You* whip the wild man?" Ned replied, who had been describing, as they came along, how a wild man had once served him, and so regarded this challenge as an insult to himself. "He'd take you and throw you over the fence, so that you wouldn't be found again for a week, even if they went to look for you with spectacles. You and the wild man—he'd show you!"

"Ned!" the angry man shouted in reply, thinking it beneath his dignity to engage with a beast, "If I couldn't whip the spotted painter and the wild man together, may I never carry a rifle again on my shoulder! Why, I'll bet ten quarts of whisky that the wretched cripple of a wild man cannot even whip that dirty catamount."

"Hurrah! ten quarts of whisky—that's a bet, Ned!" the mob shouted.

"All right," Ned replied. "Boys—ten quarts of whisky that the wild man chaws up the catamount, and picks his teeth with his short tail. Hu—pih! and now to set them to it."

"Gentlemen!" the Frenchman now shrieked, "the half-hour is up. I must beg you to go home, now, and keep the peace. Gentlemen, you understand me?"

"All right, old tortoise!" Ned said, smiting him on the shoulder so that his knees gave way.

"Hurrah! Long live the Frenchman!" the crowd now shouted and laughed. "All right; we'll go home, but the fight first."

"Shall we let 'em out here, or how is it to be managed?" Ned now asked, without troubling himself further about the owner of the animals. "Hurrah for the whisky! Give us an axe to open the cages."

"Gentlemen!" the Frenchman said, now seriously terrified, as he sprang between the men who were preparing to open the cages of the catamount and the chimpanzee; "let it be—it's my property—you must not lay hands on my property."

"Oh, go to grass!" Ned replied, contemptuously, hurling him on one side. "We don't want to lay hands on your property; your property shall settle it among themselves. Hurrah, boys! lend a hand here."

One came up with an axe, to liberate the prisoners, when another discovered the doors of the cages, and was going to open them, when Bertrand prevented it at the right moment.

"Stop, monsieur, stop!" he shouted, and anger began to gain the upper hand even with him. "Back from the cage! If you open it the catamount will escape, and we shall never see it again—five-and-twenty dollars lost!"

"I said so," Ned replied—"I said so. The wild man will chaw up the catamount, and the beast knows it, so it shows the white feather. Give him the chance to bolt, and he'll run up as far as Missouri before he stops to look back."

"That's all you know about it, I say," Bill, his opponent, said; "he may bolt, that's possible, but not from this dirty cripple of a wild man, but because you are making enough row here to frighten a cart-load of catamounts. Give him a fair and honest fight, and I swear that he'll chaw him up, body and bones."

"Hurrah, boys!" Bob now said; "we can so arrange matters

that the two beasts can fight fair and not bolt. If we thrust the two traps close together, and open the doors when they are opposite each other, the animals will pay each other a visit."

"That's a good idea; and now make haste, boys, before it grows dark!" Ned shouted, as he laid hold of one of the cages. The Frenchman tried once again to interfere, and summoned those present to aid him; but the majority were against him, and he, therefore, hurried as quickly as he could across to the hotel, to tell the judge, who had arrived an hour before, of the wild and illegal behaviour of the mob, and appeal to him for assistance. But, as is too often the case in America, where the laws are excellent, but cannot be always carried into execution in these wild countries, so it was here. The judge no sooner heard of the chance of a disturbance, than he took a lawyer friend of his by the arm, and went for a walk in the woods. He was perfectly well aware that little or nothing could be effected here by main force; and being in no way inclined to make these rough fellows his enemies, or expose himself to any danger, he prepared to get out of the way, and so could not be found. The constable did the same; and Bertrand, after being sent from one house to the other without finding the persons he sought, at length discovered that he was hopelessly left at the mercy of the mob, and determined, after the Arkansas fashion, on taking the law into his own hands.

In the meanwhile, a mad scene was taking place in the poor Frenchman's exhibition. Bob, with the aid of the others, had dragged the chimpanzee's cage close to that of the catamount, and the two doors were about to be pulled up, when some of the backwoodsmen interposed, and tried to persuade the drunken men not to destroy a stranger's property in such a wanton manner.

"Hang it!" said Ned, impudently, "we paid the fellow entrance-money, and now wish to have our sport for it; and, besides, there's a bet which must be settled—so clear the course."

"Look out, Ned!" a voice shouted at this moment, and as the daring young fellow turned a shot passed over his head, and the aim was so close that he could hear the bullet's whistling. The danger had been imminent; for Bertrand, now driven to extremities, had seized his fowling-piece to shoot Ned, as the leader of the gang; and very little punishment would have been inflicted on him for it. A friend of Ned's, however, knocked the barrel up at the right moment, and the Frenchman down; and, while a couple dragged the unconscious man away, to prevent further mischief, Ned shouted contemptuously, as he took up the gun—

"Devil take him! to fire at a man with such a thing—I have a great inclination to open all his traps. But hang it, boys, we are wasting valuable time. Now to work, that we may earn the ten quarts of whisky."

Throwing the gun on one side, and opening the two cages in spite of all objections, all pressed round to see the result of the fight between the two animals.

The catamount, being probably terrified by the disturbance around, cowered for a time in a corner of its cage, and only turned its large, cat-like eyes quickly and timidly on the men who surrounded the cage, but would not get within reach of its claws; while the chimpanzee leaped up and down the iron bars, and had not yet noticed the open door.

For a while the crowd also remained quiet, but then the catamount's eyes first fell on the open door, which it observed suspiciously; but, as it would not advance, the men began to grow impatient, and Ned shouted—

"Seize him, my boy, seize him! If the wild man in there knew that he had a catamount within arm's length—hu—pih!—how he would fall on it!"

"We'll introduce the cat to him," Bill replied, with a laugh; "then he will have no excuse"—and, seizing a stick, he stirred up the catamount, which bit and snarled, and then retired to the other end of the cage. By this it drew nearer to the opening, and being still annoyed by the stick, and probably supposing it to be a means of escape, it slipped through, and, by doing so, caused the chimpanzee no slight terror, for it now sprang up the bars and looked for a way of escape; while the catamount, on finding the cage occupied, hurriedly tried to retire.

But the attentive Bob had already cut off retreat by shutting down the door; and the cat, as if expecting an attack from the strange animal, retired to the furthest end of the cage, showing its claws and teeth more in defence than for attack.

"I'll be hanged if the wild man is not the greatest coward I ever saw in my life!" Ned said, in disgust; "he's got such a brute of a catamount before him, and don't pin him. I believe his good heart prevents him—he thinks it would be murder."

"Ha-ha-ha-ha!" Bill laughed. "Seize him, Catty, seize him! Catch hold of his tail, and see if he has any feelings—seize him!"

"Hu—pih!" the mob shouted, and the dogs outside barked and whined; while some of the wild fellows, who had committed all sorts of crimes on the Indian frontier, raised the war-cry of the Choctaws.

"Seize him, coward!" Ned also shouted, infuriated by the cowardice of his champion—and struck at the terrified ape, which was clinging to the bars. It loosed its hold and sprang back, but then fell on the hissing catamount, which seized it at once in its claws.

"Hurrah! hip, hip, hurrah!" the mob shouted. "Seize him, Catty—give it him, Jimmy!" they yelled, in mad excitement; and the chimpanzee, probably in mortal terror, and now driven to extremities, seized the catamount and bit it over the left eye, so that it sprang back to the other corner in consequence of the pain.

It would be impossible to describe the rejoicings when this took place; but, whether the cat was excited to fury by the pain, or the yells of the spectators drove it into a state of desperation, as the ape turned away instinctively in the hope of escaping, the cat bent down for a spring; and while Ned hallooed, "Take care, Jimmy, take care—play fair," it sprang on the back of the ape, and threw its claws around it.

The chimpanzee, however, one of the strongest apes of its race, was not at all disposed to give in without a struggle; for, as the cat leaped, it turned round and met the bite with jaws hardly less powerful. The catamount, however, succeeded in pinning its enemy by the throat, and it hung on, however much the ape might resist and try to get loose. They fell to the ground, the chimpanzee at top, biting the cat's head and ears savagely; but the cat held on, and, as the poor wild man's strength gradually gave out, it took a fresh grip.

"Enough, enough!" Ned now said for his man; "enough, beast! that's false play—let loose!"—and he thrust the stick into the catamount's side. But the brute held on in its bloodthirsty fury—the ape loosed its hold; and when the catamount, attacked on all sides, was finally compelled to let go, it left its opponent dead on the battle-field with his throat torn open.

The confusion that now arose was really uproarious. One party rejoiced and yelled, the other quarrelled and swore. A couple were sent for the whisky to drink the lost bet on the spot, while others danced and leaped round the confined space as if perfectly mad. Ned was the noisiest of all; and when he had yelled down all the others, and forced them to be quiet, he declared that he demanded justice for the wild man, who had been unfairly attacked and murdered by the beast of a cat, and they must hold a trial over the catamount, which he hereby accused of a cold-blooded and premeditated murder.

A loud shout of assent was the reply, and, for a moment or so, nothing could be heard save confused cries—"Choose a jury"—"A judge"—"Murder"—"Hanging," &c., until the chaos cleared up a little, when Bob sprang on the catamount's empty cage, and summoned the meeting to chose a jury and commence proceedings.

In a minute twelve men were selected, some of whom, however, were challenged by Bill, who had declared himself the advocate of the cat. At length the number was full, and Ned was just about to bring forward his charge, when a disturbance began again outside, and the Frenchman, who had recovered from the blow, now tried to enter his circus with a knife in his hand. The first two or three gave way; but, as he sprang forward, half-a-dozen put out their legs—he stumbled, and in a minute found himself, bound and unarmed, in the power of his torturers. In vain was the opposition of the more quiet persons, who thought the affair had been carried far enough; the arrival of the whisky drowned every sensible word, and the cry, "Silence in court"—"Out with the disturbers"—with the

"O yes! O yes!" in imitation of the sheriff, stifled all objections. The Frenchman was dragged out of the circus, and handed over to his own men, lest worse might befall him, and then the maddest trial ever held on earth began.

The catamount was charged with murder, and, in spite of its defenders' assertion, that everything had been done to force it to make the attack, after a sitting of nine or ten minutes it was condemned to be hanged by the neck till it was dead—dead—dead; and the only difficulty seemed to be in carrying out the sentence.

In the meanwhile night set in, and dry reeds were brought up to illumine the place, on which, however, there stood no tree to carry out the sentence. Still they did not require to go far; scarce twenty paces off was a clump of magnificent oaks, to which the cage, with the infuriated beast inside, was now dragged. There was a greater difficulty in fastening the noose round the animal's neck, and then carrying the rope out of the cage; and though the first was effected by means of a small wooden fork, all attempts to bring the rope through the door and pull the cat out seemed for a long time futile, until Bob seized the rope cautiously through the half-opened door of the cage, and fastened it round one of the lower branches of the oak. Then they let the cage go; and the beast, being pulled through the opening by the neck, for a moment held the whole weight of the cage on its claws. But it was too heavy; it was forced to leave hold, and hung twirling round to the shouts of the mob, till it suddenly seized the cord with its claws, and swung itself up. Some of the men were going to fetch a pole to beat it down; but the terrified animal, by pulling at the noose desperately and furiously, began to throttle itself, and at last fell back dead from the branch, and began slowly swinging round.

The mob hailed the cruel deed with coarse shouts, and then retired triumphantly to continue their drinking bout till late in the night.

Stewart had, from the beginning, taken the Frenchman's part, and done his utmost to bring the drunkards to their senses, though in vain. He it was, too, who at last prevented Bertrand rushing among the mob and stabbing right and left. Nothing could be done by force against their superior numbers, and they would have, probably put a bullet through his head into the bargain.

It cost some trouble, indeed, to bring the outraged and ill-treated Frenchman to cooler thoughts; and only the perfect certainty of being able to do nothing against the mob compelled him to visit the judge—whom he could not find till eleven o'clock—and lay all the circumstances before him.

The judge, a very quiet and reasonable man, listened to him attentively, and, by Stewart's assistance, inquired into the minutest details. Then he took the Frenchman on one side, and told him that, though he was sure of obtaining a verdict in his favour, he would not secure sufficient compensation from these people, who had only a horse and a rifle, and not a sufficient amount of property to be seizable by the law. Still he promised him his aid, told him to keep quiet, the next day to lay out the dead ape on a sheet, like a corpse, and wait for the rest.

The next morning, as Ned was lying fast asleep, wrapped up in his blanket, a young man, a lawyer from Little Rock, walked in, shook him, and sat down quietly by his side to await his awakening.

Ned rose on his elbow, and looked round him in surprise. The remembrance of the past evening still lay heavy as lead on his eyelids, and he could not shake it off at once.

"Well, Ned," the strange visitor said, after giving him quite sufficient time, as he considered, to wake, "are you sober this morning—eh?"

"Sober?" Ned repeated, rubbing his eyes in amazement. "Who the devil are you, and what do you want here?"

"I am a good friend, Ned," the stranger said, with indescribable coolness; "and should like to do you a service."

"Who the deuce asked it of you!" the young backwoodsman growled. "You're a lawyer, aint you?"

"Yes, Ned," the stranger replied, quietly cutting a splint from the chair on which he was sitting, and proceeding to whittle.

"And what have I to do with a lawyer, except it is Willmers, who is conducting my cause against Osthorn?"

"You were very jolly yesterday, eh, Ned?"

"Yesterday—who—I? Oh, yes, I believe so. Hang it all, we must have drunk a little too much, my head is so heavy. What nonsense 'tis that a man never knows when he has had enough!"

"Yes, Ned, that's a bad thing, and has often brought misfortune on men," the lawyer said slowly, and shook his head earnestly.

"Misfortune!" the young fellow repeated, springing up half anxiously and half angrily. "What on earth is the matter with you, and what do you want of me? Oh! I remember now, we set the mad Frenchman's beasts fighting—ha-ha-ha-ha! I suppose he will be trying to get damages. I wish him luck. Serves him right, the fool. Why does he bring catamounts into our settlement, where we are too happy to shoot them? And as for his coward of a wild man, why——"

"That was not a beast, Ned," the stranger said, sternly.

"Not a beast!" Ned said, growing frightened; "what was it, then?"

"You can answer that question as well as I can," the lawyer said, dryly. "But a wild man is not a beast, that is clear. And if a wretched human being goes wild in the forest, humanity and our duty as Christians, bid us take care of him and preserve him from injury. But if we hound wild beasts on him, against which he has not any arms to defend himself, that is a very bad affair, and a just jury must bring it in murder."

"The devil take it!" Ned said, and the anxious glance he turned on the lawyer proved that the allusion had been sufficient to make the young fellow regard the matter in quite a new light. At first he tried to laugh the whole affair away; but the stranger begged him to come with him, and led him to the Frenchman's tent, where they found the corpse of the wild man stretched under a blanket.

This sight produced the right effect. Ned saw himself in the desperate position of a murderer; and the only chance of escape, according to the lawyer's advice, was to come to some settlement with the Frenchman, and persuade him not to bring a charge. The sharers in the last night's revelry were, therefore, secretly and hastily collected, and they decided on sending a deputation to the judge, and asking his opinion.

The judge replied evasively; he would not give them any advice. His position prevented him expressing a judgment about a matter which might be brought before him during the assizes; but, were *he* mixed up in the affair, he would come to a settlement with the Frenchman, even if it cost him all he was worth.

On the same morning, M. Bertrand had a private interview with Ned Holly; the court commenced sitting, but the Frenchman brought no charge, and on the next morning his wagons were all ready packed and prepared to start.

He had given the chimpanzee a decent burial on the previous evening; skinned the catamount, and laid it out to dry on one of the chests; but, instead of his little pony, which was now fastened by a rope to the last wagon, he rode Ned Holly's splendid stallion, which he had brought to Francisville for sale, and had good reasons for believing was worth three hundred dollars; and in the catamount's otherwise empty cage were two large parcels of otter and deer skins.

M. Bertrand has turned his wagons once more eastward to Memphis, and not to Little Rock. He appeared to have made no bad bargain, for he grinned pleasantly as he patted the neck of the chestnut which bounded under him, and noticed the gloomy glance with which Ned Holly followed the movements of the splendid animal; but that was the last wild man he would risk for a new adventure, and he thought it advisable to seek more civilized districts.

Under a stately oak, at the corner of Sycamore and Washington Streets, Wilson and Stewart threw up a mound over the grave of the wild man, and the women of the settlement avoid the spot with superstitious alarm to the present day, because they assert that, on the night of the first Sunday in September, the ghost of the wild man is seen, and, by its whining, entices the catamounts which are seen in such numbers during this month.

Ned Holly is still happy that he got out of that awkward affair so cheaply.

WHO DID IT?

WHO DID IT?

A Prairie Tale.

CHAPTER I.

SMITHSON'S MURDER.

IT was a cold but pleasant afternoon, in the month of February, when a solitary rider left the town of V——, in Illinois, and followed the broad road through the prairie. He was a young man of some seven or eight and thirty years of age, with good-tempered, dark eyes, but nothing further could be seen, for, in accordance with the custom of those cold regions, he had buttoned himself up in a great white flannel coat, so that only his bright eyes, with the upper portion of a pair of cheeks, reddened by the cold north-wester, peeped out between the raised collar of the coat and under the protection of a fine, dark-brown, otter-skin cap.

The lower parts of his legs were also wrapped up in a large piece of blue flannel, which was fastened together under the knee by green garters, and so formed a species of gaiter. A plain iron spur was attached to his right heel, and on his left shoulder he carried one of the long and handsomely-worked Kentucky rifles through which the inhabitants of that neighbourhood have gained the reputation of being such excellent shots.

The rider, however, seemed not at all prepared for hunting, in spite of the gun, for neither shot-belt nor powder-horn could be seen upon him; but he trotted sharply along the hard-frozen road upon his little rough-haired pony, and scarce deigned to cast a glance on the prairie hens that continually rose on all sides. He had perceived a single rider before him, and now tried to catch him up, in order to render the tedious journey through the monotonous prairie, which was covered, as far as the eye could see, with parched, yellow grass, more supportable and interesting by pleasant conversation.

This tremendous, yellow, heaving plain was a sorrowful sight. In the east, heavy masses of cloud lay over the verge of the grassy sea, and were endued with a still more gloomy and wild aspect by the patches of blue sky that peeped out among them; the cold north-wester blew sharply and cuttingly from the great lakes over the wide plains, and even the beams of the midday sun could not warm the half-frozen rider, who continually cheered his little active pony to canter along and shake a little warmth into him. He at length caught up the rider before him, and stopped his pony by his side, to keep pace with the other's contentedly-trotting animal.

"How are you, Doctor? How are you?" the latter cried, as he recognised him. "Have you been to town, too, in the cold? This *is* the weather; the north-wester reaches one's very marrow. But it wont last long. Do you see the long black patches on the clouds? They all run from east to west—that means rain or snow, and the cold will then yield a little."

"I hope so," the young man said, offering the other his hand, which he shook heartily. "But tell me, Smithson, aint you half-frozen? The cold gets through my flannel coat, so that my very bones chatter, and you set there bare-necked on your horse as comfortably as if it were August instead of February, and the wind came from the left and not from the right."

The person thus addressed was a hearty old man, with snow-white hair, which curled under his old, worn-out felt hat. He wore a dark-blue woollen hunting-shirt, ornamented with scarlet fringe, trousers of the same stuff, though without the ornamentation, and coarse yellow, home-made shoes. His clean white shirt was open in front, in spite of the bitter cold, and displayed his neck, which the sharp breeze had dyed of a dark-red hue. The wooden handle of a bowie-knife projected from the brown leathern belt that confined his hunting-shirt, but he carried no other arms. He looked kindly at the Doctor, and answered—

"You sit too much in your room, Doctor, by the fireside, and when you go out you wrap yourself up so that your nose can scarce be seen, and every cold draught makes you shudder. Yes, yes—if our blessed country were not so flat that the rain in evaporating in summer produces the dangerous prairie fever, there would be very few of us countrymen among your patients. But tell me, Doctor, I thought you never went out shooting, and now I see you with a famous rifle on your shoulder. Hang it! I must have seen it somewhere before—did you buy it in town?"

"No! This morning, when I went to the gunsmith's to get a few bullets for my pistol, he asked me to take the rifle with me to my house, and send it to John Singer's on the first opportunity."

"John Singer! I thought so. I have lain many a night in the woods with John and the gun; and now I see why I didn't recognise it immediately—John has had the brasswork taken off and iron put on instead. It's much better, too; I always told him that brass glistens too much in the wood, especially if the sun plays upon it. But I can save you any further trouble about the gun. John Singer only lives half a mile from my house; and my Jim rides past every morning when he goes to school. He can take it with him to-morrow morning, for I shall reach home to-night, if I have to ride till twelve o'clock."

"You will do me a great service; for, to tell you the truth, the heavy lump of iron has already pained my shoulder."

"I saw it, I saw it!" the old man said, laughingly, "directly I cast my eyes upon you: the way in which you held the rifle told me you were not a sportsman. Now, *I* feel as if I wanted something if I haven't a gun on my shoulder—I am so used to it. But, Doctor, one good turn deserves another, and you can save me a ride of thirty miles, to-morrow, from my house to your town. I have got to pay these hundred and five dollars to a trader of the name of Rosenberg, and you would do me a kindness if you would take the money for me; but have a receipt, for I have not much faith in the fellow, for he's got a crooked nose, and his black hair is so curly; and the little German who lives near me says all sorts of things about him. Will you do it?"

"With great pleasure, my good friend; the money shall be punctually paid, and I'll have a receipt."

"Well, then, here's the money," said Smithson, as he handed the young man a little, worn, brown leather pocket-book. "Leave them in it," he said, as the Doctor proceeded to take out the bank-notes, in order to return him the book; "I don't want it just now, and you can give it me at another time. But, Doctor," he continued, as he laid the rifle on the saddle before him, "haven't you any powder by you? I don't care about carrying an unloaded gun, and shall probably see a deer or two before nightfall."

"Yes, I've some powder, but no bullets; I bought a quarter of a pound for my pistols; for the powder Rosenberg sells is shameful, and yet he has the impudence to ask a dollar a pound for it."

"Well! I've got a bullet in my pocket. It belongs to my rifle, and will fit John's gun, if I take a thick wad: he often used my bullets, but his are rather too heavy for my rifle."

With these words he stopped his pony, got down, and pulled a bullet out of the depths of his trouser's pocket.

The doctor also dismounted, and, after throwing the reins over his arm, began stamping and jumping, to restore the circulation in his half-frozen feet.

"But you haven't a gauge, Smithson," he said to the latter, as he offered him the powder.

"It's of no consequence. Pour the powder into the palm of my hand till it covers the ball. Stop!—not so quick. There, that's about enough. See!" he continued, after he had carefully picked the nipple with a feather, that was placed for this purpose in a hole bored in the butt. "See, with this piece of leather the ball fits famously; and now," he said, as he drove it down the barrel slowly, but with a strong arm, "I should like to see the buck that comes within eighty or a hundred paces of me."

The two men mounted again, and rode some seven miles together, telling anecdotes, and discussing the events of the day, until their roads parted, and the young Doctor stopped his pony.

"Here we must say good-bye?" he cried, shaking the old man's hand heartily. "I long for a comfortable room; and, if I cannot warm myself thoroughly by riding, I shall turn in at Mansfield's, and spend the night there."

"Good-bye, then!" the old man said to him, as he turned his pony to the left-hand path, while the Doctor rode away in a northerly direction. "Good-bye! and next week, when it's election day, I shall come up and fetch my receipt."

"Good!" the Doctor replied; "in that case you must stop for the night at my house.

They were now about a hundred yards from each other; and, after another hearty "Good-bye!" each trotted merrily along the hard-frozen road.

Smithson had nearly twenty miles to ride before he could reach his farm, and he drove his spur several times into the side of his little active pony, which, after a few high bounds, cantered across the plain with extraordinary speed.

The sun was still about an hour high when he approached a little wood, which lay in a long, dark strip across the horizon, and formed the first boundary of one of those immense prairies that extend in a southern direction from the lakes almost to the Ohio river.

When he reached the edge of the wood he allowed his pony to walk, and looked attentively through the open forest on each side of the road, in order to discover and kill some unsuspecting deer, and take a good piece of venison home with him.

On arriving at a little thicket, about half a mile from the prairie where the road made a circuit to avoid a group of fallen trees, he suddenly heard, close to him, the cry of a turkey, and stopped his pony to see where it was. At this moment, not fifteen paces from him, a flash of fire gleamed from the low bushes; a loud crack followed, and the old man fell from his saddle, mortally wounded, upon the hard ground. Once he raised himself convulsively, fell back, stretched himself, and died, his warm heart's blood pouring in dark streams over his blue hunting-shirt, into the ruts upon the road, while his horse, startled by the accident, flew along the road towards its stable.

The old man lay quietly some five minutes; the blood had ceased to flow, and had congealed on the road. His face assumed the livid hue of death, while his widely-opened eyes looked fixedly upwards towards the blue sky, as if seeking help thence, or invoking vengeance on the murderer. The bushes by the roadside were then moved apart, and a little, remarkably pale man, looking round quickly and timidly, leaped into the road.

He was dressed in a leathern hunting-shirt and leggings, wore on his feet a pair of strong, coarse shoes, and a cap of fox-skin on his head; but his face, disfigured by pockmarks, revealed, with terrible rapidity of succession, all the predominant passions; as satisfied revenge, fear, daring, and contempt, which gave it an almost supernatural look of horror.

In his hand he held a long, heavy, smooth-bore rifle, which had just dismissed the death-bearing bullet.

Gently, quickly, and almost noiselessly he crept up to the corpse, and bent, with cold malice in his glance, over the livid face of the old hunter, from whose features the painful, sudden death had not removed all the traces of good-humour and placidity.

"You will not despise my smooth-bore again, and say it's only fit for children; it has hit the mark this time—right through the heart," he muttered softly to himself, as he raised the corpse by the left shoulder. "Fortunately it has gone through, so that my bullet will not betray me when they find the body; but now for the money, old fellow;" and with timid, eager haste he began feeling the person of his victim in order to find the money which he supposed the old man possessed, for he had heard in the town, during the morning, that he would take a certain sum home; but no money was to be seen, and more and more furiously and eagerly he searched; he even opened the box in the butt of the rifle, to see if the old man had hidden the money there; but in vain.

"Damnation!" he cried, as he raised himself, threw his cap on the ground, and stamped his foot furiously. "Made the old sinner cold for nothing, absolutely nothing! But it is impossible," he interrupted himself; "he must have it on him;" and he began anew his terrible task, and examined all the places where he could conjecture that the money would be hidden. It was useless, and, gnashing his teeth and exhausted, he seated himself at last to rest on one of the fallen trees. The danger to which he exposed himself, of being found and apprehended near the corpse, soon conquered every other feeling.

He sprang up, walked to the corpse, and lifted the old man's rifle, which had fallen to the ground.

"The bullet has gone through him," he said to himself; "and if I fire the old fool's rifle, the people who find him will believe that he has shot himself by some accident. That has often been the case; it would be too cruel for me to find no money and be hanged in the bargain."

With these words he fired the rifle in the air, laid it by the old man's side in such a position that it might appear probable that it had gone off by some unhappy accident, seized his own gun and cap, and fled to the wood, where he had bound his horse, at about a quarter of a mile from the spot. He mounted and rode off at full speed in a northerly direction, in order to show himself in some public-house, and so avert any possible suspicion that might attach to him.

Mansfield's was the first house he reached by nightfall, and he was just going to ride up and call, when he saw a boy going towards the stable with a horse he had just watered.

"Whose horse is that?" he asked the lad, when he came close to him.

"Dr. Middleton's," was the reply; "and who are you?"

"A traveller," he replied, shortly, trotted along the high road to a public-house about two miles distant, and without being noticed by any one, entered the little store of a low block-house, which served as a drinking-room.

The murderer had quitted his victim scarce half an hour, darkness was still struggling with the light, and striving to conceal the terrible spot, while several ravens, attracted by the scent of blood, were swinging on the topmost boughs of the neighbouring trees, in readiness to commence their disgusting meal with the earliest dawn, when two horsemen came at a hard gallop along the same road poor Smithson had so lately fallen on.

When they had arrived at the scene of the murder, the two horses suddenly shied, and stood trembling with fear and horror. The men were good riders, and yet the suddenness of the bound had nearly thrown them from their saddles, and, though somewhat alarmed themselves, they tried to calm their frightened animals.

"Wo-o-o! you brute; can't you be quiet when I bid you!" one of the riders angrily said—a tall young man, who gave himself all possible trouble to calm his horse. "Hark, Tom, there must be some dead animal lying in the road, for that's the only thing that can make my old fellow bound so; he is generally as quiet as a lamb."

"Well, my horse must pass," his companion said, who was built more powerfully than the other, and whose accent revealed the German, as he struck his spurs again into his rearing animal, and urged it on. But the attempts of the two riders were all in vain to pass the spot the horses feared.

"Confound it!" the taller of the two said, whose name was William Preston. "I'll see what there is lying in the way;" and with these words he sprang from his horse, threw the reins to his comrade, and walked nearer the mysterious spot, while the German (his name was Thomas Vollheim) remained quietly awaiting the result of the examination. With a wild shout of horror Preston, however, sprang back, when, by the last gleam of the expiring daylight, he recognised the pale features of a human corpse.

"Look here, Tom," he called, as he bent over the body, and tried to see the features of the dead man. "Good God! it's old Smithson!"

The German had sprung from his horse, bound the reins on the projecting branch of an oak, and walked with an internal shudder but firm step to Preston's side.

"What shall we do now?" the latter asked, as his comrade stood solemnly by his side, and regarded the face of the dead man. "Shall we ride to my house, it is only five miles distant, or back to town and fetch the police?"

"I fancy the latter is the best," Vollheim replied. "But how on earth did this horrible thing happen?"

"It's too dark for us to see anything," Preston said. "Let us light a fire here, close by, and by the light we will examine everything more carefully, and consult what had best be done. To tell the truth, I feel a little uncomfortable here in the dark, and yet I am not usually a coward."

Without saying another word, the men struck a light, and soon after a bright flame sprang up, fed with dry leaves and wood, which threw a light like that of day over the terrible spot, while they now prepared to examine in what manner Smithson had perished.

Vollheim decides to remain by the corpse

CHAPTER II.

DR. MIDDLETON FOUND GUILTY.

"LOOK here, Tom," said Preston, who had knelt down by the corpse and bent over it, "the ball entered his right side, and —his own gun has been lately fired."

With these words he raised the rifle from the ground, and looked carefully at it.

"Yes, indeed," said Vollheim, who took it from him; "can the old man have fallen from his horse and shot himself? That would be strange, for he was such a famous rider."

"Hark, Tom," Preston continued, "that appears to me very improbable; only see how disordered his dress is! I am afraid that the old man has been shamefully murdered, and perhaps had money by him. The shot must have been mortal, and—his trousers-pocket is turned inside out. Look here—and here," he cried, stooping down, and remarking the distinct footmarks in the soft ground round the fire; "a man has been stamping here—they must have surely been struggling together."

Preston now examined the slightest traces he could perceive by the flickering light that might lead to the discovery of the murderer; for the sharp-sighted man did not doubt for a moment that a murder had been committed, while the German seriously and mournfully regarded the remains of the worthy old man, who had been respected and loved by all who knew him.

"Listen, Bill!" he at length broke the painful silence; "the most sensible thing we can do is to ride back as quick as our horses can carry us, and fetch the constable. A shameful murder has been committed here; and, in any case, we shall be able to find to-morrow some traces that will lead to the discovery of the murderer."

"You are right, Tom, quite right, and the sooner we do it the better, for look how the sky is growing covered. We shall have snow as sure as I stand here, and then the murderer will be secure; and, indeed, who knows whether the weather will hold till to-morrow morning. We must return to-night with torches and track the villain. But shall we leave the body thus exposed, and the wolves, perhaps, find it and gnaw it? And still I should not like to disturb it, that the magistrate may find it in the same condition as we did."

"I'll tell you what, Bill," the German quietly remarked, "you'll find the road to the town in the dark, so ride back without me, and I'll keep watch by the body. If the wolves scent anything living, there'll be no danger from them."

"But wont you feel afraid to remain alone with the body?" his comrade said, with an inward shudder.

"I've a good fire, and the time will soon pass; if you make haste, you can get back by two o'clock; besides, I think I hear the sound of a horse's hoofs. By George, yes!" continued the German; "its our old friend Douglass. Hi! Douglass! Here!"

Douglass rode up, and Preston hurriedly told him how they had found old Smithson's body.

"And, Douglass," continued he, "will you stop here with Vollheim while I ride back to the town."

Douglass readily consented to remain while Preston mounted his pony, and went at a sharp trot along the road by which he had come a short time before, while the other men took the saddles and cloths from their horses, laid them by the fire so that the flame was betwixt them and the corpse, and then stretched themselves out—the one to sleep, the other to watch.

After a few hours Vollheim fell into a restless slumber, but he woke up, probably startled out of some terrific dream; and, shuddering as he remembered the circumstance that detained him there, sought to distract his thoughts by stirring up the fire, and piling great logs of wood to keep up as much light as was possible.

After midnight, several wolves that had scented the blood began howling, and came nearer and nearer, making wide circles round the spot; but the presence of the men and the bright fire kept them aloof.

At length, when Vollheim's watch was pointing to a quarter to three, they heard the anxiously expected sound of voices which were to release them from their sorrowful post.

The examination the new-comers commenced with some torches they had brought with them was very careful, and they came to the unanimous conclusion that the dead man had been assassinated and then robbed. The bullet could not be found, to show from what rifle it had been fired; but the wound showed that it must have been a large bore.

While searching the place, Preston found, close to the thicket where the murderer had concealed himself, a powder-horn, with the roughly-cut initials, P. M. M. D.

None of the men recognised the horn, nor could they guess the meaning of the letters. Vollheim now came up, and, after examining the flask, asked Preston what Dr. Middleton's Christian name was?

"Paul," said the latter; "but why?"

"Merciful Heavens!" the German muttered; "the name agrees, but he cannot have committed such a frightful deed!"

"Who—the Doctor?" Preston quickly asked. "Ridiculous! He assassinate anybody! I would just as readily believe it was my own father. No, no, that's folly. Besides, what is the meaning of the two letters, M. D.?"

"Paul Middleton, Medicine Doctor," Vollheim said, in a monotonous, serious voice.

"Nonsense, nonsense!" Preston cried; "and yet—I saw the Doctor leave town yesterday soon after old Smithson; and, if I'm not mistaken, he had a rifle on his shoulder. God! that would be too horrible. His poor wife—his old mother!"

He seated himself on one of the fallen trees, and leaned his head on his hand, as he gave way to very sorrowful reflections.

"Come, Preston," said Vollheim, "let us follow the trace. You are as good as a bloodhound on a track, and perhaps we shall, in that way, catch the right man."

A guard was now left by the corpse, another sent to inform the unfortunate man's family that they might fetch the body home, and the rest now began, each provided with a light, to carefully follow the track of the murderer in the soft ground, which was a tedious task, for the shadow thrown by the torches gave a very uncertain illumination to the ground.

At length, when day was just breaking in the east, they reached the spot where the man had mounted the horse, and now followed with greater ease and speed the hoofmarks.

The sky had become clouded during the night, and just as the men recognised in the distance the house of Mansfield, the magistrate, to which the track led straight, and along an unfrequented road, it began snowing, and increased so rapidly, that before they reached Mansfield's a white covering hid the track from their sight, and rendered any further search impossible.

"It's lucky," said one of the jury, "that we followed the track betimes; a couple of hours later, and we should not have known whether to go north or south."

Preston made no reply—he was melancholy and thoughtful. This chain of circumstances, which threw suspicion on the Doctor, whose conduct had been always so upright, rendered him very sorrowful, for he was almost like one of his family; and yet he could not have acted otherwise than he had done. Still the hope continually recurred to him that the Doctor was incapable of such a deed, and that they would surely find traces of the murderer at Mansfield's house.

When they reached the magistrate's double block house, breakfast was just served, and he compelled the men immediately to come in and eat a mouthful, as they must have started betimes to reach his house at so early an hour. He called to the girl in the kitchen to broil some more ham and poach some eggs, and then joined his early guests in the keeping-room.

"Judge," said Preston, then, after the first friendly salutations were over, "did any one stop the night with you?"

"Yes—Doctor Middleton. Why?"

The men exchanged glances of conviction.

"Did you notice anything peculiar in him?" one of the jury asked further.

"He was as cheerful as usual, was he not?" Preston hurriedly asked.

"Peculiar!" the Judge slowly repeated, without noticing the last question. "Peculiar! No—and yet he seemed to me very restless. His wife is ill, as he said, and he rode off at daybreak this morning; I have not seen him since."

"Good God! if it was true!" Preston groaned, and threw himself quite exhausted into a chair.

"But, men, what's the matter—what has happened?" the Judge now asked, himself disquieted; and in a few clear words Preston told him all, from the moment when they had found the body, up to the spot where they had hit the murderer's track; showed him the powder-horn with the initials, and called one of the men as witness, who had given old Smithson one hundred and five dollars the previous morning in good Ohio, Illinois, and Indiana notes. "But no!" he cried, as he finished his narrative; "and were he himself to tell me that it was he that shot the old man, I would not believe it—by Heaven, I would not!"

Judge Mansfield, a venerable old man, who had known the Doctor from his earliest youth, turned deadly pale when he heard the terrible accusation; and although he did not doubt that there was some mistake, still he could not deny the request of one of the jury, who asked for an order for immediate arrest, and he sent the constable, a young man who lived in his house, along with them.

Preston at first would not go to the Doctor's house, but the Judge begged him to do so; for he hoped, as he stated, that the whole had originated from an unhappy combination of circumstances, and the actual murderer would be discovered.

It was about ten o'clock when Preston, Vollheim, Douglass, the three men from the town of B——, and the constable, reached the Doctor's house.

Judith, a young Irish, rosy-cheeked girl, who attended to the household work (as the Doctor's wife was in weak health, and had even been ill for several months), but was treated more like a member of the family than as a servant, opened the door for them, and was not a little surprised, as it seemed, on seeing a number of men enter at such an early hour. Preston was the last; and a slight blush crossed the pretty girl's cheek as she took the young man's offered hand, but it speedily made way for a feeling of anxiety, when she noticed young Preston's pale and disturbed face—for he was a welcome guest at the house, and one by no means indifferent to her.

"Is the Doctor at home, Judy?" he asked, with such a serious, melancholy face, that Judith quite forgot to answer; but looking timidly at each of the men in turn, ejaculated—

"In Heaven's name, what has happened, Mr. Preston—you look so solemn? And all these persons—the constable, too!—what can have happened?"

"Wait, Judy, I will tell you all afterwards; but now say if the Doctor is at home—we should like to ask him a question?" the young man continued very seriously.

"He is up-stairs," the girl said; "but tread gently," she continued, as she saw all the men preparing to follow Preston, "Mrs. Middleton is very poorly, and only fell asleep at dawn."

Doctor Middleton, entirely unaware of everything connected with the terrible event of the past day, was sitting alone in his study when the men entered. He was counting the money old Smithson had delivered to him, in order to pay it when he went out to the tradesman, who lived not a hundred yards from him.

He kindly offered his hand to young Preston, and several others he knew, and begged them to sit down; Preston, however, held his hand firmly, and said, looking seriously and timidly in his face—

"Doctor, old Smithson was murdered last evening!"

"Murdered! Good God!" the Doctor exclaimed, really terrified at the horrible news, as he only quitted the old man at a late hour in the afternoon.

One of the men, who had been fetched on the previous night from V——, had walked to the table in the meanwhile, and now said, seriously and menacingly—

"Those are the notes I myself paid old Smithson yesterday morning; that is the pocket-book in which he put them, and there is the identical red tape which he bound round it before my very eyes."

"Dr. Middleton, you are my prisoner," the constable said, who now advanced and tapped the Doctor, who was speechless from surprise and terror, on the shoulder.

"But, for God's sake, folks!—Preston, Vollheim, Douglass!—you don't believe—— Great God! am I dreaming? You do not really believe that I killed and robbed the old man?"

A terrible pause ensued, but then Preston cried, in a loud voice, as he seized the Doctor's hand—

"No, no, Doctor, the devil take me if I believe it! If you were to tell me yourself you had done it, I could not believe you."

"Thank you, Preston," said the Doctor, and pressed his hand heartily. "I thank you; I was quite sure that you, at least, must know me."

"Doctor, it is a harsh duty I have to perform," said the constable, much moved, "but you are aware—it is my duty, and you must go with me."

"God! My wife!" the poor man muttered to himself, as he now thought for the first time of his beloved wife's weakness and nervous excitement; "she will not survive it when she hears it."

"Calm yourself, Doctor," Preston said, soothingly, "your innocence must be proved, and if you are forced to remain a couple of days from home, your wife will not know where you are. Trust in God's mercy, and I and Vollheim will stop here, and explain the affair to your mother, and calm her, if possible."

All considered this the best course, and even the Doctor feared at this moment that he might not be sufficiently master of his feelings to take leave of his wife and mother. He went down into the stable, saddled his own horse, and in a few minutes was on the road to V—— with his companions, in order to be taken to prison, and await the result of an examination.

But young Preston's hope of seeing the Doctor's innocence speedily proved was not fulfilled; the proofs against him became continually stronger and more telling. The rifle-smith testified that he had come to him to get some bullets for his pistols, and that he had powder with him in a piece of paper, which he (the gun-smith) was certain of, because he had wrapped it up for him in a coarser piece of paper, as the other thinner piece had begun to tear. As soon as he heard there was a rifle there for John Singer, he had immediately offered to take it with him, under the pretext that he should certainly see Singer in a few days, and *this rifle, lately discharged, was found by the corpse.* The trader who had paid old Smithson the money for pickled pork, stated on his oath that the notes found at Dr. Middleton's were the same as he had given him, and the pocket-book the same in which he had placed them. The powder-flask bore Dr. Middleton's initials, and though the latter obstinately denied ever having seen it before, still the other evidence spoke too strongly against him, especially as he confessed to having caught up the old man a few miles from the town, and had ridden with him until their roads parted.

Unfortunately, the snow that had fallen so unseasonably prevented them from examining the footmarks more closely, and, spite of the Doctor's continued assertions of his innocence, the case looked terribly black against him.

The assizes, which were to decide the fate of the unhappy man, were fixed for the 23rd. The jury assembled, and the case commenced. Middleton's counsel defended him warmly, called the whole neighbourhood to prove his irreproachable conduct to every one, appealed to his whole past life, and the friendly terms on which he had always stood with old Smithson. It was useless. The jury retired, consulted scarcely ten minutes about a case which was so clearly and palpably proved, and returned a verdict of "Guilty."

The Doctor sank back fainting in his chair when he heard the terrible word.

On the afternoon of the next day, Preston was sitting, pale and downcast, in the parlour of Dr. Middleton's house. Before him stood Judy, and from her swollen eyes bright tears were falling down her now pale and wasted cheeks.

"Go, go, Mr. Preston," she said, in almost a broken voice, as she turned from him; "what use are all your kind words to me? You're one of those who led my poor master away to prison, and if the poor lady up-stairs dies, which is sure to be the case when she hears her husband's fate, which we can no longer conceal from her, then you never need call me your Judy again—my heart will be broken too," and the poor girl wept bitterly.

"But, Judy, is it my fault? Could I have acted otherwise than I did? Oh! could I have an idea, when we found the corpse, that —that suspicion would fall on our good doctor?"

"And you really believe that he committed the murder?" Judith asked, as she quickly turned to him.

"No! by Heavens, girl, you are too hard upon me. The Lord above knows that I would gladly do all in my power to help the poor doctor, who, I am firmly convinced, is innocent, although I cannot understand how the evidence all turned so against him."

"Will you do all in your power? Will—will you do all you can to save the poor Doctor?" Judith now said, laying her little hand on the arm of the man who was dear to her, and entreating him, at the same time, like a child, with her large, blue eyes fixed upon him.

"What do you want me to do? What can I do? The verdict is uttered, and the sentence will be carried into effect on the 26th."

"Listen to me," Judith continued, with much emotion. "He is

confined in the little prison at V——; his poor mother was with him yesterday, to see him for the last time and cheer him; his wife is wrestling with death in this house; the truth must kill her as soon as she hears it; the Doctor himself was your friend—your benefactor—and the day after to-morrow—the day after to-morrow, man, he will be hanged."

"But, Judith!" the young man begged, astonished at such passion on the part of the usually so quiet girl.

"Stay—do not interrupt me—you can be in town before daybreak to-morrow; go to him, persuade him to escape, and assist him. He will—he must fly! You cannot say that it is impossible to liberate him," she continued, "for you yourself once told me that the gaol is a poor one, and a prisoner could easily escape from it if the bars were cut through with a fine saw. Here is everything you want—saw and file. The German, Vollheim, procured them for me, and here," she whispered and blushed, "here are fifty dollars. It is all I have saved—I—had intended it for another purpose, but I would gladly give ten times as much if I had it to free my good master, and save my poor dear mistress from death."

"But the gaoler, Judith?" Preston objected, half undecided.

"The Doctor saved his wife and child when attacked by fever, and never took a cent for it; and although he dare not let him out himself, he will not watch him so closely, and you are young and active. Here are the tools," she continued, more calmly, and almost whispering. "Go, and when you have freed the poor man, and when he has escaped to Texas and we follow him thither, then—then——"

"Well, Judy?" Preston asked, gently, as he took the blushing girl's hand; but she could not answer him. Sobbing loudly, she threw herself on the young man's chest, then tore herself from him, and fled like a startled fawn.

Preston was gained. It was his firm conviction, in spite of all evidence and proof, that the Doctor must be innocent, and with a light heart he started for the town, in order to fulfil Judith's and his own wishes. But he found impediments at the very place where he least expected them.

The Hostelry—A clue to the real Murderer.

CHAPTER III.

THE REAL MURDERER.

AFTER Preston had gained admission to the Doctor on the next morning, and had informed him of his plan, the prisoner declared firmly and decidedly that he would not quit the prison, but would even summon the gaoler if he heard the slightest sound indicating an intention to liberate him against the will of the law.

"There are many good people," he concluded his remarks, "who, even if I suffer the disgraceful death to which I am condemned, will fervently believe in my innocence; but if I escape, not one of them will doubt but that I actually committed the horrible crime of which I am accused, and I would sooner die a thousand deaths than live in a foreign land under the crushing weight of this suspicion. No, Preston, I will not escape: my life is in God's hands; and, if I must end it in this terrible fashion, His will be done; He alone knows whether I was capable of committing such a deed."

Preston quitted him in great emotion. He tried, it is true, to offer him some hope, but he himself could not believe in it, and, desponding, and not knowing whither to turn, he rode slowly into the town, with his reins thrown upon his pony's neck.

A few hundred yards from the inn where he had fed his horse, there stood another hostelry; and loud quarrelling, singing, and shouting reached him from the open door; but the rough noise and the wild merriment did not at all harmonize with the feelings which pervaded Preston's bosom, and he was just going to ride past, when Vollheim walked to the door, and made a sign to him to come in for a moment.

He threw his horse's bridle over a hook outside the door and walked into the well-filled room, telling his friend the conversation he had just had, and the result.

"I knew it, I knew it," Vollheim replied. "He is innocent, and will not fly like a guilty man; but the little girl would not give up her entreaties, and I was obliged to get her the tools. I am very glad, though—very glad—that the Doctor is true to himself. He is a man of honour, and I would give my right arm if I could save him."

Loud laughing and shouting soon rendered any conversation in a low tone incomprehensible, and they walked to the bar among the guests who filled the room. They were, for the greater part, strangers, who had arrived to be present at the execution, and were now conversing about the morrow's spectacle.

It cut Preston to the heart to hear them speaking in such a way about the death of a man whom he loved as a brother, and, after hurriedly swallowing a glass of brandy-and-water to recruit his exhausted strength, he was just going to force his way through the throng, when a man came up to him, who seemed to have been paying too much attention to the whisky bottle, and addressed him like an old acquaintance.

"I say, Preston, how are you? I've not seen you for an age. Well! I'm delighted to meet you again, for you're a precious good fellow:" and he made a movement as if about to embrace tenderly his old friend.

"What, Messworth!" Preston said, by no means pleasantly impressed, as it appeared, by the drunkard's recognition of him, for he kept him at arm's length. "But where have you come from all at once? I fancied you were in Texas."

"Been there, too, old boy!" Messworth exclaimed, as he seated himself on an old tree-stump just before the door; "been there, too, and only arrived here this morning, as I heard in St. Louis that a friend of mine, Dr. Middleton, was going to be hanged. Serve him right, too—what did he shoot people for?"

"Good-bye!" Preston cried, and turned to his horse, to escape from the man, who was a regular vagabond, and had formerly lived in V——, but had gone to Texas some six months before, and had now again sought his former place of abode, probably from old associations. But the latter, who suspected what he intended, caught Preston by the arm, saying—

"No, old boy, no; you're not going in that way. We must have a drink together—we have not had one for such a long time, and I feel tremendously thirsty. The devil take it! my throat is always so dry, and the water is so miserably bad here."

Preston exerted himself to get rid of him, when the other suddenly seized the powder-horn Preston wore (the same that had been found in the bushes on that unlucky day), and exclaimed—

"Confound it! how did you get my powder-horn?"

Preston and Vollheim started at this inquiry as if electrified, and exchanged a glance of surprise; but Messworth was not daunted by it, but proceeded zealously—

"Yes, my powder-horn! although you look at one another in as much surprise as if you had never met before. It's mine. Did I not lend it to that scamp Curneales a little while before I left, and the son-of-a-gun never came near me again, so that I was obliged to have another made?"

"But," Preston replied, almost losing his speech, in half-joyful, half-doubtful surprise, "are you quite sure that it is yours, and that you lent it to Curneales?"

"If I'm certain? Devil take it—isn't my name and my birth-place clearly enough marked upon it? You can look for yourselves—'P.,' Philip; 'M.,' Messworth; from 'M.,' Milford, in 'D.,' Delaware. Well, who else does it belong to? More by token the horn cost me a dollar and a half, for the cover is good silver, as the German pedlar of whom I bought it told me."

Preston stood for a moment helpless and speechless; such various feelings overpowered him; but the more thoughtful Vollheim handed the drunkard a dollar and a half, and begged him to leave him the horn, as he had taken it in exchange, and disposed of it to Preston, but did not know, at the time, that the person he had it of had no right to it.

Messworth, well satisfied with the ready money he held in his hand, assured them that he set no value on the horn, and that they could keep it, and wanted the more to have them back into the store to help him spend the money, but they got away from him, leaped on their horses, and were soon in the open prairie before the town.

"Victory! victory!" Vollheim cried, when they had the last houses behind them. "We are on the track!"

"But where shall we go now," Preston asked, "to find this Curneales? Who knows where he is? And suppose he denies it?"

"Only come with me," Vollheim said, in the highest stage of delight; "only come with me. I know where the bird is to be found. But we'll ride past the Doctor's house, and cheer the poor women with a few words."

He then told his friend that he had seen and spoken with this Curneales on the previous evening, and that he was stopping at a store about five miles from the Doctor's house, in which he had been residing for some time, and employed himself exclusively in hunting; that he wandered about gloomily and thoughtfully, and hardly spoke with anybody. According to the landlord's statement, he was only waiting for some fifty dollars, owing him by a trader in V——, and, as soon as he received them, he intended to go to Texas and settle there.

At a sharp trot the two horsemen rode, with light hearts, and filled with joyful anticipations, over the frozen prairie, and in the afternoon reached Judge Mansfield's house, in order to inquire more closely if, on the evening of the murder, no other suspicious person had been seen there. No one could give them the slightest information, and Middleton was the only living being that had shown himself. But the little stable-boy suddenly remembered that he had seen a stranger soon after dark, whose features he had not been able to recognise; but his voice had seemed to him very familiar.

The Judge had joined them, and expressed his opinion, as he shook his head, that that would not help the poor Doctor much.

"Stay, Judge, stay!" Preston now burst out, no longer able to master his impatience, "his innocence will be proved; we are on the track of the murderer!" And then he told him all the circumstances connected with the powder-horn, and the suspicion cast by it upon Curneales.

With a beating heart and glowing cheeks the old man listened to the statement, and his eye grew gradually brighter.

"Yes," he at length said, "our Lord will not suffer the innocent to perish. The murderer will be seized, and the poor, hardly-tried man will stand free and acquitted before his fellow-men!"

"But, Judge," Preston continued, "my horse is nearly dead; I have scarcely quitted its back since yesterday morning and——"

"Take my best saddle-horse, Preston," the old man interrupted him; "take and ride it to death, if you like, but catch the villain, and try to make him confess. I will make out a warrant and send a constable with you. My Jim shall, in the meanwhile, carry a letter to the town, to put off the execution till I arrive there, and I will myself ride to the Doctor's house to console the poor women, who require it badly enough."

The old man made these several arrangements quickly in succession, and the hope of saving the Doctor, whom he loved like a son, seemed to have rendered him twenty years younger. Preston, Vollheim, and the constable galloped away to the store, selecting a nearer road than that past the Doctor's house.

The sun had set, and the shades of night were closing in, when they perceived, at the skirt of a little wood, the house, through whose solitary window the melancholy light of a tallow candle gleamed.

When they arrived, they delivered their horses to a young Irishman who performed the functions of ostler, and walked into the little store that was almost blocked up with various goods.

"Is Curneales here?" Preston asked the trader, who was comfortably extended on the counter, and appeared to take no more notice of his new customers than by calling out "How do you do?" to them.

"Curneales! yes, in the other house. But you can't see him now —he's asleep—he drank a little drop too much, and his head has grown rather heavy—he has been asleep for nearly a couple of hours."

"But we must see him," the constable replied sharply, and walked before the other two; but Vollheim took him by the arm, and requested him to let them go in first, as they hoped to make the man's evil conscience a traitor to him on their sudden appearance. He consented, and the two friends entered the little blockhouse, which was only separated by a passage from the other in which the shop was, but was under the same roof with it.

The trader's wife was standing at the fire preparing supper, and, stretched on a bear-hide close to the chimney, lay Curneales, employing an old Spanish saddle as a pillow, on which he held his fox-skin cap with his left hand, in order to lie softly. He was not asleep, but half rose at the entrance of the two men, and looked wildly at them, when he perceived in them the persons who gave the first information about the murder that had been committed.

"Curneales," Preston said, after the customary salutation, "I should like to show you something; will you be good enough to come here to the fire?"

He arose silently and angrily, and then asked, in a growling tone—

"What the devil brings you here so late to disturb a Christian at his rest?"

"Do you know this?" Preston asked quietly and loudly, as he held the powder horn close before the man's restless eyes, who could scarce suppress a cry, and fell back a step in terror, while he pressed his right hand convulsively to his heart beneath his hunting-shirt. At this moment, the constable, who had entered unnoticed, laid his hand on his shoulder, and said, calmly and firmly—

"You are my prisoner!"

But like a flash of lightning, a broad, heavy knife glittered in the murderer's hand, and with a firm leap, and brandishing it wildly, he took advantage of the first surprise of his enemies and bounded through the open door. His triumph, however, was only of short duration, for he was struck to the ground by the fist of the powerful trader (who had seen and heard all that had taken place, and did not doubt for a moment that he had committed some terrible crime), and was immediately seized by the men who were close at his heels, and thrown down and bound, in spite of his desperate resistance.

Foaming at the mouth and gnashing his teeth, he writhed in the hands of his foemen, but Preston's arms held him as in a vice, and at last, perceiving that all resistance was useless, he remained quiet, and lay as if dead on the ground. He gave no reply to the questions addressed to him except the most awful oaths, and swore that they should suffer bitterly for maltreating him.

They allowed their horses a good hour's rest; but then Preston grew impatient, and could not stop any longer in the room.

He begged Vollheim to assist the constable in guarding the prisoner and leading him to the town, threw himself again on his horse, and galloped, as rapidly as the animal could bear him, to the Doctor's house.

Oh! with what joyful feelings he now flew towards the desired object. As he reached the open prairie, the lights of the usually so cheerful house gleamed before him, in which, since the melancholy event, pain and sorrow had taken up their terrible abode, and he drove his horse to fresh exertions, so that it flew with him over the plain. At length he reached the gate, sprang from the saddle, and, throwing the reins of his trembling, steaming horse to the groom, he entered the door that Judith opened to him.

But the young man's powerful body was no longer able to bear up against the immoderate exertion—his knees trembled, his pulse ceased beating, and when Judith came to meet him, he had scarce strength enough to cry, "He's innocent! we have the murderer!" before he fell fainting at the feet of the terrified girl.

"He is dying! he is dying!" she shrieked, and threw herself, forgetting all else save the danger of her lover, upon him, and tried to lift him up. "Oh! Holy Mother! he is dying under my hands, and I—I have killed him!" She clasped the lifeless body passionately, and sank half-unconscious by his side.

Mansfield, who had come to console the ladies and prepare them for fresh, joyful hope, now came up, and his and the servant's united exertions succeeded in recalling the exhausted man to life.

They bore him to a bed, where he slowly recovered; but he had scarce regained his senses and recognised those that surrounded him, before he tried to spring up; Mansfield, however, held him with a firm hand, and bade him keep quiet.

"I must go!" Preston exclaimed—"I must go to the town. Have the Doctor's fastest horse saddled; but haste, haste! for a human being's life depends on every moment."

"No," said the Judge; "that would be folly to let you go in your present condition; you are so weak that you can scarcely move an arm."

"Oh! I am as strong as a bear," Preston said, eagerly. "But do let me go, if mine and the Doctor's life are dear to you; the Doctor is innocent—we've got the murderer! Oh! I must, must go!"

"And if the weakness were to overpower you again on the road, and you fell fainting from your horse, who in V—— would hear a word of what you are now so anxious to impart to them? No; a strong, healthy man shall ride over to them, and that, too, on my own horse; but it will be neither you nor I. We will stop here, and prepare the ladies for this change of fortune, for it is long since the poor creatures have experienced such a joyful hour."

Preston saw that he was really too exhausted to bear the fresh journey, and ten minutes later a rider was galloping over the frozen plain, carrying a letter to V—— from the Judge, in which he promised to deliver the real murderer on the next day.

Preston was now obliged to tell all in detail; and Middleton's old mother, who came down now, as the Doctor's wife was slumbering peacefully, through the hope with which she had been inspired, fell thankfully on her knees, and thanked God in fervent prayer, not for her son's innocence, for she had never doubted that, but for the proof of it; and Judith, with an unspeakably soft smile, offered her hand to the young man, who raised it joyfully to his lips.

What need have we of saying more? It would be useless attempting to describe the joy of the good beings when the Doctor again hurried into their arms, acquitted and honourably discharged by his judges. But for a long while he felt the after-pangs of the terrible suspicion that had rested upon him, if only for awhile, and a violent fever confined him to his bed; but both himself and his wife eventually perfectly recovered.

Although he was now almost adored by his neighbours, who did everything in their power as reparation for their former suspicion, and to recompense the Doctor for the sufferings he had endured, still he could never forget that he had been esteemed a murderer and robber, and condemned as such by those whom he had ever loved as his friends. The next year, in spite of old Mansfield's prayers, who did all in his power to prevent him, he removed across the Mississippi into the State of Missouri.

It is scarcely necessary to remark that a second little family emigrated with him to the Far, Far West, and that William Preston and his young wife did much to render his life in the quiet forests of his new home easy and pleasant, so that he soon forgot, in the society of those kind beings, how he had been once mistaken and suspected.

Vollheim followed the two families a few years later, and acquired a considerable fortune through lead mines he found on his land, and which he worked himself, as well as through several foundries he established.

Curneales, when confined in the prison of V——, confessed the murder, but escaped on the day before the execution, through Messworth's aid, as it was said; but this could not be proved, and he himself only remained for a few days in that neighbourhood after Curneales' flight. It was believed that Curneales fled to Mexico.

LOST AND FOUND.

LOST AND FOUND.

A Tale of Indian Life.

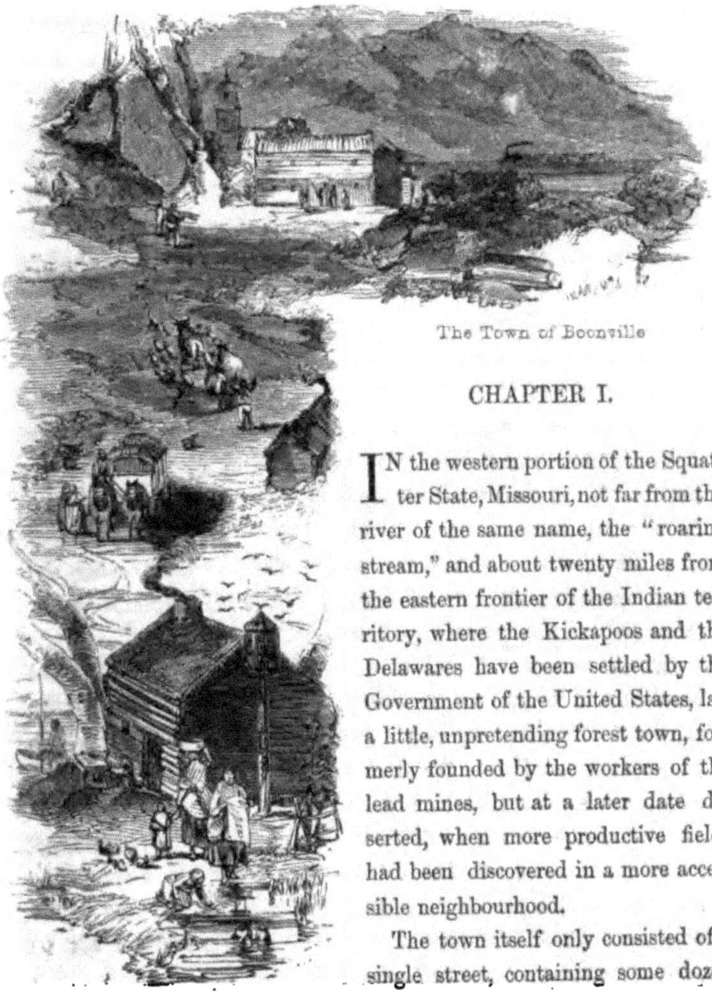

The Town of Boonville

CHAPTER I.

IN the western portion of the Squatter State, Missouri, not far from the river of the same name, the "roaring stream," and about twenty miles from the eastern frontier of the Indian territory, where the Kickapoos and the Delawares have been settled by the Government of the United States, lay a little, unpretending forest town, formerly founded by the workers of the lead mines, but at a later date deserted, when more productive fields had been discovered in a more accessible neighbourhood.

The town itself only consisted of a single street, containing some dozen houses, the largest of which was the meeting-house; the most comfortable that belonging to the trader or storekeeper; but the smallest and neatest was inhabited by a poor widow, a Mrs. Rowland, who lived there with her adopted daughter, in great retirement, but universally loved and respected. As my little story principally relates to these persons, my readers will possibly like me to explain to them at once, and in as few words as I can, a few things necessary for the understanding of the story, and with which they must have become acquainted eventually.

Mrs. Rowland was the oldest settler in the whole town, for her husband had discovered the lead mines here on a hunting expedition, and had commenced work, as the pioneer of civilization, amidst the then hostile Indians. But he would not be warned by the fate of thousands, who, before him, had sought the red son of the forests in his home, and insulted him by their arrogance. Trusting in his strength and his clever management of his rifle, he despised every danger which might menace him from an enemy or a rival—and fell. A chief of the Delawares had been insulted by him. A few days later he heard the cry of a turkey close to his cabin; he took down his rifle to make sure of the easy prey—went out—and never returned. The sound must have been a snare of the treacherous Indian. A few moments later, the dusky, dread forms flocked round the now unprotected house; and when the unhappy wife recovered from the fainting fit into which the first shock had thrown her, she found herself beneath a tree in front of the smoking remains of her cabin, and her son, her only darling child, had disappeared.

In vain she sought the whole long day, with her bleeding and burnt fingers, through the smouldering remains of her peaceful home: she did not even find the body of her son, to give it Christian burial. In a half-frenzied state she flew through the forest to the nearest cabin, many miles distant, and eventually went in her hopeless sorrow to reside with her sister at St. Louis. Here she lived fourteen long years in retirement; but, although time had assuaged her sorrow, she never forgot the dear one of whom she had been robbed by the murderer's hand; and, most of all, the thought allowed her no peace or rest—that she had never had positive proof of her child's death. Although she was forced to yield to the conviction that her husband had fallen a victim to Indian vengeance, still she could not, either awake or dreaming, dismiss the idea that her boy had perchance been stolen, perchance had escaped, lost his way, and been sheltered by farmers, or possibly by travellers.

When, therefore, she heard of the establishment of the little town of Boonville, scarcely a mile from her former abode, she determined on taking up her residence there, as she was now alone in the world, with her little niece, a pretty child of twelve years of age, whose mother was just dead. There, at least, she would be in the neighbourhood of the spot where she had lost all that she had loved upon this earth; and there, too, she thought her hope would be, if ever, fulfilled.

But six long years had again passed, without her finding a trace of the lost one; and although all the inhabitants of the little town, acquainted as they were with the poor mother's lot, had given themselves the greatest trouble to back up her researches, all appeared useless. The lost one was not to be found; and the poor aged woman gradually drew nearer and nearer to the grave, for which she had been yearning more than ever in the last years, as the sole spot which would unite her to those she fondly loved.

It was a pleasant, sunshiny evening in August; from the north-east a cool, refreshing breeze was blowing, and before the doors of the several houses, beneath the shade of fruit-laden hickories or chestnuts, and surrounded by vessels, from which issued a dense smoke to disperse the troublesome mosquitoes, sat the inhabitants of Boonville; the women engaged with various sorts of needlework, ceasing from their labour at times to cast an eye on the supper cooking in the house, and the men, in *dolce far niente*, whittling pieces of wood, or lazily reclining on buffalo skins extended on the ground. The only chair disengaged was before the pedlar's house, for the mistress was busied with a burning face at the kitchen fire; while Zachariah Smith was serving two Indians, who had come into town a short time before, with their bundles of skins and game, in order to exchange them for things they required: gunpowder, knives, tin cups—and whisky.

They were two warriors of the tribe of Kickapoos, if the name of *warriors* could be given to two of the most miserable specimens of the Indian race. The dirty and torn woollen blankets which they wore scarcely sufficed to cover their nudity; and their hair, no longer rising in the proud scalp-lock, but unkempt and unshorn, and bound into masses by burrs, hung down their brown backs like the hair of a horse's mane. The one wore a shirt; but whether it had been originally made of white stuff or coloured calico, could no longer be distinguished. The blood of the slaughtered game had formed a species of crust upon it which only appeared broken off at the shoulder through carrying the heavy and clumsy rifle; their leggings were patched with pieces of untanned hide, and their mocassins looked as if they would go to pieces at any moment. A belt made of twisted hickory-bark held the little scalping-knife and a short reed pipe; and their inexpressive, monotonous features did not brighten up till they noticed, in the trader's store, the whisky casks. The bargain was very simple, and, therefore, soon arranged; the necessary quantity of powder they received and put in their horns, but the remainder-price they naturally demanded in "uiski," and they soon sat down with it in a corner, between salt and meal tubs, and began their carouse without any further preparation.

They only possessed one cup, and the younger Indian looked on with widely-opened eyes, almost ready to start from their sockets, when the elder poured the yellow fire-water into it; his broad mouth was expanded into a still broader grin, and two rows of splendidly white teeth became visible. One hand he extended at the same time, almost involuntarily, towards the celestial draught; and a gentle, gurgling laugh was heard, as his comrade raised the cup first to his lips. But the smile disappeared; the corners of the mouth again contracted, although the lips were still parted, and the eye assumed a still more fixed and anxious expression, when the friend, no longer behaving as such, seemed to be glued to the tin cup.

"Ugh!" the first drinker at length said, removing the cup, after a long, long draught of bliss, and looking over it at his comrade, whose features, however, suddenly resumed their hilarity; he stretched out his hand, seized the cup, which he did not let loose again, and now appeared determined on taking full and entire revenge on the person who had caused him to undergo all the martyrdom of expectation. Thus they drank in turn, each observing with breathless anxiety the disappearance of the seductive poison—each, when the turn came to him, forgetting his former feelings in the consciousness of his happiness, which excluded every other thought. And before them, on the counter, holding his right knee with both hands, his body bent a little back to maintain his balance, and, with his smiling eyes fixed on the tippling couple, sat the trader, to all appearance excessively amused at the scene.

But though the savages had been serious and word-sparing at first, they grew more cheerful as the dire drink coursed through their veins, and its fierce spirit attacked their brains. They began singing little fragments of war chants, probably praising—for Smith understood their language very imperfectly—their own excellent and unsurpassable qualities; and it seemed as if their frenzied hilarity increased in proportion as the tide ebbed in the bottle which was cruising so rapidly between them.

"Ugh!" one of them cried, as he tried to fill his cup again, and found, to his horror, that the bottle, which he had just raised to the light, and thence calculated must contain at least a cup and a-half, now only permitted a decent drain—"what that? uiski in it, and wont come out!"

While the other bent over to him curiously, and in great alarm, he turned the bottle up, and found, to his far from pleasurable surprise, the heel.

"Wah!" he cried in astonishment, "great hole here; white man has great hole in bottle—ugh—bad—Indian have bottle full—nothing in hole."

"Ugh, bad!" the other chimed in, and showed, by a nod of his head, that he perfectly coincided with the sentiments just expressed.

"Eh, Indian," the trader replied, "look at the other bottles; there's the hole in all of them; they hold the right measure, and are made so on purpose. If it was not for the hole, the bottle would be made smaller."

"No need," the speaker growled again; "white man has got skins whole—only bullet-hole in them—can be mended up again—white man must mend this hole, too."

"Ah, ah, ah!" Smith laughed, "that's a comical notion, too. How could I pour in at top and bottom both? But besides this, you've both had as much as you can comfortably carry."

"No harm," the second Indian growled, and pointed to the bottle—"stop the hole."

"Well, if you must have it," the trader laughed, and jumped down from the counter, "I don't care for the couple of drops. Here, Kickapoo, hold the bottle—but stand firm; why, fellow, the drink's got in your head already, and still you want more."

"No harm," the savage grinned, "very good more—much better word than less—less bad word."

"So then, not less hot, less hungry, less thirsty," Smith laughed as he stooped down to the cask.

"No, no," cried the Kickapoo, and his eyes already devoured every drop that was measured out to them, "always more thirsty—thirsty very good—very, very good."

The hole, however, had not yielded so much as they had possibly expected, for they kept its contents a long while stationary between them, and talked much and zealously in their own language; but at last they emptied it; and when the trader remained inexorable, and would not give a drop more, one of them produced a little packet from his blanket, which he unfolded, and took out a finely-prepared otter skin. It was evident that they had not intended to sell this for whisky, but probably exchange it for other pressing necessaries for the squaw at home, who usually prepares objects of this nature; but the terrible greediness which the red sons of the forest, once tempted, feel for the destructive enjoyment of the fire-water, soon ended the struggle which was probably going on within their breasts.

The Indian threw the skin, which the American carefully examined, on the counter, and asked at first for half a bottle of whisky, afterwards something else; they only intended to spend a portion of the property intrusted to them in drink. With the draught, however, their desire for it increased; and cup after cup was poured out for them by the head-shaking and dissatisfied trader, until the last cent had been swallowed, and their indefatigable throats required more still.

"More uiski," one now stuttered, with bloodshot eyes, and stretched out his arm with the bottle to the American, "more uiski —skin worth a bottle more."

"You shan't have any more," the trader replied in the most decided manner; for he feared, and that justly, the wild, unbounded temper of his guests, who, however peaceable they might be in a sober condition, in a state of intoxication frequently ran a-muck, and were capable of the worst. "You two have drunk more than would have done six of you good, and it is better for you to sleep off your drunkenness for a couple of hours."

"Drunkenness—sleep!" the elder of the two stuttered, as he seized the bottle by the neck, and hurled it in a corner, where it broke into a thousand fragments. "White man, more—Po-co-mo-con sober as a young bear. White man drunk, totters like a young birch—ha! ha! ha!—more uiski, pale-face, more uiski!"

"You'll not have a drop more," the trader said, and pointed to the broken bottle. "Are you good Indians? do good Indians do that? do sober young bears do it? Pack up your traps, and I will take you to my storehouse; there you can snore till the morning, and then you shall have each a cup-full—are you satisfied with that?"

"Yes," said the elder, "yes, very good—cup-full—very good—but now, not to-morrow—to-morrow another!"

"You're a clever fellow. No, have a sleep first."

"Pale-face cheats," the younger now yelled in his passion, "cheats red man—pale-face gives nothing away."

"Will soon give uiski," the other stuttered, "if he—hic—knew—hic—knew what I do—hic."

"Possibly," said Smith, laconically.

"Not possible," the Indian cried, aroused by the white man's calmness—"no—hic—not possible—certain. Indian knows great secret for white men—hic—great secret of the Konzas—hic—but uiski, more uiski."

"No, you don't," laughed the trader, who naturally thought that the savage was trying to deceive him in order to get another cup of whisky. "You can keep your secret and I my whisky, that will be the best."

"You'd give a cask-full—hic—" growled the savage, "for secret; white man—hic—ugh—two casks-full—hic—white man among Indians—ugh—a tall man—hic—great warrior—ha! ha! ha! ha! worth two casks-full—hic!"

The younger, who did not appear so intoxicated as his companion, and perhaps had a sort of foreboding that they might be exposed to unpleasantness through his chattering, seized his arm, and tried to drag him away; but the other thrust him back with an angry exclamation.

"More uiski—haih!" and his war-yell echoed along the street, so that the children ceased their sport, and the few persons who were still seated before their doors raised their heads in surprise to listen to the fearful sound, which probably summoned up heart-rending reminiscences for many of the number. Smith had also grown attentive. A white man among the Indians! Something of that sort was evidently meant by the confused speech. He did not know whence it came, but almost involuntarily the thought of Mrs. Rowland crossed his brain, and he determined on pursuing the trace as rapidly as possible.

"Hulloh, Indian! is that true what you're saying?" he addressed him, and walked round the counter.

"Aha!" the red-skin grinned. "Po-co-mo-con right? heik—Pale-face give whole cask-full—heik—heik—for story—here's the cup."

Smith filled it, with a shake of the head, from a jug that stood on the counter, and looked inquiringly at the Indian; but the latter had carried it too far. With glassy eyes and a sickly smile he raised the vessel once more to his lips, but he could not swallow any more.

"Heik," he stuttered, and the whisky poured down his brown chest and shirt; "heik—white man—good—but uiksi better—much better—heik."

And the cup fell from his hand. Po-co-mo-con moved forward a step to maintain his balance, but slipped on the wet floor, and would have fallen had not the trader seized him. But there was no chance of carrying on any conversation this evening; even the younger man seemed so intoxicated, or at least pretended to be so, probably to escape any questioning, that there was no chance of a reasonable reply from either of them. Smith, therefore, did the only thing left him under these circumstances—he dragged the unconscious Indians, without further delay, into his warehouse, threw them on a pile of deer and bear skins in one corner, and carefully locked the door upon them, with the determination not to let them go the next morning till they had confessed the whole story, and whether things were really as he now fancied them.

But when the morning came, and Smith went to the store with the intention of waking his prisoners, he found, to his intense surprise, the nest already empty, and no trace of the Indians; on closer examination, he saw that they had broken through a corner of the low roof, which they could easily reach by means of the rough beams, and had taken with them two famously-smoked deer hams, which he had only purchased the previous day for a silver quarter-dollar a-piece. The loss of the hams he felt least; they had drunk, and would probably wish to eat. He would have given them the hams, if he had only known the real case about the secret. The wish, however, remained a wish; and if he thought at the first moment of pursuit, he immediately gave up the idea again as impossible to be carried out; for of course the savages would take all possible trouble to leave no trail, or at least visible one, behind them.

But what to do now? Smith, in his reverie, whittled away a couple of pieces of wood, which, in quieter humour, would have lasted him the whole day, and still came to no resolve; for, to tell Mrs. Rowland anything of the matter, without a certainty, would have been a cruelty to the poor old woman, whose death would probably result from her hopes being unsatisfied. Then, might it not be presumed that the treacherous savage might have invented the whole story in order to get another draught of whisky? But the other had evidently been frightened when the elder mentioned the subject. Ha! there was a man passing whom, in the present state of the case, he most desired to see.

"Hulloh, Tom—oh, Tom!" he cried.

"Hulloh, Smith! What, up so early?" the person addressed said, in a cordial tone. "Good morning."

He went across to the house, and stood in the doorway, resting on his rifle.

Tom Fairfield was a tall, powerful man, a real backwoodsman hunter, body and soul, and never happier than when he was out in the forest following a trail or setting a trap. He seemed now to be on an expedition; he carried his rifle in his hand, the light Spanish pack-saddle and bridle on his shoulder, to look for his horse in the forest; and had the woollen blanket bound round him, to camp wherever night surprised him.

"Listen, Tom," Smith said, with a much more serious face than he usually assumed, and at the same time drew the young man into the store. "You are well acquainted with the Rowlands. Well, you needn't blush, my boy; here, take a drain; it's dogwood and sherry bitters, and will do you good—the whole township knows that you are courting Rosy."

"Nonsense, Smith," said Fairfield, and, to conceal his embarrassment, emptied the glass at a draught.

"Bah! man," the latter said, "why do you want to deny it? Don't try to persuade me you provide them with firewood, game, and so on, out of mere friendship."

"And pray whom could two helpless females——"

"Ah! pack of nonsense; that's all stuff. Rosy is a nice, good girl, and you're a handsome young fellow, a good hunter, and a good workman; then what should prevent you from setting up housekeeping? But there's something I want to ask you about. Would you do the Rowlands a very great service?"

"Rowlands! What is it? Tell me," Tom cried, evidently startled by Smith's seriousness. "Is it in my power?"

"You are best judge of that," said Smith. And then he told him, in a few words, what he had heard the previous evening from the Indians, and his own ideas on the subject. Fairfield listened silently, and with the most eager attention; he seemed to watch every word as it escaped from the speaker's lips, and only nodded at times, when the trader made any remark that agreed with his own thoughts.

"And you fancy that Mrs. Rowland's son is living among the Konzas?" he at last asked, when the trader stopped and looked at him inquiringly.

"I don't really know," said Smith, "what I ought to believe; but if a white man is living there as an Indian—and the drunken rascal's remark leads me to believe it—why should it not be young Rowland as well as any one else? The journey would be the only thing; but that is, in truth, no trifle, and it requires just such a man as yourself to undertake it. How far do you fancy it is to the village of the Konzas?"

"I don't care for distance," the young hunter said, thoughtfully; "but the tribe's large and widely dispersed."

"How old would the boy be now?" Smith asked.

"Two-and-twenty. Mrs. Rowland was speaking about him only yesterday, and said his birthday was just at hand. But," he added, in a gentler tone, "she must not know a word about it, for the anxiety and expectation would kill her."

"That is just what I was thinking," said Smith, "and made me so glad to see you. But her joy when you return with him!"

A similar scene seemed also to flit by Tom's mind, for he smiled silently, and then passed his hand across his brow.

"Smith," he said, and bent down to him, "you seem to take an interest in them, and I am glad to see it. But you do not know, and you could not, indeed, how happy the fulfilment of the poor old woman's earnest wishes would make *me*; and on that account alone I owe you unbounded gratitude for giving me even a prospect of realizing her hopes. I will go to the Konzas, and that within an hour."

"What, directly?" Smith cried in surprise; "but that is not possible. You must surely make more preparations for a journey of a hundred and twenty miles than if you were going to the next watercourse, to shoot a bear or a stag."

"Why," Tom laughed, "is it not all the same, whether I camp out for a week in this neighbourhood, or go a little further? I shall be still in the woods, and what need I take for my comfort?"

"Provisions at the least."

"Those the forest will provide me. I have my blanket and my pillow," he pointed laughingly to his saddle; "and what more do I want?"

In fine, spite of all the trader's representations, Tom could not be persuaded to give up his expedition; and all he was induced to do was to roll up a piece of bacon, and maize bread, and some pounded coffee, in his blanket—the bacon serving as fat for the lean deer and turkey meat. Half an hour later he took a cordial farewell of the trader, begged him once more not to mention a word of the matter, even to his wife—(at the idea of his intrusting a secret to his wife Smith burst into a loud laugh)—and, five minutes later, had disappeared behind a low thicket of sassafras and dogwood.

Smith stood for a while close to his house, whence he could see the young man as long as he was in sight; and it was not until the morning sun, that rose cheerily above the forest, threw his shadow far across the yard and the quickset hedge, that he suddenly returned to the store, opened the back door, and called into the kitchen—"Mrs. Smith, if any one should happen to call for me, I am going over to Cowley's." And Zachariah Smith walked, with his hands folded thoughtfully upon his back, slowly down the street towards the house mentioned.

"Hm!" Mrs. Smith said directly afterwards, and her sharp nose, somewhat reddened by the heat of the fire, became visible between two glistening grey eyes. "Hm! gone to Cowley's: that's always the way. 'I'm going to Cowley's,' and the wife never goes there: she can stay at home and attend to the shop, and run in whenever any one comes. Well, I'm tired of it. And what's in the wind now? My husband up this morning before daybreak; and these secrets about Mrs. Rowland! Oh! I heard it all, my dear Mr. Smith;" and she turned, with a look of malicious triumph, towards the quarter where she now expected her husband was. "Mrs. Smith hasn't got cotton in her ears when she wants to hear anything. Mrs. Rowland spoke about him, he said—and young Rowland among the Indians—and Mr. Tom sent to fetch him. Oh! Mr. S., I'm not such a simpleton that I can't put two and two together. So, we've found the boy at last—he'll have grown a nice specimen—and my husband is in the secret—is always having to do with those nasty Indians. What a dreadful disturbance that was again last night! Good Mr. Billy-goat will shake his head when I tell him that—and I don't hear a word of the whole story—the beautiful fellow doesn't tell his lawfully married wife a syllable, but goes over to Cowley's. Mr. and Mrs. Cowley, they must hear every morsel of news, and have their fingers in every pie. But only wait, Mr. Smith. I'll find it all out, even if I'm forced to go to Mrs. Rowland's to make inquiries. I've put up with it long enough; but now my patience is exhausted, and I'll try whether I can't see as far through a millstone as Mr. Smith can."

And with this laudable determination she suddenly dived again into her kitchen, leaving the tin coffee-pots and iron saucepans and pans, which hung on the surrounding walls, in unbounded astonishment over the splendid harangue they had just heard.

But although Mrs. Smith, in the first outbreak of insulted curiosity, had formed such a desperate design of taking Mrs. Rowland by storm, and insisting on knowing what secrets were going on between that lady and her own lawful husband; still, in cooler blood, she appeared to yield to quieter feelings, and first tried her powers of persuasion on her husband. But he remained for twelve whole days deaf and dumb both to the *tiraillerie* fire of insinuations and the heavy battery of direct questions; and as, during all this whole time, Tom Fairfield was not seen in Boonville, and some persons began expressing their anxiety lest something had happened to him, she could no longer bridle her curiosity, but really decided on paying Mrs. Rowland a visit—a duty she indeed owed as a neighbour. She felt, at the same time, firmly convinced that she would have no difficulty, during the course of conversation, in obtaining a glance at the circumstances which so nearly interested her, and were guarded with such secrecy.

The fourteenth day since the Indians' visit to Boonville had arrived, and the first of the month of September as well, which, however, had been announced by heavy storm-clouds, and the gloomy mist lay in compact brooding masses over the groaning and heaving forest. Mrs. Rowland was seated, warmly wrapped up with pillows and shawls, in a roughly-made but comfortable arm-chair—for the wind whistled cool and sharply over the clearing, and the old lady had felt worse for the last few days than she had ever done before. At her feet sat Rosy, the pretty, charming maid, with her left arm lightly resting on her aunt's knee, and holding a little Testament, from which she was reading to the aged woman "The Sermon on the Mount." She had just finished a chapter, and a tear glistened in her eye, as she let the book fall, and looked up to the pale, care-worn face of her more than mother; she gently touched her hand, and whispered—

"Shall I read any more, mother?"

"Stop now, dear child," said the matron, as she laid her thin hand on the young girl's smooth tresses; "stop now, you have exerted yourself too much, and have other matters to attend to. Suppose you were to go over to Cowley's, and beg them to send us their man for half an hour, to bring us in some firewood—only a little: Tom is sure to return to-day."

"There's plenty of wood," Rosy said, quietly. "I went early this morning into the forest, and fetched an arm-full to boil your soup; and when I came back Mr. Cowley had sent his Tim with a whole cart-load, and he was just beginning to cut it into lengths. You were still asleep, mother."

"They are very good people," the old lady whispered. "May God requite them! It is wretched, though, to be so alone in the world, without a son, without a friend."

"Mother!" Rosy entreated in a reproachful voice.

"You are right, my child; I am perhaps unjust to you and Tom Fairfield. But if he did not return—if he, too—— Do not be vexed, my child," she proceeded, after a long pause; "you know how sorrowful and wretched I must feel on this day, the anniversary of that terrible morning. I see everything in darker colours than perhaps is right; and, at times, cannot understand how I, a weak old woman, could survive all those strong healthy beings!"

"Mother!" the niece implored, as she rose, and, hiding her face on the old lady's shoulder, whispered in a soft voice, whose utterance was almost choked by tears, "if I cannot be to you as a son, still I love you like my own mother."

Mrs. Rowland made no reply, but threw her arms affectionately round the lovely girl, and held her tightly pressed to her bosom. At this moment there was a loud knock at the door, and in joyful surprise, and with beaming eyes, Rosy hastened to open it. Mrs. Rowland, too, raised herself, and looked with interest towards the door, for that was just Tom's knock, and for how many miserable days had Rosy awaited it with ever-increasing anxiety. Quickly, and with a trembling hand, Rosy drew back the bolt, and threw the door open; but an "Ah!" of painful surprise escaped her lips, and Mrs. Rowland, too, sank back on her pillow with a gentle sigh, when the good-tempered, but still sharp and most unwelcome face of Mrs. Smith was seen in the doorway. There was no chance of turning her away. The lady scarce saw the breach open before she rushed in with laudable zeal; straightway took a chair by Mrs. Rowland's, and then made a thousand excuses that she had come in without any preparation; the storm had surprised her on her road to Cowley's, and she could not refrain from taking advantage of this opportunity when she was in the neighbourhood—she lived about five hundred yards from Mrs. Rowland's—to visit them, and see how the dear, dear patient was.

Mrs. Rowland replied to all this in a gentle voice, and with all possible conciseness. She hoped, perchance, that in this way, by giving Mrs. Smith no opportunity for conversation, she might shorten her visit. But if that had been her intention, she was little acquainted with Mrs. Smith, or at least gave her credit for much less sociability than she really possessed. The good lady asked once, and at starting, whether she disturbed them; and on receiving a polite, though hesitating "No," in reply, she did not lose a moment in making herself as comfortable as possible. She laid down her great cotton umbrella, took off her mittens, pulled from her pocket a short pipe, which was already filled, or "loaded," as Mrs. S. sometimes called it, lighted it at the fire, and soon felt, to use her own expression, thoroughly at home. Mrs. Rowland was gradually so exhausted by the conversation, although she needed to make hardly any reply, that she at last sank back in her chair and closed her eyes. Even Mrs. Smith fancied she must allow the old lady some peace, but made up her mind to begin upon the younger lady instead.

"It will soon be lively in this house," she remarked, when Rosy had arranged her aunt's pillow, and taken her place near her, or rather between her and their visitor, to deaden the sound of conversation as much as possible. "Yes, when there's a man in the house, things are very different."

Rosy, poor girl, blushed down to her neck-ribbon, but, at the same time, looked with astonishment at the talkative dame.

"Come, come, miss!" Mrs. Smith continued, somewhat annoyed at the idea that the young girl showed no readiness to confide in her, "you needn't pretend to be so terribly innocent. I know the whole story; but I'll keep it a secret—not a person shall hear a syllable from me."

"But, dear Mrs. Smith——"

"But, dear Rosy Baywood, if you don't like to talk to me about it, I've no objection. But how long has he really been lost?"

"Lost! Oh, do you really believe that he is lost?" Rosy now cried in her alarm for the man she loved; for she naturally thought that the remark referred to him.

"Is! Was, dear miss," Mrs. Smith said, with a smile. "But after such a length of time to find a man again among those terrible red savages seems to me very remarkable. But what I was going to say—how long is it since Mrs. Rowland lost him?"

"Mrs. Rowland?" the young girl repeated, now quite astray, and the old lady, either aroused from her half-sleep by her name being mentioned, or listening probably to the conversation with closed eyes, turned her head gently towards the speaker, and looked up to her. "Mrs. Rowland? I really do not know."

"Well, it must be some twenty years," continued the undaunted Mrs. Smith, who was determined to let them know that she was perfectly acquainted with all the circumstances. "I can remember very distinctly, that my dear departed John Rosbeard, of Connecticut, who found a lead mine here, spoke about it. But I hope they'll wash him before they bring him in. Good gracious! one of those painted men is a terrible sight, with his blue cheeks, a yellow nose, red ears, and green lips, and the scalp—only think, Miss Baywood, when my late husband described the scalping to me, and showed me his scalp, still safe and sound on his head, I really fell down like a log of wood, in a fainting fit. If they only wouldn't scalp I could put up with all the rest; but scalping is horrible."

"Mrs. Smith!" the old lady here suddenly cried, starting from her chair in terror and painful surprise, for her visitor's remarks, so exactly in accordance with what she had been thinking of during the whole tearful day, drove the blood, with terrible rapidity, through her veins, and her heart beat almost audibly.

"Mother!" Rosy implored; "mother, it is only a mistake."

"Good gracious, Mrs. Rowland," the amiable lady went on, "I really didn't think you would hear it. No! he wont think any more about scalping, if he did it before. The terrible fellows cannot refrain from that. They are their war trophies, as they call them; but Mr. Billygoat will teach him the duties of a good and pious Christian. Oh, Mr. Billygoat is an excellent gentleman!"

"Mrs. Smith," the patient said, gently; and the hand which Rosy seized trembled as if from ague. "*Who* will not think any more about scalping? *who* wears the colours and marks of the savages? who—the whole room is going round with me—who was lost twenty years ago, and has—has been found again?"

"But, dear Mrs. Rowland," the worthy trader's wife asked, good-humouredly, "why are you so secret with me? I know the whole story. Hasn't Tom Fairfield ridden off to fetch him? I don't know with what tribe he is, for I couldn't catch the name rightly; but if you don't wish it, I'll really not say a syllable about it to any living being."

"Tom Fairfield gone to fetch him—from what tribe?" the old lady repeated, in a trembling, half-suffocated voice, and held her brow between her icy-cold hands. "Am I dreaming, or have sorrow and pining driven me mad?"

"Well, I never saw such a woman!" Mrs. Smith said, shaking her head, though now somewhat alarmed by the excitement the sick woman displayed.

Rosy started up—a thought of what was meant, and, perhaps, was even then being done, crossed her mind; and, casting only one glance on the unhappy old lady, she made a sign to Mrs. Smith not to utter a syllable about it, whatever it might be. But it was too late; ere the trader's wife understood what she was to do, or ere Rosy could bend down and whisper to her, Mrs. Rowland again raised her head, and her glance met that of her niece, fixed so reproachfully on the chattering dame. She quickly comprehended her meaning, and was by it the more concerned in the painful certainty, which she did not dare to express, through fear of dispelling the charm which held her senses enchained in a sweet, though perchance fearful dream. But in the same way as the maniac contrives to deceive the watchfulness of his guardian, the old lady employed the opportunity, with almost convulsive haste, of drawing from the dame the secret which contained life or death for her.

"You are right, Mrs. Smith," she said, and tried to smile with torture gnawing at her heart, "we do not want to keep anything longer secret from you."

"See now, dear Mrs. Rowland!" the lady cried, now perfectly appeased, with triumphant delight; "I told you so from the beginning—though my husband—"

"And Tom Fairfield has gone to fetch him—to bring him to Boonville?"

"Dearest mother!" Rosy implored in her terror, for she dreaded, not without reason, the fearful consequences which such excitement must produce on the patient.

"Quiet, my child, quiet!" the sufferer soothed her. "I am perfectly well now—quite well, Rosy. And Tom Fairfield, ma'am?"

"Well, he really cannot be much longer; but it is true, now, he'll bring him—eh?"

"Him? Yes, certainly. You mean—you mean—"

"Why, your son!"

"Ha!"

The old lady uttered a cry which cut them both to the heart. Rosy threw herself immediately on her fainting form, crying, in a reproachful tone—

"Oh! Mrs. Smith, what have you done?—you've killed her!"

And the worthy dame stood at first very much frightened, for she did not yet comprehend the whole affair, although the idea was gradually dawning upon her that she had played an extremely stupid trick, and had got herself in a very unpleasant position. In this she was speedily confirmed by Rosy's explanation; and when she heard that neither of them had known the cause of Tom's departure, she was perplexed indeed. The best-hearted woman in the world, and the very last to purposely injure one of her neighbours—least of all the worthy, unhappy old lady—the idea became insupportable to her, that, through her chattering, which she could not now sufficiently blame, she had caused such a misfortune. She would not quit Mrs. Rowland's side, did everything in her power to lighten Rosy's burden, and would not grow calm until she saw that the old lady had recovered from her fainting fit, and had sunk into a sound sleep, the probable result of exhaustion.

Extraordinary was the change which had taken place in her since hearing Mrs. Smith's news. She remained the whole day so calm and resigned, inquired several times whether *they* had not come, and made Rosy promise not to conceal their arrival from her; but she avoided mentioning his name—the word "son" had not yet crossed her lips. Thus five o'clock arrived. Mrs. Smith had inquired several times how the old lady was, and was begging pardon for at least the twentieth time for her foolishness, when another knock was heard at the door, and Mrs. Rowland started up in her chair with a half-suppressed cry; for when the door opened, Tom Fairfield entered—but alone.

Rosy started also; but, before Tom could utter a word, Mrs. Rowland stretched out her arm towards him with a fixed, unshrinking eye, and said, in a scarcely audible voice—

"Where is he?"

"Heavens!" said Tom, in terror, and looking at Rosy; "how does your mother know?"

"Where is he, Tom? If you wish to kill me, hold back your reply!"

"She knows all!" Rosy affirmed, tearfully; and Tom, who soon found that all his preparations were unnecessary, calmed the poor woman so far by assuring her that he had found her son, and brought him; that he was well and happy, but that she must calm and prepare herself that evening, and he would bring him across the next morning.

But the mother would not hear a word of it. "To-morrow!—why not to-day—now? Was she less calm now than she would be to-morrow? Certainly not. The long night of expectation would exhaust her strength, and she would see her boy—whom she had mourned for so long—at once."

No representations were of any use; and as Tom himself felt how right she was under the circumstances, he promised to bring her son in half-an-hour, and only begged her to keep calm and quiet, and not give way to her maternal feelings too much. In the meanwhile, Mr. Smith was busied at home in converting the savage—who was proved to be Mrs. Rowland's son by several marks he bore—into a respectable white man. In the first place, the various pigments were washed off, with which he had bedaubed his face, even more than the Indians did, in order that his whiter skin might not be visible through it. Then he was obliged to lay aside, to his evident regret, all the ornaments with which he was begirt—especially all which caused any reminiscences of scalping, and similar horrors—and, last of all, put on—and he was clumsy enough in them—"human trousers," as Smith called them, and not in such cut-away things, which left off just where respectable trousers ought to begin. Besides this, he received waistcoat, coat, shirt, and shoes. Although, however, he appeared tolerably satisfied with all, or, at least, put up with them without opposition, he threw off the latter immediately, because they pinched him, and he could not lift his feet from the ground. He also spurned, in the most obstinate manner, the splendid black hat which Smith pressed upon his brown, bushy locks with visible delight. He would not listen to any persuasion; and, at last, nothing was left but to lead him to his mother, bare-headed and barefooted.

The word "mother" was the only charm which had led him hither from his wild, free life, to the village of the pale-faces. "Mother!" the sound struck him like a melody heard in youth, but long forgotten; and though gently, with such force that he felt his heart beat, and he could not but follow the celestial sound. And now he stood at the door, which the white man at his side pointed out to him, and he timidly turned his eyes to the right and left, as if wishing to fly from the interview he had so longed for. Convulsively, and as if seeking help, he seized Tom's arm, who walked close at his side, and he felt ashamed that a pale-face should see him in such a state of excitement.

"Ugh! how cold I am!" he whispered, and drew his coat firmly over his chest, as he had been wont to do with his blanket.

And within the house, her cheeks reddened by internal excitement, and with sparkling, animated eyes, sat the old lady, holding her niece's hand firmly in her own, lest she might leave her at this moment; for without she heard steps—voices—and in breathless excitement she listened to the sounds, striving whether she could distinguish—Heavens, how her heart beat!—the voice of her child—her son!

And now—now the door opened, through which the trader walked with a polite and kindly salutation; and behind him Mrs. Rowland saw Tom's open, manly brow, and at his side a brown, uncovered head. She raised herself in her chair—all the weakness of her illness had left her—she stood strong and alone, held by no one, supported by no one.

"My dear Mrs. Rowland," said Smith; but the mother regarded not the stranger who separated her and her child.

"My son, my son!" she cried, extending her arms yearningly, imploringly towards the men. And now the half savage could no longer be silent; he tore himself loose from Tom, who sought to hold him back, pushed the trader on one side, and flew with a hurried bound, and the gently, joyfully-uttered exclamation of "Mother!" into the aged woman's arms. They held him in a firm, close embrace, as if they would never be loosened again during life; but the mother's strength gave way in the one feeling of blessed delight, and she only felt herself supported from falling by the arms of her son. "My child—my son!" she said, soothingly, as she at length fell back in her chair, and he sank on his knees before her, half involuntarily, half drawn by her. "My dear, dear child! the lost one found at last; years of sorrow and suffering requited, before life had quitted this old, weak body—my dear, dear child!"

John remained long and silently in her embrace; and it seemed as if he were ashamed of being so weak and womanish before "white" men; at least he threw a timid glance round the room when he raised his head; but he was alone with his mother. All had quitted the room; even Mrs. Smith, who, now that her precipitation had produced no ill consequences, had come with good spirits to be present at the meeting; but she was taken, very much against her wish, by the arm by Mr. Smith, in a much more affectionate manner than usual, and led out of the room. Mother and son remained

The Indian Village.

long alone. The latter had soon overcome the last feelings of timidity, and now sat by his mother's side, patted her head, and called her, in his broken English, by all the sweetest, most endearing names he could think of. It was not till the expiration of half-an-hour, and when they had both grown calmer, that the others returned; and Tom was obliged to tell at once how he had found the lost one, and induced him to accompany him. He did so, though, in a few words.

The tribe of the Konzas he had reached on the fourth day after his departure from Boonville, and immediately commenced his researches : but he could gain no decided answer from either warrior or chief. A part of those he addressed pretended not to understand him. A part denied any knowledge of a white man among their nation. But this very denial confirmed the American in his belief that they did not speak the truth; for some regarded him with surprise, as if they could not comprehend how he had learned it; others grew confused, and said they did not know exactly, but believed there had been a white man among them once. At last he found among them a Canadian-Frenchman, who quickly put him upon the right track. On the same evening he led him to the village where the "White-deer," as he termed him, lived; and, although the latter would not at first have any communication with the pale-face, and even obstinately refused to speak a word of English to him, still he gladly heard the village of the white men spoken of, and even began to listen attentively when the stranger spoke of his mother, who had been waiting so many years in sorrow for his return, and had hoped to see her son once again ere she died. Tom had caused an immense impression upon him when he at last said, as the savage could not be induced to follow him—"And then the White-deer wishes his sick old mother to sink into her grave, and have no son to cover her wigwam, to kill game for her, and make it ready to strengthen her? Shall strangers dig her grave, lest wolves and vultures should desecrate her remains?" "Ugh!" the savage shouted. "White man right—White-deer bad son!" and he sprang up and rushed out into the forest.

Tom Fairfield was not a little astonished when the White-deer had disappeared the next morning, and could be found nowhere; he searched through cabin after cabin, and met many an angry word, many a threat, when he entered the wigwam of any warrior hostile to the pale-faces.

He was just giving up all hope of finding the fugitive, and had mounted his horse to return to the adjoining village, where the Canadian had raised his wigwam, when suddenly the White-deer came up on his rough-haired pony, fully equipped for war, and offered to accompany him. Some of the tribe at first opposed it and would not suffer a man who had become one of themselves to be carried away from them in such a manner. The White-deer did not appear, however, easily intimidated; with bold words he repulsed the dissatisfied; and, his war-club in the right, and his rifle in the left hand, he bounded dauntlessly through the crowd, who made way for him, and did not actively attempt to stop him or his companion.

Thus they arrived at Boonville; and John Rowland stooped down over his mother's hand affectionately, and she begged him, for the few days she would still remain on earth, never, never to leave her.

A whole month passed thus without any event of importance occurring at Boonville. But, although the matron, in her happiness at recovering her child, had for the first few weeks revived, and appeared to have forgotten all her weakness and illness, still the natural exhaustion which must follow such a state of excitement, even in a healthy mind, soon returned, and she became daily weaker. As regarded John (for he had given up his name of White-deer from the outset), he felt himself more at ease with the civilized life of the townsmen than might have been expected; he at least wore the clothes which had been given him—after some time, even shoes and hat; ate at table with fork and spoon, and seemed especially happy by his mother's side, by whose bed he sat for hours, with most pleasure when she was asleep, and looked silently and seriously on her face. With this exception, people did not get on well with him; he was wild and domineering, as he had been accustomed ever since he had become a warrior, and seemed ill-disposed to alter now.

Rosy managed best with him; the gentle, amiable girl exercised great influence over him; and whenever, in dress, manners, or language, as was often the case, he fell back into his old habits, it only required a word from Rosy, or even only a glance, to bend his temper, which in some instances would not even yield to his mother. But there were three persons in Boonville whom John escaped from when he could, and for whom he in the course of time felt a species of hatred. The first was our good but talkative Mrs. Smith, who from the outset had so tormented him with questions and inquiries, that he was really afraid of her; and once even, to the horror of his mother, who could not imagine what was the matter with him, he jumped out of the window as she came in at the door. The second was the Reverend Pastor, who in his saintly zeal thought it his duty to convert the poor, blind pagan. At first, and especially as it caused his mother great delight, John listened attentively to his remarks; and although afterwards he could only be induced, by Rosy, to remain quietly seated as soon as the preacher—or the medicine man, as he persisted in calling him—had laid his hand upon him and commenced his exhortation, still in that he only remained faithful to the beautiful Indian custom of never interrupting the speaker, but let him end his discourse, and listened to him at least with external attention. But the pastor was greatly mistaken if he thought for a moment this was the result of John's devotion. John hated the old man like sin, or perhaps worse; still at first they remained on a tolerably peaceful footing, and the preacher seemed satisfied when his new convert remained quiet for the proper season.

The third person was, strange to say, no one else than Tom Fairfield—who must be regarded as the chief cause and instrument of his return. At first the two young fellows appeared inseparable. Tom took all conceivable trouble to initiate the lad in the mysteries of civilized life; and John, although with visible repugnance, willingly acquiesced in every change which the backwoodsman, whom he found to be a famous hunter, and consequently respected, recommended him. But the longer he lived in his mother's house, where Tom Fairfield was a daily guest, the more he withdrew from his society, answered his inquiries syllabically, avoided his company, and became quarrelsome towards him, if he could not escape him otherwise; which was not his wont, even with the preacher. This became more apparent as autumn advanced, and Mrs. Rowland's condition grew daily worse. At this time Rosy was confined almost exclusively to the bedside of her mother. John also quitted the house very rarely, and only when he went to the forest to shoot a stag or turkey; but when he had a store of meat he would look on for hours, while Rosy nursed his mother, or, when she had fallen asleep, pushed on one side her usual employment—the large, whirring spinning-wheel—and seated herself with her sewing at the foot of the bed.

November came at last, and, although the glorious autumn—called, in this its fairest season, the Indian summer—brought pleasant and warm days, still the north-west wind frequently howled over the tops of the trees, which were clothed in all the gorgeous panoply of the fall. And when the foliage had died away, strength and life faded from the heart of the old lady. For years she had courageously borne suffering, offered her brow to sorrow; now, with the return of joy, her heart yielded to feelings which were too overpowering for it. As the sap disappeared from the foliage and branches of the trees, the stream of life ebbed in her veins, and she daily felt the nearer approach of dissolution.

And yet she would have lived so gladly now—for it had not escaped her that the son, ransomed by such faithful patience, no longer felt happy or comfortable in the family circle. He clung to his mother with all the strength of filial love, and remained by her bedside for hours together, scarcely ever going into the forest, his usual home.

But what would happen when she was gone, and the bond was severed which alone connected him with civilization? There was only one chance of enchaining him afterwards, and that the poor lady saw alone in the union of her niece with Tom Fairfield, who had become an actual settler in Boonville, and had lately proposed in his blunt, honest fashion for Rosy's hand. With them John could remain—in them he would ever find faithful and affectionate relations, and they would surely succeed in restraining her son from returning to that horrible life among the savages. Yes, even for Rosy's sake it was good and necessary that she should be provided for, and have a male supporter, before she lost her aunt; and Mrs. Rowland's only wish was to see their union effected as speedily as possible. Most peculiar was the effect which this announcement, which he heard from his mother's lips, made upon John. He replied not a syllable—he did not raise his eyes from the ground, and his mother asked him twice whether he had heard her, and was glad that his cousin had found such a protector against the storms of fate.

"And will Rosy have white man?" he asked, gently, and as if already acquainted with the answer.

"They have loved each other for several years, and Rosy believes she will be happy with him."

"Good! John is glad!" said the young man, as he got up and left the room. He did not return for the whole day, but remained till late at night in the forest, whence he returned with his pony heavily laden with game, and, without speaking to a single person, climbed up from outside into his bedroom. From that day John was completely altered. Usually silent and peaceable, he became obstinate and quarrelsome. With the exception of his mother and Rosy, he conversed with nobody, and frequently vented his spite upon those who came across him, or had excited his enmity. Towards the worthy Mrs. Smith this temper was displayed in a mischievous fashion. If she had addressed him by chance, she might be sure that when she was cooking the supper that evening, a stone or piece of wood would come down the chimney; or else some one, who could never be discovered, would fire off a gun close to her, when she would usually be "frightened to death;" or else her chickens would be restless all night; and sometimes a few were missing from places where neither owl nor opposum could have reached them.

But the poor clergyman, who considered it a point of honour to convert the obstinate savage, fared much worse. If he succeeded in catching the "benighted savage" in some place where he could not escape, he would give him an exemplary discourse; then John began to cut the most horrible faces, gnashed his teeth, drew nearer and nearer to the terrified preacher, and perhaps at last yelled the war-cry of the Konzas so close to his ear that the pious man would fly in horror from the room, and hear the savage's contemptuous laugh ringing after him. After every such meeting, he might be certain, however, that on the same night one of his hogs would be missing, or his fence pulled down, and the herds driven a-field; or at times a bullet killed his best and fattest cow. If the sufferers attacked the fancied culprit, they only made the matter worse; and the whole town began to regard the converted savage, as he was at first called, as a nuisance whom they would be glad to get rid of at the earliest opportunity. It was remarkable, however, that John never played any tricks on Tom Fairfield, though his feelings were so hostile towards him; on the contrary, he even saved his life, with great danger to himself, one day when out hunting. Tom had caught an old bear lapping in the neighbourhood of Boonville, but had fired a precipitate shot through a sudden movement on the part of the animal, which brought the slightly-wounded and furious bear upon him directly. The bear had killed one of his dogs, and the

John's struggle with the Bear.

other was too weak to give him any effective assistance; his knife, which met a bone, broke at the first stab; and he would have been wounded dangerously, if not killed, by the beast, had not John thrown himself undauntedly on the furious enemy, and pierced him to the heart so skilfully that he fell dead on the spot. Tom wished to thank the young man, and extended his hand with affectionate words, but the other turned away growling, and disappeared in a neighbouring thicket, without troubling himself further about hunter or prey. At home he did not say a word about it; and when Tom came home and told the story, and the mother patted his cheek with glistening eyes, and Rosy took his hand tearfully, and called him "her dear, dear brother," he became gentler than he had been for many a long day; and on this occasion the pastor even would probably have escaped unpunished, had not this worthy man come for some time past to the determination to leave the pagan savage to his own devices for the sake of his hogs.

Thus matters stood, when the old lady felt one day very weak and ill. Her children no longer quitted her side; and John, especially, sat by her bed, and held her hand firmly in his own. But the sand had run which had been allotted to the sufferer on earth, her strength departed, which till now had sustained the frail edifice.

"Rosy!" she whispered, as the evening sun was opposite her bed, and the red gleam imparted to her ashy features a deceptive brilliancy. "Rosy—Tom—I feel so wondrous light and happy—I do not feel my limbs any more, which confined me like lead to my bed—I believe death is approaching—promise me ever to love my poor boy as your brother."

"Mother!" Rosy sobbed, and laid her face on the shoulder of the dying woman.

"He shall be as my dearest brother!" Tom said, with deep emotion; "yes, these words could not render him dearer to my heart than he already is. John shall never want a friend as long as there is a drop of blood in my veins."

"And, John!" the mother whispered, "will your mother's grave be as dear to you as she was when living?"

John had evidently fought a hard struggle with himself: he was ashamed to weep in the presence of another man, or to display any signs of weakness, and sat silent and motionless, with his eyes fixed immoveably in one corner of the room; but now, at this direct appeal to him, when his eye told him, who had looked on so many dead, that the dear being could live but a few moments, he could no longer endure it; he sank on his knees by the bedside, hid his head in the blanket, and his whole body trembled from the overpowering grief he felt.

"Good John!" the mother whispered, and her hand rested on the son's hand to bless him—"good, dear John!"

"Mother!" Tom Fairfield cried suddenly, for a strange spasm flitted across her face—a peculiar convulsion of her features terrified him. John started suddenly, and fixed his eye for only a second on the dear features.

"My mother!" he sobbed, and the bright tears poured down his sunburnt cheeks; "my dear mother, are you really going?"

The dying woman made no reply—the last pressure of her hand was given to the child—her closing eye was fixed on the setting sun; and with its disappearance behind the gold-glistening foliage of the forest her faithful eyes closed for ever.

On the next day after his mother's death, John dug her a grave on the spot where his father's cabin had stood. She had desired to rest there; and nearly all the inhabitants of the village accompanied the corpse to its last quiet home, under the rustling, waving trees of the forest. John remained there three whole days and nights; and when he at last returned, he was serious and sorrowful, and seemed to have quite lost his former wild manner. He behaved gently as a child to everyone. Even towards the preacher he was affectionate; so affectionate, indeed, that at first he frightened the poor old gentleman more than by his former wildness, as he fancied this was only a mask, behind which he intended to play him fresh tricks. But in that he was mistaken. John always remained the same, and now avoided those very persons whose proximity seemed to have delighted him so much hitherto.

Although he still retained his old bed-room in his mother's house, the young girl scarcely ever saw him; he rose before daybreak, brought in wood, lighted the fire, ate his breakfast in his house; then, however, he avoided Rosy for the whole day, and at night she could only see him climbing to his room from without and seek his couch. He procured game enough for the house, and prepared soft skins for her after the Indian fashion, and sewed moccasins and coloured blankets for her. But he did not do this at home, but in the forest, whatever weather it might be : and she could only make him happy by accepting what he brought her, generally in the morning.

Thus the day drew nearer, so longed for by Tom Fairfield, for his marriage with Rosy; and Tom had invited all his acquaintance and friends to be present. In festive procession, the happy couple went to the magistrate's house, and even John was not absent on this occasion. At Tom's side, towards whom he had lately become as affectionate as in the first week of their acquaintance, he entered the magistrate's house, and was witness to the solemn ceremony; but when the bride had uttered her modest and still so glad "yes," and when her *husband* drew her gently to him, and pressed her to his bosom, then he escaped noiselessly and unnoticed from the room—from the house—and across the street into his own little garret.

It was night, and bright beams were pouring from Tom Fairfield's new house, and the merry sounds of the violin echoed down the street; the merry couples were dancing hornpipes and quadrilles, reels and jigs; the cup was going merrily round, and at times loud peals of laughter deafened the shrill sound of the music.

But past the house, through the autumn storm which howled through the leafless trees, walked a hunter, with his rifle in his hand, his tomahawk in his belt, and his blanket on his shoulder. He was rapidly passing Fairfield's window, when the silvery sound of a laughing female voice struck his ear. He stopped, hesitated for a moment, and then approached the house; he climbed up the fence, and looked for several minutes solemnly and silently through the little window into the brilliantly lighted room, and upon the merry beings who were dancing and whirling in the confined space. Happiness and joy beamed on every face on which his gloomy glance fell; but it turned dissatisfied from all in search of the *one*.

Ha! there Rosy joined the circle; the happy young *wife* on her husband's arm, and the light of the lamp fell cheerily and brightly on her face. John's eye was fixed upon her; but not a sound escaped his lips—not a motion, with the exception of a convulsive quivering of his lips, betrayed the struggle going on within him. At last he nodded, as if taking farewell, but almost unconsciously, towards the spot where he left all he still loved in this world, and who would have made his happiness their care; then he slowly descended, and threw his rifle across his shoulder.

When he again reached the ground, he had regained his former calmness. He drew his woollen blanket tightly across his shoulders, and, following the path which led to the west, past his mother's grave, his dark form soon disappeared in the gloomy shade with which the virgin forest closely and densely begirt the clearing.

And whither did he bend his steps?

He was never heard of again. But he had not returned to the Konzas; for a few weeks later the Canadian-Frenchman, who had put Fairfield on his trail before, came from them, and he knew nothing about him. Even Tom himself visited the tribe in the spring; but no one could give him any information about the White-deer—he had disappeared and left no sign.

THE PLANTER.

The Slave Sale.

THE PLANTER.

In Two Parts.

PART I.

FINE MEN AND WOMEN FOR SALE.

IT was the month of October, 1840; the sun was rising out of the dark shadows of the level land which forms the eastern bank of the Mississippi; the mocking-bird was rocking backwards and forwards in the tulip-trees, and swarms of merry, fluttering "silk-tails" were intoxicating themselves with the seductive berries of the China-tree; huge, snow-white herons were sailing slowly along close to the surface of the river, or standing in earnest posture on some tree that was lying in the water, to await the appearance of some little fish. Nature was holding its Sabbath, but not so man.

Upon the road which runs along the bank of the Mississippi, between the Levée and the plantations, a troop of negro slaves, men, women, and children, was coming down from the Atchafalaya settlements in double file, and followed by an ox-team, on which the luggage of the blacks was laden. They were not chained or even bound together with ropes, but on each side of the band rode two overseers armed with loaded double barrels, and the leader of the caravan carried not only rifle and knife, but had two immense holster pistols in his belt. The negroes, however, seemed to pay but little attention to this savage escort, for, laughing and singing, they walked along side by side, and rendered their journey less tedious by jests and stories.

Was it indifference for that which impended over them? Was it the levity peculiar to this race, which bade them take advantage of the happy, idle moments—that they cared not for the future? The answer is—that they were slaves. No plan they could form for their own behoof; no end they might try to gain, would be of any avail to them, but the present moment was their own, and that must not pass away unapplied or unemployed—it would never return again, and to-morrow, probably, they would be writhing again beneath the whip of the heartless overseer.

The higher, however, the sun rose, the more animated the road became, and the negroes frequently found themselves caught up by Creoles and American settlers, on their fiery little mustangs,* who exchanged a few words with the leader, surveying the slaves for a moment, or made them defile past them, and then galloped, with hanging rein, in the direction of the river, to the court-house of the

* Small wild horses, caught on the prairies.

Pointe Coupée. There, in the meanwhile, the majority of the planters in the whole settlement had assembled, to be present at the sale of the "moveable and immoveable property" of a Frenchman who had lately died at the "Great Bend," and the auction soon commenced, after the usual form, by putting up plantation, buildings, and "wild land" of the deceased. The slaves at length arrived—one-and-thirty in number—at their destination, and were arranged by the overseers partly in families, and partly individually.

The thoughtless carelessness of the negroes had now disappeared; the serious import of the next hour, which must decide their future destiny, appeared to weigh upon their minds, and a slight whisper might be heard at intervals among the unfortunates. With nervous timidity, their eyes passed from one to the other of the purchasers, who were carefully examining them, in order to read beforehand, from their looks, what lot awaited them if this one or the other bought them.

At length the Sheriff gave the signal to commence, and a powerful negro, with broad, good-tempered features, and truly herculean arms, was first led forward. He was followed by a young, sickly woman, with hollow eyes and sunken cheeks, who led a child by the hand, and had an infant in her arms.

"NERO," the Judge read from the catalogue, "Nero, a male slave, thirty-five years of age, of powerful build and healthy constitution; by trade a smith, and can manage an axe excellently. Maria, his wife, remarkably useful in the cotton field. Scipio, their child, three years of age—an infant of the female sex."

"Wont you sell the man alone, Judge?" called out a planter of Feliciana parish. "The woman seems preciously thin."

The unhappy wife pressed her child to her bosom, and looked with an anxious glance around, and the man seized her hand, as if fearing to be torn from her.

"No!" the Judge replied. "The families will not be separated."

And with a deep sigh, that seemed to come from the bottom of the heart, the poor woman became calmer.

"Six hundred dollars!" said a Creole from False River.

"Six hundred and fifty !"

"Seven hundred !"

"Eight hundred !"

"A thousand !" cried a little fat man, with a good-tempered face, who had just ridden into the court-yard, and knew the slave who was now under the hammer.

"One thousand dollars !" the Sheriff repeated, as an immediate pause ensued. "Gentlemen, one thousand dollars ; the man alone is worth twelve hundred !"

"One thousand and fifty !" a tremendously tall man, in a blue tail-coat and nankeen trousers, bid.

The negro cast a glance of entreaty towards the little fat man, which he seemed to comprehend, for he nodded to the Sheriff, and said—

"Fifty more !"

"Master Turnbull," the long man whispered, as he walked up to him, "do not outbid me, and we shall afterwards be able to make a bargain about the man."

"Do you think so ?" Turnbull asked, looking at him sideways. "You want to separate them, eh ? you're a slave-dealer, I suppose ?"

"That's my trade," the tall man answered ; "but let me offer, and when they are knocked down, as I said before, we will soon come to an arrangement about the smith."

"Twenty more !" he now cried, raising his voice and walking away from Turnbull.

"One hundred more !" the latter shouted, and the eyes of the two slaves sparkled with delight.

"Go to the Devil !" the slave-dealer muttered, and walked to the other side to examine the other slaves.

"Twelve hundred and twenty !" the Sheriff said. "Twelve hundred and twenty for the first, the second, and the third time !" he repeated, and, on the last word, struck his hammer on the railing. "Mr. Turnbull, they are yours."

The two negroes had anxiously awaited the fall of the hammer, but now they hurried with joyful haste up to their new master, for Turnbull was notorious as the best-hearted man in the whole parish, seized his hands, kissed and squeezed them, and behaved like children that have received a new toy.

"I was afraid massa wouldn't come," said Nero, as he again seized his new master's hand, and then patted the frisky little animal on which he was seated.

"Be off," Turnbull said, with pretended anger. "Be off; confound you—you'll tear the clothes off my back. But, Nero, go with your wife into the public-house close by, and make them give you something to eat; you need only say it is for Turnbull."

With these words he returned to the auction, which had recommenced, and the slaves, happy in having obtained such a good master, hurried to obey his commands.

The sale now proceeded quietly. Turnbull purchased a lad of twelve and a girl of seventeen years of age, whose parents had died very recently, the first for 400, the latter for 600 dollars; and the slave dealer bought two whole families, which, as he stated, he intended to take to Kentucky. Among them was a girl of about sixteen, nearly white, the daughter of a mulatto woman, for whom several planters offered him a considerable sum. He asserted, however, that he could obtain a much better price in the North for the handsome Southerner; and, after delivering the downcast slaves to his overseers, he crossed with the ferry-boat to Bayou Sarah, and thence went up the Mississippi in a steamer.

"Why does Hawthorn stand there so despondingly, Turnbull?" a young planter of the vicinity asked the latter. "He didn't bid once, and I heard him heave a deep sigh once or twice."

"On the first Monday in November his property will be put up to auction," Turnbull answered sympathizingly. "There must be a queer feeling about his heart when he thinks that the same thing as this impends over him in four weeks. He has gone into too many speculations, and cannot pay his debts. I am sorry for him, as well as for the splendid slaves he has got—at least fifty-two head; they will now be separated."

"It is not that which is gnawing at his heart," a young Creole interrupted him; "he has just told me what it is. The cholera has broken out on his plantation, and he says, since yesterday afternoon up to this morning, when he rode away, seventeen have already died."

"The deuce!" the man said in terror.

"Yes, yes! it is no joke," the Creole assured them. "He ought, really, not to go about in this way among us. Confound it, he may be infected himself."

"Well! that was all we wanted in addition to the bad times," Turnbull said, shaking his head. "A little cholera among the negroes, so that we may speedily get rid of our property, and then we can go with the volunteers to Texas. We shall have a rifle and a horse left. But here comes Hawthorn; he must tell us if he thinks the matter dangerous."

The man of whom they were speaking was of tall, almost slender, form, with very projecting cheekbones, and grey, lively eyes, which did not remain for five seconds fixed on the same spot, but turned continuously from one of the assembly to the other. But heavy cares seemed to weigh upon his heart, and his face was pale, his hair and his dress in disorder. With a slight bow, he was going to walk past the men, when Turnbull, who had dismounted and was leading his horse by the bridle, moved in front of him.

"Hi, Hawthorn! what has happened to you since we last met? You don't look in your usual spirits. Bless my soul, man! you mustn't take a contrary wind so much to heart. Who knows whether it will not blow from a better quarter to-morrow?"

"Turnbull," the planter replied, as he seized his kind comforter's hand, "a man can endure much misfortune, and even the most frightful things. When they burst upon us in all their terror, they will not easily hurl a strong man to the ground; but when they come in succession, drop by drop, always wounding the same spot, then they don't merely bow down the spirits, but they cause the heart to break."

"Courage, Hawthorn, courage!" Turnbull exclaimed, "we live in a land where sudden changes of fortune are no rarity; a single good speculation can make you as rich as before, if not richer."

"It's all over with me!" said the American, shaking his head; "for five years misfortune has been pursuing me. The first year it began with the loss of the cotton crop—but none of you fared better; but the next year my cotton gin was burnt down, probably set on fire by a negro, and nearly half my crop went with it. In 1837 a pestilence carried off the greater portion of my flocks. In the following year I tried the speculation in Texas, bought 300 mules there, but was attacked and plundered, as you know, by the Cumanches, and saved my scalp only by a miracle. Last year I was persuaded to put my money in the Consolidated Bank, which stopped payment directly afterwards. Far from being bowed down by all this, I hoped, at least, by the sale of my slaves, to be able to satisfy my creditors, and remain an honest man, and now this plague has broken out among them—my son, the doctor, fears, indeed, that it is cholera—and Heaven knows whether I shall not, within eight days, be—a beggar!"

He was silent, and Turnbull looked sympathizingly in his face.

"But if you were to remove your healthy slaves into another parish, so that they might escape infection?"

"Dare I do it?" Hawthorn replied; "they, as well as all my property, are offered for sale, and you know yourself that I have no longer any right to dispose of them."

"I will ride over with you," Turnbull said, after a pause of painful silence, "and have a look at them myself."

"What use is that?" Hawthorn answered; "you cannot help them, and will expose yourself to the risk of catching the infection."

"I will accompany you, however, if only to convince myself whether danger threatens the adjoining settlement. But whom are they bringing there? The sale doesn't appear over."

This exclamation was drawn from him by the appearance of a negro, whom the Deputy-Sheriff now brought up, almost clothed, we may say, in chains. He was a captured mulatto, whose owner could not be discovered. He himself asserted that he was free, but could not prove it in any way, and was now going to be sold, in the name of the State, to the highest offerer. The chains were laid upon him because he had already broken out of three different prisons, despite all precautions, and on the last occasion had nearly murdered the turnkey. Everybody was afraid to buy him, and in vain the Sheriff offered him for the low sum of 200 dollars. A planter from the neighbourhood of New Orleans, who was accidentally present, at length decided on purchasing him, and employing him on his sugar plantation. He obtained him for 201 dollars.

"He can't escape at my place," he said, with a laugh; "he must swim through a lake, and there my alligators keep guard—famous beasts in that respect. They have already, it is true, shamefully 'chawed up' three slaves of mine, one of whom escaped with difficulty, without legs, and two without arms. But it served as a warning to the others; not one would go up to his waist in water, even to save his own father's life. But how shall I get the fellow to Waterlow?"

"There, you've got a chance," said one; "here comes the little Frenchman who drives the bread-cart; you can lay him in there."

"That's a good idea!" said the planter from New Orleans; and, holding the negro by one end of the chain, he led him up to the cart, which was just rattling past, drawn by a single lean pony.

"Hullo! you fellow in the cart!"

"Monsieur!"

"Can you take my slave with you to Waterlow, and deliver him at George Pleuvier's?"

"Impossible!" the driver said. "The cart is crammed full, and here isn't room enough for a dog, much less for a full-grown nigger, and a hundredweight and a half of chains!"

"How would it act if we were to fasten him up behind?" the planter said. "He doesn't want to ride. You would deliver him properly?"

"*Certainement!*" the Creole said, with a laugh. "Lock him up firmly behind, then he can help to push; but, if he's accustomed to walk slow, I am very sorry I can't arrange matters for his convenience. I am in a hurry, and he will have to trot a little."

"How far is it, then?" the planter asked.

"Only twelve miles; and I generally do the distance in an hour and a half."

"Oh! if it is no further," the former expressed an opinion that "his joints will be brought into good condition by the exercise."

Without further ceremony, the unfortunate was now fastened, by means of two large padlocks, to the rear of the light cart, and they started at a sharp trot, in which the negro was forced to join, unless he had wished to be dragged along the ground. His only consolation was, that he could lay the greater portion of his chains upon the back of the cart.

Turnbull and Hawthorn had, in the meanwhile, crossed the river, and rode through Bayou Sarah and St. Francisville, both little flourishing towns, to the latter's plantation, which was about six miles distant.

There, though, all looked gloomy and desolate—all labour had ceased—the hedges were torn down, the windows of the dwelling-houses open, as if the inhabitants had removed. The horses were grazing in the garden, treading down the flowers, and gnawing the fruit-trees. The usually so cheerful plantation more resembled a place that had been attacked and plundered by robbers than the principal abode of a Louisiana planter. Here and there the negroes were standing in groups and conversing together. They did not even appear to notice the arrival of their master, except that one of them quitted the others, came up to the two riders, and stood by the side of Hawthorn's horse.

"Well, Hannibal," the latter asked, "how do matters look? Are the patients any better?"

"In the last three hours four have died, and William and Celeste are lying in their last agony," the old slave answered monotonously and with deep sorrow. "I am not well myself," he continued, after a short pause. "Hannibal's time will soon come now!"

"Horrible!" Turnbull exclaimed. Hawthorn made no reply, but looked, with dry eyes, gloomily and wildly, on the ground.

At this moment the door of a little building in the centre of the negro-huts was opened, and two wide coffins were carried down the little steps by twelve negroes. The surrounding slaves joined the procession, and all, with the exception of Hannibal, who remained with his master, soon disappeared in a little magnolia thicket which bordered one side of the plantation.

"And why only two coffins?" Hawthorn asked after a pause,

during which Turnbull had been gazing after the procession with horror in his looks.

"The time is too short, massa, to make a coffin for each. They die too quickly. Out of your seven carpenters, two already lie in that mound, and were forced to work hard enough while alive; but they cannot keep up now with the deaths."

"Good, good!" said Hawthorn, and waved his hand impatiently. "Do as you please; I am satisfied. Were I only at rest! Will you not visit my hospital?" he then turned and said to Turnbull. "It's worth while looking into it. If I had the sick of a whole town under my charge, it could not look worse. I have cleared out my overseer's house for it, and taken him into my own."

"Thank ye, thank ye," said Turnbull, timidly retiring a step. "We should not expose ourselves uselessly to danger. The sickness is contagious, and I should not like to take it home with me. But who comes riding there?"

"It is one of my negroes," Hawthorn replied. "My overseer sent him this morning to the adjoining plantation to procure provisions. I see he has come back with the baskets."

The slave rode up to his master and threw the empty baskets from his horse.

"How's this, Scipio?" the latter asked in surprise. "Why haven't you brought what was ordered?"

"Wont let nigger upon any of the plantations," said Scipio in an angry tone. "Was at all—Lobkins, Wharton, Heckmann, Sayers, and the rest; they all said nigger might go to the Devil; he brought the plague with him."

"I thought so!" Hawthorn sighed. "I'll ride back with you, Turnbull," he quickly turned to the latter. "I must have some distraction. If I stopped a day among my people I should grow insane!"

"Come, then!" the latter said, who was not sorry to quit the dangerous proximity of the sick; "perhaps there may be ways and means to help you. A real man must not despond as long as he has a horse to ride and a head to speculate with. Come to my house, where you can recruit yourself a little, and perhaps the sickness will exhaust itself in the meanwhile; or, at any rate, you will escape the danger."

Silently the men turned their horses back upon the road, and left the spot to its horrible solitude and desolation; but, before they left the clearing and entered the forest, they heard the wild wailings of the negroes, who were lowering their friends and relations into the grave.

The eve of departure.

PART II.

SOUTHWARD, HO!

IT is a peculiar feeling that seizes even upon the boldest and most undaunted, when he approaches a place in which a contagious disease rages, and where death breaks out from its ambush, and seizes its victim before he perceives the proximity of the terrible enemy. Many a man would boldly face a row of bristling bayonets, but his foot hesitates when he must tread the soil on which pestilence is reaping its horrible harvest; he would attack the enemy into whose face he can look, with fresh courage; but here, when he must presume death in every friendly pressure of the hand, in every breath he draws, he turns and flies the curse-laden spot. Such was the case with the inhabitants of West Feliciana parish; none again visited Hawthorn's plantation, and when the death-news arrived of a more terrific nature each day, when they heard, at last, that the corpses lay unburied on their beds, a strict cordon was drawn.

Four weeks later, at the end of the month of October, several men had assembled at the landing-place of Bayou Sarah, in order to await the arrival of the packet-boat from New Orleans, when a young planter of the neighbourhood galloped up, and gave his horse to a negro that was standing near. He was Hawthorn's nearest neighbour, and all surrounded him with questions about the fate of the heavily-tried man.

"It's all over with him," he said, looking round sorrowfully.

"What! dead?" they all exclaimed, as if from one pair of lips.

"Dead!" the planter repeated: "I have just come from a place where one of his still healthy female slaves fetched provisions each morning—less every day—and heard the terrible news. The day before yesterday, the last of his male slaves, his faithful Hannibal, died, who had been busily engaged in nursing the sick, and had held out for an incredibly long time. Hawthorn, whose son has also escaped the infection, could not survive the loss of his faithful servant, and blew out his brains this morning, as the girl told me."

"Horrible!" they all cried.

"His son, the negroes said, was nearly mad, and bitterly reproached himself for not calling in other physicians."

"The fellow ought to be hanged," said Turnbull, who had just come up. "I told the old man the boy knew nothing. No, he must play his quacksalvering tricks with the niggers till he put them all underground. If I was one of the creditors, he should not escape punishment. But what do they intend to do now? How does it look with the sale on next Monday?"

"God knows!" a trader of Bayou Sarah answered him. "Since the pestilence has been raging there, no one has thought anything more about the sale. I am one of the creditors, but we have given up watching for the last fortnight. At first, we kept a sharp eye on the plantation, as we thought, not without good reason, that Hawthorn might be off with his slaves to Texas, or some other safe place. Now, of course, this cannot be feared, and, although I lose a good bit of money by him, I am sorry for the poor devil!"

"And where is his son, the doctor?" Turnbull asked.

"He mounted his horse," the planter replied, "directly after his father's suicide, and rode away, no one knows where."

"We must go out in any case to-morrow," Turnbull said, after a little reflection. "It cannot last any longer. We cannot answer for it to God and the world if we leave the few human beings who are still there without help. The disease must have exhausted itself."

"I will not go," the planter asserted. "This morning I could smell the dead bodies, as the wind blew right across from there. I shudder at the very thought !"

"I wont go !" said the trader. "I have lost enough already in the affair, and will not risk my life in the bargain."

All had some excuse, or openly said that they were afraid of the contagion; and Turnbull was obliged to give up his philanthropic design, as he could have done nothing alone.

But how did matters stand, in the meanwhile, on the plantation, which was avoided by all, and seemed left a prey to the evil spirits? Desolate silence reigned there; the carrion crows flew, in short circles, round one of the negro huts, and thence into the neighbouring trees, there regarding, with greedy eyes, the spot where such a glorious banquet awaited them, had it not been for the hoarding that closed the entrance.

The sun now sank behind the summits of the magnolias into its green bed, the deserted settlement became gloomier and more cheerless, and here and there a pale star was glistening in the azure vault above, when suddenly, but cautiously, five negroes, wrapped in dark blankets, assembled from various directions and walked towards Hawthorn's dwelling. When they arrived at the back gate, one of them struck his knife against an old tin coffee-pot that had been, as it seemed, carelessly thrown there, and repeated the signal five times before the door opened, and Hawthorn walked out, dressed entirely in the fashion of the western backwoodsmen, with leathern hunting-shirt, leggings, mocassins, rifle, and knife, and, stopping for a moment on the threshold, looked sharply round.

"All safe, Hannibal?" he then asked, turning to one of those who had just arrived.

"Yes, massa!" the faithful slave replied; "there is no danger now. No one dares approach this terrible place in the dark. But it is time to start!"

"And have you the boats in readiness? Is the path through the magnolias free? Have you taken all your precautions in case we meet any one?"

"All arranged, massa!" Hannibal answered with great self-satisfaction. "The young gentleman is at the boats with William and Scipio, and six others, and the remainder of us are enough to carry all our baggage, for what we took last night to the swamp by the bank of the river lies safe, and we can take it on board as we row past."

"We'll make haste then; my boy!" Hawthorn said with a smile, as he kindly tapped the old slave's shoulder. "You shall not be a loser, Hannibal, for serving me so faithfully and zealously—nor any of you! But now let's be off; minutes are precious, and we have a long journey before us."

At a sign from him, Hannibal hurried back to the house, opened the door, and said a few words. Directly after, the desolate apartments became all alive, a confused sound of voices was audible, and a number of negroes—men, women, and children—rushed, with shouts of joy, into the open air.

"Stop!" Hawthorn cried laughingly, as he raised his hand to quiet them; "the dead must not make such a noise for fear of disturbing the living. Quiet, children! till we are in Texas; then you can dance and sing; but now hold your row. Hannibal and Nelson will show you the things which must be carried to the boats, and mind and keep on the hard-trodden footpath, that no marks may be seen on the edge of it."

The blacks went actively to work, and in a short time each had lifted his burden. The signal was given, and the train was set in motion.

Close to the western boundary of Hawthorn's plantation, a small thicket of evergreen prickly palms and splendid magnolias commenced, which extended for nearly three miles on each side of a deep ravine, through which a little stream ran down to the Mississippi. In this ravine, and through the cane-covered brakes, a small footpath led to a little blockhouse that had not been inhabited for a long time, as a murder had been formerly committed in it, and it had been, consequently, deserted by the inhabitants. In this hut the cautious Hannibal had ordered all the goods brought down on the previous night to be concealed, and he now moved noiselessly along the path, followed by the other slaves. It was a glorious night for such an undertaking; a gloomy, damp fog covered the stars as with a thick veil, and thunder rolling in the distance announced an approaching storm. Hawthorn at first followed the procession with his rifle on his shoulder, but now pressed through the bushes to give some directions to Hannibal, when the latter suddenly stopped, and, with outstretched finger, pointed to something white in the bushes.

"There!" he whispered in a scarcely audible voice, "fire, massa, fire at the white spot; it has no business in the forest."

"Who's there?" the American shouted, and moved a step forward, with his rifle raised. "Who's there? Answer, or I fire!"

The figure seemed, for a moment, undecided what to do; but the danger was too imminent to delay long, and, with a firm step, it walked up to Hawthorn and stood opposite to him.

"Raley!" the latter exclaimed in surprise, "what brings you here?"

"The suspicion that all was not exactly here as rumour said," the young man answered. "Hawthorn, Hawthorn! you have played a shameful game, and God has sent me hither to punish you."

"Curses on you!" Hawthorn said, grinding his teeth. "Your confederate, that worthy Morris, of course, formed this plan to watch me? What will you be paid for it?"

"I was, certainly, formerly in Morris's service," Raley replied, drawing himself up to his full height, "but now he knows nothing of my actions. I came here on my own account, for I suspected the disgraceful stratagem. But do not believe you will escape just punishment, and then reap the curse that you have sown."

"Do you think so?" said Hawthorn, with suppressed passion, as the other turned from him. "Do you really imagine I should be fool enough to let you go, now, that you may spread the news about? Pish! You must consider me a precious fool!"

"Dare to lay hands on me!" the young man exclaimed, as he drew a pistol from his belt. At the same moment, however, Hannibal seized his arm with an iron grasp, and, in spite of his resistance and cries for help, he was speedily bound and gagged.

"Ascribe that to your folly and impudence," Hawthorn said, as he again placed himself at the head of the troop. "You will, at any rate, make the journey with us to the borders of Texas, and then, perhaps, become more sensible."

"I doubt it greatly," said Hannibal, with a grim glance at the young Creole.

"What?" said Hawthorn, as he turned sharply round.

"That—that he'll grow more sensible," the black replied, with some hesitation; then delivered the prisoner to two of his comrades and hurried after Hawthorn.

They soon reached the swamp. The burning sun had, however, dried it up, with the exception of a few deeper parts, which were connected by narrow arms, and they continued their journey without any remarkable interruption till they reached the willows that overhung the river. The deep-sounding cry of an owl was heard on their approach, which Hannibal answered with the cry of the whip-poor-will, and, directly after, the young doctor walked out of the thicket, and heartily welcomed the new arrivers.

"All in order?" his father asked, as he looked round for the boats.

"All," the doctor replied. "Everything went on famously; not a soul noticed us, or believes that we are still walking on the earth."

"One, though," his father said, "whom we have brought with us in bonds."

"Do you know him?" the doctor asked.

"Yes, it is Raley, the young Creole."

"The devil! the spy whose cursed watchfulness we have to thank that we could not leave the country a fortnight back. Morris's creature! And what do you intend doing with him?"

"Taking him with us to the Texan frontier," old Hawthorn said.

"Or, at least, a part of the distance," Hannibal muttered to himself. "Will the charge of the villain be given to me?" he then asked in a louder tone.

"Do as you please," Hawthorn answered, as he went down to the boats; "only keep him so that he cannot betray us."

"Ai, ai!" the negro laughed, and, at a signal from him, some of the blacks carried him down into the smallest boat, in spite of his strenuous resistance.

"Bind his feet together—that will do," said Hannibal, now on board; "we must be on the other bank in safety by daybreak, and must row at least fifteen miles up the stream. Quick, my boys, quick!"

The blacks, four young men, pulled actively, and they soon lay in the shade of some immense cotton-wood trees beneath the small, deserted hut. On a signal being given, Hawthorn's overseer, who had here guarded the goods, appeared on the bank, and, after the exchange of a few words, they began loading the boats. Then they raised their sails, favoured, as they were, by a fresh south-west wind, and glided up the Mississippi, as near the bank as possible, to avoid the powerful current.

Hannibal had taken the smallest boat, and in this the prisoner lay, bound hand and foot, and not able to move. The negro might have easily outsailed the others, but he purposely allowed the broad sail to flutter a little, remained a cable length behind the others, and kept further out in the stream. The heavy splashing at the bow soon showed that the small boat was labouring against the whole mass of water; and after he had set the sail to catch every breath of wind that blew from the Gulf of Mexico, he touched the shoulder of his prisoner, who lay in the bottom of the boat, without paying the slightest attention to what occurred.

"Massa Raley!" the slave said, and a devilish smile crossed his dark features; "Massa Raley, do you remember how you had Hannibal bound and beaten, last spring, in Bayou Sarah, because he would not stand as guard while you were paying a visit to your friend's wife? You, of course, had a different excuse: the nigger had been impudent, and had even threatened, and that required punishment. My master was not there, and you knew the law was on your side."

The white man bit his teeth together firmly, and looked up inquiringly to the dark figure that bent over him. For a moment it seemed as if he was about to speak, but then he sank back into his former position, and the negro, who had watched him closely, continued—

"Do you remember, too, how you fired a charge of duck-shot at my brother, four weeks afterwards, because he had gone to Bayou Sarah without a pass, though every child knew him, and tried to escape twenty-four hours' imprisonment by returning to his plantation? You had the law on your side, what did you care that the poor fellow was obliged to keep his bed for months in violent pain? Do you remember all this?"

The prisoner looked with a startled, wild glance up to the dark form that bent over him with a threatening expression, but did not stir.

"Good!" Hannibal continued in a suppressed tone. "You have certainly not forgotten it; and blessed be the day on which I revenge my poor brother! Recommend your soul to God, for you have not another quarter of an hour to live!"

The prisoner had listened with a loudly-beating heart to the negro's threatening words, but had only believed that he was employing the power intrusted to him for a short while, in throwing his fury and hatred in the teeth of a white man. But now, when the horror of his situation rose clearly before him, and a terrible prescience of his fate dawned upon him, he tried, with the strength of despair, to burst his bonds and liberate himself. Hannibal, however, had foreseen this; the cords were tough, and, after a few minutes of useless exertion, the unhappy man fell back into his former position, while the cold perspiration poured from his brow.

"It is all of no use," Hannibal said with a laugh, as he pushed a fresh plug of tobacco into his mouth. "To work, lads! Overboard with him! We must return to quieter water, or we shall lose the others. I cannot see their sails now. Help him over!"

The negroes quickly obeyed the command—as it seemed, gladly. The unhappy man was raised up, in spite of his resistance, hung for a moment hovering in their powerful grasp, and then flew, accompanied by a loud "A—hoy—y!" from the leader, into the stream, that splashed up and closed over his head.

Hannibal had, in the meanwhile, loosened the sail, so that it fluttered in the breeze. The boat, no longer driven up the stream, stopped in its course, and the negroes carefully watched how the drowning man rose again, sank, and then emerged once more. But when the gloomy waters closed over him this time, Hannibal seized the tiller, without uttering a word, and, with swelling sails, the light boat flew towards the bank, and glided along it swiftly and noiselessly.

The morning was breaking when the fugitives stopped at the mouth of a little stream that falls into the Mississippi below Tunica.

"Here is the place," said Hannibal, who had now sailed up to his master's boat; "if we lay by here for the day, not a soul will find our hiding-place. To-morrow night we can reach the Atchafalaya, unload, and continue our journey by land, before the timid Creoles have dared to approach the 'Pesthole,' as they christened our plantation. How they will open their eyes when they find the dead cows in the hut!"

"Good!" Hawthorn replied; "we will follow your advice, but not forget the sentries. Have you kept your prisoner secure?"

"He is safe," Hannibal answered, and glided with his little boat first into the mouth of the stream.

Five weeks after these events had occurred, Turnbull received the following letter:—

Texas, 4th of December, 1840.

"My dear Sir,—As you are the only man in Louisiana whose opinion is not a matter of indifference to me, I feel impelled to give you a brief explanation of my apparently dishonest conduct, which will partly justify me in your eyes; or, at least, moderate the verdict which you have already pronounced upon me in your heart.

"You know in what a desperate position I found myself; that I was on the point of losing, by a public auction, everything that was absolutely necessary for my future existence. I saw myself at the edge of a precipice, from which my own energy could never have drawn me out. I was forced to keep the means of action, and was just about losing them through the greediness of my creditors, especially that Morris. Watched by his spies, I had no other choice but to invent some method to drive both friend and foe back from my plantation, and that could only be done by a disease which caused terrible ravages among my slaves, while the terror felt by the other doctors favoured in leaving the cure of the pretended pestilence to my own son.

"I easily induced my faithful negroes to help me, for, if my plan succeeded, they could all remain my property. I had always treated them justly and kindly, indeed, like a father; while, on the other hand, by a public sale their fate would be rendered uncertain, and they would assuredly be dispersed. Hannibal was remarkably useful to me in the affair; his clever head guided the whole conspiracy. Empty coffins were kept in readiness, and as soon as a stranger showed himself on the plantation they were buried, at first with a solemn procession, but afterwards with gloomy, ominous silence. We soon gained our point. The neighbours drew a cordon to defend themselves from contagion, and, from that time, we lived in tolerable security. But to increase the suspicions, we killed two cows, and kept the crows from them, so that any one who approached the place must inevitably smell the corruption, and believe that it was the unburied bodies of the unfortunates who died so rapidly one after the other.

"Our plan was successful. We took boat and sailed up the Mississippi, lay for the first day in an osier-bed, which concealed us and our boats, reached the Atchafalaya on the second night, and sailed down it without any further apprehension of discovery. Not far from the Mexican Gulf we were to find mules, with whose help we should continue our journey by land. But we waited in vain a whole day for the promised animals—they did not arrive; but, instead of them, a steamer, which bore us, in a much easier and swifter fashion, to the shores of the promised land.

"After reaching Houston, we wandered with fresh spirits further into the interior, and now the axes of my negroes, and the crashing of the overpowered trees, sound all around me. Texas is still a young and healthy country, and with the means I at present have at my command, I have the best hopes of being a wealthy man again in a short time, and paying my debts gradually, without becoming a beggar myself. Remember your own words, my dear sir, 'a true man must not despond as long as he has a horse to ride and a head to speculate with.'

"I will not yet tell you of my place of abode, although I am not afraid of seeing any of my creditors here. I will first prosper again, and then you shall hear once more about old Hawthorn, and I hope that, at a later date, we shall drink many a glass of brandy-and-water together, and have a chat together, whether it be in Texas or Louisiana. In the meanwhile, believe me, in all sincerity,

"Yours, dead and arisen,

"WILLIAM HAWTHORN."

IN THE BACKWOODS.

IN THE BACKWOODS.

IN October, 1840, two Germans started from Little Rock, in Arkansas, in a north-westerly direction, in order to look at a little patch of land situated on the Little Cypress river (at a distance of about fifty miles from Little Rock), which had been offered them for sale, and, at the same time, praised in a very energetic manner.

In America, we know, people from all countries come together, and characters come in contact there which would never have found one another in the old land, or, had they done so, would never have agreed. Thus our two travellers, an apothecary and a tailor, had formed an acquaintance and a liking for each other in a strange town, where they were surrounded by Americans, and scarcely understood the language.

The tailor was a passionate sportsman, and, in order to be attired in true hunter's fashion, had bought, in Little Rock, a pair of mocassins and leggings, upon which he looked down with no slight satisfaction from either side of his horse. Nothing in the world, though, would have induced him to doff his light blue, elegantly-finished tail-coat, with which he hoped to make an impression on the country people, as he well knew how expensive cloth coats were in the west of America, and how rarely a backwoodsman can spare the money to buy one. Besides this, he wore a tall, black beaver hat, but his shirt collar was open, for he wished to be "at his ease," as he expressed himself, in the forest. Over his shoulder hung an English double-barrel, with a game-bag, a double shot-belt, powder-flask with patent charge, and a percussion cap-box, all new.

His comrade was dressed simply, but by no means *à la* hunter. He wore a dark frock-coat and a brown skin-cap, with his usual feet and leg-casings; and he had not even girded on a pair of spurs, which formed a material part of the tailor's equipment. He, too, had a double-barrel and German shooting appendages, but appeared not at all to share the attention with which his comrade looked along the road, or up into the trees, to discover either a bear or a turkey, as it had been his opinion till now "that the creatures must run about in the woods in swarms."

The apothecary seemed to be looking more upon the ground and devoting his attention to the plants, on account of which he had already dismounted a countless number of times, partly to examine them, and to dig out others by the roots and place them in a long tin box, a species of herbarium, which he carried in his game-bag. They had ridden away from Little Rock on the previous day, and had spent the night with two young men, a German and a Russian, who had bought land on the roadside a few weeks previously and settled there.

"Dolle!" said the tailor, suddenly addressing his companion, who, in the distance of nine miles they had now gone over, had dismounted some twenty times—"Dolle! call me Joseph, if you are not more on the road than in the saddle! You startle all the game we might find by your eternal getting up and down!"

"But, good gracious!" said the man thus addressed, "we have ridden who knows how many miles, and have not seen a single head of game—not even a squirrel or a bird along the road."

"But it may happen at any moment," said the other in great excitement. "Are we not advancing further into the back-woods every step, and may not all those clumps we see before us contain herds of bears? To speak the truth, though," he continued, when Dolle had again mounted and they rode slowly along together, "I pictured the backwoods very different; the trees are not taller and thicker than they are in our forests, and the couple of creeping plants I have seen are scarce worth mentioning."

"But we are in the hills, Burg," the apothecary answered, "and, in the bargain, in very barren, unfertile hills, where the trees cannot grow so tall and thick—but, in truth, what is that in front of us?"

"Where? where?" the tailor asked, starting as if electrified, and touching his horse's stomach with his spurs—on which he had not thought—so that it gave a tremendous bound and would inevitably have thrown its rider, had he not, with true contempt of death, let his gun fall, and hung tightly round his horse's neck. As he pulled up his heels, while performing this operation, so high that the spurs lay on the saddle-cloth and no longer disturbed the pony, it immediately grew quiet—for it was by no means of an ill-tempered disposition, and had been chosen by its rider at Little Rock on account of its quietness—and enabled Burg once more to seat himself firmly in his saddle.

"But, Burg, you will have an accident with your gun if you let it fall in that way?" Dolle exclaimed in terror, as he pulled back his horse. "It was a mercy it did not go off—and the barrel is pointed at me into the bargain!"

"The confounded spurs!" Burg said, sitting upright in his saddle again, and carefully groping for the stirrups, with his heels turned outwards. "That is the third time it has happened to me. It is fortunate that I have such a firm seat, for any one else in my position would have certainly been thrown."

"You had better say it is fortunate that your horse is such a sheep, and stands quiet. Just look at your Bucephalus—he has really gone to sleep!"

"Come up!" Burg cried, as he gave a "cl'k!" and struck his horse with his clenched fist, but took good care not to touch him with his spurs. "Come up! but you mustn't believe, Dolle, that the beggar's asleep when he's got his eyes shut. He is only inventing new leaps, by which to get me out of the saddle."

"Well, as long as the saddle-bow holds," Dolle said with a laugh, "there will be no danger. But why don't you get down and pick up your gun, or do you mean to let it lie there till we come back?"

"Call me Joseph," said Burg, with a timid smile, "if I'm not afraid to get down through these confounded spurs. It's strange, but let me turn and twist as I will, I've always got my heels just at the very place where they ought not to be."

Dolle had, in the meanwhile, dismounted, good-temperedly enough, and had handed him his gun, which Burg gratefully received, and they slowly set their horses in motion again.

"By the way, Dolle," cried Burg, "now I remember why my horse bounded in that fashion. What was it you wanted to show me? What was it; a stag or a bear? I saw nothing."

"The remarkable creeper twining round that tree," Dolle answered very quietly.

"And made a disturbance about a miserable creeper, just as if it were something wonderful," Burg said, angrily. "I fancied a bear or even a panther was running across the road."

"Well, we will get on all the quicker now," Dolle replied, driving his own horse at a sharp trot; but his companion could scarce keep up with him, for his gun was continually in his way.

They had reached the declivity of the dividing ridge, where the road wound down with extraordinary steepness into the valley, towards the waters of the Fourche la Fave, and Burg stopped his horse at the top, and remarked to his companion, as he pointed to the precipitous road—

"Dolle, call me Joseph, if I risk my neck down here, and remain on my horse. I'll get down and lead it; it looks just as if we had to ride down a wall."

Dolle made no answer, but did what his comrade had been speaking about, and took his horse by the bridle, and then walked up to Burg and begged him to give him his gun till he had dismounted, for an accident might happen.

Burg was perfectly willing to do so, and reached the ground with uncommon precaution, and without tickling his horse this time with the spurs; but he pulled his foot up directly he reached the ground, for he had trodden with his unsoled mocassins on a sharp stone, for this simple reason, because there was nothing else but sharp stones there.

"Au !" he called out, as he held his foot, "the confounded stones have too many corners here."

"But who told you to put on mocassins !" Dolle said, angrily, as he walked down the hill before him. "You have been accustomed all your life to wear leather boots——"

"Calf-skin," Burg corrected him.

"Well, calf-skin boots, if you like; and now you've got that thin rubbish, which feels just as if you had nothing at all on your feet."

Burg followed slowly without any reply, and concealed his pain when he trod on a stone that was too sharp, and sank irretrievably on his knees; at the same time the spurs continually slipped under his feet, as the mocassins have no heels, and he had fallen twice very seriously. At the bottom of the hill, though, where he hurt himself dreadfully, by being tripped up by his own spurs, he stopped angrily, and, as he stooped down to remove the sharp irons, he said furiously—

"No; and if I mustn't ride again in my whole life, I wont rend my own flesh with them. So," he said, as he thrust them into his pouch—"so, lie there till I take you out again, and that will hardly be till I've got a pair of reasonable boots on my feet again."

The two riders now mounted again, and followed the broad road which ran along through the valley from this point, and presented no further difficulties.

In the afternoon they reached the little stream, were ferried across, and asked, after they had some dinner and fed their horses, for the road to the Cypress, and the station of a certain Farmer Dennis, the same whose land they were going to look at.

"Well," said the ferryman, a powerful, low-statured man, as he came to the door, after both had mounted, and pointed with his hand to the fence—"well, if you want to find the road, you must ride along this fence, and leave the road at the corner, and keep along the fence till you come to the other end; from there the trees are fresh blazed, and if you keep to the little footpath, you can't make a mistake."

The riders thanked him, and followed his directions, found the fresh marks on the trees and the footpath, and were now obliged to ride one behind the other, as the road was so narrow, and bushes hung over it.

"Halloa!" said Burg, as his tall beaver hat was caught by a little branch, and thrown down—"Halloa! the bothering trees had better take up the whole of the road. I've been riding for a quarter of an hour with my nose on the saddle-bow, and the first moment I lift it up, off goes my hat. But, tell me, Dolle, where does this road go to? the forest is growing thicker, and we can scarce find it."

"Yes, dear Burg," the apothecary said, as he stopped and looked round, a little doubtful himself; "there, you ask me too much; but it must be the right road, for we have seen no other leading to the right or left."

"Well, I hope so," Burg said, with a sigh; "but I'm beginning to long for my fellow-men. The sky looks to me very suspicious, as if we were going to have a violent shower, and then lose our way. Bur!" he continued, giving himself a shake, "if I have to pass the night in the wet forest, with my thin coat on!"

Silently they continued their road, each engaged with his own reflections, and reached the dividing ridge between the Fourche la Fave and Cypress rivers, upon which the road led for a short distance, through roughly-broken stones and dense hickory and oak-clumps, and then wound down a steep hill into the valley of the Cypress.

"Dolle," said Burg, as they stopped for a moment at the top, and surveyed the wide valley which lay before them, of a dark green tinge, looking gloomily in the approaching twilight and the heavy masses of cloud that were collecting—"Dolle, I wish we could see the blue smoke rising somewhere, for this solemn silence does not agree at all with my constitution. I feel quite uncomfortable; the forest seems dead. Would a man's child believe that we have been riding since daybreak in the backwoods, and have not seen a single head of game—not a turkey, no, not even a squirrel, if it was only to try if our guns would go off? I really believe that a man could have here in the wilderness every convenience for—starving."

"I should prefer eating leaves and bark before I let it come so far," Dolle remarked, with a shake of his head; "but our prospect, as regards a lodging for the night, is a poor one, for it is quite dark down in the valley, and not so particularly light up here."

"According to my calculation, we must have ridden at least ten miles since we left the old American's house," Burg asserted.

"Yes, and it was only seven to the nearest house," Dolle remarked, as he anxiously took out his watch, which, alas! only too fully confirmed his fears as to night setting in. "Come, Burg," he continued, as he dismounted and led his horse down the steep hill, "let us make haste and get on."

Burg got down this time without Dolle's assistance, and limped, growling, yelling, and complaining about his feet, behind the other, till they mounted again at the foot of the hill and rode at a sharp trot along a little stream whose course the path followed. It grew darker and darker the while, and heavy storm-clouds collected more menacingly from all quarters, which made them apprehend a rough, inhospitable night; still the two Germans drove on their horses the faster, till, passing through a stream, they lost both the path and Burg's hat, and, although they found the latter after a long search, the other was and remained covered by the darkness, and it was now beyond all doubt that they must irretrievably pass the night in the woods.

"I will halloa once, though," said Burg, and before Dolle could make a reply, he yelled in such a frightful and ear-rending manner that the former sprang back in terror, and begged him, for goodness sake, to be quiet.

"Who the deuce do you think would hear your yells? Halloa loud, or not at all."

"But I can't halloa any louder," said the tailor, angrily. "I have something the matter with my throat."

"Well, then, I'll try," said Dolle, and shouted with all his strength five or six times, but no one answered him—not even the echo thought it worth while—and very despondingly the two men began holding a consultation as to what would really become of them through the night.

"At any rate, I will not remain here in the valley," said Dolle; "it's so gloomy and desolate, and the trees all look as if they would fall on our heads every moment."

"But on the hill there's such a draught," Burg objected; "and I in my thin blue coat."

"And who told you to put such a thing on to go a journey? and why did you not accept the German's offer, where we stopped last night, to lend you his coat?" the apothecary answered sharply. "Well, then, you stop in the valley; I'll go up the hill, for I can see what's going on from there at least."

With the seeing it was not quite so correct, for it became pitch dark, and again rain began to fall, wet and coldly, upon the two unhappy wanderers.

Dolle now made preparations to mount the hill again, and Burg followed him, for he had no intention of remaining alone in the gloomy valley, sighing and complaining of his feet, which had been wounded by the sharp stones. Still they progressed only very slowly, for they had to lead their horses, and were caught every minute by thorns and creepers.

"You were complaining this morning that you hadn't enough creepers," said Dolle, as Burg had walked into a thicket and was searching in the prickly branches for his hat, which he was continually losing. "I should think you had quite enough of them now."

"Well, that was all I wanted," Burg complained, in a sorrowful tone, "that you should begin laughing at me. Call me Joseph, if I have a sound place on my hands, and I wont speak about my feet; I gave them up long ago. When I get back to Little Rock, I shall be obliged to have both legs amputated."

"Get back to Little Rock!" Dolle now complained. "Ah, if we were only at the top of the hill! we will not even think about Little Rock."

"Well," said Burg, who had regained his hat and put it on, "but what wonderfully fine things we shall find on the hill, I really do not know. I wish nothing more than that we were down it again."

Dolle may, on the whole, have been of Burg's opinion, so he made no reply, but climbed silently and doggedly up the steep hill, whose summit both at length reached, quite worn out.

The thin drizzle had now degenerated into an actual shower, which wet them through and through. Burg declared that his heart, his hat, and his feet were as soft as butter, and Dolle fastened his horse to a bush, and seated himself beneath a tree to have some little shelter.

"You will catch cold, Dolle," Burg said, "if you sit down in the wet grass—bur! I really don't like to touch myself, I'm so damp; and my poor coat!" he sighed, as he folded his hands moodily, and looked on the ground. "If there was only a stable here, in which we could put our horses," he at length continued. "Surely I mustn't stand here the whole night and hold the bridle?"

"Why don't you fasten it up? there's a tree close to you," Dolle answered, angrily.

Burg stretched out his arm with the bridle, to follow this advice, but sprang back with a yell of agony, and cried, as he held one hand in the other, "Donnerwetter! there are needles in that tree!"

"It is probably an acacia," Dolle said very quietly.

"Herr Dolle, I forbid all remarks!" the tailor now said, in a terrible state of excitement. "If I did not look upon you as a dead man—for your wet seat must certainly give you a mortal cold—I should express myself in much stronger language on the subject, but I call God and the world to witness that I am treated here in a most shameful manner. If my death ensues, and it must almost inevitably be the case, I have been murdered—assassinated !"

"But, good gracious, man, whom do you accuse of such terrible crimes ? Are we not ourselves to blame for them ?" Dolle asked.

"We—I ?" the tailor answered in astonishment. "Do you believe that I would have penetrated into this wilderness with my blue coat, if I had had a foreknowledge that no human being existed in it ? Did not the treacherous ferryman speak of seven miles, and have we not ridden and walked at least seventeen, and I without neckerchief, with mocassins on my feet, which I put on to be able to creep up to the game unheard ? And now I would give my blue coat if I could halloa so that the neighbourhood could hear me—if this desolate spot, by the way, possesses any neighbourhood."

"Sit down, then," Dolle said ; "you surely don't mean to stand there till six o'clock to-morrow morning and philosophise ?"

"To-morrow morning at six o'clock," the tailor gloomily muttered to himself, "I shall be found leaning against these trees, converted into an icicle, for I feel that my heart's blood is frozen already. Oh dear, Dolle," he continued in a gentler tone, "I have always been a good man, never did any one an injury purposely, and now I must perish here in such a miserable fashion !"

"Halloa !" Dolle shouted as he sprang up, "now I've a good idea. We'll wrap ourselves in our saddle-cloths, and lay the saddles here under the tree and sit upon them."

"That idea was sent direct from Heaven !" Burg said with delight, while he sprang to his horse and felt, with trembling hands, for the buckle on the saddle-girth, which he at last discovered, and was soon wrapped up in the cloth and sitting on the saddle by Dolle's side, to await the break of day.

But the two comrades in misfortune did not long keep their seats, for their limbs felt as if petrified, and they were compelled to give them some motion to restore the blood to circulation.

The apothecary sprang like a madman round the tree, but the tailor's feet hurt him so terribly that he did not dare do it, on account of the sharp stones; so he looked out for a tolerably smooth and soft spot, upon which he continually hopped from one foot to the other, and attempted to whistle once or twice, to make his companion believe that he felt jolly, though the result was dismally unsuccessful.

At length the first beam of day broke in the distant east; the rain had ceased a little, and now and then a piece of blue sky peered out through the misty veil of clouds.

Although Burg must have been wet through, he was actually leaning against a tree and sleeping, when Dolle suddenly fancied he heard the crowing of a cock. He listened, and, in truth, the delicious sound was repeated in the distance, which announced the vicinity of human habitations, a fire, and a cup of coffee.

"Burg, Burg!" he shouted as he shook him.

"Seven yards," the tailor said, still asleep, "will be quite sufficient."

"Burg—confound your seven yards—there's a cock crowing!"

"A cock!" Burg now cried, as he opened his eyes in alarm, and soon perceived the melancholy situation in which they were—"a real cock!"

"Yes, only listen—there again—and over there another!"

"And why are we still sitting here?" Burg asked, as he sprang up like a madman; "is it to see how the country looks by sunrise? Hi! why are we not flying? Oh, my goodness!" he suddenly interrupted himself, "I've lost the use of my limbs, and my feet are swollen and as wet as sponges. Well! I shall like to see the doctor's bill and the visits—he can take his residence with me at once for eight weeks at the very least."

Filled with cheering hopes, the two saddled their horses, which took them at least half an hour, for it was the first time in their lives that they had ever performed this operation, and Burg especially insisted that the saddle-bow went behind, as he perfectly well remembered that he had held on by the broad end yesterday. After several attempts, they at length accomplished it, however, led their horses, which had stood quietly the whole night—for they were used to this sort of thing—down hill, and reached, after an hour's ride, wet and stiff, the long looked-for house, where they were heartily welcomed and kindly entertained by the old farmer.

Burg, however, was more dead than alive, and no power on earth would have dragged him out on that day to look at the land for which he had ridden some fifty miles. He swore that he had seen more of the country than he wanted, and he would live and die in a town. Country life was not made for him, and the hunting in Arkansas was so miserable that it did not repay the trouble of lugging about a gun.

Dolle certainly walked over the farm, but the excursion had had an evil effect upon him as well, and on the next morning both returned, accompanied by a guide, who took them as far as the broad, well-worn road to Little Rock, where it was Burg's first employment to cut up the mocassins, in which his feet had suffered so terribly, into very little pieces, and then take to his bed and drink tea, to rest from the horrible fatigue to which he had been exposed.

THE FAT WIDOW.

THE FAT WIDOW.

CHAPTER I.

A PLOT.

I MUST take my readers with me again to Little Rock, the distant capital of Arkansas, which, at the time of our narrative, was a very unpretending place, but has grown considerably in late years, and has pushed its boundaries further and further into the dense backwoods that closely encircle it. Public buildings are now erected, stately houses have arisen out of block and board huts, and it bears scarcely any resemblance to the little half-Indian spot, composed of wigwams and shanties, that formed the first foundation, the seed of the later city.

Little Rock did not present so stately an aspect some thirteen years ago. In rainy weather it was necessary, in that portion of the town which is now the busiest, to look for fords through, and slippery boards over, foaming rivulets, and, as for paving, a portion of the inhabitants alone knew it by reminiscence. The city was then confined to several narrow streets, running parallel with the river, and the few brick-houses served, at times, as objects of admiration and astonishment to the hunters who came in with deerskins or game.

It was at that time, too, that artizans could carry on a roaring trade in the little settlement, for nearly all who had emigrated thither had done so in order to earn money quickly, and become rich, but by no means with the intention of working. Thus, for instance, there was only one cobbler who really made new shoes; he was a mulatto, and earned an immensity of money. Carpenters found famous wages, tailors and locksmiths were invaluable, and so on; in short, any one who really liked to work had no necessity to sit with his hands in his lap for a moment.

About this time, a little tailor, of the name of Julius Merir, came to Little Rock "on spec," and really with no further hope than of gaining his daily bread, and wandered for a whole day in melancholy mood, and with an empty stomach, about the town. His passage on the steamer had stripped him of his last cent, and he did not dare address anybody, because, as he afterwards stated, "he was not acquainted with the police, and they might possibly go about dressed like other folk." But hunger is a painful thing, which he could not endure long, and his good fortune guided him to another German, who, although he had not been any length of time in America, was somewhat better acquainted with the manners and customs of the country.

Charles Fisher, as the latter was called, first put himself in possession of our little tailor's whole history, which was certainly simple enough, and required no great breadth of canvass. Merir, who had come to New York from Bremen, in the emigrant ship the *Hope*, had joined a company in Bremen who intended to found an immense social settlement, had gone with them to the western part of Tennessee, but there he had soon arrived, with the others, at the conviction that they had all been cheated in the matter of their land purchase; and afterwards, when the whole society dispersed in various directions, he had sprung on board the first, best steamer, that stopped at the nearest wood-yard, and, as it was bound for Arkansas, it bore the young adventurer quickly and safely to look for a fortune.

As soon as Charles Fisher knew how he stood with his little countryman—whom he already liked, as he was exactly the same height as himself—he speedily procured him work and shelter; and Merir, who was industrious and honest, devoted himself with such energy to his labours, that he not merely soon earned sums of money which he would never have deemed possible in his most daring dreams of masterhood, but, after the expiration of a few months, had his own *atelier*, where he snipped and sewed, so that it was a pleasure to see him.

Fisher had certainly been forced to talk seriously to him, and inspire him with courage; for the old prejudices had still too deep a root in his mind. He would not be persuaded at first, or allow himself to be convinced, that such a glimmering light as himself, who in Germany had scarce finished his apprenticeship to his honourable profession, could here become a master at one breath, and even have journeymen, without asking permission beforehand, or any one saying a word to the contrary.

Nor was "the cutting out" anything so very brilliant, for it was a thing which he had never undertaken before, and was obliged to study from his own head and on the bodies of his customers, some of whom asserted, without any regard for his feelings, that the clothes he made them fitted them nowhere except on the shoulders, and hung on their bodies for their own convenience more than for that of the wearer. That could all be put up with, however.

"A master never fell ready-made from the sky," was Merir's consolatory proverb.

His customers might look where they could find consolation; and as he, with only one tailor to rival him, continually obtained more work, and more practice in consequence, his circumstances improved daily.

Before long, Merir was, according to his own opinion, a rich man, and, with a pocket full of silver, he commenced, though unfortunately too soon, a different mode of life. He took into his lodgings a negress as housekeeper, who soon showed, by her remarkably good clothes and other adornments, that her situation was anything but a bad one; at the same time he gambled, and accustomed himself to the enjoyment of the usual strong drinks, bought shooting apparatus, and began wandering about the woods all day long, through which, as a natural consequence of such behaviour, he neglected his work and his customers.

Such a life could not last for ever, though; and the treasure, that had seemed to the little spendthrift inexhaustible, soon came to an end. Then he ran into debt, and tried to keep his head above water as long as possible in that way; but, as that did not last long, and the cautious Americans would not give the good-for-nothing workman any more credit, he was at length obliged to return to his board, and, with a sigh, he again took up needle and thread, scissors and goose.

Just as it frequently happens, however, in this terrestrial life, that we poor mortals neglect the right moment, in our blindness, and then begin suddenly to pull with all our strength when the rapids have already seized our boat, and are hurrying it with frightful rapidity to the yawning cataract; so was it with Merir, who now found, first to his surprise, and then to his terror, that circumstances were very different in Little Rock from the time when he commenced his artistic career. Two other "merchant clothiers" had arrived from some corner of the United States; and, as they worked with the industry which Merir had displayed at the outset, it may be easily conjectured that the most custom went over to them; and they deserved it sooner than "the little blackguard Dutchman"—the honourable cognomen Julius had obtained in the course of time in the town.

Merir was in despair. Where was now his prospect of a reputable connexion? How could he hope, with his couple of "shabby customers," to satisfy even his most necessary wants, much less obtain the luxuries which had already become his second nature? His propensity to gambling and drinking could not be so easily extirpated; and Merir, instead of attending more zealously to his business, and making the far more honourable attempt to regain his old position by industry and talent, thought of other means, and calculated and contrived what was to be done, and how to help himself.

But, however cleverly Merir was able to use his needle, it was quite a different case when it was requisite to develop any mental energies; and his hours spent in reflection and biting his nails, had no other visible result, except that he usually jumped up on the expiration of one or two hours, seized his hat and ran straight, hair on end, into the little boarded bar which Charles Fisher had erected a few months before, and stocked with the different wines and liquors required in such a place.

Here Merir rejoiced and recruited himself with the spirituous liquors, to which he certainly rendered all possible justice, and also with the *spirituel* conversation of his friend Charley, as the Americans and Germans called him for shortness. On the occasion I am writing of, he had his third glass of mint julep before him, while Charley was sitting close beside him on the counter, whistling "Yankee Doodle," and beating time lightly with his heels.

"Charley," Merir at length said, after a tolerably ominous pause, during which he had been sucking at the straw, and staring fixedly at the glittering lumps of ice and damp, cool mint leaves before him—"Charley! I must stop payment; ready money is rare, and Julius Merir will declare himself insolvent. Julius Merir, at least, knows no way by which he can escape another terrible necessity."

Fisher suddenly stopped his whistling, looked at Merir in some embarrassment, and said nothing at all for a long while; then he proceeded with five or six bars of the melody that had been so abruptly interrupted, broke off again, and finally asked, as he turned on the counter till he was full-front to the drinker, with whom he was alone in the room—

"Escape a terrible necessity! H'm—and that is——"

"That other people declare me insolvent," Merir replied, without removing his lips from the straw, with which he was sucking up the last drops from the glass.

"H'm!" Charley said again, and wheeled to the right, as he returned to his old position: "h'm, that looks rather windy—Merir, that looks very windy!" and he recommenced his concert with augmented vigour.

Charley had every reason to be daunted by this discovery, which he had, however, long feared, for Merir owed him a by no means inconsiderable sum, on which he had been reckoning for the purpose of erecting a new house. If the tailor were really without any means, he saw no possibility of obtaining his money, for he knew the little fellow too well not to feel certain that, after once becoming a rake, he would not so soon make a fresh start and try to live respectably.

"Very windy," Merir said, though quite calm and resigned, after the first drum-and-fife burst had ended; "stormy, indeed, Charley—stormy, with wind and hail, as the almanack says, and no prospect."

"And Mrs. Broadly?" Charley asked, and winked to his young

friend opposite. "Mrs. Broadly, Merir? Do you know she lately received 4000—say 4000 dollars? I saw the boxes myself."

"But they will do my mother's son no good," Merir muttered, gloomily. "Insolvency hangs over my head by a single hair, like the sword of Damocles; even the fleshy widow will not save me from it—she has a heart of marble."

Julius Merir was accustomed, when he spoke privately with Charles Fisher about Mrs. Hosiannah Broadly, to employ the distinguishing, though somewhat familiar expression of the "fat, or fleshy widow."

"Merir!" Fisher said, and again wheeled to the front, "I have an idea!"

Merir was astonished at it, and gave vent to this feeling by an "Oh!" of surprise that almost involuntarily escaped his lips. Fisher, however, was not baulked by it. In his brain a chain of ideas had really been formed, which threatened to break forth with all possible speed. With his finger to his nose, he sat silently for a few seconds, but then proceeded, with a slight nod that expressed his perfect satisfaction—

"Yes, yes, Merir! the fat widow can and must make your fortune. But good sense is required—intelligence, Merir. Be wise as dov——. No! be harmless as doves, and wise as serpents. The fat widow loves you, Merir—she feels herself attracted to you."

"But she is as tough as a Macintosh," the tailor growled, and got up to prepare his fourth glass of mint julep; "tough as a warm, elastic galosh, is the fat widow. She will never consent to lend a stranger even a miserable hundred dollars; the unlucky key of the money-box is continually mislaid."

"H'm!" Fisher said further, and smiled with silent pleasure to himself; "that speaks remarkably for the lady's carefulness, my little Merir—very remarkably it speaks for it. To a stranger she ought to give nothing—not a cent ought she to give to a stranger. But she will not lock up her money from her—bridegroom!"

"Her bridegroom!" said the tailor, and turned in horror to Fisher; "surely I'm not to marry the fat widow?"

Fisher laughed loudly, but did not reply directly; for, in fact, it was a matter of perfect indifference to him whether Merir married the fat widow or not, so long as he had his money, and, at the same time, the prospect of keeping an excellent and *paying* customer in the little tailor. Thus much he saw, though, that Merir would, on no consideration, willingly consent to enter into the bonds of holy matrimony with this lady; and as, besides, he had entertained quite a different plan originally, he did not delay any longer in imparting it to his friend, in a cautiously suppressed tone.

The plan really consisted in nothing less than a feigned promise of marriage, which, made with all seriousness, would, in any case, serve to draw a sufficient sum from the rich widow, at least, to pay the little tailor's debts. Fisher, at the same time, represented to him, with more than Indian eloquence, how he could then commence a fresh life free from care, and easily regain his old customers, without being continually pressed by his creditors, and deprived of the enjoyment of his existence.

"But the widow?" Merir said, shaking his head seriously. "Give the Devil a little finger, and he soon gets the whole hand. If I promise her marriage, it's all up with me—she'll marry me whether I like it or not."

"Let me manage that," said Fisher, with a laugh; "I must have lived so many years in Little Rock to no purpose, if I did not know how to cook her goose. No! my little Merir, she cannot marry you, even if she would—she dare not."

"But why? She is of age, Heaven knows!"

"Yes, certainly, twice or thrice. But may I ask where is her husband?—where is Mr. Broadly?"

"Broadly! why the whole town knows that he was attacked, six or seven years ago, by the Cumanches, on the Santa Fé expedition, and killed. I thought the story was well known, for Mrs. Broadly is not the woman to keep a thing of that sort quiet. She has told me all about it, with the most circumstantial details, more than twenty times. I know it by heart."

"And where are the proofs of her husband's death?"

"Proofs? Oh! she has not been able to procure any yet. The savage red-skins are not in the habit of giving any certificates of death."

"Good! that is all I wanted to know," Fisher said, hurriedly; "I built my plan upon that. You have, for the present, nothing further to do than to make her a proposal, and the rest will come of itself. You run no chance of a refusal. The widow will certainly not die of a broken heart, even if she don't have you, and would just as soon take any one else, for she will not marry a second time for *love*. But all Little Rock knows the reason for that."

"The reason?" Merir said, in surprise. "Well, what reason has she? If all Little Rock knows about it, I must belong somewhere else—I don't know a syllable of it."

"Eh! she doesn't want to be called the 'fat widow' any longer," Fisher said, laughingly, "and will have a husband at any price, so that she can get a proper name. No one else will marry her—that she must be certain of by this time—so she will take you. At the worst, Mrs. Merir always sounds better than the 'fat widow;' and, speaking the truth, it is probably her last chance of getting rid of the odious name."

Thus the eloquent little landlord harangued his friend earnestly and lengthily, till Merir, after many objections, many anxious doubts, at length consented, and, at last, even made the condition that, if Mrs. Broadly had a generous fit, Fisher should make out his bill one hundred dollars more than it really was, so that he might have a little money in case of need. And now, matters being so far arranged, the two worthy little fellows fetched a round-bellied bottle of real Madeira from a cupboard usually kept carefully locked, then seated themselves in a quiet corner, and laughed and drank, and talked and giggled to one another, till the sun had sunk far behind the green tree-tops, and a white, milk-like cloud lay in heavy, impenetrable masses on the river.

On the next day, Julius Merir—who had neglected himself more and more lately, and seldom thrust his heated face, with sleepy eyes, before mid-day, out of window, in order to judge of the probable time by the position of the sun—appeared, to the great surprise of his neighbours, at seven in the morning, in his light blue tail-coat, with glittering gilt buttons, new waistcoat and cravat, new boots and inexpressibles, new hat, new gloves, and new pocket-handkerchief; in hort, so smart and gay, as if just taken out of a bandbox, as the varnished signboard, which he had bought in better times for a heavy sum, and upon which, though certainly in rather a forced position, two gentlemen were depicted, dressed in the very latest fashion—one in a chamois-coloured coat, the other in a rich surtout—and with locks which, as the backwoodsmen said, curled like "pigs' tails," holding their hats in one hand, and with the other their walking-canes to their lips.

Before anything else, he went to Charles Fisher's, where he breakfasted, and willingly accepted his invitation to drink "fresh courage" in a bottle of Madeira; and then—but that has remained a mystery. He was certainly seen to go into the widow's house two or three times in the course of the day, and his face bore, when he came out, but more especially when he went in, an expression of serious and reverent solemnity.

In the afternoon, Mr. Fisher was requested to visit Mrs. Broadly, and the conference, held with closed doors, lasted above an hour; but, on the next morning, the gossip of the town was, that the blackguard little Dutchman was going to marry the old rich widow Broadly—of course, only for love—and afterwards take the Arkansas Hotel in Front-street.

But how did the people know it? Good gracious! who ever yet traced out the origin of town gossip? As when a pane of glass is broken in a well-organized family, not a soul did it—"it must have been cracked before—it fell out of itself." The town gossip, too, is told by some one, somewhere else, and some one else's sister has then imparted it to some one's acquaintance, by whom it is again carried, though, of course, only as a report, into some other company, and then, like a bomb-shell, it is scattered into twenty various directions.

Thus much was, however, certain—Charley Fisher went about for a day or two with a very cheerful face, and Merir had money in abundance, but did not appear at all disposed to attack or wear out its joyful existence by paying too many of his debts.

Julius Merir had really proposed for Mrs. Broadly's hand, and, at the same time, had the satisfaction of receiving anything but a refusal. Mr. Fisher was witness of the affecting betrothal, and the course of events was exactly as the watchful little Charley had foreseen.

The lady proceeded, after a few sportive reproaches, suppressed by a kiss, to pay all the debts without hesitation, and the marriage was appointed to take place on the first Monday in the next month, just as if the affair had been a sessions.

The first Monday in June certainly arrived, and Mrs. Broadly was radiant as a cabbage-rose, in yellow satin and orange blossoms. All the young ladies who lived opposite to her, and had kept the windows in a state of siege the whole morning, would have paid, with the greatest pleasure, a dollar a-piece as admission, only to look at Mrs. Broadly for a quarter of an hour in full dress; and, oh! how the roguish creatures would have laughed afterwards! But all the window-blinds were pulled down, and the watchers were only able to perceive at intervals a transient shadow, which ever shot past their eyes like a bright, yellow gleam. Their expectation was raised to the highest pitch through it, for the appointed hour passed away, and another, and another, without the bridegroom being seen or heard.

The blind that afforded a prospect of the street running to the river was now raised more frequently. At times, the lower portion of a very red face became visible, and the lady's impatience had reached the highest pitch, when Merir hurried up, in highly unusual haste for a bridegroom, quickly disappeared in the house, the door of which opened like lightning, and brought the watchers without to such a state of desperation by not reappearing, that the ladies unanimously declared that they "would not waste another moment over the ridiculous marriage, but leave the windows directly;" though the declaration was not carried out, for not one quitted her post.

But they would have been really astonished could they have looked into the interior of the little apartment, in which a lady in yellow satin, red-hot with passion and excitement, reclined on a sofa, and convulsively crumpled up in her hand a letter, which had already been kneaded into the smallest possible compass; while opposite to her, but in such a position that he had the immense round mahogany table between him and the furious lady, stood Julius Merir, and his features wore a peculiar mixture of fear and dogged obstinacy.

And the letter?—ran thus.

"J. Merir, Esq.,—You are on the point of committing a crime—you are about to marry another man's wife. Do you know what threatens you if you do it purposely? The House of Correction! Mr. Broadly lives, a prisoner in Santa Fé; but arrangements are made to release him. He may be already on the road, hastening to the arms of his wife—and you?

"Take care. I warn you as a friend. I have also warned your bride, who is hurrying to her ruin. There is still time; the next hour may see you exposed to the vengeance of the law or of an outraged husband.

"Weighty reasons force me to conceal my name for the present, but soon it will not be necessary. In the meanwhile, I will call myself simply your

"SAVIOUR!"

CHAPTER II.

A COUNTERPLOT.

"AND you believe that rubbish, sir?" the lady asked, and hurled the crumpled paper at the bridegroom's head. "You listen to such anonymous trash, and my word is held of no account by you!"

"But, dearest Mrs. Broadly!"

"Silence, sir!" the fair one majestically commanded. "You only increase the disgust I am beginning to feel for the whole false male sex. What do you intend to do?"

"Dearest Mrs. Broadly!" Merir now stuttered in confusion, as he was thus driven to explain his views without any concealment, "I really don't know. You—you will find it reasonable. Six years' imprisonment, if your honoured husband——"

"Enough, enough, sir! I now know more than will be beneficial for my weak nerves," madame groaned, and concealed her face for an instant in her white handkerchief. "Leave me, I request you. But one thing more—swear to me first, sir, that only the fear that my poor husband may still be alive, induces you to defer a union of which you yourself said to me, a few days back, that it alone could render you happy."

"Mrs. Broadly!" Merir said, in embarrassment—for he was not really so bad that he would give his word to back a lie—"you really would not believe that I——"

"Swear, sir!" the yellow satin bride called in a commanding tone; "or, by Heaven! I must consider you a disgraceful, shameful hypocrite, whom Heaven's vengeance may, perhaps, reach through my weak hand."

She sprang up, and took one long, determined step towards the little man; while the latter, fearing the worst from the angry lady—like a dog that draws nearer his master, to escape the threatened blows—walked close up to her, seized her hand, and whispered in a soft voice, apparently trembling with internal emotion—

"Hosiannah! and you could thus mistake your Julius? No! That was not seriously meant; you only wished to try your betrothed. But see, I have gone through the trial pure as gold. I do not tremble at your angry words; for I feel that a few months—Oh! were they weeks, days, hours!—will show you whether my heart is capable of a false thought. Send a messenger to Santa Fé, and when he returns to us with the melancholy news—no, I mean the joyful announcement—which will fulfil my wishes, then, Hosiannah, then you shall see how terribly, how unjustly, you have accused the heart of your Julius—then you shall open your arms penitently, to receive him whom you now try to repel with harshness, but in vain."

"Enough, enough!" the lady replied to this fiery address, though in a strangely cold tone. "I will believe your assertions; but, in that case, you will have no objection to sign these few lines temporarily."

She walked quickly to her desk, and wrote a few hasty lines—

"Do not be afraid, sir; it does not contain another word beyond those you have just solemnly uttered. I request your signature."

Merir hesitated, but there was no way of escape, and, with a trembling hand, seized the pen, and in a few seconds Julius Merir's autograph was at the bottom of a promise of marriage, which would be held binding by any court in America.

"So, sir," the lady said, quietly, as Merir let the pen fall and retired, "now leave me, I will change my dress. You will understand that my present costume cannot summon up any thoughts that are favourable to you."

"Hosiannah!" the tailor whispered reproachfully.

"Enough!" madame interrupted him syllabically, and Merir soon found himself half pushed out, half of his own accord, in the passage, whence he hurried, as fast as his feet would carry him, to Fisher's little bar. Here, however, he soon regained his jollity; when once removed from the magic circle of his beloved, his pristine levity returned. The two little fellows drank and laughed far into the night, and were as happy as sand-boys together.

A surprising piece of intelligence awaited them, however, the next morning. Mrs. Broadly had disappeared; and the only thing which could give her sympathizing neighbours the slightest hint as to the direction she had taken, was the certainly vague report, that a boat, rowed by two men, and carrying some dark object in the stern, had left the landing-place at daybreak, and gone down the river.

Merir felt disquieted by it—he really did not know why—there was something so mysterious in this silent departure. But, however it might be, it did not trouble him long. The road to Santa Fé lay for several hundred miles through a desolate wilderness; and a single messenger would not have been able to reach the town—nay would not have attempted it for the highest reward—for his capture by the red-skins, perhaps even his death, was inevitable. The regular caravans did not start, either, till the 1st of May in the next year, and did not return till autumn, at the earliest; so he had eighteen months before him. Till then much might alter, and Merir had reason to conjecture that, by that time, he should not have much to trouble Little Rock about.

Thus eight days passed; that which at the beginning of the week had been almost exclusively the subject of town gossip, was now almost forgotten, and Julius Merir, who had certainly settled Fisher's demand, but had cleverly kept back the money intended to pay his other debts, lived gloriously, and managed in some way or the other—Charley Fisher, at least, could not comprehend how—to procure fresh credit to a considerable amount.

On a sunny afternoon, though—Oh! he was sitting so happily in Charley's garden, and admiring the polish of his boots—he was startled by a very affectionate note from the "fat widow," inviting him to pay her a visit that evening.

How had the lady returned? No steamer had stopped—no one had seen her arrive—and, most assuredly, she could not have fallen from the clouds. What was the meaning, too, of this half-mysterious, half-affectionate *billet-doux?*

Charley Fisher also shook his head ominously when he was informed of this peculiar circumstance. But the little rascally tailor had no choice; go he must. And he at length started; but with a heart heavy as if he were going to have a tooth plucked out. The feeling possessed him involuntarily, and he could not get rid of it.

Fisher had a number of visitors this evening, for a steamer from Fort Gibson, which was going to start for New Orleans the first thing next morning, had arrived, and a part of the passengers were drinking and chatting, while others purchased provisions for the voyage. At ten o'clock the last visitors returned to the boat, and Charley was just putting up the iron bar across the door for the night, which shut him up from the outer world, when some one tore the door open, and Merir entered, pale and exhausted.

He did not leave his friend long in the dark as to the cause of his terror, but first helped him to close the door again, and this time bolt it properly, and then said, in a hurried though whispering tone, that the widow had returned, and had brought her brother, who was a Justice of the Peace at goodness-knows-where, who had not only been present at the unlucky expedition to Santa Fé, and had been a witness that Mr. Broadly had been tomahawked and scalped by a Cumanche Indian, but was also in possession of a letter, written by a friend, who also saved his life—referring to that event, and the death of "poor Broadly" more especially, circumstantially.

What to do now? Both did not doubt for a moment the widow had invented all this—probably, with her brother's assistance. But how to prove it? It was impossible, and the tailor walked desperately up and down the room, with long steps, and with his hands behind his back.

Charley at length advised him, quite openly, to bite into the bitter apple, and marry the widow.

Merir swore, though, that "he would sooner suffer death at one blow, than be tortured slowly." He knew the widow well enough to be aware what he might hope from a marriage with her. Besides this, there was another special reason, which he now imparted to his friend. He had, in the four days immediately following the widow's disappearance, while he was still regarded as her future husband, and himself firmly believed that she would not return, or, at least, not so soon—run considerably into debt in her name, as not a soul would trust him in his own. Woe to him, if the matter came to light after he had delivered himself, bound hand and foot to the widow, by marrying her.

As matters stood thus, hesitation did not appear advisable. Fisher himself advised him to get out of the way as soon as possible; and as, fortunately, the steamer about to start next morning afforded the best opportunity for flight, the two conspirators did not delay their preparations any longer, and completed them about an hour before the required time. Fisher went on board when the first bell rang, and carried Merir's luggage down.

There he accidentally met the captain—for captains are seldom up so soon on board the boats—who was also uncommonly polite to him, and entered into a long conversation, which was quite contrary to his usual custom. Fisher was, at length, obliged to break it off, as the second bell was ringing, and excused himself by stating that a person, who intended to go by the *Roaring River*, was waiting for him ashore, and then hurried back to his house.

He had scarce disappeared behind the houses, when a stout lady and a tall gentleman, without any luggage, walked down to the landing, across the broad gangway, and up the cabin steps, when they disappeared through one of the numerous doors.

The piercing sound of the bell was now heard for the third time across the silent and still foggy river. The first golden streaks, showing that the sun-god was awake again, appeared on the eastern horizon, and all belonging to the *Roaring River*, who were still on shore, hurried to the snorting, puffing, wheezing steamer, which was still held, though, by powerful ropes. Two men also hurried down from "Fisher's store," one of whom carried a little carpet-bag, and the other a leathern bag, with a stout iron padlock. The first of them was Charles Fisher, the other Julius Merir.

"Now, Merir," Fisher said, as they reached the plank, "make haste on board. I can't go any further, for fear of the boat starting with me aboard."

He put the carpet-bag down on the broad gangway that ran round the boat, and wiped the perspiration from his brow.

"Oh! Mr. Fisher, have the kindness to come up here for a moment," the captain said, who had just walked out on the boiler-deck. "We must have a glass together. You have, at least, five minutes."

"The boat wont start directly?" Fisher asked, still rather mistrustful.

"Certainly not, as long as you are on board," was the consolatory reply.

And Fisher felt, as he told Merir, no further objection. He sprang rapidly up the narrow stairs, while the cabin-boy followed with the luggage, and the captain himself opened the door for them. Merir, however, who was now in front, was almost seized with a slight apoplectic fit, for, before him—was he awake, or was a terrible dream mocking him?—close before him stood, in yellow, rustling satin, her kindly, smiling face surrounded by a huge wreath of orange-blossoms, and a heavy gold chain upon her fat neck—Hosiannah Broadly, the cabbage-rose; while, by her side, in a solemn black coat, white cravat and waistcoat, with a hat in his hand, and a heavy book under his arm, stood Mr. Jonathan Halloway, J.P., from Montgomery county, and brother to the charming bride.

Fisher, who followed at Merir's heels, had scarce thrown a glance upon the lady's form, before he rapidly retreated, and was just rushing down stairs again, but was stopped by the captain, who took him affably by the arm, and began conversing about the weather and the crops, and soon drew him into the cabin, laughing and chatting, but not losing his hold for a moment.

What most surprised him, however, was the extraordinary calmness with which both himself and Merir were received; all appeared to have been waiting for them some time. They were not left in doubt for a moment, for the captain of the *Roaring River* had scarcely got Charley so far in safety that he could not again escape from the cabin, before he said, with a reverential bow to the fair bride—

"Mrs. Broadly—as I shall only have the honour of calling you for a little while—this is in accordance with the request of this gentleman, who asked me last evening to allow your marriage to be solemnized on board my vessel instead of in the town."

Merir looked up to him in terror, but the captain continued in the same calm and affable tone—

"I consented with the greater pleasure, as it afforded me, as well as Mr. Charles Fisher, the opportunity of being present at the ceremony. Your kindness in accepting my invitation justifies me in hoping that you will place no more difficulties in the way of the young and ardent bridegroom; and I believe we can proceed with the ceremony without further delay, as my time is short, and my boat must be under weigh within a quarter of an hour at the most. Mr. Merir, the lady will take your arm; Mr. Fisher, on this side, if I may request. And now, my good Mr. Halloway, I think we can begin."

Merir allowed them to pull him about like an automaton, though a clumsily made one. He raised his hand, wrote his name, uttered a loud, distinct "Yes!" and fell on his young wife's neck by word of command—even suffered Mr. Halloway to take off the heavy leather bag, and hand it to Mrs. Broadly—he had become a helpless machine. It was not till he left the vessel with his wife that the thought of his future misery occurred to him, and then his knees gave way and he cried bitterly. Mrs. Merir, however, knew better what was befitting; she walked through the row of grinning waiters, who easily comprehended what had taken place, and left the boat hastily, with her "husband" in tow, while Mr. Halloway remained with the baggage, and formed the rearguard.

"Well, Mr. Fisher," said the captain, and turned with a smile to the worthy little man, "and what will you take to drink—brandy, rum, whisky?"

Mr. Fisher stood there exactly like a person who suddenly wakes up at night in a pitchy dark room, hears his name called, and cannot for the life of him find the door.

"Pray, Mr. Fisher——"

"Captain Bowling!" the landlord stammered.

"Mr. Charles Fisher!" the American repeated.

"Go to Bath, sir!" Fisher burst out, as he was now forced to see that their scheme had been betrayed, and they had been frightfully humbugged. He pressed his hat over his eyes, and rushed up the cabin-stairs, over the plank, on shore. He would at that moment have given anything to be deaf, and not be compelled to hear the peals of laughter that saluted his retreat.

And Merir?

For a whole month he endured the blessings of matrimony; for a whole month he bore abuse and cuffs in the house, and sarcasm and ridicule in the streets—a whole month he suffered and endured, like an Indian chieftain bound to the stake, without complaint, without murmurs, drowning his fury now and then, when he succeeded in gaining a moment's peace, in oceans of brandy and mint julep. One morning, however, he had disappeared; the whole night through, a light had been burning in Mrs. Merir's room, and she had probably been waiting with continually increasing wrath for her husband, but he did not return. No steamer had started, no boat was missing, and still he did not make his appearance. Messengers were sent in every direction; in all the newspapers was an accurate description of the traitor; Charley Fisher himself was examined, though without any favourable result—it was all fruitless.

Merir had again launched himself upon the stormy sea of life, without money, without linen, and without anything, save what he had on his person. What awaited him, did not appear, even in its gloomy uncertainty, so horrible as what he here really suffered; and when, after weeks and months, no news arrived of him, there was not the least doubt but that the "wretched little Dutchman" had fortunately escaped. Mrs. Merir was, however, called afterwards, as before, the "Fat Widow."

FINIS.

CPSIA information can be obtained
at www.ICGtesting.com
Printed in the USA
LVHW022013120422
716028LV00006B/208

9 783752 591767